Cops & Clobbers in Deadwood

"Anyway, I can't just go to Detective Hawke and tell him that I need those clocks because there are a bunch of *others* coming to kill me."

With an official bounty out on my head now, the word "bunch" might not be adequate. A slew of *others* might be better. Or a troop. That sounded more ominous. Like a wild battalion of bloodlust-filled monkeys.

I grimaced and ate another chip.

"Those clocks are a key part of the monitoring process," I said aloud, repeating what Harvey and I both knew.

"Sure as a dead man stinks."

"Eww." I wrinkled my nose at him. "I'm eating here."

"Which is why we have to figure out how to hijack them clocks out from under Johnny Law's nose." He snatched the next chip from me before I could stuff it in my mouth. "And that there is the makin's of a *caper*, plain and simple," he said with a smug look while popping the stolen chip into his mouth.

"Fine, maybe this is sort of caper-ish. But if we're going to take this to the next level, we can't say a peep to anyone."

"That right there is how the cow ate the cabbage."

I was glad he agreed with me. "Especially not your nephew. He's probably allergic to capers, breaking out in a rash of handcuffs and Miranda rights at the mere notion of one."

ALSO BY ANN CHARLES

DEADWOOD MYSTERY SERIES

COPS & COBBERS IN DEADWOOD

BOOK 14

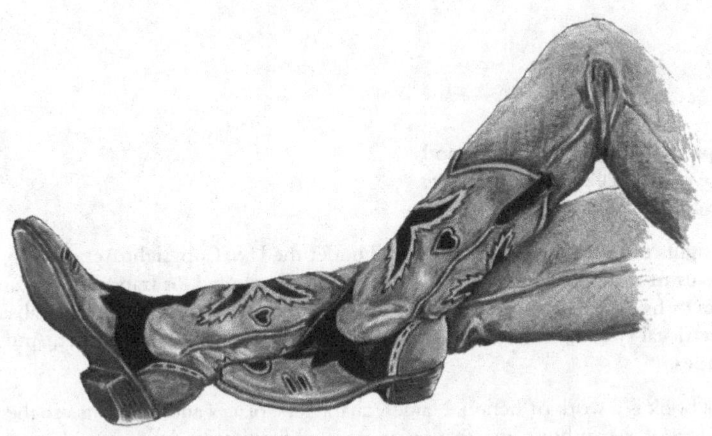

ANN CHARLES

ILLUSTRATED BY C.S. KUNKLE

This one is for David, my brother.
You are a wonderful example of compassion and love.

Dear Reader,

As I write this, I'm mentally sitting in a tent down in the Yucatán jungle, sweating my buns off in the humidity. Up in Deadwood with Violet in this fourteenth book you're about to read, we are stuck in a polar vortex with subzero temperatures and finger-freezing winds. It's going to take me a couple of weeks of research and writing to get used to being in the heat instead of the cold. Plus I'm switching months of the year. In real life, where I'm physically sitting in Arizona, we're having beautifully warm fall days and freezing nights. It's only November at home, versus Violet's world in *Cops & Clobbers in Deadwood*, during which we celebrate Valentine's Day. Don't even ask me what month we are in down in the Yucatán. Months don't matter in the jungle where we are just trying to survive from sun up to sun down. This bouncing around throughout the year and settings is why I walk out of my office each evening after a day of writing and have to stand still for a moment to determine what month it is in reality. I don't even try to figure out the day of the week without help.

I hope you enjoy this latest tale. I try to make each book in Violet's world feel a little different while keeping in mind the overall series arc. I believe this makes binge reading all of her books more fun, with each one having a different theme and sometimes more of a certain genre element than another. For example, some books have more action and supernatural elements, some stories have more adventure and mystery, and others focus on the relationships between characters in addition to solid doses of humor.

Cops & Clobbers in Deadwood took me longer to write due to life interfering and keeping me out of the writing chair, but I'm back to work now. I'm looking forward to catching up with all of the characters in my different series over the next year, and I hope you are, too! Thank you for your patience as I found myself and my "voice" again.

*"It takes an awful lot of time to **not** write a book."* ~Douglas Adams

Happy reading!

Ann Charles

www.anncharles.com

ACKNOWLEDGMENTS

I am so lucky to be surrounded by so many wonderful humans (and a few *others*) who help and support me from the start of a book through to the final promotional push after it's released. Thank you to all who follow and many more not listed who have been so kind over the last year:

My husband, Sam Lucky, for your love and hugs and all you do to help me write and create a book; my son, for dropping everything at a moment's notice to take a weeklong trip with me to South Dakota during a winter storm; and my daughter, for helping me with story ideas and brainstorming character development.

Violet's First Draft superstars: Mary Ida Kunkle, Becky Binder, Kristy McCaffrey, Marcia Britton, Paul Franklin, Diane Garland, Michelle Davis, Vicki Huskey, Lucinda Nelson, Stephanie Kunkle, and Wendy Gildersleeve. You were so much fun to tell this story to one chapter at a time!

C.S. Kunkle for making time to draw when you had so much excitement going on in your own life. Eilis Flynn, my amazing editor, for your patience as I continued to push back one deadline after another. Violet's WorldKeeper, Diane Garland, for hanging out with me in Florida and for helping me remember the finer details of Violet's life prior to this book. Michelle Davis and Mark Davis for always being willing to help out even when troubles are doubling up on you. Becky Binder for your determination and smiles. Wendy Gildersleeve for your help whenever I need it on whatever project comes your way. Cheryl Reavis, an amazing author, for writing one of my very favorite books, *One of Our Own*.

Violet's Beta Team for your willingness to help me in whatever timeframe you're given and for your wonderful feedback. You give me the confidence to publish without needing to hide under the bed … for too long. Violet's Deadwood Deputies, readers, and friends for your kindness, awesome support, and helpful reviews. Without you, Violet wouldn't be able to find new readers to join us all in this wild and woolly series. Finally, my brother, Clint, for always hanging in there no matter how bumpy the road gets.

Violet Lynn Parker (1–14)—Heroine of the series, real estate agent
Willis "Old Man" Harvey (1–14)—Violet's sidekick and bodyguard
Dane "Doc" Nyce (1–14)—Violet's boyfriend, medium
Detective "Coop" Cooper (1–14)—Deadwood and Lead's detective
Zoe Parker (1–14)—Violet's aunt and mentor in life
Layne Parker (1–14)—Violet's nine-year-old son
Adelynn Parker (1–14)—Violet's nine-year-old daughter
Natalie Beals (1–14)—Violet's best friend since childhood
Jerry Russo (4–9,11–14)—Violet's boss, owner of Calamity Jane Realty
Mona Hollister (1–9,11–14)—Violet's coworker and mentor in realty
Ray Underhill (1–9,12,14)—Violet's ex-coworker and nemesis at work
Benjamin Underhill (1–9,11–14)—Violet's coworker
Jane Grimes (1–9,11–14)—Violet's previous boss
Cornelius Curion (3–14)—Violet's client; so-called ghost whisperer
Reid Martin (2–14)—Captain of the fire dept., Aunt Zoe's ex-lover
Oscar "Ox" Martin (12,14)—Reid's son
Prudence (2–9,11–14)—Ghost residing at the Carhart/Britton house
Zelda Britton (2,4–9,11–14)—Owner of the Carhart house in Lead
Dominick Masterson (4,7–9,11–14)—Previous client of Violet's old boss, Jane, and well-known Lead businessman
Mr. Black (2–4,6,8,9,11–14)—Mysterious, pale-faced Timekeeper
Hildegard Zuckerman (12)—Friend of Mr. Black and Ms. Wolff
Ms. Wolff (5,8,9,14)—Previous resident of Apt. 4 in the Galena House
Rosy (6–9,12)—Camerawoman from TV series, *Paranormal Realty*
Hope & Blake Parker (9-10,12-14)—Violet's parents
Susan Parker (1–10,13-14)—Violet's sister; aka "the Bitch from Hell"
Quint Parker (1–3,7–10,14)—Violet's brother; Layne's hero
Freesia Tender (5–9,13-14)—Owner of the Galena House
Stone Hawke (5–9,11,13-14)—Coop's ex-partner on the force; detective called in to solve cases
Rex Conner (3–9,11,14)—Biological father of Violet's children
Eddie Mudder (3,6–9,13-14)—Owner of Mudder Bros Funeral Parlor
Theodore Weatherly (14)—Deadwood's Town Archivist
Madame Oliva Contraire (14)—Medium (possible) hired by Vi's boss

"I love it when a plan comes together."
~**Colonel John "Hannibal" Smith**
The A-Team

CHAPTER ONE

Friday, February 8th
Deadwood, South Dakota

Apparently, hell had frozen over.

But I had bigger troubles these days—the ticking kind.

"It's colder than a polar bear's ass in here, Sparky," Old Man Harvey said, shivering in his thick Sherpa coat.

He wasn't stretching the blanket on that forecast. In fact, I wished we had a blanket to stretch across us, the thicker the better.

"You can borrow money on that. My toes stopped radioing in ten minutes ago." I rubbed my gloved hands on my thighs to keep my legs from turning into flesh-cicles.

My self-appointed bodyguard and I were two peas in a pod on this late afternoon in the Black Hills. The "pod" being a dark and quiet pickup truck with windows growing frostier on the outside and foggier on the inside by the minute. Our breaths steamed the air inside the cab, but not enough to beat back winter's bitter-cold fingers. Mother Nature had shaken Deadwood's snow globe really hard, leaving us in a mire of swirling doom.

Harvey grunted. "You're gonna have to face the facts head-on, girl. We hit a knot and there ain't no goin' forward."

"Quit your bellyaching." I cupped my hands in front of my mouth, blowing warm air into them. "It won't be much longer."

"You've been singin' that tune for the last hour."

A blast of wind rocked the vehicle, peppering the windshield with pellets of icy snow.

Harvey turtled deeper into his collar. "Besides, you and I both know we'd have a better chance at tryin' to lasso a snowflake than sneakin' a bunch of creepy clocks out from under Johnny Law's big nose."

Maybe so, but I was trying to remain optimistic in spite of being backed steadily into the corner over the last few months.

"We've herded cats before," I reminded him.

I snuggled into my cashmere scarf and tugged my stocking cap lower on my forehead, wishing I had a trapper hat with furry flaps to cover my ears like Harvey.

He snorted. "Sure, but them there were practically tame kitties. Not to mention the weather was downright pleasant compared to this mess." He thumbed toward his half-fogged-up window.

It was ten below outside. At least that was what the pickup's temperature gauge had displayed the last time Harvey had started the engine in hopes of stopping our blood from freezing solid. But that number didn't take into account the wind blasting in from the north. Every time I sniffed, my dang sinuses froze halfway to my ears.

"If it gets any more unfriendly out there," he continued, "we're gonna have dogs stuck to fire hydrants all over town."

"We just need to lay low here a bit longer."

"Fine, but I'm gonna start 'er up and warm my vittles again," he said, reaching for the ignition.

I caught his sleeve. "Not yet."

"Why not?"

"It's still light enough to see the exhaust and there should be another cop car rolling by any minute now."

"This wind will blow the exhaust away before anyone sees it."

"Give it five more minutes." I tugged his arm my way. "Please."

He scowled and pulled his arm free, but then nodded. "Fine, but you owe me a hot cooked meal for this one, and pizza doesn't count."

I didn't bother reminding him that he was the one who'd invited himself along on my stakeout this afternoon, not the other way around.

I frowned out the windshield at the old multi-story boarding house sitting a hop, skip, and a short sprint up the street. The darkening sky behind Galena House painted a chilling scene, but not because of the dwelling's blood-stained history. According to the weather reports, western South Dakota was about to be slammed by a polar blast that would keep us frozen solid for a week or two. That sky promised frost-bitten toes and fingers—or worse—for any unfortunate souls stuck outside for too long.

A glance at Harvey found him with his hands stuffed in his armpits. "Much more of this cold," he said between chattering teeth, "and you'll have to dress me in a pine overcoat and tuck me in for a dirt nap."

"You know the saying—if you can't handle the cold, get out of the freezer."

"That ain't a sayin', and it sure as hell ain't motivatin' me one way or the other." He scoffed under his breath. "I think your funny bone done froze up and broke off, Sparky."

I raised the binoculars I'd brought along to keep an eye on the boarding house from a safe distance. I could see light in several windows on the two main levels of Galena House, except for the downstairs apartment at the lower back quarter of the building, which was exactly where I needed to go to get those damned creepy clocks.

Unfortunately, there was more than a trek through the Black Hills' ice box and a locked apartment door in our way. Detective Stone Hawke, the rent-a-detective from Rapid City, who was temporarily helping out the local police, had taken up residence in that particular corner of the building. The grandstanding blowhard was already trying to pin multiple murders on me, so I didn't need to add any more charges to my list of possible crimes.

Harvey sighed. "Well, hell. I done lost all feelin' in my left ass cheek and for what? We ain't seen hide nor hair of that badge-totin' fool comin' or goin' out of that old haunt."

As old haunts went, Galena House had a solid reputation for tragedy over its century-plus history. Some of the deaths had been of the human variety, some not so human. But its fatal reputation wasn't on my mind today. I was waiting and watching for a whole other reason. Make that, for a whole *other* problem.

"True, but I'm playing the long game these days," I said.

"You're too short on time and long on talk, if you ask me."

Headlights turned our way from up the street. I lowered the binoculars and slid down in my seat, motioning Harvey to follow. "That's the cops on their next scheduled drive-by," I whispered, checking the time on my phone. This one was running a few minutes late. After monitoring the scene for the past few days, I'd learned their vehicles and routines.

"Why are you whisperin'?" Harvey asked. "Smoky can't hear us." He hunkered lower as the cop rolled closer, the top of his trapper hat hidden by the steering wheel.

"Just humor me, old man."

"You wanna know what I'm thinkin', Sparky?"

"That feels like a trick question."

Harvey's thoughts tended to center around his wild escapades with women over the years and often involved some state of nudity. He usually made sure to include enough tawdry details to make my cheeks burn.

"Gettin' caught might not be so bad," he continued in spite of my hesitation.

I held my breath as the vehicle passed by the pickup at a slow crawl, its tires crunching on the hardened slush and packed snow.

Harvey inched upward, watching via his side mirror as "Smoky" drove away. "At least they keep the jail cells nice and warm. I hear the toilets are purty clean, too."

I cringed. "Not clean enough."

I knew that fact from hand-cuffed experience thanks to Harvey's nephew, Deadwood's regular irksome long arm of the law, Detective Cooper.

Fortunately, Cooper and I had reached a compromise after being forced to work together lately more often than not. He'd even agreed to stop threatening to arrest me. We also shared a love for Natalie Beals, my best friend since my tree fort–making days, who happened to be rubbing ankles under the covers with the prickly law dog most nights now.

"My prostate ain't likin' this cold sittin' business any more than my tail feathers." Harvey struggled fully upright and turned to peer out the back window.

I followed his lead, watching the taillights of the Deadwood Police rig fade in the growing gloom. "I told you it was a cop."

I'd gotten good at recognizing the police department's cruisers, SUVs, and pickup trucks from a distance.

As soon as the taillights were swallowed up by the windy gloom, I turned back to the front. The coast was clear at the moment, and the tip of my nose was starting to tingle from the cold.

"Okay, run the engine and warm us up again."

Harvey grunted and leaned forward. The truck started with a bit of reluctance.

"We need to leave it runnin' longer this time. If it gets much colder, it might not want to start." He patted the steering wheel. "The old boy gets a tad cantankerous when it's nut-and-bolt-freezin' weather."

My cheeks were almost too cold for me to smile. "Are we talking about the pickup or you?"

That earned a small grin in response, but his expression sobered again in a blink.

I leaned closer, taking a longer look at him in the glow of lights from the dash. The ornery sparkle was missing from his blue eyes, and his silver beard seemed more straggly around the edges. Come to think of it, I hadn't seen a gold tooth peeking out from his smile in days.

"Are you feeling okay?" I asked, sitting back in my seat. "You seem a quart low on piss and vinegar the last few days. Are you catching a cold?"

He waved me off. "I'm fine. I'm just down in my joints thanks to this polar plunge."

"So, it has nothing to do with one of your old flames giving you some heart pains?" Or was it a lack of women making him a sad sack?

Harvey usually had a pretty rose waiting for him to stop by and water her petals. During the last week, though, he'd been eating both breakfast and supper at my aunt Zoe's house, leaving only long enough to sleep and bathe.

He shrugged and then cleared his throat. "I've been thinking …"

Oh no. I cringed in preparation but played along as his stakeout buddy. "About women?"

He shook his head. "About this here caper of yours. We need a name for it."

I blinked in surprise at his sharp right turn in the conversation. "I told you when you picked me up from work that this isn't a caper."

We'd no sooner rolled out of the parking lot behind Calamity Jane Realty's office than he'd started spouting off about planning one.

"All great capers have groovy sorts of names," he said, clearly ignoring me.

"*Groovy?*" I rolled my eyes. "Are you still talking to my moondust-sniffing mother every day?"

My mom had barely evolved beyond the hippie era of her younger years. The yoga-loving wildflower continually preached to me about peace and happiness, especially when it came to getting along with my sister, Susan, who had been as crooked as the devil's backbone since childhood.

Lately, Mom had taken to chatting up my friends. I suspected this was her attempt to keep tabs on my mental stability after Christmas, when I'd learned that Susan had stolen my identity and used it to marry some rich dying fossil who'd keeled over soon after the wedding. Lucky for me, their vows didn't stick due to a previous marriage that had never come to an official end, so I remained Violet Parker, single taxpayer, at the moment. However, there was still the big fish's will, into which Susan had finagled her way, and I didn't want even one slimy penny the dead guy had set aside in my name. Or the money for my kids, either, whom Susan had pretended were her offspring.

My sister had promised my mom she'd fix this mess, but Susan had a history of running off when shit got too deep and leaving me facedown in the muck. I had doubts about seeing any sunshine at the end of this particular sewer tunnel anytime soon.

"Hippie Hope and I like to share recipes and talk about the good ol' days," Harvey said with a shrug. "How about this for a caper name: The Timekeeper Tomfoolery?"

"That sounds like a nursery rhyme."

"You're right, plus it's too much of a mouthful." He scratched at his bearded cheek. "The Grand Clock Cavort?"

"That's even more words."

"Yeah, but it's about half the syllables. Wait! I got it. The Charge of the Cuckoo Brigade."

"It's almost turning into a full-on sentence now."

He shrugged. "I sorta like the military feel in that one."

"Yeah, well, for the umpteenth time, this is *not* a caper so we don't need an official name."

"Then what are we doing here?" He shifted in his seat. "Besides givin' my aches and pains plenty of reasons to caterwaul."

"I told you, we're on a stakeout." I lifted the paper lunch sack from the console between us. "We even have snacks like they do in the movies, remember?"

"Of course I remember the snacks, Sparky. I'm the one who made the sandwiches and chips. If it were up to you, we'd be nibblin' on crackers for hours on end while our bones started protrudin' through our skin."

I harrumphed. "It would take a lot longer than a few hours to start seeing either of our bones."

I'd done a bang-up job of putting on a pound or two over the holidays. Or maybe five, but who was counting besides the scale, and I'd thrown that stool pigeon in the garbage can a few days after New Year's with a shout of "Good riddance!" and instructions where it could shove its insulting numbers.

"I noticed you've been bendin' your elbow more lately at the table," Harvey said with a teasing wink. "Spoonin' on your winter weight, are you?"

I held up my fist between us. "Careful, bucket mouth. Them there are fighting words. Besides, it's always good to have some extra pounds stored up in case of an emergency."

He playfully knocked my hand aside. "This might be a stakeout, Sparky, but you gotta admit that it also feels like the beginnin' of a good ol'-fashioned caper."

"How do you figure?"

I pulled a grilled pastrami and provolone sandwich from the bag. The bread was golden brown and sprinkled with salt, looking pretzel like, with the pastrami piled thick in between. It smelled like a piece of deli heaven.

"A stakeout is where you're watchin' a person or a place," he explained.

"Exactly." I tried not to drool as I held out his half of the sandwich "snack" he'd made for us. "We're watching the boarding house."

He took the sandwich half and then stole the paper bag away from me. "You forgot about the fresh-baked parmesan chips I packed."

"I'm planning to get to those after I finish with this sexy baby." I took a bite of my sandwich. The bun was crispy, and then soft and delicious, mimicking a big pretzel. The tender, salty meat and rich cheese almost made me forget about how cold my cheeks were—both sets. "Oh my molies, Harvey. This is so good."

Harvey dug into the paper sack and pulled out two sealed bags of cheese chips, tossing one my way.

I swallowed my mouthful before saying, "And since we're here watching to see when Detective Hawke gets home, that's two for two." I opened the bag of homemade chips. "So, it's officially a *stakeout*, and that's all it is. No catchy name needed."

Actually, the apartment in which Detective Hawke was squatting was not really his "home." According to Freesia Tender, who owned Galena House, the previous renter's name was still on the lease. "Ms. Wolff" was the name, whom I hoped was resting in peace since I'd unwillingly played a major part in her demise, but only after I was coerced—well, blackmailed even, sort of—into taking on her role of keeping track of "time" with those damned clocks left behind in her apartment.

I took another bite of sandwich, and then another, thinking about "time" as I chewed. Not the normal moon-to-sun-to-moon minutes in a day, but rather the amount of time that non-human troublemakers, aka *others*, traveled inside this particular realm. Without those clocks, which acted like warning alarms, I was blind to the potential danger coming my way.

Sadly, the sandwich was gone too soon, just like Ms. Wolff, who'd paid her rent a year in advance according to Freesia and still had another seven months left on the contract. In my opinion, that meant Detective Hawke was taking advantage of a dead woman. However, Cooper had a slightly different view on that front. More important, though, the furnishings inside the apartment still belonged to Ms. Wolff, including a shitload of custom-made Black Forest cuckoo clocks that I needed to do my Timekeeping job in order to maintain balance between good and evil here in the Black Hills.

Like some overzealous hen, Detective Hawke was sitting tight on the nest of cuckoo clocks inside the apartment, while he kept squawking, "Police evidence!" over and over. The dopey bird refused to let any civilians inside until Ms. Wolff's killer was found and the murder case closed.

I wiped my mouth with the napkin Harvey had included in his snack bag. Somehow, I had to figure out how to get past Detective Hawke to collect his ticking evidence while evading the suspicious nincompoop, and a jail cell while I was at it. Unfortunately, my name was always the first on his suspect list no matter the crime.

"It's a caper," Harvey reiterated while finishing his sandwich. "You're just in denial about it."

"*Not* in denial." I opened my bag of cheese chips, savoring the smell of baked parmesan.

"Bull hockey. We're not just watchin' for that silly peacock to return to the coop." He nodded toward the boarding house out the windshield. "We're here to come up with a plan on how to get into that apartment he's holin' up in and nab those clocks." He pointed a chip at me. "And that's what you call good ol' premeditation, girlie, which is leadin' up to a caper."

I shook my head, glancing out at the bits of snow the stiff winds were blowing this way and that as I tried to daintily nibble on a cheese chip before giving up and cramming the whole thing in my mouth. Dear Lord, these chips! I had to fight the urge to play horse and feedbag with the rest.

" 'Premeditation' sounds too ominous," I said between chips. "I don't want to do anything criminal."

At least not today.

And especially not with Harvey in tow. Cooper would chew me up one side and down the other for getting his uncle stuck in this latest mire, and that law dog had sharp teeth.

"You mean you just don't want to get caught," Harvey said, staring at me with one bushy eyebrow raised.

I shrugged. "Hawke doesn't really need those clocks to solve the case of Ms. Wolff's death."

"Because you killin' her had nothin' to do with the clocks, right?" He snickered.

"You can sit on that sarcasm and spin, wiseacre." I mock-glared at him while shoving another chip in my mouth. "And I didn't kill her. She wanted to be done with this life, remember? She sacrificed herself in order to pass this damned Timekeeping task on to me."

"No need to go cockin' your shotgun in my direction, Sparky."

He held up his hands in surrender. "I know you had to sacrifice that particular cow to save the herd."

I took a deep breath and plucked another chip from the bag. "Anyway, I can't just go to Detective Hawke and tell him that I need those clocks because there are a bunch of *others* coming to kill me."

With an official bounty out on my head now, the word "bunch" might not be adequate. A slew of *others* might be better. Or a troop. That sounded more ominous. Like a wild battalion of bloodlust-filled monkeys.

I grimaced and ate another chip.

Anyway, what was even worse, these hunters were coming for my daughter, too. Addy was already showing signs of following along in my ancestral line of killing, between her natural ease with weaponry and her psychic dreams. My son, Layne, wasn't out of the woods either, since he seemed to be some sort of innate monster beacon, luring deadly fiends for me to execute. Criminy! As if worrying about my kids being bullied at school wasn't bad enough.

"Those clocks are a key part of the monitoring process," I said aloud, repeating what Harvey and I both knew.

"Sure as a dead man stinks."

"Eww." I wrinkled my nose at him. "I'm eating here."

"Which is why we have to figure out how to hijack them clocks out from under Johnny Law's nose." He snatched the next chip from me before I could stuff it in my mouth. "And that there is the makin's of a *caper*, plain and simple," he said with a smug look while popping the stolen chip into his mouth.

"Fine, maybe this is sort of caper-ish. But if we're going to take this to the next level, we can't say a peep to anyone."

"That right there is how the cow ate the cabbage."

I was glad he agreed with me. "Especially not your nephew. He's probably allergic to capers, breaking out in a rash of handcuffs and Miranda rights at the mere notion of one."

"We might need Coop's help, though, especially with throwing Hawke off our scent, and any other law dogs sniffin' around."

Harvey had a point. It would be good to have someone on the inside when it came to the police. Not that Detective Hawke trusted anyone much these days if they had any ties to me; not even

Cooper, his official partner in crime fighting.

"I don't know," I said, chomping on another chip. "How about mum's the word until we've worked out any kinks in our caper plans." I pulled off my glove and held out my little finger. "Pinkie swear to silence with me, ol' man."

Harvey leaned forward and sniffed a couple of times, then frowned at my pinkie as if I'd been sticking it in places the sun didn't shine. "I'm not touchin' that. I don't know where you had it last."

I gaped. "It's just my pinkie."

A pair of headlights blared through the back window, lighting up the cab like we were sitting on stage.

"Get down!" I whispered and slid southward again.

Harvey stayed put, trying to block the bright light reflecting in the rearview mirror. "I'm not sure hidin' is gonna do us any good this time, what with the engine runnin'."

Crud. He was right. We'd been made.

I heard the dull thump of a car door in spite of the wind's buffering attempts. Struggling back upright, I brushed the chip crumbs from my scarf and lap. "If it's Detective Hawke, let me do the talking."

"You gonna put a hex on him again, Witchy Parker?" Harvey wiggled his fingers at me, pretending to cast a spell.

"No, Mr. Smarty Suspenders. Playing witch with the dufus usually lands me in more trouble." Although truth be told, every time I talked to Detective Hawke, I seemed to dig the hole in which I was standing a few feet deeper no matter how much I tried to toe the line. "I'll just say that we're waiting for Natalie to finish up inside and join us. It's not against the law to loiter outside a house with good intentions, is it?"

"That probably depends on how deep your hands are in your pockets and your definition of *good*." Harvey wiped at his steamy window, looking out at his driver's side mirror. "Hold onto your britches, Sparky."

"Why?"

"Here comes Pecos Bill ridin' in on a tornado." He sat back, grimacing my way. "It looks like he's chewin' on a mouthful of barbed wire to boot."

"What do you—"

Boom-boom-boom!

A gloved fist pounded on the driver's side window.

Detective Cooper's scowling face filled the glass.

"Open up, dammit!" he barked.

CHAPTER TWO

When Harvey rolled the window down, a blast of wind reached inside and slapped us both in the face.

"Criminy," I grumbled, shivering clear to my toenails.

"Howdy, boy!" he hollered to Cooper, smiling wide. Or maybe his lips had just flash-frozen that way. "You wanna join us? It's colder than a bucket of snowman piss out there."

Cooper's gaze locked onto me and squeezed into a hard squint. "I should have known you'd be with Parker."

"What's that supposed to mean?" I asked, his tone spurring me to glare back.

His focus returned to his uncle. "Dispatch got a call about a couple of knuckleheads who appeared to have gotten stuck in the snow up here, so I volunteered to check out the situation on my way to Nat's place."

"We're not stuck," Harvey said, pulling his fur-lined collar tighter around his neck.

"Then what are you two doing here?"

Before I could come up with a good explanation that wouldn't make Cooper coil up and start hissing, Harvey fired back a question of his own. "Hey, Coop, you're still plannin' to play poker with us tonight, aren't ya?"

Usually the guys' poker night was on Wednesdays, but my boyfriend—actually, Doc Nyce was now my secret fiancé—had been pulling some long hours of late, what with him being in the financial advising business and tax season in full swing. To make things easier on Doc, Harvey had rescheduled poker night to this evening, since Doc hadn't booked any appointments for Saturday morning.

Cooper held his arm up as another gust of wind rocked him on his feet. "Yeah, but aren't Parker's kids gone this weekend?"

Natalie must have told him about my parents taking my fraternal twins for an early birthday getaway weekend. Addy and Layne would hit double digits this year—the big 1-0—and my parents thought it'd be fun to take them to an inside amusement park resort down in Denver.

"Why do my kids being out of town matter when it comes to playing poker?"

The kids would normally be home with Aunt Zoe and me while the guys had their beer-and-cards fun over at Cooper's place. Make that Doc's house, since he was renting it to Cooper and Harvey while he shacked up with me and the kids at Aunt Zoe's.

I probably needed to start thinking about eventually moving to Doc's now that marriage was in the picture. Of course, I'd fantasized about this happening during the months we'd dated, but now that it was more than a daydream, I wasn't sure I was ready yet to leave Aunt Zoe and the home where we'd created so many memories.

Cooper shrugged. "I just figured Nyce and you would want to enjoy some time without kids."

Harvey scoffed. "She and her stallion can screw around together every night, Coop. They have plenty of time to play *poke-'er* under the sheets. What Doc needs is to shake off her bridle now and then, so he can horse around with us." He paused, his face scrunching. "I think that mighta come out sideways through my back teeth, but you get my meanin'."

"You certainly painted a picture," I said, still shivering.

Cooper winced as a freezing gust hit him. "If you aren't stuck, then what are you two pains-in-the-asses doing here?"

"Nothing, Cooper." I stuffed a cheese chip in my mouth while glancing the other way. I was afraid my tell-tale nose twitch might give away my little white lie. My peek back in his direction ran smack-dab into his eagle-eyed glare.

"Let's try that again," Cooper said. "Uncle Willis, how about you fill me in on what you two are doing out here." This time it clearly wasn't a question.

"I'd sorta rather keep my business to myself," Harvey said,

shooting me a worried frown.

"That's your right, of course. But I could call a pal of mine who's now at the Bureau of Alcohol, Tobacco, Firearms and Explosives, and put a bug in his ear about that cannon you bought off the internet from an unlicensed dealer."

I leaned toward the nosy detective. "Blackmail isn't a pretty color on you, Cooper."

"Yeah? Well, orange jumpsuits and your crazy blond curls would make you look like a jail cell clown, Parker, so one of you two turkeys better cough up the truth before Hawke gets word about you being within breathing distance of those damned clocks."

Harvey looked at the boarding house for a couple of beats, and then turned to his nephew. "We ain't doin' nothin' much. Just havin' a little polar picnic."

Cooper lifted his walkie-talkie to his mouth. "Dispatch, Detective Cooper here. I might need you to put a call into ATF."

Harvey flinched, holding up his hands in surrender. "Okay, Coop. You win. Sparky and I are just doin' a little premeditating, that's all."

The detective's steely gray gaze lasered back and forth between his uncle and me. "Premeditating about what?"

When Harvey hesitated, I came up with an answer. "Tomorrow's breakfast."

"Bullshit, Parker. Try again." Cooper lifted his walkie-talkie to his mouth, focusing on his uncle while his thumb hovered over the Talk button. "Or do I get ATF on the horn?"

Harvey sighed, cursing under his breath. "It's nothin' to get all huffin' and puffin' about, Coop. Sparky and I are just ponderin' the idea of plannin' a teeny-tiny caper to sorta borrow some—or maybe all—of those clocks from your ding-a-ling partner, so we can save the world from some very, very bad, sharp-toothed critters."

Hell's bells. Harvey had sold me out for a cannon.

Cooper's face hardened into a full-fledge scowl so fast he might have cracked a molar. "You're planning a caper with *Parker?*"

I bristled. "What do you have against me?"

I had a great batting record when it came to sneaking around in the dark and not getting caught.

Well, a pretty decent record, anyway.

Mostly.

Cooper guffawed. "You two can barely walk side by side without tripping over each other's feet."

Oh, that was rich coming from him of all people. I crossed my arms. "Remind me, Cooper, who has ended up with a broken nose and multiple black eyes at previous crime scenes? Was it your uncle or me?"

Cooper pointed his police walkie-talkie at me. "That's because you're an irresponsible investigator. You need to leave crime scenes to the professionals and stick to real estate."

I held my hands out palms up. "Show me some professional crime scene investigators and I'll happily back away. Until then, when it comes to solving crimes, I'm stuck with you and a barking mad version of the Sheriff of Nottingham."

Harvey sat forward, keeping me from doing something stupid like throwing the bag of my remaining cheese chips at the insulting ape outside the window.

"Now don't you two start peckin' at each other again," Harvey said. "Besides, it's just a li'l caper, Coop."

The walkie-talkie crackled to life. "Detective Cooper, you want me to contact the ATF?" the dispatch officer asked.

"Negative on that. I'm *out* for the night." He stuffed the walkie-talkie inside his thick coat as another squall rocked the truck. "Unlock the doors," he told his uncle.

"Why?" I asked warily.

"Because I'm going to use simple words and non-complex sentences to explain to you bumbling yahoos why this caper idea of yours is an incredibly foolish risk, and I'm not going to freeze my ass off in the process." He held up his gloved index finger. "Sit tight. I'll be right back."

Harvey rolled up his window while Cooper dashed back to his vehicle for whatever reason. "Hot peppers, Sparky."

"What about them?"

"That boy seems to have a couple of fiery ones jammed up his tailpipe this afternoon, and I figure he'll be spittin' fire at us from the other end when he gets back here."

"Well, if you'd have kept quiet about our caper idea."

"Yeah, yeah." He pursed his lips. "But I can't lose that cannon before I even get a chance to light 'er up."

"What do you even need a cannon for?"

"Shootin' whangdoodles," he said, as if a sillier question had never been asked.

Whangdoodle was the name Harvey's grandpappy had given the odd inhabitants back in Slagton, an old mining town that supposedly had gone sour along with the water after years of mine tailings contaminating the creeks and wells. At least that was the government's story. The truth was much darker and involved some of those bad, sharp-toothed critters Harvey had mentioned to Cooper.

But Slagton and its whangdoodles were way down on my list of worries these days. I had sharp-clawed trouble on the verge of blindsiding me, and I needed those dang clocks to help me bob and weave. Unfortunately, now that Cooper had his tail lit up about our caper notion, the hill in front of me just got higher.

The headlights glaring through the back window went dark. A couple of seconds later, a shivering gush of cold air slid into the backseat along with a frosty cop. How wonderful.

"It smells like feet in here," Cooper said, tugging off his black stocking cap. His short blond hair stuck out this way and that, reminding me of upside-down icicles. "Same as it did last night at the house. Did you bring some of those parmesan chips along?"

Harvey held up his half-full bag of cheese chips.

"I'll be confiscating that." Cooper reached forward and grabbed it, shucking his gloves so he could pluck out a chip. "Damn, that imp sure did a number on your interior."

He was right on that. Harvey had to duct tape the seats and door panel that the imp had shredded a couple of weeks ago.

"I'm waiting for some new seats to come in at the body shop, then I'll take it in and get 'im back to as good as new."

"So, was it Parker's harebrained idea to plan this stupid clock caper?"

"All I had planned was a stakeout," I said, turning in my seat so I could snarl at the detective when necessary without having to twist my neck. "Your uncle talked me into the caper part."

Harvey scoffed. "Did not. I just pondered why you dragged me out here on this hairy afternoon, proposin' that maybe what *you* were noodlin' was actually a caper."

I scoffed louder than him. "You *proposed?*"

He shrugged. "I s'pose you could say 'hinted'?"

"I distinctly remember repeated mentions of the word 'caper' on *your* part, not mine."

A growl came from the law dog in the back seat. "You know what? Whichever of you two crackpots came up with this caper concept doesn't matter, so long as you realize it's a bad idea that you should forget about, like last week's meatloaf."

I narrowed my gaze. "I made last week's meatloaf. What was wrong with it besides me burning the top a bit?"

Harvey snickered. "It never did quite make it into the 'loaf' stage. More like a pan of congealed chicken hearts and livers drizzled with gooey, ammonia-smellin' snot."

I gaped at the old goat. "Those were mushrooms and beets under some melted brie, all of which are perfectly good foods. Besides, you can't blame a mom for trying to cook something healthy for her growing children."

Cooper shuddered visibly. "I've seen better-looking three-day-dead roadkill on a summer afternoon. You should stick to store-bought pizza and leave getting those clocks to me."

I shook my head. "I'm tired of waiting for you to get them. You keep giving me excuses when I ask you about sneaking a single damned clock, let alone a bunch of them."

"Those aren't excuses, Parker. They're logical reasons correlating to laws, and they clearly explain why you need to wait a little while longer to access that apartment."

"Just a little longer, huh?" I thumbed toward the boarding house. "You and I both know Detective Hawke isn't going to leave that place anytime soon."

"Which is why Sparky and I are gonna come up with a way to light a fire under that turkey hawk's tail feathers," Harvey added with a can-do nod.

Cooper's jaw set. "It's not going to work."

"Jeez, Cooper." I sighed. "Someone needs to take a pickaxe to the chunk of granite sitting north of your shoulders that we keep mistaking for a head."

"Don't come swinging for me, Parker. I know when to duck."

"Your crooked nose says otherwise," Harvey pointed out,

chuckling.

Cooper's mulish gaze shifted to his uncle. "Whose side are you on, Uncle Willis? Parker's? Or me and your cannon's?"

"The cannon's." There wasn't even a slice of hesitation on Harvey's part.

I wrinkled my upper lip at the bearded buzzard before returning to his nephew. "How can you be so certain our caper won't work when we haven't even told you our plan yet?"

Not that we had a plan, but for all Cooper knew we'd already tunneled our way into the basement of Galena House and had wheelbarrows lined up and ready to haul everything out but the kitchen sink.

His lips tightened to a thin, stubborn line. "I don't need to hear your cockamamie plan, Parker. From my position within the police department, I can tell you with certainty there is no way you can get your greasy mitts on those clocks without causing a hell of a ruckus that would send Hawke on a rampage and end with both of you meatheads in jail and me demoted to handing out parking tickets just by association with you two."

Harvey harrumphed under his breath. "Maybe Coop's right, Sparky. Maybe we can't make the grade here."

I did a double take. Harvey didn't usually change tactics so quickly, especially when it came to notions that made his blue eyes sparkle like this possible caper had for a moment.

"There's no *maybe* about it, Uncle Willis." Cooper rubbed his hands together, apparently trying to use friction to make up for the truck's inability to fight off the frigid weather outside. "You two don't seem to understand yet how much Hawke would love to lock Parker and her broomstick behind bars, so he can mark these cases as 'Closed' and head back down to Rapid City, where he believes a promotion will be waiting for him. Possibly even a dream opportunity for him to step into some FBI shoes."

My chest tightened while flares of anger shot upward, heating my cheeks. "It's bullshit that this is about furthering his career. Never mind that my family is in danger, and that my neck might be on the chopping block any day now if I can't get to those clocks."

I knew another asshole who'd recently tried to use me to further his career—Rex Conner, my kids' sperm donor. To make matters worse, Rex was still working up in Lead at the defunct Homestake gold mine that was now a science research center, which meant he kept popping up in my sea of life like a bloated shark carcass. I wouldn't mind taking a pickaxe to Rex, too. Only I'd aim lower when it came to the selfish, cheating bastard.

"This is partly about Hawke's career," Cooper said. "And partly about his pride. You've poked that bear too many times, Parker. Something I warned you about more than once."

"Yeah, yeah, yeah. You keep hacking on that stuck hairball."

"Only because you keep screwing up and making things worse." He ignored my middle finger rebuttal, focusing on his uncle. "At least one of you is coming to your senses about this caper crap. What was your grand plan, anyway? Blow a hole in the side of the boarding house with Uncle Willis's cannon, grab the clocks, and run?"

"Oh, come on!" I rolled my eyes. "Give me and Yosemite Sam here a little credit."

"Hey, that's not a bad idea," Harvey said, grinning my way. "You think Freesia has her insurance paid up?"

The image of Detective Hawke standing in the middle of the apartment with gunsmoke-singed cheeks and smoking hair popped into my head. I snickered. "She'd probably have to get an additional policy rider before we try that."

"That's not even a tiny bit funny, Parker," Cooper snapped. "Don't encourage Uncle Willis. He's hot to trot and already a-saddled to light up that cannon."

"Oh, get that stick out of your blowhole, Detective Buzzkill. Harvey's kidding around." I looked back at the cannon owner. "You are, right?"

"Maybe." He scratched at his beard. "I guess we could hold off on the cannon for now and figure out a way to replace all those clocks with lookalikes."

Cooper pshawed. "Where are you two going to find that many Black Forest clock replicas?"

"Online." I threw that out just because I didn't like to be pshawed at, especially by someone who wasn't even willing to put any thought into this clock caper.

"The cost of shipping alone would be astronomical," Cooper continued. "Plus, Hawke has had those clocks thoroughly documented with photos. I've seen some of the paperwork on them myself."

"Sparky, what about that clockmaker you met back in Slagton when Coop and I were blowin' holes through those crazy saber-toothed turkeys down the road?"

Actually, the clockmaker wasn't in Slagton. I'd gone into a dark realm thanks to a mental medium trick, and Doc had opened a door into somewhere *else*, which happened to be the threshold of an otherworldly clockmaker's workshop. My inter-realm traveling pal, Cornelius Curion, aka the "Spirit Miser" because of his ability to lure in all kinds of ghostly sorts, had been there with me that time. Unfortunately, Cornelius had been instantly smitten with the clockmaker's ethereal beauty, while I'd been overwhelmed by the fact that I was no longer in Kansas or Oz, so neither of us came away from that field trip with anything more than a sense of awe.

"I don't know how easy it would be for Doc to guide me back through the dark to the clockmaker's workshop. Honestly, I'd rather be in jail than go back into that mole-like realm, especially considering all the creatures that might be sniffing around in there, looking for someone to eat."

Not to mention that a certain orange-eyed demon named Kyrkozz might still be stuck there after our last scuffle in the dark, waiting for a new opportunity to rip out my throat and leave my head posted on a pike.

"Good point," Harvey said. "Making a bunch more clocks would probably take too long anyway."

I nodded. "And there's always the chance of something coming back from the dark with me, which could make things even worse in Deadwood than dealing with a cranky detective during a polar vortex." I nodded toward the backseat. "Or two."

"Kiss my frozen ass, Parker." Cooper leaned forward so he was shoulders deep into the front of the cab. "You know, it sort of sounds like you two are trying to come up with a plan, and I thought we all agreed you were *not* going to do anything caper related."

"I didn't sign on any dotted lines, did you, Harvey?"

Cooper bared his teeth at me.

"Down, boy," Harvey said. "We're just shootin' the shit here." He drummed his fingers on the steering wheel. "Sparky, you remember how Ms. Wolff did that time loop deal with you?" At my nod, he continued, "Well, now that you're walkin' a mile in her Timekeeper shoes, what if you tried one of those loops and headed back in time to grab the clocks off her walls? I mean back before Hawke joined the police party."

Cooper guffawed. "Jesus, Uncle Willis. You're suggesting time travel as a plan? Did you pack some hooch in your snack sack, too?"

I ignored Cooper, actually holding up my hand to block his face from view as I answered Harvey. "Being new at this job, I'm not sure how that would work. But Mr. Black might have an idea since he's been doing this clock gig longer than me."

Tall and deadly, the pale-skinned *other* was my partner in Timekeeping. However, Mr. Black's kind were not human hybrids like me and my *Scharfrichter* ancestors. With my luck, my DNA would cause a hiccup in the time loop, and I'd end up who knew where or when and with what.

"You're forgetting something, Parker," Cooper butted in. "Mr. Black and your boyfriend both have warned you against playing with time for your own benefit. Remember that story about one of your ancestors who messed around with time to try to save her husband and ended up losing a kid in the process?"

"I have not forgotten any of that, Cooper." Nor would I ever be able to erase the nightmare I'd had after hearing that ghastly story, or the gut-wrenching image of my daughter—in pieces.

"Alrighty then," Harvey said, waving us both off. "So we're agreed that jugglin' electric eels is preferable to goin' back in the dark or fiddlin' with time."

"We're agreed that we are *not* going to pursue acquiring those clocks until I say we are in the clear," Cooper stated, clipping his consonants for emphasis.

"Boy howdy," Harvey said, adding a grunt for emphasis. "Plannin' this caper with you, Coop, is like tryin' to move a bull out of the kitchen."

Cooper sputtered. "We are not planning a caper. Not now. Not ever. Wrap your hard head around that, Uncle Willis."

"Maybe we could distract Detective Hawke with a bigger problem," I suggested. "You know, like a more sparkly murder case to solve so that he hands off clock duty to Cooper."

"No." Cooper didn't even take a moment to think about my idea.

"Why not?"

"Short of getting fired, Hawke won't let Ms. Wolff's murder case go, because he's dead set that you killed her." His eyes narrowed. "Which you did, Parker."

Cooper had been right there next to me in that apartment when it all went down—most of it, anyway. "Yeah, but not on purpose."

He smirked. "That defense isn't going to spare you from a prison sentence if Hawke can find even a hint of motive or evidence linking you to Ms. Wolff's death, such as you stealing the clocks from her apartment."

"So, let's get the jackass fired then," Harvey said.

"And how are you two going to do that?"

"We could nail him for police harassment," I said sourly. "He's a ham-handed cretin when it comes to women."

"It would take multiple infractions in order to get him anything more than suspended."

"If he's suspended," Harvey said, "then maybe he'll head back down to Rapid City to lick his wounds. Then we can get those clocks without anyone noticin'."

A scoff came from the monkey playing detective between us. "So, you think the Deadwood police will simply lock Ms. Wolff's door and let the cobwebs spread during Hawke's suspension?"

"One could hope," I said.

"Please, Parker. *Hope* is that batshit crazy voice in your head telling you to 'give 'er a try,' when common sense is shouting, 'You're a fool if you do!' "

I wrinkled my nose at him. "You really need to invest in better motivational posters."

"Listen, over the last couple of months, Hawke has gone above and beyond to make this case a big deal at the station. The chief will most likely assign the task of monitoring the apartment to someone else until Hawke returns."

"Maybe they'll assign it to you," Harvey said.

"Sure, and then when the clocks disappear on my watch, how do you think that will look for me since I'm already tangled up in Parker's messes? Not to mention that everyone in town knows I eat supper at her aunt's place most nights of the week." He shook his head. "I don't want clock duty while Parker is around."

"Yeah, but—" I started.

Cooper held up his hand, stopping me. "Let me finish telling you two why getting Hawke suspended or fired is a bad idea. There's a chance that with him out of the picture an outside entity will be called in to help, and trust me, we don't want the Feds nosing into this any more than they already have. You may not like Hawke, but he's acting as a buffer at the moment for even bigger problems for Parker."

"So, you're saying I'm between a Hawke and a hard place," I said with a grin.

Harvey let out a hoot of laughter.

Cooper scowled at my incredible wittiness. "Stick to selling real estate and leave the jokes to Nat."

I ignored him and fished out the last cheese chip from my bag.

"What if we don't get rid of Hawke completely?" Harvey asked. "We just give him a good scare one night in that spooky apartment so he decides to hole up somewhere else for a while."

"Scare him with what, though?" I asked. "He carries a gun, remember. I'm not as fond of bullet scars as Cooper."

"Parker already screwed up any scare tactics by pretending to be a witch and then acting like she could talk to the dead."

"I can talk to the dead." I was thinking of a particular dead Executioner, who lived up in Lead in a beautiful house overlooking the vast Open Cut, a bygone pit mine left over from the town's gold-mining past. "Well, sort of, anyway. We just need someone to act as Prudence's megaphone."

Harvey grumbled under his breath. "Let's not talk about Prudy. You might shake her tree too hard and wake her up, and I'm downright tired of her squawking in my head."

Prudence, the uppity ghost who took great pleasure being overcritical when it came to my screwups as a killer, had taken it upon herself to possess Harvey, my volunteer bodyguard. Unfortunately for Harvey, she had a habit of showing up to the party whenever she pleased, no matter where he was, even if he was in bed with one of his old flames. Prudence had put a crimp in his giddyup, and until we could figure out how to help him rein her in, he was stuck with the dead Executioner rattling around in his head.

"Have you thought about what could happen if Hawke learned more about your true calling?" Cooper asked between chews while finishing off Harvey's bag of chips.

Yes, and none of what came of those thoughts had involved sunshine, rainbows, or even a single unicorn. However, I just shrugged at Cooper. "What do you mean?"

"He's already told everyone at the station that you're a witch, but nobody really believes him. If you continue to play at this supernatural shit in front of him, he might find out *what* you really are, and I don't think he'll swallow that pill as easily as I did."

"Ha!" I aimed a chip at him. "You choked on that pill for weeks."

That was until Cooper joined Doc and me and a couple of others for a séance one night, during which we lured out a nasty ghost that blasted through Detective Skeptic in the backseat and opened his third eye, as Cornelius would say. After that, Cooper could see ghosts, and his doubts about Doc's and my tales of spectral fun and games had dried up.

"Exactly. Trust me, we don't want Hawke knowing more. Let's stick to broomsticks, warts, and spells. You being a witch in his eyes is dangerous enough."

Cooper eased back and tugged on his black beanie cap. Apparently, he was done telling us why we couldn't get the clocks.

A blast of wind rocked the pickup, throwing a small tree limb at the hood.

"I guess Coop knows best, Sparky."

"About what?" I asked, looking over at Harvey in time to catch his wink.

"You and I just aren't wily enough to pull off a caper."

"Damned straight," Cooper said, zipping up his coat. "Hawke has that apartment locked down like Fort Knox. It would take a team effort to even get close, including some recon and surveillance crews, as well as someone who knows how to get around security devices. It wouldn't hurt to have an ace who can shadow Hawke without getting caught, too, and maybe even a couple of movers who could relocate that many clocks without damaging them. Not to mention that Parker would have to be practically hand-in-hand with Hawke the whole time the caper is taking place in order for her alibi to be rock-solid."

I made a face at the thought of holding Detective Hawke's hand. "I'd rather get licked by a demon in the dark."

Cooper slid his gloves on. "You two need to get out of here before Hawke comes home and finds you. I doubt he'll be as friendly as I've been." He eyed me in particular as he reached for the door handle. "Uncle Willis doesn't need to end up in jail tonight. We need him for poker."

"I love you too, Cooper," I hollered at his back as he climbed out into the wind.

He slammed the door.

I turned back to Harvey. "You know, your nephew is a real Dudley Downer."

He smiled wide at me, his two gold teeth shining in the glow of the dash lights.

I recoiled slightly. "What's that about?" I asked, pointing at his happy face.

"Coop mapped out a startin' plan for us."

I thought back on Cooper's parting remarks. Reconnaissance, security detail, surveillance, tailing, relocation. Hmm. The big know-it-all had also said it would take a team, not just Harvey and me.

"We just need to round up the herd," Harvey said, voicing my next thought.

I nodded, grinning myself now. "And see who's willing to join our game of clocks and robbers."

CHAPTER THREE

Saturday, February 9th

No plan ever goes according to plan, even if Harvey claimed we were going to pull off the caper of the century.

I reminded myself of this bit of wisdom the next morning while nearly stumbling into my dresser as I tugged on a pair of black cashmere tights. I'd learned this lesson the hard way last month when my plan to trap and exterminate one persnickety pain-in-the-ass imp had taken a left turn, and I'd ended up saving the little shit from a much bigger, smellier, longer-clawed menace instead.

I grabbed a thermal undershirt from the pile of clean clothes on the chair by my bedroom window. Thanks to the deep cold seeping through the glass, the fabric was chilly enough to make me shiver as I pulled it on. I rubbed my hands over my arms, creating my own heat. Not even the thick curtains could keep winter's touch at bay on a day as frigid as this one was already gearing up to be.

Something thumped in the closet, making one of the doors rattle.

"I heard that," I called out, reaching for the black sweater dotted with faux pearl beads that I'd laid out on the bed before hopping into the shower.

From the other side of my closet doors, a single strangled-sounding *squawk* came in reply.

I hauled the sweater over my head and zipped it up to my chin. "I told you before, my closet is off limits."

To give credit where it was due, that dang imp had run

interference for me in the thick of the chase, a kindness I'd chalked up to me being the enemy of its sharp-toothed enemy.

I grabbed my suede gaucho pants from the back of the chair, stepping into them.

But that didn't explain why the imp had hitched a ride home with me after the fight was over. An unfortunate twist of fate followed, ending with my animal-loving daughter finding the imp lurking in the backyard early the next morning.

I buttoned my pants, tugging at the waist where they were tighter than usual. Hmmm. Much more elbow bending at the supper table and I was going to have to start joining Doc at the Rec Center for some unpleasant types of repeated bending. And jumping. And maybe even jogging, God forbid.

A wet snort came from the direction of my closet. I grimaced toward the doors.

Dang my tender-hearted daughter.

Of course, Addy had taken pity on the shivering critter, which I was almost certain had been an act on its part to gain my kid's sympathy. After all, imps were known to be very tricky and incredibly smart.

Behind my back, Addy had fed the imp some honey, its favorite treat. Then she'd dressed it in one of the sweaters my mother had crocheted for Elvis the chicken, another mischief maker Addy had rescued last summer. Before I could explain to her why keeping an imp for a pet was a very bad idea due to its tendency to wreak havoc, she'd given the darn thing a name: Daisy. My favorite flower. As if that would endear me to the little red-eyed, raisin-skinned devil.

When I'd threatened to toss Daisy the imp out into the cold, Addy had cried up a storm, complete with wretched wails and crocodile tears behind her glasses. She'd sworn on the life of her favorite stuffed animal, Buck the pink-horned unicorn, to have dreamt that Daisy would save my life someday, but only if we let the imp stick close to us.

That dream bit had given me pause. The same went for Doc and Aunt Zoe, who'd been in the kitchen with me during Addy's maelstrom. All three of us had exchanged worried frowns, because Addy had a history of dreaming about events starring me that were either happening at the moment or yet to come.

What had Doc called it after the first couple of times it'd happened? Some kind of psychic deal. Was it precognitive dreaming where she could predict future events? I think that was what he called it. Or was it telepathic dreaming, during which Addy could tap into my consciousness and reveal any struggle I was dealing with at the moment?

Whatever the name, this psychic dreaming business was apparently part of Addy's growing skillset as a *Scharfrichter* in the making. That meant that if there was any truth in that imp dream of hers, then maybe there was a reason Daisy had tailed me home.

So, along with Elvis the chicken, Rooster the dog, Bogart the cat, and a silly gerbil named The Duke, we now had Daisy the imp, who happened to be visible to only me, Addy, and—surprisingly— Layne. Aunt Zoe figured that my son's developing powers of a Summoner included the ability to see all *others*, both deadly and not-so-deadly, since in the end, Layne was basically monster bait.

The kids hadn't seemed to realize yet that Aunt Zoe and Doc (or any other visitors) couldn't see the imp, since we'd all agreed to pretend otherwise for the time being to keep questions at bay.

Another thumping sound came from the closet, this time followed by more guttural squawks.

I scowled at the doors. Currently, Daisy was hiding in my closet with Elvis the usurper. The imp had taken a liking to the chicken instantly, probably because Daisy liked chicken meat, especially if it was honey-flavored wings. However, Addy had been strict with the imp that Elvis was a friend, not food, and Daisy liked my daughter most of all, so this particular chicken was off the menu … for now.

I had no idea if Elvis could actually see the imp or not. Chickens weren't usually psychic. Or were they? I wasn't sure if any studies had been done on that.

At the moment, I could tell it was these two particular screwballs in my closet, because while one kept trying to fool me into thinking it was a feathered fowl by making silly squawking sounds, the actual bird was loudly warbling, which was Elvis's version of talking in her sleep.

"That's it," I said, yanking open my closet door.

Elvis popped awake with a loud *bah-gawk*, which surprised a *hiss* out of the imp. Then feathers flew and shoes scattered as the two made a dash for the shadows at the other end of the closet.

I grabbed a squirt bottle full of water and aimed it at them. "I may have promised Addy that I wouldn't throw you two out in the cold while she was gone, but I will drag your asses back down to your fancy basement condo, kicking and squawking, if you don't get out of my closet right now."

With that, I pulled the other door open enough for them to escape and then squirted some water in their direction.

Both shot off toward my bedroom door, the imp loping on all fours while the chicken flapped her wings and hop-scuttled along behind it. I chased after them out my door, down the stairs, and into the kitchen, where I ran into another strange bird, only this one was sitting at the table eating vanilla cookies from my aunt's Betty Boop cookie jar while wearing a black Cossack hat and a zebra-striped scarf.

"Cornelius," I said, detouring to the coffee maker after Elvis and Daisy escaped through the flap in the door leading to the basement. "To what honor do I owe this visit from the great Tsar of Siberia so early in the morning?"

It wasn't actually that early, but late-morning resurrections tended to fit Cornelius's biorhythm chart better, which was an actual lined graph detailing his intellectual, emotional, and physical energy levels. He'd shown me this chart somewhat recently after I'd picked on him about sleeping in each day as if he were royalty. I should have known better than to call his bluff. After all, I was dealing with a man who liked to add lavender oil to his bathwater because it encouraged the ghosts to join him for a rub-a-dub in the tub.

"I've recently come across Edith," he told me while nibbling on the edge of a cookie. "And she has given me an idea on how to locate lost spirits."

I poured myself a cup of brain rocket fuel. Apparently, I was going to need all the help I could get right out of the gate today with Cornelius the Spirit Miser.

A glance out the kitchen window above the sink found smoke coming from the chimney of my aunt's workshop. Aunt Zoe had several specialty glass orders to create for a couple of Valentine's Day weddings, so she'd been putting in long hours at her glass furnace lately. I'd left her alone last night to work while Doc was off playing poker, instead choosing to settle for a quiet night alone on the couch with a pint of peanut butter fudge ice cream for company, along with a heartwarming book about a cop from the Navajo Nation, a put-upon nurse from back East, and a child caught in the middle of two cultures that both wanted him as one of their own.

I planned to talk to Aunt Zoe about Harvey's and my caper idea before I headed off to work this morning, but first, I had a ghost whisperer waiting.

"Who's Edith?" I asked, joining Cornelius at the table after adding a splash of milk to my coffee. "Is she into tarot cards, too?"

Over the last couple of weeks, Cornelius had been focused on using a tarot deck to help predict how my day would go. Personally, I'd rather not know every morning that the sky could fall on my head at any time. Stupid Tower card.

"Edith tends to dislike working with tarot cards."

I liked Edith more already. "Is she solid or wispy?"

"Both." He offered me a cookie, which I took because they were some of Aunt Zoe's homemade vanilla delicacies. Winter weight aplenty or not, I only lived once and who knew how long I'd keep breathing these days with the sky falling and whatnot.

"How can Edith be both?" I dipped the cookie in my coffee before gobbling up the sweet vanilla goodness.

"Well, she's made of black tourmaline, so that makes her mostly solid."

Tourmaline was a type of stone, last I knew. "Mostly? Is this black tourmaline in a molten state?" I jested.

"Well, rocks are matter, which is made of atoms, each with a nucleus containing moving protons and neutrons. And, of course, we mustn't forget that there are electrons orbiting this nucleus, so in essence—"

"Cornelius." I hit him with a hard stare over the rim of my coffee cup. "I'm about five seconds away from kicking your shin with my mostly solid foot matter."

He scooted out of reach. "As I was saying, Edith is mainly solid. However, she is a guiding spirit, so there is a substantial amount of wisp to her."

Wisp? I took a big swig of coffee while I pondered how to proceed in this conversation without feeling like I was chasing my tail around and around. "Is this chat session going to end with some kind of a riddle?" I asked. "Because you know how twitchy I get when you riddle me in circles."

"Edith is often prone to riddling me to the edge of madness." He grabbed another cookie.

I snorted. "I think I tumbled ass over teakettle into that swirly abyss months ago."

He inspected me for a few beats. "As Aristotle supposedly said, there's no genius without some touch of madness."

"Yeah, but how much is a 'touch'? Like a glancing blow?"

He shrugged. "I would theorize a smidge more than a brush but not quite a full-on smear."

"Yeah, well, let's just hope it doesn't rub off."

"I recently cleansed Edith, so she should remain clear." One of his black eyebrows climbed upward, toward the Cossack hat. "Unless you have muddied the ethereal waters again with your physical medium abilities and inconveniently manifested another meddling haint. Or worse."

He made it sound as if I had a handle on my medium abilities.

"Uhhh, I don't think I've manifested anything lately." I glanced toward the basement door. There was an imp in my life these days, but I hadn't conjured up that sucker, I'd just accidentally sort of helped free it from a cage and then batted it through a window to freedom. "And since I've recently showered, we should be muddy-water free."

He looked at my hair. "That would explain why I keep thinking of my great aunt's toy poodles." After he dodged the cookie I tossed at him, he asked, "On a more serious note, I trust you have flushed your chakras this week."

I set my mug down. "Cornelius, you know me well enough by now to realize that when you speak to me in strange tongues first thing in the morning, I tend to bite."

"You bite all day long, in my experience. To keep from contracting rabies, it's simply a matter of knowing how fast to retract one's fingers."

When I playfully gnashed my teeth at him, he slid a few more inches away. Then he reached into his vest pocket and pulled out a necklace chain with a pointy black stone attached to it.

"Violet, I'd like you to meet Edith the Arbiter." He held out the necklace toward me.

"You're talking about the stone, right? Not some invisible guest you brought along without telling me." While I could see the imp, my ghost vision was cloudy most days.

"Edith is not just a stone. She is the clever spirit who guides me when I use this particular pendant for pendulum divination, helping me to find the answers I seek."

He tapped the pointy stone with his index finger, making it swing slightly over the tabletop. "Edith, this is Violet the Executioner."

"She can just call me Violet," I said, and then I remembered we were talking about a stone spirit and made an effort not to roll my eyes.

He set the pendant down gently on the table. "Today, Edith is going to help us find something we have lost."

"Let me guess, you misplaced your car keys again." Cornelius had a way of losing the use of his modes of transportation one way or another.

He shielded the black pendant with his hand. "Please," he whispered. "Do not speak of keys in front of Edith. The mere word alone will send her into a spin that would be the envy of any whirling dervish."

I mimicked zipping my lips and waved for him to continue.

"The lost object to which I'm referring is actually a certain ghoul who recently tried to lure you into its parasitic embrace while keeping you trapped in your deceased coworker's office."

Actually, Jane hadn't been my coworker. She was my boss until a petulant *other* had torn her to pieces for shits and giggles and then tossed her into the Open Cut pit mine in Lead. I cringed at the memory of both Jane's demise and my haunting *tête-à-tête* with the terrorizing ghoul Cornelius was hoping to find with Edith's help.

"I told you and Doc that I didn't think reaching out to that ghoulie asshole in a séance was a good idea," I reminded him. "Especially after it tried to cleave my head in two with a letter opener."

Cornelius's pale forehead lined. "I do not believe a letter opener could produce the same results as a cleaver at such close range. Perhaps claiming a potential piercing of a soft spot, such as an eyeball, would be more accurate when retelling that moment."

I tossed another cookie at him, hitting him in a soft spot—his scarf.

He brushed the crumbs from his scarf and then crammed the broken cookie pieces in his mouth. "Anyway," he said after swallowing, "this will not be a séance." He lifted Edith by her chain again, letting the pendant dangle between us. "We will not be reaching out to the parasitic ghoul, merely using a psychic flashlight, if you will, in order to see where this malevolent spirit might be hiding while it waits for its next opportunity to lure you into an orphic web."

I sat back in my chair, watching Edith swing in a small circle over the table as I digested what he'd said. "So, you're telling me that a pointy stone can find a hiding ghoul?"

"As I specified, her name is Edith the Arbiter. Calling her a pointy stone is insulting, and as we need her help with this task, you should try not to vex her."

I had my doubts—too many to count—about everything here at the table so far, except for the cookies and coffee. However, Cornelius and his many bags of psychic tricks had come through for me in the past.

"Why black tourmaline?" I asked, knowing Cornelius well enough to figure he had a certain reason for choosing this particular stone for the mission.

"Because of its protective qualities. I also think it will allow us to *see* without the risk of being seen in return."

"You 'think,' " I repeated, not liking the crack in the door he was leaving.

"If we were looking for something less hostile, or an inanimate object, then I might have brought Millicent or Winifred along instead."

I opted not to take the bait regarding the other two names he'd mentioned. "Are you going to hypnotize me with Edith?"

"Of course not. Edith is no pythoness."

"That sounds like some kind of female snake goddess."

He let out a small snort. "Oh, Violet. You have so much to learn. But first, we need to locate a certain ghoul." His gaze shifted to the black tourmaline. "You will need to bond with Edith before we start."

I crossed my arms. "You want me to cuddle with a stone?"

"What did I say about insulting her?" He pointed at the pendant, which was suddenly swinging quickly back and forth. "Now look what you've done. She is clearly agitated by your lack of appreciation for her insightfulness."

"Tell Edith I'm sorry." And I meant that. Sort of. After all, Cornelius—and Edith—were only here to help. "I just need more coffee before this Saturday morning divination class."

"You must speak to Edith regarding your acknowledgment of offense. It will have more value coming from you."

I looked from Cornelius to the stone and then back at him. Was he serious? After months of this oddball friendship of ours, I still couldn't clearly read his tells.

The last time I'd stepped in the ring with this particular tricky ghoul Cornelius wanted to locate, it had tried to use Doc's voice to lure me into the darkness, and then my own voice to show off its abilities. I didn't know to what end it was practicing such subterfuge, but its powers seemed to be growing stronger.

My guess was it was waiting for me to slip. Before that happened, I needed to get the upper hand here, especially considering my theory that the ghoul could do more than simply mimic Doc's voice if it got anywhere close to him and gained access to his mental medium skills. Or worse, got its ghostly hands on his Oracle abilities and started opening metaphysical doors into the dark realm where all kinds of nasty *others* roamed, including good ol' Kyrkozz, my pustule-covered, demonic nemesis.

With a sigh, I pushed my skepticism aside and went all in with Edith, leaning toward the stone. "I'm sorry for being disrespectful this morning, Edith."

The black stone stilled suddenly, hovering between us with only an occasional small shudder.

"That's weird," I said, pulling back slightly.

"I told you there is more to Edith than simply protons and electrons."

"You did not say that."

"Regardless of who said what, and the fact that you seem to be having memory issues, Edith the Arbiter appears to accept your apology." Cornelius's cornflower blue eyes locked onto mine. "Now, are you ready to find a ghoul, Violet the Executioner?"

I gulped down the last of my coffee. "Let me get some more

gumption first." A few seconds later, I was back in my chair with a full mug of caffeine steaming on the table next to me while I cupped Edith the stone in my palms.

"First, you need to clear your chakras."

I glanced up at the Betty Boop clock over the kitchen sink. "Do we have time for that? I need to be at work in an hour."

He inspected me as if I had a black light shining on me showing all my lint. "You're right, most of your chakras are undoubtedly fouled up beyond quick repair. Let's focus on your crown chakra for now, since it is where you connect to spirits, and see how far that gets us."

"Sheesh, it's not like I don't keep clean."

"Let's be real here, Violet. Spiritually, you're usually sprawled out in the gutter with an empty bottle of tequila next to you and gum in your hair." He wrinkled his upper lip. "At least we hope it's gum."

I weighed the pros and cons of stealing his Cossack hat and letting Elvis lay eggs in it. "How about you zip it with the insults and tell me how to clear my dang crown chakra?"

"Fine. How are you at doing headstands? We could collect a pillow for this exercise, if needed."

There would be none of that. "Have I mentioned my temperament issues in the morning?"

"Right, so that option is out." He stroked his pointy goatee, pursing his lips. "Usually, this involves a little more time along with meditation, but my grandmother taught me a quick cleanse method long ago. First, close your eyes." After my eyes were closed, he said, "Now imagine a violet-colored lotus flower floating over your head."

"Violet because it's my name?"

"No. The crown chakra is often associated with shades of violet and bright, glowing white light."

"Okay." With my eyes closed, I imagined the purple lotus flower. "Flower in place."

"Now breathe in through your mouth and on the exhale hum through your nose. Do this five times." After my fifth exhale, he instructed, "I want you to picture a candle floating in the air in front of you."

I stiffened. "That tends to get me into trouble."

I'd stumbled into too many creepy beings while playing with candles in the dark of my mind.

"Don't worry, you're not going to reach into the dark. This will just be a sweeping of the clutter that might get in our way. And make sure the candle is black with a single wick."

I remembered him telling me before that black candles release negative energy and offer protection, so I nodded and pictured the candle in front of me. "All right, the black candle is in place and lit." I resumed humming as I exhaled.

"Now burn some mental sage in the candle flame."

That was different from anything we'd done in the past. "Why?"

"Because I forgot to bring sage along with me this morning."

I imagined an aromatic waft of the smoke flitting through the room. "Sage smoke is here."

"Do you see Edith?" When I started to open my eyes, he clarified, "In your mind, Violet."

Eyes fully closed, I focused on the black candle again. Sure enough, the pendant lay at the base of the flame, its polished sides reflecting the candlelight.

"I see her."

"Good. Then we are ready to begin. Open your eyes."

That seemed too easy, but he was the boss. I blinked in the bright yellow kitchen. The stone in my hands felt warmer than before.

"Hold the end of Edith's chain between your thumb, index finger, and middle finger, suspending her over the table." After I had the pendant dangling, he ordered, "Keep your elbow on the table so that your hand is as still as possible."

"I'm trying."

"You must focus and stop shaking."

I palmed the pendant and held it toward him. "Maybe you should do the holding."

He reared back, hands raised. "I can't. Edith will only tell truths to the holder, so you have to be the one."

I took a deep breath and let the stone dangle again, working to steady it and my hands with success this time.

"Let's see how Edith responds to you." Cornelius scooted closer. "This will also tell us if she is ready to work with you."

"Do I need to woo her some more? Whisper sweet nothings in her ears."

He stared at me with a straight face. "Edith has no ears."

"I was speaking metaphoric— You know what? Never mind. How will we know if Edith likes me enough to help us find the ghoul?"

"Don't be absurd, Violet," he said, as if I were the silly one who'd given such a quirky name to a pointy black stone. "You simply need to ask her a yes or no question that you believe is true, and then one that you know is untrue."

"That seems rather rudimentary."

"Well, it's merely pendulum dowsing, not rocket science." He pointed at the black tourmaline. "Let's start with something basic. Ask her if your name is Violet."

"She already knows that, remember? You introduced us."

"Humor me. Have I steered you wrong before?"

"Yes. Multiple times. Dangerously so, more than once."

His gaze narrowed on me. "Or did you steer yourself incorrectly each of those times, assuming it was what I wanted of you?"

"Cram it, mister." I focused on the still pendant. "Edith, is my name Violet?"

At first, the pendant remained unmoving. Then, ever so slightly, it began to swing back and forth, gaining momentum as I watched.

"It feels like she's shaking her head no," I said, looking across at him.

"Typically, affirmations tend to be forward and backward, but you might not be normal."

I scoffed. "Story of my life these days."

"I've seen this before with other mediums, although you are the first physical medium I've had fondle Edith."

I wrinkled my nose. "I am not fondling her."

"To fondle is to touch or stroke in a loving or tender fashion. You were definitely fondling her moments ago."

"Let's just agree to disagree on this and move on. The clock is ticking."

He nodded. "Now, for the untruth." He indicated toward the stone.

"You want me to lie?"

"No, I want you to ask Edith the same name question, only using a false name."

"Gotcha. Edith, is my name …" I paused, trying to come up with something different. "Junebug?"

Cornelius's eyebrows crinkled slightly.

The pendant slowed, shifting to swing front to back.

"There you have it," he said. "Movement in that direction means no for you."

I stared at my own arm, trying to see if I was somehow making the pendant swing differently, but I was truly trying to keep as still as possible.

"It appears now that you and Edith have made a connection." He pointed at my free hand. "Hold that thumb under the pendant with the pad side up."

"Why my thumb?"

"Because it gives off neutral energy and will still Edith."

The skeptic in me was having trouble digesting this, but I did as told anyway. Edith quickly stilled with only slight vibrations as she hovered over the pad of my thumb.

"That's trippy," I whispered.

"Edith does have a way of bewildering the doubtful."

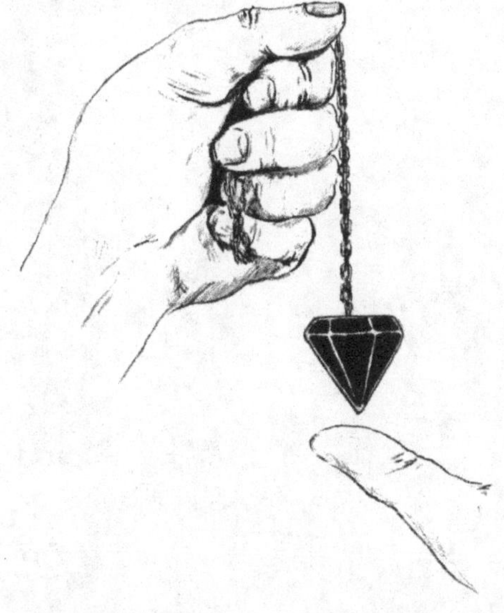

I looked over at him. "So, how do we figure out where a lost item is if all I can ask are yes and no questions?"

"We have to be creative. Keep in mind that Edith is simply acting as an extension of your own intuition." He rubbed his hands together. "As you are the first physical medium that Edith has ever worked with, I'm excited to see what sparks will fly."

I cringed. "Are we sure we want flying sparks? I mean, have you considered all of the ways this could go south?"

"Here." He held up a cookie. "This talisman will keep you safe."

"That cookie is a talisman?" Did he think I'd fallen off the back of a turnip truck recently?

"Yes." He set it on the table in front of me. "Now eat up. It's time to play peekaboo with the boogeyman."

CHAPTER FOUR

How had it come to this? I wondered as I swallowed the last of the cookie.

I stared at Edith the Arbiter, trying to take this pendulum consulting business seriously. Unfortunately, I had no idea how else to find a phantom ghoul without taking soul-sucking risks that had my heart palpitating from the mere worries of it all.

Frowning, I attempted to focus on the task at hand—or rather the shiny, pointy piece of black tourmaline. How much trouble could possibly come from talking to a spirit connected to a stone? Hell, I'd been involved with some crazy crap since moving to Deadwood last year—surely this couldn't spin out of control. Not with me sitting safely at Aunt Zoe's table on a plain old Saturday morning in February.

"Uhh, Edith," I started but then paused, glancing at Cornelius for some sort of confirmation that I was going about seeking the stone's counsel the right way.

Should I whisper? Speak confidently in a deep voice? Think about a certain color while asking questions? Imagine light shining out of one of my chakra orifices the whole time?

He waved for me to continue in the midst of biting into another cookie.

"Do you know where the ghoul is hiding?" I asked Edith in my regular voice.

The stone held steady, as if my thumb were still under it.

"It's not working," I told Cornelius.

He crossed his arms. "That's because Edith does not suffer simpletons. Ask a more intelligent question."

Simpletons? I resisted the urge to dump the whole jar of cookies in his lap. "Edith," I spoke again to the stone dangling in front of me, "is the ghoul still hiding in Jane's office?"

That was where I'd last seen it, so I figured I'd start there.

The stone began to swing from front to back.

"No," Cornelius said, confirming what I saw. "Keep going, but remember that while you are asking Edith questions, you are actually tuning into your own intuition with her help. That's why I wanted you to envision her next to the candle in your mind before we started, so we could tap into your physical medium abilities."

I continued to watch Edith swing. "So, should I picture a candle flame while asking my questions, like when we do a séance?"

He pondered that while chewing, then shook his head. "Just try to remain focused on the task at hand—you know, finding where that unruly scamp scurried off to."

The word "scamp" seemed too playful for what we were dealing with, which was why I'd been so hesitant to reach out to the parasitic vermin in the first place.

My concentration returned to the stone. "Edith, is the ghoul hanging out in the Hellhole tunnels?"

The bastard had been hiding in the closet in Jane's office for part of the time when we'd battled, calling out to me in Doc's voice and then mine. In that closet was a trapdoor that allowed access to what we'd come to not-so-fondly refer to as a Hellhole. This grate-covered hole in the crawlspace under Calamity Jane Realty in turn gave way to a network of underground tunnels leading in several directions, including a direct line to the basement of the courthouse across the street. Another spur went to Mudder Brothers Funeral Parlor.

I wasn't willing to go spelunking at this time to explore the other unmapped branches down there, no matter how much Natalie tried to double-dare me into it, especially after I'd already run into one or two creepy boogeymen on a previous hair-raising occasion. The old *Here there be monsters* mantra applied tenfold in those dark passageways.

Edith the stone swung front to back in answer to my question.

"The ghoul is not hiding in the vicinity of the Hellhole," I said under my breath. I looked up at Cornelius, who was pulling another cookie from the Betty Boop jar. "That's a relief."

He pointed the cookie at me. "I have been meaning to tell you that my cameras have not recorded any ethereal movement in the haunted office since your last escapade in there."

Damn. I worried my lower lip. That meant there had been no sign of Jane's ghost either. When I'd faced off with the ghoul that last time in her old office, the entity had carved a message into the desk that said she was gone, but I'd been hoping since then that it meant only for the moment, not for good. That hope spurred a new question.

"Edith, did the ghoul do something to make Jane's ghost disappear?"

Or had Jane moved on of her own accord? It seemed too coincidental that she had left after the ghoul lured me into her office.

"Violet," Cornelius said through a mouthful of cookie. "I believe that is a side road meant for another journey."

"I want to know if this asshole hurt Jane."

"Jane is dead."

"I know. I meant, like, gobbled up her ghost's energy or sucked it up into a spirit vacuum."

"You are limited on availability this morning, remember?" He glanced pointedly toward the clock.

Of course I remembered, but Edith the stone was now swinging side to side, which meant yes.

"So, the ghoul did do something to Jane," I said to the cookie monster sharing the table with me. "You know what this means, don't you, Cornelius?" I didn't wait for him to answer. "We're going to have to try to help Jane."

"Rein in your focus, channeler. We need to narrow down a location on the ghoul at this time. The well-being of other entities will have to wait."

I sighed. "Fine. Edith, is the ghoul still in Deadwood?"

The stone continued swinging side to side, which was good because if it had done something to Jane's ghost, like siphoned her energy, there still might be a chance to get her back.

"Is the ghoul currently exploiting another entity?"

"Where are you going with this, Violet?" Cornelius had paused with another cookie midway to his mouth.

"I was thinking about how the thing was supposedly attached to Ms. Hessler when Doc and I brought it into this realm or plane or whatever, so maybe if it's still tapping energy from another entity, like Jane, we might have more of a chance at locating it."

The stone swung side to side with even more vigor.

"So, that's a definite yes," I said. Finally, we were getting somewhere. Now, how did we find a parasitic ghoul that might be hiding inside of another ghost?

"I do not see how this is helping us locate the ghoul," Cornelius said. "It appears to me that you are simply adding even more variables to consider."

I narrowed my eyes at him, but bowed to his knowledge of Edith's skills. "What should I be asking, then?"

"We need a definite location where we can perform a séance to try to reach out to it."

"I still think reaching out that way is too risky." This slimy devil was way too slippery.

"In my experience, situations such as this eventually come to a head." He shrugged. "A case of cure or kill. There is no tiptoeing around the conundrum."

Was Cornelius referring to the cousin he'd lost years ago to another malevolent entity during an exorcism? Or was this from another …

Focus!

Okay, back to the problem at hand. The ghoul remained in Deadwood, but it was not in Jane's office or in the Hellhole and its surrounding tunnels.

I put my thumb under the stone's point, bringing it to a standstill. "Shall I just start listing off places?" I asked him.

"That is a method to which Edith is accustomed during my sessions."

I pulled my thumb away. "Edith, is the ghoul somewhere in the courthouse?"

The stone shivered for a second, and then it began swinging front to back in a negative response.

"Is the ghoul in Mudder Brothers Funeral Parlor?"

Edith continued to give us her version of a thumbs-down.

Several minutes later, the stone was still swinging forward and backward, and we had still not gotten a single yes response.

"This isn't like hide and seek," I said, reaching for a cookie in defeat. "It's more like the game where you try to blindly hit your opponent's ships by calling out coordinates. Maybe we should return to trying to find whomever the ghoul is attached to now."

Cornelius clasped his fingers together, his eyes narrowing slightly. "During your struggles with the entity in your late boss's office, was anyone else in the building?"

"Besides you?"

Cornelius had been upstairs at the start of the entity's song and dance, watching the scene via one of his video cameras until the screen had gone dark.

"Actually, by the time you were fully engaged with the entity," he said, "I was outside of the building trying to gain access downstairs. Was there any other living person in there with you?"

"My coworkers were all gone by then, but Cooper showed up right before the ghoul disappeared."

He frowned at the stone and then back at me. "Ask Edith if there is an entity attached to the bristly detective."

"I thought the ghoul only attached to ghosts."

"We don't know the limits of this ghoul's abilities."

"Right. Shit."

While Cooper was a burr under my saddle most days, he was a crucial part of our little motley team, and I didn't relish the idea of trying to dislodge a parasitic ghoul from his hide. Someone would undoubtedly get shot during that exorcism, and it would probably be me. Not to mention there was the whole part about Natalie and Cooper trying their hands at a happily-ever-after to consider.

I put my thumb under Edith to bring the stone to a standstill, wanting to start fresh to be certain on this answer.

"Edith, is the ghoul attached to Detective Cooper?"

It held still for a long three seconds, and then the stone swung front to back. Whew!

"That's good news." I reached for Edith, pausing her mid-swing. "The last thing I needed was a possessed version of Cooper coming for me with his guns blazing."

When I looked across at Cornelius, he was watching me with a lined forehead. "Is there a chance the ghoul followed you home?"

"I wouldn't think it could make it through the sigils and wards

Aunt Zoe has protecting this house."

He glanced toward the back door. "I forgot about your aunt's protection measures."

"But then again," I said, remembering a tale Aunt Zoe had told me that had happened in this very house in the past. "There is an imp now inside of this house. Years ago, another imp had attached itself to Reid and made it through her blockades somehow."

Reid Martin was Deadwood's fire captain, who had a killer smile that rendered most local females giggly. Except for his ex-girlfriend, my aunt, who just wanted to render Reid most days, when she wasn't smoldering about him against her will.

One of Cornelius's black eyebrows climbed upward. "Could some parasitic entities, such as imps and ghouls, require specific wards to keep them at bay?"

"Let's see." I focused on the stone, trying to keep my breath steady in spite of the fear beginning to tickle my lungs. "Edith, is the ghoul in this house?"

The stone began to move forward and back. Before I could breathe a sigh of relief, it shifted, moving side to side, only to then return to the previous front to back motion. Then it seemed to give up and simply spin in a small circle.

I looked to Cornelius. "What does that mean?"

He scratched his head under his Cossack hat. "Edith can't determine the answer. Something you're thinking is blocking her sight." He tipped his head to one side. "Violet, are you daydreaming about fornicating with the Tall Medium instead of focusing on the task before us?"

My cheeks heated lickety-split. I scoffed. "Am I—no! Jeez, contrary to what you and Harvey think, I'm not some horny toad just waiting for my next ride on Doc's Ferris wheel of love."

"How interesting." He leaned back, observing me, giving me vibes similar to being handcuffed while sitting under a spotlight in the Deadwood police station. "Toads and Ferris wheels typically aren't grouped in such a promiscuous fashion. Do you find *Alice's Adventures in Wonderland* to be an erotic tale of uncurbed desires with libidinous characters?"

"What does Alice have to do with a toad and sex?"

He shrugged. "Who are we to judge others' appetites? Your

horny toad is another man's busty Queen of Hearts. 'Off with his head' can be quite a lure when delivered by the right siren."

I pointed at him. "That's just weird."

"Don't get me started on the queen's ambrosian stolen tarts."

"Anyway," I said firmly, steering us back to the matter at hand. "I haven't thought about Doc once since I came downstairs." Wait, there was the glancing moment I was thinking fondly of his talented hands while pouring my first cup of coffee. "Make that not once since I joined you at the table."

Cornelius returned his focus to the stone. "Sometimes when I work with Edith, that spinning action means *maybe*."

"So, maybe Edith doesn't know if the ghoul is here."

"Or maybe the entity is here with us. Let's narrow this down. Ask about me," Cornelius ordered. "As we discussed previously, I was in the apartment above Jane's office before your battle with it began."

I hesitated. "If it is inside of you and I get affirmation of that, couldn't it react angrily here and lash out at me?" I pictured a scene from that 1980s movie *The Thing*, where the characters were testing each other's blood for signs of an alien species. "Should I have some sort of self-defense weapon at hand, like the bat in the hall closet?"

"My great-grandfather lived by the motto, 'Expect the unexpected.' Which is why it is curious that he didn't expect a wrecking ball to be the death of him. However, you are an Executioner, are you not? Surely you are not afraid of the likes of a simple human such as myself."

I scoffed. "You are not a simple human. Not with all of those hair-raising terrors Prudence and Doc say you keep locked away behind that metaphysical door in your head."

He waved me off. "I've had that door closed most of the time since childhood. What are the chances of it bursting open today?"

I wasn't interested in finding out. "How about you scoot a couple of feet back from the table just in case."

After we had more space between us, I stilled the stone again and then asked, "Edith, is the ghoul attached to Cornelius?"

This time, Edith gave me a definite negative response.

Cornelius and I traded raised brows. If it wasn't attached to him, then ...

"When the ghoul got into your head," Cornelius started, following along my line of thought.

"It tried to get into my head," I interrupted quickly, not liking the wary uncertainty I was seeing in his eyes. "But it didn't get all of the way inside."

"Violet," he said, his voice ominous. "Are you certain?"

"Yes. Pretty much." But not totally. I licked my suddenly dry lips. "I fought it off when we went into the dark together." I could still see it clearly, standing at the edge of the candlelight, watching me from under a caped hood. "I watched it run away from me while it was engulfed in green flames."

He nodded slowly. "Could it have left something behind?"

Shit. I hoped not. But what if it had?

I closed my eyes, trying to feel for it. Everything seemed the same as always—just me, myself, and I in my thoughts. Could it have created a rift, though, for future visits? Like how Prudence had cut a pathway into Harvey's mind.

I opened my eyes, focusing on Cornelius. Could he feel the terrors locked away behind that door in his own head? Maybe I needed to do whatever ritual he'd done to keep his monsters caged, just to be safe.

"There is one way to find out, Violet." He pointed at the black tourmaline. "You need to ask Edith."

I shook my head. "I don't want to."

"And this time," he continued, ignoring me, "I want you to close your eyes and picture a white candle before asking the question. This will strengthen your connection with Edith." He frowned slightly. "Although it could also strengthen your connection with the ghoul, if there is any sort of tether attached."

"So, I'm damned if I do, and damned if I don't?"

He nodded. "But wouldn't it be better to know now what we're dealing with?"

"Not necessarily. Sometimes ignorance truly is bliss."

He gestured toward the ceiling. "Your children sleep in this house just down the hall from you."

I growled under my breath. "You had to hit below the belt, didn't you?" I closed my eyes and pictured a white candle in front of me. "A single wick?"

"Yes, but be sure to retain control of the flame. Keep it small and focus on the blue within it."

I didn't bother asking what difference that made, just did as I was told. My kids' lives were at stake. No more screwing around. "Are you going to hum?"

Often, Cornelius would hum during our séances, which seemed to increase my ability to channel clearly.

"No, we certainly don't want to invite the entity to join us at the table. This is, after all, a spy mission."

"Right, but maybe you should grab the bat out of the hall closet just in case."

"I've seen you in action, *Scharfrichter*. If you decide to go rogue, I will need more than a single bat." His chair creaked, followed by the sound of footfalls on the linoleum floor. His voice sounded farther away when he said, "When you are ready, ask the question."

I took a deep breath and steadied my nerves. My children were safe at the moment, far away. So were Aunt Zoe and Doc. This was just me and Cornelius, and he seemed as ready as could be for whatever might come his way.

"I still think you should have some protection in place," I told him.

"I am holding onto my cannon in my pocket as I speak."

From anyone else, that would have made me cringe, but Cornelius actually carried a miniature die-cast cannon in his pocket for protection as a lucky charm.

Apparently, we were as ready as we were going to be.

"Edith, is the ghoul here with me?"

I kept my eyes squeezed shut, afraid of the answer.

"It's moving," Cornelius said.

"Moving how, dammit?"

"Front to back."

"Oh, thank God." I blew out the candle in my head.

"Hold on," he said. "It's shifting."

I opened my eyes. Sure enough, the pendant was taking on a side-to-side course now.

"Is that a yes?" Cornelius asked more to himself than me. "No wait, it's circling again."

The circle flared wider, around and around.

"Crap." I lowered the stone pendant to the table, letting go of the chain. "Maybe it is or maybe it isn't."

Cornelius stayed in place over by the counter, one arm wrapped around the cookie jar. "Keep in mind, Violet, that you are a physical medium."

"And that matters how?"

"Your ability to pluck entities from other locations and bring them back to your reality could be confusing Edith." He fished out a cookie. "On a high note, it appears the bristly detective and I have escaped the ghoul's sticky fingers."

I made a face at him and his attempt at positivity. "Now what do we do, besides hope that Aunt Zoe's protective measures are still working?"

He pointed his cookie at the clock. "You go sell ghost-inhabited properties while I cleanse Edith of your touch."

That made me feel like I had cooties. "I meant, what do we do about finding the ghoul?"

He took a bite, speaking through a mouthful of crumbs, "You are not going to like my answer."

I pushed back from the table and carried my coffee mug to the sink. "Probably not, but try me anyway."

"We do this again later with the Tall Medium using Millicent."

He was right. I didn't want Doc anywhere near anything having to do with that ghoul. "How is Millicent different than Edith?"

He glanced at the black tourmaline resting on the tabletop. "Millicent is a shaman stone. She has been known to enhance supersensory abilities while offering an even more powerful psychic shield."

"So, I might be able to see the ghoul *and* still protect Doc and me?"

He shrugged. "Or you might die trying. There is always the possibility of death when it comes to malicious entities with spiteful agendas."

"When you say stuff like that, I tend to not want to play medium games with you anymore." I walked over and took the cookie jar from him. It was way too light thanks to Cornelius. "Now, I have to head to work where they actually pay me to deal with nutter-butters like you." I started to turn away but then remembered something I needed to ask him. "Oh, hey, Harvey and I are plotting a caper. You want in on the heist?"

He brushed the crumbs from his scarf and coat, his hands seeming to tremble slightly in the process. "Will we be stealing brains?"

I took a step back. "Brains? Why in the world would we steal brains?"

"The pathologist who performed the autopsy on Albert Einstein is said to have kept the genius's brain upon finishing and stored the organ in a jar for years," he spoke quickly, his words rushing together. "It would seem reasonable that you might do the same with one of the creatures you have recently executed for further investigation, possibly measuring the gray matter for size and weight. That is assuming these creatures' brains are gray. For all we know, they could be blue. A big blue brain. I would like to see such a brain, although I can become squeamish at the sight of raw organs."

I wrinkled my nose. "First and foremost, I'm a killer, not a mad scientist. Second, I wouldn't touch a brain with a ten-foot pole, let alone store one in a jar like it was a big cookie …" I looked down at the Betty Boop jar in my hands and flinched, taking it over to the table and putting the lid back on it before continuing. "Our grand heist is all about cuckoo clocks."

"Ah, a nick of time, if you will." He nodded spiritedly. "Even better, a five-finger ticker sticker. Oh, I know, a chroniker crime! A mugging of minutes. A—"

"Cornelius! How many cookies did you eat?"

"I lost count after a baker's dozen. Will we be absconding with the town clock? Holding it for ransom? Leaving it on Main Street covered in tinfoil for the mayor to unwrap?"

"Yeah, you've definitely had too much sugar."

"I am feeling the need to sing all of a sudden. Maybe dance a jig. You don't happen to have a set of bagpipes, do you?"

"No, thank God, and don't even get me started on mini flutes. As for the caper, we're going to return to that apartment in Galena House where you and I had the séance with the Tall Medium and Freesia."

He squeezed the bridge of his nose. "So many clocks, so little time."

"Exactly. We're going to sneak all those clocks out from under Detective Hawke's big beak."

"Is this detective you speak of the rumbumptious grumbletonian that Natalie listens to through her floor vent?"

"A ramgrumptious bumbletonian is more like it."

Both of his black eyebrows peaked. "Can I perform a sleight of hand during this clock caper?"

Since Harvey and I had no set plans yet, I couldn't think of a single reason to shoot him down. "Of course."

He smiled, albeit with a twitch. "Then I look forward to participating in the subterfuge."

"Great. I'll let Harvey know to count you in." I thumbed toward the front door. "Now take Edith and hit the road, or I'm going to round up my inner *Scharfrichter* to execute you for hogging so many of Aunt Zoe's cookies."

CHAPTER FIVE

I'd no sooner stepped inside the back door of Calamity Jane Realty than Mona Hollister was at my side.

"I need to talk to you, Vi," she said, glancing down the long hallway toward the front of the office, where I could hear several voices—a couple familiar and a couple not, along with the deep rumble of Jerry's laughter in the midst of the conversational din.

My mentor looked very business classic this morning, dressed in a knee-length pencil skirt and a cream vintage-style blouse with blue glass buttons climbing up the high neckline. Her shoulder-length auburn hair was twisted into an elegant updo that reminded me of a 1960s starlet, complete with golden highlights and silky swoops.

"How do you do that with your hair?" I asked as I hung up my coat. Even with liberal amounts of leave-in conditioner and smoothing serum, my curls usually ended up looking like a janitor's cotton yarn mop after being left to dry in the sun.

"That's not important right now." Mona took me by the elbow and dragged me into Jane's old office—the last place I wanted to be after playing cat and mouse with the ghoul in this very room not long enough ago.

"Don't close the door," I said, catching it before she could fully shut it. The entity had kept me prisoner in here before, somehow locking the door by sheer ghostly will. Short of breaking through the glass, I'd been stuck until Cooper showed up and interrupted its lockdown.

Mona frowned at me, but left the door open a crack. She stepped close enough that I could smell her sweet jasmine perfume. "I'm worried about Jane," she whispered, even though I doubted anyone out front could hear her.

"Why?" I glanced toward the big desk on the other side of the room. The ominous carving in the wooden top telling of Jane's demise remained covered by the calendar I'd placed over it last week. "Did she contact you again?"

Ever since Jane had been killed, Mona had been receiving ghostly messages from our old boss here and there, such as cryptic notes left on her computer screen and words drawn into the Zen sandbox on her desk. The two of them had been good friends for years, their bond much more than employer–employee.

"No." Mona wrung her hands together. "I haven't heard a peep from her in almost two weeks now. In the past, she's gone quiet for a few days at most, but that's it."

Damn. I didn't want Jane's ghost to truly be gone. I had been too late to save her from the menace that had cut her life short last year. Was I too slow yet again to help the ghostly version of her?

"Have you talked to Cornelius lately?" Mona pointed toward the ceiling.

As a matter of fact, I had a half hour ago, but the purpose behind our breakfast ritual was not something I wanted to share with Mona. "About what in particular?" I played dumb.

Mona knew about some of the supernatural shenanigans going on here in the office, including Doc's abilities as a mental medium and Cornelius being a pied piper of ghosts. But she only knew a little about what I did outside of trying to sell real estate. Ignorance was more than bliss on that front. Knowing too much about my other responsibilities could put her life at risk.

"To see if he's seen any signs of Jane lately," she said. "After hours, I mean, when the rest of us are gone. I keep hoping she's just laying low in the daytime because of how much traffic has increased in the office since the final two *Paranormal Realty* shows aired."

The hum of conversation coming through the crack in the door was an indication of our office's popularity in spite of it being winter, which I'd been told was usually much slower client-wise. Didn't potential clients listen to the news? It was too cold to scurry around looking at houses right now. Most of the "interested" clients I'd had on the hook over the last couple of weeks had said as much, holding off on coming to Deadwood to look at more houses until it warmed up a little.

I had jumped for joy when the final episode in the three-part series about haunted real estate in Deadwood and Lead had rolled credits. Now I could move on from my career as a reality TV star and return to being a regular real estate agent. Although with the ghost-loving clientele now frequenting our office, wanting to visit some of the houses and buildings showcased on the series (to take photos of themselves there more often than make offers), life wasn't giving any signs of returning to its previous version of normal.

"I talked to Cornelius somewhat recently," I said, not adding that it was in between him cramming vanilla cookies in his bazoo. "He didn't mention anything about seeing evidence of Jane in the office, but he was a little distracted at the time as he often tends to be." So many ghosts, so little time for our quirky spirit miser these days. "You could text him. I think he's home at the moment."

I'd assumed that was where he'd gone after I shooed him away from the cookie jar. Although I hadn't seen his rental vehicle in the parking lot, now that I thought about it. I had seen the Picklemobile, however, which meant Doc was next door in his office, probably rearranging numbers and figures on his computer screen. Unfortunately, I was running late thanks to Edith the stone and the Cookie Monster, so I didn't have time to stop in and try to distract Doc from his calculations today with a cup of coffee, or a stolen kiss, or a little touchy-feely fun, or a maybe even a quick …

I hit the brakes on my libido before it rolled any farther down that road, returning my thoughts to Cornelius, who was living above Calamity Jane Realty currently, keeping an eye out for ghostly inhabitants while his hotel on Main Street went through extensive renovations.

Months ago, Jane's ghost had begun harassing Jerry, aka her ex-husband, who was working in the very office in which I was standing. Jane had repeatedly moved the furniture around at night, going so far as to trash the room once or twice, which Mona and I had assumed was a sign of her unhappiness with some of her ex-husband's decisions for the business she'd worked so hard to build. After a bit, Jerry had been spooked enough to call in help.

That was where our buddy upstairs had come into the picture. Or actually into the building. After hearing that Cornelius was a self-proclaimed ghost hunter, Jerry relocated from this office to the front room with the rest of us and hired Corny to use all of his fancy gadgets in search for signs of Jane's ghost.

Within a short time, Cornelius had installed cameras and microphones throughout Calamity Jane Realty. However, it turned out Jane was camera shy, preferring to leave cryptic messages for Mona. Every now and then, she'd even leave notes for me about the non-human terrors trying to mess with me—and that was another reason why we had to find her. I needed all the help I could get at scouting out trouble before it came swinging for me.

"I'll run up to his apartment when things slow down out front and talk to him in person," Mona said, her forehead tight as her gaze bounced between the door and me. "I don't want Jerry to overhear me asking about Jane. He still doesn't know how often she was visiting, and I'd like to keep it that way. The last thing we need is him wanting to sell this building because his ex-wife won't stop haunting it."

I hadn't thought of him selling. My heart sank at the idea. "You don't think that was what he was up to the last few weeks with all of those trips to Rapid City, do you?"

Her expression shifted into a smirk. "I know for certain that's not what he was up to."

I pointed at her face. "Why do you look like you just bit into a lemon? What do you know? Please tell me he hasn't signed us up for another ghost show."

"Not another show." She hesitated.

"Out with it, Mona."

"Well, it's sort of a show, depending on whether you believe the woman is legitimate or not."

Mona clearly believed the latter based on the curl of her upper lip.

"What woman?" I asked, feeling like I'd skipped a page in the script.

"Madame Olivia Contraire, Medium Extraordinaire," she said with a French accent.

I tipped my head. "That sounds like a cartoon character."

"Unfortunately, she's not only a real—and highly eccentric—

woman, she's also sitting out front across from Jerry's desk waiting to meet you."

"Why me?"

"Because Jerry has a new marketing idea, and you're his first guinea pig."

I crossed my arms. "What marketing idea?"

"He's offering clients the option of having a medium join them while touring homes with their agent. This way they can see ahead of time if there are any ghosts in the homes or not, and they can then buy according to their wishes."

My jaw dropped. It would have bounced off my toes if it hadn't been attached. "You gotta be fucking kidding me."

She held up her left hand, the other hand on her heart. "No lie, your honor. Turns out Jerry has been interviewing potential mediums down in Rapid City, touring a supposedly haunted house to test them out. Little Ms. Contraire and her psychic act passed with flying phantoms, checking all of his boxes." Her lips thinned. "Although, with the way she bats her golden eyelashes at him, I suspect her obvious flirtations didn't hurt her ranking in his test group."

"Is she young?"

For some reason, I'd pictured an old woman with deep wrinkles fanning from her eyes and lining her cheeks under a messy nest of white hair complete with a twig and a leaf or two. Someone with gnarled fingers, like my great-grandmother, who'd carried a bag of rune stones in her pocket and spoke in a croaky voice.

"Probably about your age or a few years older. It's hard to tell with all the sparkly makeup on her face."

Sparkly? Considering that description and Mona calling her "little" Ms. Contraire, I was now picturing a fairy nymph with glossy wings and glowing orbs floating all around her. Although a few years older than me would put her around forty, so not quite the usual sweet-faced cherub used in Hollywood's version of fairies.

"She only showed up a few minutes before you got here," Mona said. "So, I haven't had a chance to learn enough about her not to judge by her whimsical looks alone."

Whimsical? Did she have rainbow-colored hair, a big red nose, and arrive in a tiny clown car? I shook that idea from my head, now at a loss on what to imagine.

"Apparently, she was extra early," Mona continued, seemingly oblivious to my head scratching. "Jerry appeared genuinely surprised when she arrived. But then she explained that he'd sent her a telepathic message to show up an hour early."

"Had he?" In my world these days, that could actually happen.

She scoffed. "Jerry has trouble sending texts most days. He prefers phone calls to finger-talking, as he calls it. Mind messages are several light years out of his league."

That was true. He usually had about a three-text tolerance before he hit the call button.

"I tell you," she said, crossing her arms. "Jerry had to resort to some fast talking to smooth Ben's and my feathers."

"Did you glare holes through his thick head?"

She grimaced. "No, but some coffee was spilled."

I grinned in spite of what—or rather who—I was about to face in the front room. "Mona, you're the best."

"Don't throw flowers at my feet just yet."

My grin slipped. "Why?"

"Unfortunately, you're stuck with Madame Contraire today during your appointment. Jerry already guaranteed her that you will be thrilled about having a medium at your side as you show houses."

I would be if it were a certain Tall Medium who shared my bed at night. But a stranger? Worse, what if she really could interact with ghosts? How would I even know if she were legit without someone who could actually see ghosts riding along with us today?

"Oh, and it turns out our little sparkly medium is a big fan of yours."

"Of mine?" My heart pitter-pattered. How did she know me? I crossed my fingers she wasn't another cult-loving dingbat who wanted to offer my womb to some demon as a baby-making oven.

"She watched all three of our *Paranormal Realty* episodes and claims that you appear to have a slight bit of sixth sense yourself." Mona winked. "How I'd love to be able to fit into your pocket today. Maybe we should start having Rosy and her cameras follow you around, too."

I nailed her with a mock glare in spite of how much I enjoyed hanging out with the camerawoman from the *Paranormal Realty* show. "Don't you dare give that mad marketer out front any more ideas."

She rolled her eyes. "Jerry drives me to drink some nights."

I had a feeling it wasn't just out of frustration for his marketing ideas.

Mona and Jerry often had sparks crackling when they were together. Something had happened in the past between them when Jane was alive. Not when she was married to Jerry, but after. However, no matter how much I'd prodded Mona, she wouldn't share the juicy details. For now, I was left with my imagination, which had seen too many late-night, steamy R-rated movies for its own good.

"We'd better get out front," Mona said, opening the office door wide.

"Must we, though?" I joked, but really meant it. It would be easy for me to grab my coat and skip out the back door, calling in sick for the day.

Except I had clients coming in soon to look at houses.

Plus, I needed more money in my bank account so that I could bring something into a marriage with Doc besides debt, hungry children, and a caravan of ragtag pets. Not to mention that tax time was on the horizon. Doc could work magic with numbers, but he claimed there was only so much he could do to help me when it came to going head-to-head with the tax collector.

"Let's go. Jerry will come looking for me soon enough, and if he finds us in here whispering, he'll know I tattled. Be sure to act surprised."

I opened my eyes wide and tried on a shocked grin.

She winced. "I said surprised, not like a maniacal murderer who just slaughtered a tent full of teenage camp counselors."

I turned my smile down a few notches and lowered my eyelids slightly.

"That's better." She grabbed my arm and pulled me into the hallway, adding in a low voice, "Maybe you'll be able to exercise more restraint than me and not accidentally dump your coffee on Jerry's fancy silk tie."

* * *

If only there were a way to determine whether someone was truly a medium or just really good at the old smoke and mirrors act. Like a litmus strip test that took a little drop of blood—or even a dribble of sweat—to prove a person could actually interact with the dead. Surely Cornelius must have a spare doll in his voodoo toolkit that we could poke with a hat pin in its psychic third eye to check if Madame Olivia Contraire, Medium Extraordinaire, squirmed in pain or not.

Unfortunately, without being able to see the wispy population with my own eyes, I was currently in a bit of a pickle. Somehow, I had to try to verify Madame Contraire's ability to play pattycake with ghosts based on observation alone.

After shivering through several empty houses with her trailing along behind while reaching out to any spirits willing to take her bait, my jury was still out. She might be the real deal … or not. I could confirm, however, that she'd done her homework on paranormal terminology and definitely had her mystical act down pat.

She also seemed to know far too much about me from the get-go. Back at the office, before my clients had arrived, Jerry had barely finished introducing her to me as "Madame Contraire," which she preferred to go by rather than her first name, when she'd taken my hand I'd offered in greeting and began her psychic sideshow routine. Without warning, she'd rattled off a few facts about my life, starting with where I'd worked in Rapid City before moving up to Deadwood, the high school I'd attended, and that I had a brother, a sister, and two children.

If the medium had been hoping to wow me with her *This-Is-Your-Life* reveal, she'd fallen flat on her face. Instead of following in Jerry's footsteps and crowing about her mental prowess, I'd nailed her with a hard-eyed, zip-it glare and tugged free of her grip.

Before she could continue to awe us any further with her stage act, the circus had kicked into action with the arrival of my clowns—aka my clients, both sporting matching *Paranormal Realty* coats. More ghost groupies. Yippee skippee. Mr. Groupie had shaken my hand so hard and fast that if my teeth weren't attached, they'd have jiggled out of my mouth and landed clacking on my desk.

Fast forward a few hours and here we were on our way to

shivering through a fourth empty house. This latest listing had been added to my tour by Jerry via a quick phone call post-departure from the office. *A bonus for the clients!* he'd declared over the line, trying to sell it to me with an extra squirt of ketchup and mustard.

I would like to have given him a bonus—a solid molly whop right to the breadbasket, because it was colder than penguin snot outside. I was ready two houses ago to scurry home and snuggle under a blanket, preferably with my kids, or Doc, or all of them. Hell, by that point, I'd be okay with even the dang chicken joining us for some extra warmth.

But I drew a line at cuddling with the imp.

Daisy needed to earn my trust first, especially after what that little shit had done to my face the last time I'd gotten too close. I was still hiding the last of those bruises and scratches under makeup. And the imp would have to be wearing one of Elvis's sweaters, too, along with some tiny leg-warmers. Daisy's skin reminded me of one of those hairless cats, and while those felines may be perfectly lovable critters, it turned out I preferred pets with fur.

This bonus house of Jerry's had me suspecting he wanted to get the most bang for his buck when it came to Madame Contraire's time. I wondered how many arms and legs her so-called spiritual expertise was costing him, and if she were paid by the hour or day.

When it came to my clients, it was obvious that another stop on the tour would be more than welcome. They'd been practically bouncing with glee in my backseat since we'd left the parking lot, their faces pressed against the windows to see what came next on our haunted houses tour.

"How many ghosts have you seen in your life, Madame Contraire?" Mr. Groupie asked from the backseat.

I looked in the rearview mirror. His black-rimmed glasses were partially fogged over again thanks to my warm SUV, which I'd left running each time we went inside a house so we could come back to thaw in between the polar blasts. He'd tugged off his stocking cap, making him look like a happy, disheveled elf from the North Pole with his round red cheeks, bright pink nose, and tufted hair sticking up due to static thanks to the dry winter air.

Madame Contraire, who sat in the front passenger seat, took her time answering. I'd noticed this same hesitation on her part at the first house we'd toured. Initially, I'd thought she wasn't hearing my clients' questions, but then I'd realized she was building suspense by making them wait for her replies. A showwoman through and through.

I shot a glance in her direction, curious if she'd go high on her ghost count for a shock effect or keep the amount to something more realistic.

Her puffy white coat made her look twice as big as the pixie that she was. With her fur-lined hood pulled up, it was hard to see her bright turquoise hair that had made me stop and blink upon first sight. But her matching gold lips, eyeliner, and mascara were a firm reminder that Madame Contraire dressed to impress—or to fool. I had to wonder if Jerry had found the medium inside one of those coin-operated fortune teller machines and wished her to life.

Then again, it could be she was just tired of conforming to society's fashion standards. Who was I to judge? I had trouble matching my socks some days.

Madame Contraire turned my way, her dark eyes holding mine for a moment before she shifted in her seat to interact more easily with my potential buyers. Although if I were to lay money on these two being serious clients or not, I'd definitely lean toward them fitting into the along-for-the-ghosts category.

"Too many to count, *mon chéri*," she told him in a deep, velvety voice.

I still wasn't sure if we were hearing her real voice, or if this was part of her bohemian-like act. The tone certainly fit the part, especially considering the many gold-colored bangles she wore on both wrists that jingled even under her coat—somehow—with her every step. I glanced down at her long thick broom skirt. Were there such things as knee bangles?

"Often times I don't actually see the spectral," she continued. "I simply experience their vibrations in the air around me."

That earned her a joint "Ohhh" from her backseat audience.

"Imagine, if you will," she continued, holding out her arms. "Small tendrils of electricity dancing over your body, tickling your skin into goosebumps. That is what ghostly energy feels like."

Hmm. That certainly wasn't what Prudence's ghostly energy

felt like every time she walloped me. That hoity-toity haint delivered a sensation that was more heavy handed when it collided with my face. A sock stuffed with an orange would be more accurate. Or even a grapefruit.

"That's so coooool," Mr. Groupie whispered in awe.

I almost let a snort fly, switching it into a sniff at the last moment.

True medium or not, as we'd toured this morning's listings, Madame Contraire had "sensed a presence" in each location. Maybe she could. Or maybe she was saying that because my clients had indicated on their registration sheet that they were looking for properties with spirits residing within their walls. Whatever the case, the couple had certainly gobbled up the idea of ghosts floating nearby like sharks with fresh chum.

It appeared that Jerry's latest marketing ploy was working like gangbusters, which sucked for me. His success meant that I needed to figure out if this medium was actually seeing Casper and his ghostly pals sooner rather than later, because ever since we'd left the office, I'd been squirming like a worm on a hot sidewalk.

If Olivia Contraire were truly able to sense the non-living, she might actually pick up on my own physical medium abilities, same as Doc and Cornelius had done even before I knew I had any such skills. I didn't need the truth that I was anything other than a mid-thirties single mom trying to sell real estate becoming common knowledge around these parts.

Make that an engaged mom, I corrected the voice of doom monologuing in my head, sneaking a smile at my reflection in the rearview mirror. There were no tiny hearts floating around my head, though, nor bluebirds with pretty ribbons, so I returned to my current leaky boat up Shit Creek.

Otherwise, if this woman were simply pulling the wool over Jerry's eyes in order to make some easy money, I needed to know so I could let my guard down and focus on trying to sell real estate to these two paranormal junkies ... and any future folks who might request a medium's presence during home-showing trips.

"Where to next?" Madame Contraire asked me while we waited at the stoplight next to the visitor center at the old Fremont, Elkhorn & Missouri Valley Railroad Station.

I had turned on my left blinker, planning to head toward the house Jerry had told me about at the edge of Central City, but then I looked straight ahead toward Main Street and had a grand epiphany.

A surefire way to kill three birds with one stone!

I could test out Madame Olivia Contraire, Medium Extraordinaire, as well as give my *Paranormal Realty*–loving clients a surprise treat, *and* get busy on a little pre-caper work all at the same time!

"You'll see." I shut off my blinker. "You'll like this one, I think."

When the light turned green, I drove straight, continuing on up the hill between the historic Franklin Hotel and what used to be a bank long ago. At the top, I took a right and cruised along Williams Street, slowing to a stop next to the wrought iron fence lining the front lawn of …

A collective gasp came from the back seat. "Galena House!" my clients cried out in unison.

Yep. Galena House. That was next on our tour. I'd have to come up with an excuse for Jerry later for not taking him up on his idea.

I shifted into park, staring up at the beautiful old gal. I knew of one ghost residing within the building's historic walls: Big Jake Tender, Freesia's great-great—maybe one more great—uncle. Doc had met Big Jake's ghost on a visit to the past during one of our séances in Ms. Wolff's place.

I'd once stumbled upon another ghost in the same apartment. He'd looked like a greaser from the 1950s. However, he wasn't a free-roaming entity like Big Jake. This other ghost had been one of multiple victims brutally murdered there on the same night. The negative energy from the horrific act had left behind an invisible scarring of sorts on the apartment. A "residual haunting," according to Cornelius, which meant that same traumatic, bloody scene would play over and over through time.

My heart still ached for the greaser. He hadn't deserved to die so violently. If only I'd been able to stop …

I blinked back to the present.

Anyway, other than Big Jake and the haunting tragedy, neither Cornelius, Doc, nor I had run into any other ghostly pals. Nor had Cooper mentioned seeing any ghosts in there, and he'd spent plenty of time in the boarding house lately, ever since he and Natalie had gotten together last month.

I turned to my clients, who were both staring out at the house with big saucer eyes, reminding me of Daisy the imp eyeing a jar of honey. "While this place is not quite what you had in mind with your 'two bedroom and two bath' request, I think you'll enjoy a first-hand look inside."

"Jerry didn't mention that you'd be taking us here," Madame Contraire said, frowning out the window at the rectangular sign in the front yard with the words *Galena House* painted on it.

Exactly. Nor had he sent any telepathic messages to her about it either, apparently.

"It's a treat for my clients."

And a test for her.

"Before we go see if there are any ghosts roaming around inside," I said, reaching for my door handle, "I'm going to make sure it's a good time for the owner to let us check out the place. Wait here."

I stepped outside, pausing to glance up and down the street. The bone-chilling wind rocked me in my boots, leaving me shivering. Detective Hawke's usual police-issued vehicle wasn't anywhere to be seen, but Natalie's truck was, and so was Freesia's Subaru. Leaning into the wind, I started up the sidewalk to the front door.

Now, I just had to convince Freesia or Natalie to run interference for me while I did a little reconnaissance to get a better idea of the current clock situation inside Ms. Wolff's apartment. My fingers and toes were crossed that Detective Hawke was preoccupied playing cops-and-robbers at the moment and wouldn't come home in the midst of me sniffing around his door.

CHAPTER SIX

Natalie opened the front door at Galena House before I'd finished climbing the porch steps. "Well, well, well," she said. "Look what the snowcat dragged in."

"I'm not inside yet." I stomped the snow off my boots on the outside doormat. "And I wish I had Reid's snowcat today. It's colder than the hinges of hell out here."

"Wouldn't those be hot?"

"Depends on which version you're talking about. Dante's Ninth Circle of Hell has troublemakers trapped in ice."

"I guess when that particular hell gets you feeling down, you could always make snow cones to cheer yourself up." She grabbed my coat and yanked me into the foyer, closing the door on Old Man Winter's freezing fingers.

"You know," I said as I tugged off my gloves, "optimism is often confused with a lack of intelligence."

"Well, these days I'm more of a pessimistic optimist."

"So, what's that mean? You expect the shot glass of tequila to be half empty so you're never disappointed?"

She smiled. "I'm always happy drinking tequila, period."

"True, you are a happy drunk."

"I was thinking more along the lines of continuing to wish upon stars even though going in I know many of them have already been dead for a few million years."

"So, essentially, you're wishing upon the dead." I stuffed my gloves in my coat pockets. "That seems optimistically goth of you."

"Goth? Maybe. Coop is a bit of a Heathcliff from *Wuthering*

Heights. All dark, mysterious, and sexy."

"Don't forget angry and morose, not to mention always looking to torture an innocent, lovely blonde who just wants to figure out the answers to a mystery or two in town."

She chuckled. "Yeah, well some of us like a little bite along with our kisses. And you're far from innocent, Nosy Parker, which is why I'd follow you to the moon and back."

"Who are you trying to kid? You only want to go to the moon for the green cheese." I gave Natalie a once-over. Her dark brown hair, yellow sweatshirt, and overalls were splattered with various paint colors. "You look like you've been standing under a bird cage at a rainbow zoo." Upon closer inspection, her face had paint freckles, too. "Did you manage to get any paint on the walls, Raggedy Ann?"

She waved off my question. "Word on the street is that you're looking for some clock-caper pals."

Harvey must have already talked to her about enlisting in our clock crusade.

"Shhh." I frowned down the hallway toward the door to Ms. Wolff's apartment, where a length of yellow and black crime scene tape still hung from one of the door jambs like a leftover party streamer.

"No need to shush me. Sherlock Homeless isn't here at the moment." She crossed her arms, leaning back against the front door. "Is it true? Are you planning to play a game of clocks and robbers?"

"Don't you mean cops and robbers?"

She smirked. "With the way your luck has been running these days, babe, it will be more like cops and clobbers."

"As long as I'm not the one getting clobbered again. It would be nice to start my day without having to cover my bruises with makeup."

Natalie pointed at my face. "Good job on hiding what's left of that black eye. I like how you smudged your eyeliner a little more than usual. Your face is all ready to take another beating from your invisible new pal."

I growled under my breath. "That damned imp."

"Ah, come on now. Daisy was simply using a bit of self-defense against the big, bad *Scharfrichter.*"

"Figures you'd take the imp's side. You always were a sucker for thickheaded knuckle-draggers. Take your boyfriend, for example."

She grinned. "I just did a few hours ago before he headed off for work. Were you watching us do the naked boogie through a hidden camera?"

"Come on!" I recoiled a step. "How many times have I told you that I don't want to hear about your sex life with Detective Crabbypants."

Her grin widened. "More like Detective Grabby-ass today."

"That's it!" I took off my stocking cap and held it up under her nose. "If you don't zip it on you two banging your pots and pans together, I'm going to cram this down your sugar pipe."

"Whatever, meathead." She stole the cap from me and tossed it over her shoulder. "I have something to show you up in my apartment." She leaned in closer, whispering, "Corny gave me a fancy little camera to use for keeping an eye on my downstairs neighbor."

Prior to now, she'd relied on listening through the vent in her floor to keep tabs on Detective Hawke. "Is that legal?"

She shrugged. "Who cares?"

"The law dog you're canoodling with surely does."

She rolled her eyes. "Relax, I already told him."

"And did Cooper threaten to arrest you?"

She shook her head. "He might have been sleeping at the time. But I did tell him. It's not my fault he chose not to listen."

"You think that will fly when he finds out?"

"*If* he finds out, I'll deal with that then. I'm sort of hoping he'll want to handcuff me again." She winked at me. "Maybe even read me my rights and give me a good tongue-lashing."

I scrubbed my hand down my face. "You really need to find a new best friend."

"No way, babe. It's you and me 'til death do us part." She pulled me closer and put me in a neck lock, dropping a kiss on my temple before letting me go. "Now, come upstairs and check out my new toy. Be careful of the freshly waxed floors. They're slippery."

"They look great, but the field trip to your apartment will have to wait." I tiptoed across the floor and grabbed my hat. "I have some clients waiting in my car, hoping to see the place. Is Freesia around to okay a quick walkthrough?"

"Don't you usually call ahead?"

"Yeah, but this was a last-minute decision." I thumbed at the door. "Jerry hired a medium to do ride-alongs."

"No shit." Natalie nodded. "You know, that's actually a good marketing ploy in these parts."

"Her name is Madame Olivia Contraire, Medium Extraordinaire."

Her eyebrows shot upward. "What a mouthful. Is she old?"

I shook my head. "Around our age would be my guess. Maybe a little older."

"Is she French? The 'Extraordinaire' part in her title makes her sound fancy. I always want to fully pronounce the 'extra' part of that word instead of blending it together, which makes my tongue feel loose in its socket." She licked her lips and repeated, "Extraordinaire." And then she gave it another whirl, with "Extraordinaire," stumbling at the end. She shook her head. "No, now it's just sounding wrong when I try. You say it again."

I angled my head and looked at her sideways. "Have you been sniffing paint?"

She held her hands out wide. "By the bucket full, schnookums. What of it?"

I knocked her hands down. "The woman's last name is Contraire. She could be French or not. I haven't gotten around to asking about her lineage, what with all of her ghost chatter."

"She sounds like a character in a Dr. Seuss book." Natalie peeked out the narrow window next to the door. "Is she legit on the ghost front?"

"I don't know. That's why I'm here. To see if she conjures up any ghosts, and if so, which ones."

"Good thinking, pilgrim," she said, trying to sound like a cowboy.

"What have I told you about imitating John Wayne?"

She turned back to me with a toothy smile. "That I nail impersonations. Besides, that was supposed to be Mae West."

"And she just rolled over in her silk-lined casket." I pointed at the wide staircase leading to the second floor. "Is Freesia up there?"

"Yeah, but she's getting over a cold, so you might want to stick to texting her."

I did so immediately and got a thumbs-up response right away with an additional note telling me to have Natalie join us if she felt up to it, since she had keys to all of the locked doors.

"She wants you to play hostess," I told Natalie, pocketing my phone. "You game?"

"Sure. I can't wait to meet Ms. Frenchie."

"It's Madame Contraire. She's persnickety about her name."

"*Oh la la,*" she said with a thick French accent.

"And remember, these are actual clients, so there is a chance—albeit very slim—that they might want to buy the place."

"*Oui, oui.*" She kicked her heels together and saluted me. "I solemnly swear I'll be *un chaperon incroyable*, General Napoleon."

"Bring it down a couple of notches, Joan of Arc. I'd settle for moderately good."

Her hand lowered. "You do know that those are figures from two very different periods in French history, right?"

I wrinkled my nose at her. "Who died and put you in charge of France's archives, smartypants?"

She tried to flick my wrinkled appendage, but I dodged. "That's 'Madame' Smartypants to you."

"Speaking of mad ma'ams, you need to help me figure out if Contraire can really see ghosts."

"And how do you propose I do that, toots? Unless you have a psychic decoder ring from a cereal box that I can borrow, I'm going into this ghost-blind."

Yeah, I hadn't nailed down the answer to that head-scratcher either. "I don't know. Try pinching her when she's not looking and see if she blames it on a petulant poltergeist."

"Pinch her? Really? That's your brilliant idea?" She scoffed. "I'd have better luck taking this up with your Magic 8 Ball."

"Well, too bad, because I left it at home." I glanced down at her paint-splattered wardrobe. "Now, you need to go change, Cindy-Lou Who, because in that getup it's *you* who looks like a character from a Dr. Seuss book."

Her gaze followed mine. "Fine, I'll go up and change into something less colorful for Madame Mary Contrary and her pretty maids all in a row."

"It's Olivia Contraire, Dopey Dwarf."

"I used to be Snow White," she said in another lousy impression of Mae West, shooting me with both finger pistols. "But I drifted."

"Go change before I toss you into one of the drifts next to the porch."

Laughing like Snow White's nemesis, the evil Queen Grimhilde, Natalie took the stairs two at a time.

I pulled on my hat, glancing once more toward the strip of crime scene tape hanging from the door leading into the forbidden realm of clocks before heading back out into the frozen tundra.

Five minutes later, I was back in the foyer again, this time with my guests in tow. They shivered off the cold from the rush through Deadwood's wintery wasteland as they took off their boots and set them on an inside mat out of respect for the hardwood floor now polished to a gorgeous shine.

"Welcome to Galena House," Freesia's understudy said as she waltzed down the stairs like a princess at a ball. "My name is Natalie, and I'll be your guide today on your walk-through of this historic masterpiece."

Okay, so my best friend was slathering the frosting a little too thick on the cake this afternoon, but as Freesia's real estate agent, I opted to keep my critique tucked away behind my teeth.

Natalie had changed into a pair of khaki pants and a black cardigan, looking quite professional except for the few dots of paint I could still see freckling her cheeks and brown hair.

I introduced my clients to her first and then turned to my special guest. "And this is Madame Contraire."

"I love your hair, Madame Contraire." Natalie's smile was all charm. "I do declare, that color is so rare and—"

I cleared my throat, shooting the wannabe Dr. Seuss a hard glare while contemplating kicking her in the derrière.

Dear Lord, now I was playing her rhyming game, too.

"And uniquely *magnifique*," Natalie finished, the glance she sent my way brimmed with glee.

"Thank you," Madame Contraire said dismissively. Her focus was locked onto the shadowed hallway leading back to Ms. Wolff's apartment. "Is that police tape?"

"Hey, Natalie," I said, ignoring the medium's question. "How about you show these folks around upstairs while I make a quick phone call? Maybe start with the attic."

Not knowing how long Detective Hawke would remain off the premises, I needed to get my snooping done pronto.

Madame Contraire nodded approvingly. "The attic is usually a location favored by spirits, allowing them a safe and quiet place to escape from the living and all of our clamoring about."

Natalie clapped her hands together. "Come along, my dear guests, to the attic per your requests."

Oh, jeez. I should have hired a mime to lead the tour.

Madame Contraire waited for the others to go first, turning my way with one raised gold-lined eyebrow. "Does our guide often speak in rhyme?"

"Only on Saturdays," I said, struggling to keep a straight face. "You should be glad it's not Wednesday."

"Why is that?"

"She fancies limericks on hump day. The bawdier the better."

Madame Contraire groaned and followed them up the stairs.

As soon as everyone was out of sight, I tiptoed down the hall toward the apartment door with the metal knocker that looked like a tiny grandfather clock. I was halfway surprised that Detective Hawke hadn't covered the knocker with crime tape, too. His clock lockdown had its limits, apparently.

If the bonehead knew why the clocks on the other side of this door were so important, I could understand his unwillingness to share. But this was spite, pure and simple, along with a teaspoon of police procedure, both born from my unwillingness to cower each time he huffed and puffed in my direction. And maybe an ounce of fear, too, since he swore on the sun and moon that I was some kind of witch.

Of course, me threatening to crush his *cojones* under my boot heel shortly after Cooper had introduced us months ago had probably given some teeth to Hawke's "suspect" suspicions. Well, that along with the fake hex I'd put on his tallywacker. And that time I tricked him into thinking I could see ghosts.

But was it my fault that he bulled his way into my china shop almost every time we crossed paths? There was only so much of his breaking and my cringing before I took him by the horns and flipped him ass over porcelain teakettle.

I lifted the clock knocker and tapped it three times, waiting, wanting to make sure Hawke was truly gone. After a few seconds of silence from the other side, I pressed my ear against the wooden door, listening for the repetitious *tick-tock tick-tock tick-tock*. Or maybe even a cuckoo or two. Or a chime. All were normal sounds for clocks, but in my line of work as a Timekeeper, they told a bigger—and sometimes scarier—story.

I heard nothing through the wood. So, I reached for the door handle, half expecting the door to creak open on its own before I touched it, like it had once before for me. But the door stayed locked. I twisted it back and forth. No luck.

"Now what am I supposed to do, Ms. Wolff?" I muttered, eyeing that miniature grandfather clock again.

Could she have hidden some kind of secret key in the fancy knocker? I leaned closer, tapping on the brass with my fingernail. It sounded hollow. Maybe if I …

"Hubba hubba. Hubba hubba," a deep voice said from my pocket.

I squeaked and hopped backward. Holy crap!

"Hubba hubba. Hubba hubba," came from my pocket again—the new ringtone I'd programmed for Doc last night while he was off playing cards.

My blood was still pounding in my ears when I answered quietly, "Hi, Doc."

"Why are you whispering, Tish?" he asked. I could hear the steady hum of an engine in the background rather than the silence of his office.

"No reason." I tiptoed over to take a peek up the stairwell. The coast was still clear. "I just don't want to disturb your concentration."

"Or," he shot back, "is it because you're sneaking around inside Galena House?"

I searched the ceiling and the corners down the hallway, looking for a video camera. "How do you know that?"

"Natalie texted me. She said you needed someone to keep an eye out for Detective Hawke, because Coop isn't answering his phone and Harvey is out at his ranch."

Of course, Natalie had called for backup. I returned to Ms. Wolff's door. "That's probably a good idea."

"She figured it was better than one of us having to post bail later, and having bailed you out before, I agreed."

"Only once," I defended, tapping my fingernail on the metal knocker again. "And Cooper let me off with good behavior that time."

"I wouldn't say it was good behavior, judging by the fact that you were kicking and screaming when I carried you out of his office after I'd sprung you."

I wuffled like a horse. "Come now, Gomez. Let's not drag that tattered, old baggage into our sparkly, almost-newlywed life."

"As you wish, *cara mía*. So, is this a good time to tell me about your clock caper plans?"

I wasn't surprised that Doc had heard the news. I put my money on Harvey as the tattler. Deadwood was a small town and the old goat had a bucket mouth.

"Clock caper plans," I repeated slowly. "That's a real tongue twister. Try saying it three times fast." I tried, dropping an "L" almost every time. "Maybe we need to call it something else."

"I don't know. 'Cock paper clans' as a code name would probably throw off a certain hawk-eyed detective."

I grinned. "Who spilled the beans about nabbing the clocks?"

"Your bodyguard. He stopped by my office this morning."

Bingo-bango! Frankly, I was surprised Harvey's verbal dam hadn't burst last night during their poker game.

"I planned to tell you all about it tonight after supper," I explained. "I just didn't want to distract you from your fun with numbers today."

"I appreciate your consideration, sweetheart." The engine noise quieted. "But you are my fiancée, which means you take priority over the dollar signs that fill my days and part of my dreams lately."

Little cupids floated around my head for a second or two while the sound of the wind whistling kicked up in the background of his call.

"I'm supposed to be the only one haunting your dreams, don't you know?" I teased.

"You're still in there, too." I heard the muffled thump of a vehicle door closing through the line.

"Really? Am I wearing one of those green accountant visors?"

"That and suspenders, but nothing else."

"You should throw an adding machine into these fantasy dreams. We could wrap me up in that paper tape like a mummy, and I'll moan and chase you around the office."

"I think your idea of a sexy fantasy is very different than mine," he said above a crackling static thanks to the wind.

"There's nothing wrong with a little monster love. What if we throw in a pair of gold lace-up, knee-high gladiator sandals with stiletto heels?"

"I don't know. I might twist an ankle."

I chuckled. "The heels are for me, wise guy. The canopic jars will be for you and your special organs."

"No way. Nobody is parting me out. Your fantasy has once again strayed into nightmare land."

"I thought you like it when I touch your special parts."

"Quit trying to sidetrack me, woman. If you'd rather not talk about the caper right now, then how about explaining why Cornelius stopped by an hour ago to ask me what I know about performing an exorcism for a parasitic ghoul that he fears may now be attached to my favorite Executioner?"

"Uhhhh …"

"And who is this Millicent he wants to introduce me to?"

I winced. "Yeah, about all that," I started, but then hesitated, because truth be told, I was still hemming and hawing about my sit-in with Edith the stone this morning. "Where do you stand on pendulums as psychic tools?"

"My answer depends on who's holding the chain. Was it you or Cornelius?"

I wuffled again. "You know, this should probably be one of those face-to-face discussions. Are you busy in about an hour?"

"Yes, but I'm available right now."

The front door opened at the other end of the hall.

A swirling blast of snow blew in, followed by Doc, who looked like he'd been dipped in sugar—all sparkly and sweet. Add some molasses cookies, ice cream, and a drizzle of honey to the scene and now we were talking about *my* fantasyland.

Doc closed the door and shrugged off the snow, pocketing his hat and gloves as his gaze zeroed in on me. "Hello, Killer."

CHAPTER SEVEN

orget the butterflies. Doc's entrance spurred a fluttery, flapping fracas in my chest, sort of like a re-enactment of Hitchcock's *The Birds*, minus all the flying feathers and screeching. "What are you doing here?" I asked, pocketing my cell phone.

"I told you on the phone, I'm curious about a thing or two." Doc took off his snow boots and set them on the rug next to the door. "I thought it'd be easier to get answers if I came over and caught the tiger by its toe."

"Eeny, meeny, miny, moe." I smiled up at him when he joined me in front of the clock knocker and crime scene tape.

His short, dark beard glistened with tiny crystals of ice. His coat collar did, too.

He caught my hand and pulled me closer. "My mother told me to pick the very best one, and you, Tish, are it. So, don't even bother hollering, because I'm not letting go until you tell me about this pendulum business, for starters."

"Don't you have a bunch of numbers to add and subtract?"

He chuckled. "Multiply and divide, too, but as I said earlier, I have my priorities straight."

"Aww, that makes me feel warm and fuzzy."

"That's nice, Boots." He leaned down and dropped a cool kiss on my lips. "And that's even nicer."

I smiled. "You smell fresh and cold, not even a hint of freezer-burn on you. I'm glad you came by to watch my back."

"And your front," he said with a flirty grin. "However, I should confess that my showing up here is due to Coop as well as Natalie."

"Well, that makes me feel cold and cringy. I thought Natalie couldn't get hold of Cooper so she called you."

"That's true." He stepped back, crossing his arms while leaning against the door jamb. "But Coop made me promise during last night's game that I'd drop everything and come running if you tried to do something crazy like breaking into this apartment to get to the clocks."

My gaze narrowed. "That law dog needs a new chew toy so he'll stop locking his jaws onto my leg." I pointed at the apartment door. "And getting inside of here isn't crazy. It's necessary to save my family."

"*Crazy* was his word, not mine." Doc frowned at the door, and then looked up at the ceiling, his gaze skirting from one end of the hall to the other. "You know, I'm surprised Detective Hawke hasn't installed any security cameras out here to monitor this door."

"He did," a croaky voice intervened from behind us, followed by a sneeze.

We both turned to find Freesia at the bottom of the stairwell. She wore a thick scarf wrapped around her neck, just below her pink nose, covering her mouth. A box of tissues was in one hand, and her other gripped the newel post, possibly to hold herself steady, judging by her glassy brown eyes.

In spite of being sick, Freesia painted a picture of warm loveliness on a cold winter's day, from her long black curly hair, down the fuzzy blue robe tied over her snowflake flannel pajamas, to her thick fleece slippers. As a curvier version of a young Halle Berry, the owner of Galena House probably wouldn't look bad even if she were pulled through a knothole backward.

"Freesia," I said, taking a step toward her. "How are you feeling?"

"Like Nat used my head for hammering practice." She rounded the newel post but then stopped, clearly keeping her distance. "I wanted to see if there was anything I could do to help with your clients."

I pointed upward. "I left them in Natalie's hands while I talked to Doc." That wasn't quite how the timeline had gone, but it rang true at the moment with his presence reinforcing my words.

She nodded, sniffing. "I eavesdropped a little on Nat while she had them up in the attic. She was doing a good job of talking up this old gal." She patted the newel post, then her focus shifted. "Hello, Doc. I'm surprised to see you here. I thought this was a daytime work visit for Violet, not the nighttime kind."

Since Freesia had participated during a past after-hours séance in Ms. Wolff's apartment along with Doc, Cornelius, and me, she knew about our dillydallying with wispy folks.

"It is a day visit for Violet. I just stopped by because I was in the area and wanted to make sure she wasn't harassing poor, hardworking Detective Hawke."

I reached over and pinched him through his coat sleeve, making him chuckle. "And there's more where that came from," I warned.

"Promises, promises."

Freesia laughed, which turned into a cough that she covered with a fresh tissue from the box before stuffing it into her robe pocket. "Sorry about that. I'm actually on the mend, even if I look like I'm teetering next to the grave."

"Glad to hear it," Doc said, thumbing toward the apartment door. "What did you mean about Detective Hawke trying to install a security camera?"

"Well, he tried to install a video camera in that corner last week." She pointed toward the end of the hallway. "But hallway cameras are against my house rules, so I had Natalie take it down." She glanced up the stairs, smiling fleetingly for a moment. "Which she did promptly, even though Detective Hawke was at the bottom of the ladder grumbling at her the whole time. But I told him that rules were rules, and I didn't care if he worked for the police department."

She paused, holding her finger under her nose like she had a sneeze coming. When it didn't arrive, she continued, "That camera would have been an invasion of the other renters' privacy, and frankly, I think there are a few too many cameras in the world already."

Good. Her rule meant we were safe out in the hallway when it came time to pull off our caper. But what about elsewhere?

"Has Detective Hawke installed cameras anywhere outside of the house that you know of?" I asked. "Like on one of the trees pointing at the house?"

Freesia held up her hand and then sneezed into another tissue. "Excuse me," she said, dabbing at her nose, sounding stuffier than before. "I don't think so, but you should check with Nat to be certain. While the detective has been keeping an eye on this apartment, she has been keeping an even closer eye on him, making sure he toes the line on my other house rules, too."

I wondered if Freesia knew about Natalie's new secret camera and where that fit in with her rules. Then again, Detective Hawke was not even legally living in Ms. Wolfe's apartment. Although Natalie had told me recently that he was paying rent now for the place after Cooper had talked to the chief of police about Hawke taking advantage of Freesia's kindness. However, according to Freesia, he still hadn't signed an official lease and claimed he had to stay put to protect police evidence.

As if her ears had been ringing, Natalie leaned over the banister above and called down the stairwell, "Did I just hear Freesia's voice?"

"You did," Freesia croaked, and then paused to cough into her tissue. Natalie had made it partway down the stairs by the time the building's owner could talk again. "I was telling Violet and Doc about our temporary tenant in Ms. Wolff's apartment and his fondness for visual aids."

I had a feeling she was being careful in case there were other ears listening. Speaking of those extra ears …

"Where are my clients?" I asked Natalie when she reached the bottom step.

"I left them in the storeroom at the end of the hall. Frenchie sensed a ghost in there, so she had everyone join hands to make a stronger channel. I told them I had to use the bathroom and to come downstairs when they're done talking to dead people." She turned to Freesia. "Oh, crap. Is your place locked? I wasn't worried about it because I figured you were in there."

Freesia shook her head. "I'll head back now since I'm not really dressed for company." She said a quick goodbye to Doc and me and hurried upstairs, coughing a few times near the top.

"Thanks for coming over, Doc." Natalie shoulder bumped him.

I turned to Natalie, keeping my voice low when I said, "You should have told me you were calling in the cavalry."

"I didn't have time. Your clients were already front and center down here in the foyer by then."

Doc unzipped his coat. "Well, now that I'm here, it's as good a time as any to take a look at what we're up against when we go through with this clock caper of yours."

"*When?*" I asked, a little surprised that hadn't been an *if*. "You're not going to try to talk me out of it like Cooper did?"

Doc shrugged. "Would it do any good?"

I shook my head at the same time Natalie said, "No."

"Exactly. Besides, you're right, we need these clocks."

"Did Harvey give you any details?" Natalie asked. "Because he didn't have any for me, just ordered me to keep an eye on Hawke and the place, including timing his comings and goings."

"I don't think there are any yet," I told them. "And I've been doing the same on Hawke's schedule from the outside for the last week."

"Really?" Doc quirked an eyebrow. "Why does that not surprise me?"

"Because you know my girl and her tendency to stick her nose into places she probably shouldn't," Natalie said with a playful grin.

"Hey! You're supposed to be on my side," I told her.

"Harvey didn't talk about any set plans," Doc said, "which I figured meant you two were still in the recruitment and reconnaissance stage. Unfortunately, my ten o'clock appointment showed up then, so Harvey took off. I was going to call him after I'd wrapped up, but then Cornelius showed up to put in a request to have me consult with Millicent."

Natalie's narrowed gaze switched from Doc to me. "Who's Millicent?"

I opened my mouth to tell them both about the pendulum divination and the possible ghoul situation, but then I heard voices echoing down from the hallway overhead. Dang it, my clients were coming.

"I'll tell you about her and Edith after supper."

"Edith?" she asked. "Are these new imaginary friends of yours or Corny's?"

I held up my hand to wait and headed over to the bottom of the stairwell, listening. "They'll be down here shortly," I whispered, hurrying back to them. "Doc, Jerry has hired a medium to accompany us on house showings."

He gaped and then cursed under his breath.

"Yeah, that was pretty much my reaction, only with more cursing than that." I paused, listening for footfalls. They were almost to the landing at the top of the stairs. I leaned closer to him. "I need you to help me figure out if she's legit."

He scoffed slightly. "I've told you before, Tish, there's no simple way to tell that."

Natalie snorted. "It's not like a piss test, Vi."

I pointed two fingers at her face, Three Stooges style. "No snorting at me."

She blocked me with her hand. "Sorry. No more snorting starting now."

I turned back to Doc. "Can you at least try to get a feel on her?"

"Not in front of his girlfriend," Natalie said, chuckling.

His fiancée, I corrected in my head, but that was a secret even from Natalie, in spite of me almost blowing it once or twice over the last week.

"Ignore Chuckles Magoo here," I said to Doc before glancing toward the stairwell again. "We can talk about this more when we get home."

"Okay, but I'm going to be a little late tonight."

It would be nice when tax season came to an end. So many percentages and dollar signs, so little time. "We can put our heads together after supper then."

"And maybe something else," Natalie whispered, elbowing Doc. "Hubba hubba."

Her tone almost matched my new ringtone.

"Definitely something else," he agreed, hitting me with a heated look.

"Stop it, Doc." I lightly pushed against his chest. "You're going to make me smolder in front of my clients."

The stairs creaked up near the landing. I scrambled over to the bottom of the stairwell. "Well?" I asked my clients as they reached the halfway point. "Did you make any connections?"

"There was definitely an ethereal presence in that room with us," Madame Contraire said from the top of the steps.

I shot Doc a wide-eyed look and sniffed twice while pretending to stretch my neck in the direction of the staircase. He took several steps backward, quietly slipping out of sight toward the other end of the hall.

No, that's not what I'd meant for him to do.

I sniffed and stretched again with more animation, trying my best to communicate via telepathy without gesturing too obviously that he needed to head upstairs as soon as we were gone to sniff around for ghosts.

"What's wrong?" Natalie joined me at the bottom of the stairs. She reached out to touch my face. "Are you having some kind of seizure?"

I reared back. "No, I have to sneeze," I lied, sighing in defeat.

Doc and I really needed to work on our non-verbal communication if we were going to raise two kids together. With Layne's big brain and Addy's wiliness, they'd run circles around us in no time.

Natalie focused on Madame Contraire. "So, is this presence you're talking about the same entity you detected in the attic?"

"It could have been," the medium said as she descended the stairs. "Without more time to channel, I can't be positive, though."

"What was the rush?" Natalie asked.

Madame Contraire nodded toward Mr. Ghost Groupie. "Someone received a phone call in the midst of our attempt to reach out to the spirit and is required elsewhere."

"We're so sorry we have to cut this short," Ms. Groupie said, heading over to get her boots. "But our doggie sitter had a situation come up and we need to get home."

Natalie's phone chirped, sounding like a police siren cut short. She pulled it out and stared down at the screen, her forehead wrinkling.

I turned toward the couple, smiling reassuringly. "That's okay. It's time to call it a day, anyway. It's supposed to drop another twenty degrees as evening comes on, so maybe it's best we all get home safely before dark."

I motioned Doc to come closer as my clients zipped up their coats and pulled on their boots, gloves, and hats. Maybe if he stood near Madame Contraire, he'd be able to pick up a vibe off her—or a psychic spark that made it clear she had some kind of sixth sense abilities. After all these years of Doc exploring his own medium skills, he had to know of a psychic tell that would give away her truths to him. Or her lies.

Doc joined me, but kept his hands stuffed in his coat pockets.

Whether the medium sensed Doc's presence or just noticed movement out of the corner of her eye, I couldn't tell. However, she did do a double take when she looked his way, her eyes widening slightly.

She tentatively reached out and touched his forearm, and then pulled back quickly, placing her hand on her chest. "Oh, you're real. I'm sorry. I just wanted to make sure you weren't the entity I had sensed upstairs appearing before me in your previous form."

"Doc is the real deal, all right," Natalie said, rushing over and looping her arm through his. Her cheeks were dark pink, clearly flushed. "All flesh and bones and ... hair. He's here to help me with a faulty ... uh ... plugged sink drain in my apartment." She pointed toward the ceiling. "Upstairs, I mean." She let out a loud laugh that was a borderline cackle and then tugged Doc closer to her, clearly latching onto him now as if the wind were trying to blow her away.

I eyeballed her. Her train seemed to have derailed and I wasn't sure how to follow. Doc wasn't either, judging by the way he was frowning down at her.

"I thought you were the building's caretaker," Madame Contraire said. Her forehead was lined, too, but her gaze was narrowed with a solid dose of suspicion.

"I am." Natalie tried to smile, but it came out wrinkly and crooked, as if she weren't quite in control of her face. "But I don't do plumbing."

"And he does?" Madame Contraire's voice was heavy with skepticism as she looked Doc up and down.

"What's that supposed to mean?" Natalie asked, bristling. "You think just because Doc looks factory pretty he can't get his hands dirty like the rest of us? Before you accuse someone of something that's not true, maybe you need to take a look in the mirror."

What in the ever-lovin' hell was going on? Plumber or not, this situation was swirling down the drain before I could grab the plug.

"Are you okay, Natalie?" Doc asked, looking down at where

she now had a white-knuckled grip on his wrist.

"I was referring to his lack of plumbing tools," Madame Contraire said calmly. "I would expect one in his profession to carry a toolbox."

"Oh, yeah." Natalie tried to smile again, but it still wasn't quite working out for her. "Well, he stopped by earlier with his tools. They're up in my apartment already." She tugged Doc toward the stairwell. "It was nice to meet you all. I hope to see you again."

Doc cast me one last frown before following her upstairs.

I rubbed my forehead, speechless. When I turned to my clients, they were sharing baffled looks.

A door slammed overhead.

"Is the docent always so unstable?" Madame Contraire asked, her focus shifting from the stairwell to me.

"Not usually. There appears to be some slack in her rope today."

Natalie had been acting easy-breezy until that text message had come through. I'd have to call her as soon as I had a free moment to find out what had caused her to jump the tracks.

"I suspect the rather energetic entity that I felt in the attic is affecting her ability to focus, eliciting chaotic mood swings." The medium slid her arms into her coat. "I've seen it happen before. An exorcism might be required if she continues to have fits of mania."

I didn't like Madame Contraire's know-it-all manner one iota, but rather than tell her where and how she could shove her psychic evaluation, I pasted on a smile and returned to my clients.

"Before we head back to my office, do either of you have any questions about this property?"

Ms. Ghost Groupie raised her hand. "Can we do a séance here with Madame Contraire?"

No way in hell.

"Unfortunately, the local police still have this building under investigation, as you'll remember from the television show. They would discourage any sort of gathering in here, and we must abide by the law, of course, right?"

They both nodded.

The husband was next with a question. "Are there any places around town where we could do a séance with Madame

Contraire?"

I turned to the medium. "That would be a question for her, not me."

She reached inside her coat and pulled out a business card, handing it to him. "Call me next week. I usually operate out of Rapid City, but we may be able to get special permission to visit a few locations run by the local historical group after business hours."

As my clients headed out the door, Madame Contraire turned to me, her lips flatlining. "What sort of game were you playing here today, Ms. Parker?"

Well, I'd been playing a few different games, some having nothing to do with her, so she was going to have to be more specific. "What do you mean?"

"You didn't bring your clients to this boarding house in order to sell real estate, did you?"

I feigned innocence. "If you'll remember, I did say that it didn't fit their needs list, but that it had been part of the television show, of which they are obviously big fans."

Her nostrils flared. "So, you are claiming you brought us here for simple entertainment?"

I shrugged. "It is for sale, and I am the seller's agent."

For a moment, I considered reminding her that she was the extra in this scene, not me or them. As far as I was concerned, she hadn't needed to come along today at all; it was Jerry's idea. However, I bit my tongue because I didn't want word to get back to my boss that I was giving his star medium a hard time. Not to mention that if Jerry had his way, she might be joining me on more listing tours, so burning this bridge already would cause nothing but future heartburn.

"You didn't bring me here for your own gain?" she asked.

I struggled not to glare at her. "What gain?"

She pointed up the stairs. "That man is not a plumber."

Well, sixth sense or not, she'd gotten that right.

"He is a distraction," she declared.

Doc certainly was that and had been for me since I'd met him. He'd seduced my heart into shopping for His and Her hand towels in record time.

"As Natalie said, he can't help the way he looks." I played

dumb as I tugged on my hat, giving her some extra leash so I could see where she was heading with this.

"I'm not talking about his façade."

She wasn't? Maybe she did have supernatural abilities.

"What are you talking about then?" I asked while reaching for the door handle.

"Oh, I think you know, Ms. Parker." She stepped past me onto the porch, pausing to glance back with a knowing glint. "And unlike you, he's the real deal."

Dammit! That was a great exit line, and I still didn't know if she could see ghosts or not.

Shielding my face from the nose-freezing gusts of wind that had intensified since we'd arrived at Galena House, I aimed one last look inside toward Ms. Wolff's apartment door. At least today wasn't a total loss. Now I knew where we were on the camera situation. Never mind that I could have called Natalie to learn that information and saved being on the receiving end of Madame Contraire's censure.

The wind yanked the door out of my gloved hand and blasted it wide open.

"Crap!" I stepped inside and grabbed the door handle again, pulling it shut tight. When I turned to leave, I stopped short at the sight of a familiar pain-in-the-buttinski standing at the bottom of the porch steps.

"Parker!" Detective Hawke barked at me, looking ridiculous in his police hat with the furred ears pulled down and a leather strap cinched tight under his square chin. His thick, black eyebrows ran together, making a parallel line below the front of his hat.

"Hawke!" I shouted back, although I didn't quite manage the level of passion he'd had because unlike the big cretin, I didn't have a walnut for a brain.

"What in the hell are you doing here?" He stomped up the steps, closing the distance between us until he towered over me.

Detective Hawke made a habit of invading my space almost every time he talked to me. At first, I thought it was an attempt to bully me, but I'd come to learn the dufus had no concept of personal space. That didn't make me like him any better, though. At this point, not much could.

"I'm showing this place to clients." I pointed toward my

vehicle, where Madame Contraire was climbing into the front seat. "In other words, my job."

Hawke scowled toward my SUV. "That woman was no client, not with that gold glittery shit on her eyes."

"You shouldn't judge a book by its cover." I braced against another blast of kneecap-rattling wind. "A detective as old as you should know that by now."

He turned back to me, all teeth and steamy breath. "Don't tell me what my job is, Parker. Unless you want to talk about me arresting you."

I sighed loudly, cranking up the drama for fun. "Not this again, Hawke. It's too cold to have a pissing contest today and my give-a-damn is frozen."

"That's Detective Hawke to you."

As comebacks went, he really needed to go back to kindergarten.

"You have to get used to me being in Freesia's place. I'm the selling agent." I pushed past him and started down the steps.

He caught my sleeve midway down. "Where's your boyfriend? I see his old Ford out front."

"He's helping Natalie with something," I said, yanking my arm free.

"With what?"

"Why don't you go on up to her place and ask her for yourself. I have clients waiting."

"Oh, I definitely will."

"You do that, Detective."

"I've got my eye on you, Parker."

"Good." Maybe that would keep him preoccupied while Harvey and the others snuck those clocks out of Ms. Wolff's apartment.

I headed for my car, done with this conversation long before it had started.

"And Coop, too," he called after me. "Especially now that he's suspended from duty."

I paused, looking back at the blowhard. "Suspended? Since when?"

"This afternoon," he said, his chin jutting. "And I'm heading up the investigation into the crimes he's committed alongside you."

I turned and walked away from his taunting smirk before I took off my boot and threw it at his smug mug.

So, that text message Natalie had received right before she'd jumped the tracks must have been from Cooper, letting her know about him being suspended. That was probably why she'd dragged Doc upstairs, so she could tell him in private about this latest snag.

Suspended. *Shit!*

That meant we had an even bigger problem than nabbing those damned clocks.

CHAPTER EIGHT

Aunt Zoe's house smelled like roast beef with a side of biscuits when I stepped inside an hour later. I tried not to drool as I shrugged off my coat and stepped out of my boots, but my stomach took over and had me practically skipping all the way to the kitchen.

"What's for supper?" I asked my aunt, who was sitting at the table with a couple of tattered books along with several sheets of paper and her notepad splayed out in front of her. With her silver-streaked hair plaited in a braid down her back and her forehead puckered in thought, she reminded me of a college student nose-deep in studies right before finals.

"Beef pot pie," she said without looking up.

Licking my lips, I headed for the sink. A cup of something hot to warm me from the inside out had been calling my name ever since I'd hurried through the freezing wind and ice to my rig after shutting down my computer and saying *ciao* to Mona and Jerry—and to the tension buzzing between them.

As much as I'd wanted to know if a certain turquoise-haired medium was what had rattled the hornets' nest this afternoon in the office while I was out, I'd kept my big nose tucked into my scarf and hightailed it out of there. I'd reached my drama limit after facing off with Detective Hawke and wanted nothing more than to smother my worries under a warm blanket.

"What are you working on?" I asked, grabbing a mug from the cupboard.

I didn't want to disrupt the cozy, calm aura lingering in Aunt Zoe's kitchen, so I kept my lips sealed about Cooper supposedly being suspended. Besides, she should probably hear the story behind Hawke's boastful claim from Cooper himself, who I assumed would be joining us for supper soon enough since he had no criminals to chase or curly-haired blondes to pester under the pretense of police business.

Pulling my cell phone from my back pocket, I checked to see if I had any new messages or had missed a call. Since leaving Galena House, I'd kept expecting to hear from Doc or Natalie, maybe even Cooper or Harvey, about what Hawke had told me, but my phone had remained disappointingly silent.

Jerry hadn't seemed to notice my somewhat distracted fidgeting as he drilled me on Madame Contraire's ghost speculations inside each house, and if I thought she'd made an impression on my clients. Since the medium had left immediately upon returning to the office, I was free to be candid. However, I curbed my tongue in the face of his eager questions, which I figured might be financially inspired, and simply assured him that my clients had appreciated the extra entertainment as we'd toured the houses.

Not that Jerry cared, but his experiment with a so-called medium had made the day quite memorable for me, too. I was still perched on the fence about what Madame Contraire was actually implying when it came to Doc's true profession. Not to mention I'd made no progress on determining if she could chit-chat with the dead or not, damn it.

"Come over here and take a look for yourself," Aunt Zoe said, lassoing me back to the present.

I tucked my phone back into my pocket, set the empty mug on the counter, and joined her at the table. The sheets of paper were actually printouts of the pictures I'd taken of the sigils in the Sugarloaf Building, the Hellhole, and at the house in Lead where the imp had broken into the garage and stolen frozen honey BBQ chicken wings.

I picked up the fourth picture. It was a shot of the driver's side door on my old red Bronco. I grimaced as the memory replayed of the Bronco going up in flames while I stood by, helpless, unable to do anything other than watch as part of the vehicle melted onto the pavement before the fire department arrived to put the flames out.

"Where did you get this one?" I asked, showing her the picture. Upon a second look, I realized that the focus was on the word that had been carved into the driver's side door—SLUT!

"From the insurance report Reid brought over after the accident."

"Accident?" I scoffed. "You mean the murder of my poor Bronco."

Stupid Lila Beaumont! The demon-hugging loon had left her mark on my door—and my nerves. I still broke out in a sweat every time I entered a certain lovely, Gothic revival–style house in Lead where Lila had tried to sacrifice me. Although Prudence's continued pain-inducing tricks did play a part in my anxiety attacks when I stepped over the threshold into her territory.

I held the Bronco door picture up closer.

Doc was the one who'd first noticed the symbol the mad bitch had etched into the paint in lieu of the dot for the exclamation mark. I'd been in too much of a panic to notice, since the Bronco had been my only vehicle at the time, and taking clients around in a SLUT!-mobile would have most likely snookered my chance of landing a sale.

I tapped my finger on the dot. "This symbol is some kind of sigil, isn't it?"

"Yes." Aunt Zoe began flipping through one of the books that appeared to have been bound by hand with some of the pages sticking out slightly more than others. "A very common sigil, unlike the one Daisy has been leaving around town."

I set the picture down, watching Aunt Zoe scan a few pages of what looked like some foreign alphabet. "What is that book?"

"It belonged to your great-grandmother at one time," she said, running her index finger down the page.

I cringed and returned to the counter. Grandma-great and her rune stones had always given me the heebie-jeebies, especially after she'd sniffed out the killer in me when I was just a kid, making creepy cryptic comments about my *eau-de*-death smell when nobody else was around.

"Another grisly family hand-me-down?" I carried the mug to the faucet.

"Far less grisly than the others."

I glanced at her while filling the mug. "Is it another historical account of my predecessors' adventures in slaying, or is it about their misadventures while being slain?"

The book didn't look like the others, but Aunt Zoe was our ancestral line's current *magistra*, which meant she not only had to train me in the ways of killing, but also act as the family librarian and recorder.

"Neither of those."

While I waited for the mug of water to heat up in the microwave, I watched Aunt Zoe skim another few pages.

"Then what is it?"

"A dictionary of sorts." She rubbed her jaw. "Or rather more of a collection."

"A dictionary collection?"

The microwave beeped. I grabbed my cup and a sachet of mint tea, taking the seat next to her at the table.

After leaning closer to ponder the images on the pages in front of her for a moment, I sat back. "Those weird symbols make me think of some sort of foreign alphabet with chicken scratches next to it. Can you actually read any of that?"

She stared at me, her brow pinched over her purple-rimmed reading glasses. "Those chicken scratches are Latin, my dear, mixed with a bit of old German. Your great-great-grandmother, a *magistra* as well, could read Latin with ease, but she struggled with writing it. She would resort to old German when memory failed her."

"That explains the chicken scratches, but what do the symbols represent?"

"They are a form of *magick*."

"Like black magic full of evil possibilities that might scare a certain annoying detective away from an apartment full of clocks? If so, I could use some of that."

"Be careful what you wish for, *Scharfrichter*." She poked my arm with the eraser on her pencil. "You know, magick isn't just a binary black or white power, in spite of what many books and movies have portrayed. It's full of all colors of the rainbow. Sometimes even the most exciting elements are simply boring beige or dull gray." She patted my hand. "And I meant magick with a 'k' at the end."

What? Come on! Most days I had enough trouble spelling my

name. "Who decided to throw an extra letter at the end of a perfectly good word? And what's the difference between the two?"

"It's a somewhat newer convention being used to differentiate stage magic—without a 'k'—from non-entertaining forms of sorcery."

I aimed a squint at her. "Are you messing with me, Aunt Zoe? Because I'm going to warn you up front that I'm in an arm-pinching mood." Detective Hawke's smug mug often tended to bring out the brawler in me.

She returned to her book. "No, Violet Lynn."

"Did you dump some Irish cream liqueur in your coffee this afternoon?" I picked up the mostly empty coffee mug next to her and sniffed the liquid, smelling coffee and nothing more.

Her gaze shifted to me, her blue eyes crinkling in the corners. "I wish, but no. This work requires sobriety."

I set her coffee down. "What kind of magic with a 'k' are we talking about then?"

"Sympathetic magick, I believe."

"Sympathetic as in Addy's pet chicken sorcerous-ly disappears while she's away with my parents, and since I've not personally had a chicken of my own, I feel sorry for Addy and offer her my shoulder to cry on?"

Aunt Zoe pursed her lips. "I thought you liked Elvis now."

"You're right, I do, even if she leaves eggs in my shoes."

"That's because she likes you."

"I know, I know. Although I have to wonder if the insides of my shoes stink like a musty straw nest."

She grinned. "I'm sure Doc would say they smell like roses."

"I don't know about that. He's not fond of my cold feet, so I doubt adding 'smelly' to the list of adjectives describing those appendages would be any kind of aphrodisiac." I glanced around. "Speaking of which, where is that chicken?"

"Last I saw her, the imp was trying to put the dog's paw-mittens on the chicken's feet, but Elvis's toenails kept snagging in the knit."

Huh. No shit. "Some days it seems like the only 'normal' example in my life is the setting on the dryer."

Aunt Zoe looked up with a wrinkled brow. "Yeah, well, normal isn't your strong suit, right?"

I was still trying to picture the imp's tiny hands struggling with those paw-mittens when it hit me what Aunt Zoe had said. "Hold the phone! How could you see the imp putting the mittens on the chicken? Addy, Layne, and I are the only ones with imp vision."

"More magick," she said, pointing in the direction of the back door.

Leaning against the wall next to the door was our family's antique, hand-me-down mirror from her workshop, which I now knew had an actual name—Arcana. Or as Mr. Black had called it, a *magischer Spiegel,* which was German for "special mirror." However, he'd meant the mirror was special because it was actually a supernatural gateway.

With a frame made of some sort of bronze that was carved with alchemy symbols, and the glass containing trace amounts of clear quartz and rubies, Arcana was definitely not made to be stared into for vanity's sake. According to my aunt, it was infused with powers and passed down from female to female. I'd learned some of the potential of Arcana's power when fighting a smoky devil last month.

"You mean you can see the imp's reflection in that mirror?"

She nodded. "You remember the story about Reid bringing that other imp here years ago by accident?"

"Yeah, you saw it in the reflection of the mirror inside the front door—the one that you made with all of the glass designs in the frame." The mirror that I'd passed on my way to joining her in the kitchen.

"Right. When I made that mirror, I charged it with a spell to reflect beings, both human and non-human." She frowned toward the front door. "Well, that mirror didn't work on our imp."

"That's weird. Isn't it? Why could you see the other one but not Daisy?"

"I don't know. Maybe I need to recharge the spells on that mirror. That incident with Reid was years ago." She shrugged, turning back to me, her slight scowl still in place. "Anyway, that gave me the idea to try the reflection experiment again, only with Arcana this time, and it worked."

"Really?" That was a good thing, wasn't it? It would be handy if Doc and Zoe could see the imp, as well as the kids and me. "Maybe we need to find more special mirrors and place them throughout the house. Mr. Black might know where we could find one or two."

She cringed. "I don't know. Magick mirrors can be bad juju, especially if you don't know their history."

That was true. Arcana the Mirror was a good example of this. When I'd looked into its reflecting glass last month, I'd seen a gory remnant of something long ago captured within it that had made my blood run cold. According to Prudence the know-it-all ghost, I needed to protect myself before looking into strange mirrors, so I didn't wind up trapped as well. I was skeptical about this until Doc had stared into the mirror while Prudence shielded him. When he'd finished, he told me there were actually six other entities locked away inside of Arcana, and from the looks of them, we probably didn't want even a single one to escape.

I had to wonder how much worse they could be than the imp living with us now. I certainly hoped never to find out.

But back to the books in front of us. "You were telling me about those symbols and sympathetic magick."

"Right." She tapped her pencil on her notebook. "It's a type of imitative magick. Or correspondence magick, if that helps."

"It doesn't. Keep explaining."

"Well, it's based on the notion that people or items can be affected via supernatural forces through simple means, such as a name or drawing or something else that represents them."

I crossed my arms, leaning my elbows on the table. "This is getting muddier by the minute."

"Okay, think about the cave art you've seen that depicts animals. Some historians believe that these drawings might have been created by shamans who were trying to manifest good results for hunts." She pointed at the symbols on the book page. "Sigils like these can be used similarly by creating an intention and then charging them appropriately."

I nodded. "Like when I smeared my blood on those sigils in the basement of the courthouse."

"Exactly. You were powering them with your blood—more important, an Executioner's blood—with the intention of confining the *lidérc*."

"Are there ways to power a sigil other than with blood?"

"Yes."

"How?"

"You could draw it on something and burn that object. Or just bury it. Or look at it through a hag stone."

"Like the stone I found in the clock designated to the *mardagayl*." That was the clock that Cornelius was storing for me in his apartment. At this time, the hands continued to spin on it, which was a good thing in this case.

Actually, the hag stone necklace had belonged to the *other*. The *mardagayl* had given it to Ms. Wolff to help see that which normally wasn't visible to my Timekeeping predecessor.

What came of me tracking down the *mardagayl* was a prime example of why I needed to collect all of the clocks in Ms. Wolff's apartment. That particular *other* had taught me three important lessons for my new line of work: First, not every traveler was an enemy here to cause harm. Second, there was a sorcerer at play now who I needed to worry about in addition to everything else giving me heartburn these days. Third, if I didn't keep the balance in the Black Hills (which I had no idea how to do), bloodshed and ruin were sure to come knocking sooner rather than later.

I sighed. If I were ever to become a harbinger of death, I was going to carry a daisy instead of a scythe or a tolling bell. My intended could pluck the petals one by one, checking to see if death loved them or not, hoping for the best in spite of my presence.

"You could draw a sigil in the sand or snow," Aunt Zoe continued. "Or draw it with your spit. Or even your urine—which would be easier if you were a guy, of course."

"Let's not give Harvey any big ideas on that front."

She chuckled. "You can sleep with the sigil under your pillow, or sit in the dark with a lit candle and draw it over and over in your mind. You could carve a sigil into ice and let the ice melt. You can even make art that is based on it."

"Like you do with your glass charms."

"Exactly, although those are a mix of sigils and protection charms."

The charms she'd made over the years had been protecting me since I'd popped out of the womb, according to my baby pictures. Thankfully, my mother, Hope the flower child, had played right along with the notion of peace, love, and protection charms when it came to her kids.

"Okay," I said, my mind wrapped around the whole sigil idea now. I picked up the picture of the one Daisy had carved into the garage door. "So, what you're doing here is looking up sigils from our family historical records to see if you can figure out the meaning of the one that Daisy has been scratching all over town?"

She nodded. "And the other ones we have witnessed elsewhere, like down in the Hellhole tunnels." She flipped another page in the book. "I have a feeling that if the *mardagayl's* final warning comes to fruition, the meaning behind these sigils might play a part in keeping you alive and fighting."

"Alive is good enough for me. I could skip the fighting part and replace it with eating beef pot pie."

Aunt Zoe smiled. "Then alive and eating is the goal."

I dropped the picture. "And how is the sigil deciphering going so far?"

"Not smoothly. At this point, I'm still trying to narrow down if there is a particular alphabet involved. You see, since sigils can be very personal, this one that Daisy keeps making," she paused, pointing at the mark Daisy had carved on the side of the Lead police cruiser, "could be based on the Honorian alphabet, which is also used in modern witchcraft as a method to hide magical writings in a grimoire. Or it could be based off hieroglyphs."

"Like Egyptian?"

She pursed her lips, staring down at the sigil. "I was thinking it looked like something from this side of the Atlantic. Olmec maybe, or late Preclassic period Maya." She shook her head, sighing. "Then again, maybe I've been staring at it for too long."

I held my hands out over the papers and her book. "All of this reminds me of one of those 2,000-piece puzzles of a single color with no pictures. The kind where you have to look at each puzzle piece and try to match it to the surrounding ones by shape alone."

"Yeah." That single word was filled with a grim note that matched the frown she gave me as she lifted her coffee mug. "What if it takes me too long to decipher the sigil?"

Rather than dwell on those dark clouds on the horizon, I shifted to something more fun. A group project this time, instead of her solo endeavor.

"When you feel like taking a break from this puzzle, how about you help me steal some time?"

"I heard about your caper idea."

"From Harvey?"

She shook her head. "Cornelius. He stopped by earlier to ask me about my protection charms. He mentioned something about a clock caper and then told me all about your playtime with Edith before suggesting you work with Millicent."

I groaned. I didn't have time to mess with some sort of ghost parasite at the moment. That asshole ghoul could take a number and go to the back of the line as far as I was concerned.

"Do you think your protection wards in the house could hold off a ghoul?" I asked.

I'd have thought they could keep out almost anything, but then Daisy had walked right through the door without a problem—well, actually, Addy had let the imp inside. Now the little shit appeared to be here to stay, eating us out of house and honey.

She finished the last of her coffee, setting the mug down.

"That depends."

"On what? The ghoul's history?"

"On if it really is attached to you, as Cornelius and I fear. These sigils are set to allow you to freely come and go. If the ghoul has managed to somehow glom onto you, I'm not sure that I could keep it out with what I have."

"Shittlesticks." I blew out a breath. "You think I should spend some time with Millicent the stone?"

"I don't know. I'd like to hear Doc's take on the subject."

"Me, too. Although, I don't feel like any entity is riding piggyback on me."

She nodded absently. "You need to be careful around Detective Hawke, Violet."

I frowned her way. "You think he has something to do with this ghoul business?"

"No. I heard from Natalie before you got home. If Hawke has managed to get Coop suspended, he may be more of a threat than you realize. Remember, while Executioners aren't easily killed by others, humans are your Kryptonite. The detective can lock you up and throw away the key, killing your chances to stop what the *mardagayl* warned us was coming our way."

"Or he could just kill me and claim it was an accident." I aimed a finger gun at the wall and pulled the trigger. "Pew pew."

Her gaze bounced from my face to my pretend gun and back. One eyebrow climbed northward. "Is that supposed to be a laser gun he's shooting at you?"

"Maybe." I twirled my invisible gun and then tucked it into my imaginary holster. "You're just jealous you don't have one, too."

The sound of the front door opening made us both look toward the dining room.

"Parker," Cooper's loud voice rang out. "I have a bone to pick with you."

I scoffed. Like that was news. He probably woke up every morning thinking about reasons to gnaw on my hide in place of the gratitudes he should be counting for me being in his life.

Aunt Zoe glanced at the clock. "It's about time to set the table." She stood and began collecting her books.

Cooper stalked into the room, heading for the refrigerator without pausing. "This place smells good, Zoe. You must be cooking tonight, because we all know Parker burns everything."

I wrinkled my upper lip at the back of his blond head while he opened the fridge door and pulled out a bottle of beer.

"It's *not* good to see you, too, Cooper," I said. "Have you ever heard of the saying, 'If you can't say something nice, then shut up or I'll plug your piehole with my boot'?"

Aunt Zoe chuckled as she carried the stack of books into the dining room, saying over her shoulder, "That's not quite how it goes, Violet Lynn."

"Close enough."

Cooper grabbed the bottle opener from the drawer by the sink. "You finally did it, Parker."

"What did I do?"

"You got us both knee-deep in shit without a shovel to be found."

"If you're referring to you being suspended, that's not my fault."

He glanced my way. "Who told you already? Natalie?"

"I ran into Hawke on the way out of Galena House."

This time he fully turned in my direction, hitting me with a hard scowl. "Jesus, Parker. Don't tell me you were there trying to get to those clocks again."

"I wasn't." At least not yet, anyway. Scouting out the situation didn't count in my book. "I had some clients who were interested in the place."

"Bullshit. You were there to scope out the apartment." He tipped his bottle, watching me with his squint still in place as he swallowed.

I crossed my arms. "Actually, Detective Wise Guy, I was there to determine if the new medium Jerry hired to tag along on house showings and talk to the dead was the real deal or just a snake oil saleswoman trying to peddle ghost tales."

He lowered his beer. "Seriously?"

Aunt Zoe returned, cursing under her breath. "What is Jerry the Giant going to think up next?"

"Lord only knows." I watched Aunt Zoe peek into the oven before I returned to Cooper. "Her name is Madame Olivia Contraire, and she claims to be a 'Medium Extraordinaire' on her business card. But I didn't find her that out of the ordinary."

However, I was undoubtedly biased due to the peculiar company I kept. Cornelius alone tipped my scales into the truly bizarre territory on a daily basis. Take Edith, for example. Or Millicent. Or … what was the name of his other pendulum pal?

Cooper opened his mouth to say something, but then took another drink instead.

"Is she legit?" Aunt Zoe asked, opening the cupboard where the dishes were kept.

Once again, I pondered what I'd witnessed throughout the day. "I still don't know."

Cooper set down his beer and washed his hands. "How was your dragging her through the boarding house going to tell you one way or another?" He dried his hands before grabbing the stack of plates Aunt Zoe had set on the counter.

"I figured it would be a control group of sorts with known variables—or ghosts, in this case. Since I can't hear, smell, or see ghosts, I thought that if Madame Contraire came up with something outlandish, considering what we already know about the ghost scenario there, then I could tell she was a fake."

"That was a good idea." Aunt Zoe opened the silverware drawer. "But since you still don't know, I take it she didn't sense any ghosts?"

"Well, she claimed to have picked up on an entity," I said while Cooper set the plates around the table. "But she didn't give any solid details, so I didn't come away with any definitive results."

Cooper scoffed. "And now you went and gave Hawke even more reasons to suspect you, and that means me, by association."

"I explained to Hawke that I had clients who wanted to see the house," I justified.

"And?" Aunt Zoe pressed.

"And those very clients were waiting in my vehicle."

Unfortunately, the bozo had focused mainly on Madame Contraire, and couldn't seem to see past her rather colorful window dressing.

Aunt Zoe set a stack of silverware on the table. "From the look on your face, there must be a 'but' in there."

Same as when I was a child, my aunt knew when I was hiding candy—or the whole truth—behind my back.

"But Hawke couldn't actually see the clients because it was

getting dark and the lights were off inside my rig." I scratched at a spot on the table. "Instead, he'd clearly seen Madame Contraire when they'd passed on the sidewalk."

"Why would that be a problem?" Cooper said, now distributing the silverware next to each plate.

"Well, she wears thick gold mascara, for starters."

"She sounds a bit eccentric," Aunt Zoe said while pulling the pot pie out of the oven. "There's no crime in that."

"And some very pretty, but glittery, gold eyeshadow."

"Okay," Cooper said. "She had gold shit around her eyes. That's no big deal."

"And on her lips. She also has bright turquoise hair, which matches her fingernails."

Aunt Zoe paused in the midst of brushing butter on the top of the hot pie crust. "Right. So, not exactly the salt of the earth look preferred by a monochromatic fan like Detective Hawke."

"Exactly."

Cooper grabbed his beer from the counter and returned to the table, taking the seat opposite me. "Did Hawke tell you how I ended up suspended?"

"He insinuated it had something to do with me."

He nodded. "To be more precise, it was you and Natalie and those damned clocks."

"Do you think he heard about Violet and Willis's plan to get the clocks?" Aunt Zoe asked.

I shot her a warning look, but she was still focused on the beef pot pie, the smell of which had my drool glands working overtime.

Cooper's gaze tightened. "I thought I told you two to drop that stupid idea."

"It's not stupid." I weathered his look and jutted my chin in return. "And you did, but only sort of."

"I believe I was very clear yesterday."

"That depends."

"On what?"

"From which angle you're looking at things."

Aunt Zoe turned toward us. "On second thought, how would Hawke have found out about the clock caper? It's only been a day, and all of us know better than to talk about it."

All of us? I cringed in anticipation of Cooper's probable

reaction to that.

"All of us?" Cooper repeated, sounding like he was grinding some charcoal into diamonds between his back molars. "Who have you and my uncle looped into this harebrained idea?"

Before I could figure out a way to evade that answer, the front door creaked opened again.

"Zo? You in here?" Reid Martin called out.

I looked over at Aunt Zoe, whose narrowed gaze now matched Cooper's.

"What's he doing here, Violet Lynn?" she whispered.

I held up my hands in surrender. "It wasn't me, I swear." I glanced toward the dining room. "We're in the kitchen, Reid."

Footfalls thudded our way. Over by the stove, Aunt Zoe turned her back to us, and then ran her hand over her hair and straightened her shirt.

Reid eased into the room, clearly exercising caution as he eyed my aunt.

Deadwood's fire captain was dressed in jeans and a flannel shirt tonight. His silver-streaked hair had a rough-and-tumble look to it, undoubtedly thanks to the wind howling outside, but his mustache was neatly trimmed and his eyes sparkled.

"Hey, Sparky," he said, squeezing my shoulder lightly. His gaze stayed locked on Aunt Zoe as she made a full-time job of inspecting the beef pot pie. "Thanks for the invite to supper, Zo."

She whirled, her cheeks sporting bright red splotches. "I didn't invite you."

"I know," he said, crossing his arms. "I was being sarcastic to hide my hurt feelings."

She huffed and then walked over to the refrigerator. "Well, you're here now, so you might as well stay." She grabbed a bottle of beer and held it out to him.

Reid took the beer gingerly, as though it was a stick of old dynamite. "Thanks." After opening the bottle, he returned to the table. "I heard you had to hand over your gun and badge today, Coop."

Cooper shrugged. "One of my guns, anyway."

He still had his armory at Doc's place to cuddle up with at night and plenty of bullets to whisper sweet nothings to when Natalie wasn't at his side.

"What the hell happened?" Reid took the seat next to Cooper, his back to the wall, leaving him the opportunity to openly watch my aunt.

Cooper pointed his beer bottle at me. "Parker happened. She moved up here last year and screwed up my life."

I pretended to play a violin. "Can you hear the sob song I'm playing for you, Detective Crybaby? It's a real tearjerker."

Reid chuckled. "Sparky sure knows your favorite tunes, Coop."

"Shut up, Martin." Cooper leaned back in his chair, scowling between the two of us. "Or I'll help Zoe kick your sorry ass out to the curb."

Reid watched my aunt as she mollycoddled the pot pie. "Zo has gotta let me stay tonight."

She turned with her hands on her hips. "Why is that?"

"For one thing, you're not the one who invited me to join you guys for supper."

"Who did then?" Cooper scowled. "Don't tell me, my uncle was the one sending out party invites."

Harvey was my guess, too, probably wanting to lure Reid onto our caper crew.

Reid shook his head. "Nyce called and told me I needed to come over."

"Doc?" Aunt Zoe looked my way. "Why?"

I shrugged. I was as in the dark as she was on this one.

"That answer has to do with the other reason you have to let me stay." He paused to take a long swig of his beer.

"Spit it out, Martin," Cooper said. "Before you choke on it and leave us all dangling in suspense here."

Reid grinned wide under his mustache. "You never were good at holding onto your horses." He pointed his bottle at Cooper's chest. "That's why you have so many bullet hole scars."

"Reid," Aunt Zoe said, now standing over him. "What's the ace up your sleeve?"

His gaze shifted in my direction. "I know how to legally get Sparky into Ms. Wolff's apartment, and there's not a thing Hawke can do to stop us."

CHAPTER NINE

I glanced around the crowded kitchen table almost an hour later, soaking up the calm before the next storm rolled in. Camaraderie flowed, along with wisecracks and playful verbal jabs, among my fellow clock pirates. Truth be told, as caper crews went, we bordered on motley, coming in just this side of deranged.

"Now you all might think I'm usin' too much tonsil varnish here," Harvey said to the group in general while spooning some beef pot pie onto his plate, "but if we don't round up an Invisible Man, we're startin' out this heist with a bad cat on the line."

I paused with a forkful of meat, potatoes, carrots, and buttered crust midway to my mouth.

"The harder our Invisible Man is to see, the better in this case," he added along with a second scoop of savory pie goodness.

On second thought, with Harvey at the helm of this cuckoo clock crusade, we were probably straddling the fence line of deranged with a toe dangling over into *loco*-ville.

"We already have a Count Dracula," I said, referring to one of the codenames Harvey had insisted we adopt for secrecy's sake. I held up my hands and counted off fingers as I continued, "Along with a Wolf Man, Frankenstein and his bride, the Mummy, King Kong, Godzilla, and … what was the other one?"

"The Creature from the Black Lagoon," Aunt Zoe said, who sat to my left, splitting up Harvey and me.

"What do you call a group of monsters?" Reid asked as he reached across the table and took the spoon from Harvey, dishing up a serving of pot pie for himself. "Is it a horde?"

"I always think of that term when it comes to a bunch of

zombies," Natalie said on her return from the refrigerator with an armful of cold drinks, which she placed in the center of the table for free picking. "A horde of zombies. Or should it be a swarm of zombies?" She handed Cornelius a bottle of hard cider—his favorite that she'd brought along especially for him.

"A group of goblins is often called a pester," Cornelius said instead of answering her. He held down the chair on the other side of the empty seat next to me where Doc usually sat when he wasn't working late, unlike tonight.

"A group of Violet Parkers is also called a pester," Cooper said, grinning. "Especially at the police station."

"Hardy har har." I wrinkled my nose at him across the table. "You know what a group of Coopers is called?"

"Oooh, I'd call that a sexy slumber party," Natalie answered.

She patted her heartthrob on the head like he was a good law dog instead of a prickly one, which was more in line with the snarly cur I'd dealt with since Cooper had walked his suspended ass through the front door.

I rolled my eyes. "Your rose-colored glasses are all steamy again, Natalie."

"A squad?" Aunt Zoe said to me, opening her beer. "You know, of cops?"

"Make that a kickass squad," Cooper said, his grin growing wider yet. "And every single Cooper would be an ace shooter."

"A group of ghosts is sometimes called a fraid," Cornelius continued with his collective noun trivia.

Harvey snickered. "A single visit from good ol' Prudy leaves most folks plenty a-*fraid*. And boogered to boot."

Reid leaned forward and grabbed a beer. "Maybe Prudence could be your Invisible Man, Harvey."

"No!" Harvey and I balked loudly at the same time.

"We're not that desperate," I told him. "Not yet, anyway."

"But she's about as invisible as you can get," Aunt Zoe said.

"Unless she chooses not to be," Cornelius said.

Harvey shook his head. "You don't have to tell a duck what to do with corn, Zoe, but that doesn't mean we should ride more than one wagon at a time here."

I lowered my fork, glancing back and forth between Harvey and my aunt, wondering if I was the only one trying to piece together Harvey's meaning behind ducks and wagons.

Then I shrugged it off and returned to my plate, scooping up a creamy bite of potato and peas. "A group of Coopers is called a cluster of hemorrhoids," I said after I swallowed, grinning around the table. When everyone just frowned back, I explained, "You know, as in multiple pains in the ass."

I chuckled at my own joke while everyone else booed.

"What do you call a collection of groans?" Aunt Zoe asked, patting my arm in pity.

"That was pretty lame, Sputnik," Natalie said staring down at her cell phone. "According to this website, a group of monsters is called a horror."

"That sounds 'bout right," Harvey said. "We're one big horror, sure as shootin', but we're still short an Invisible Man."

Reid twisted off the top of his beer. "You know, I can be pretty sneaky and light on my feet when I try. Maybe I should be your Invisible Man."

Aunt Zoe let out a squawk of laughter. "You definitely turned invisible after you walked out on me. I didn't see you around again for how many years?"

Reid scowled across the table at her with his beer bottle midway to his lips. "Be like Buddha, Zo. Don't dwell on the past, focus on me, sitting here right now—just a poor longsuffering fireman who's trying to win back his old flame by boasting about his ability to tiptoe around like a ballerina."

Aunt Zoe laughed some more. "Please, Martin. The hippos in *Fantasia* are more graceful than you."

"Only a little bit, but I'm quieter. Mice have nothing on me when I go into silent mode."

She scoffed. "You're about as quiet as a drunken sailor wearing a tin can necklace trying to climb out of a porcelain bathtub."

Reid shook his head. "Why would a sailor be in a bathtub, Zo? That doesn't make any sense. You're just pulling silly stuff out of the air now because you're fighting those mushy warm feelings making your heart swell up."

"Give it up, Martin." Cooper cracked open his beer. "Zoe trimmed your tail feathers on that one, and you know it."

Harvey pointed his fork at the fire captain. "Reid, you're Frankenstein, plain and simple."

"Why? Because I have big feet and carry around a long hose," he said, wiggling his eyebrows at Aunt Zoe.

She did a face-palm and then reached for her beer.

"Because you start fires wherever you go," Harvey explained and then shoulder bumped Aunt Zoe. "Like how you're setting her woods on fire right now."

She set her bottle down on the table with a clunk. "My woods are definitely flame free."

"Or are they smoldering?" I countered, winking at Reid. "I do believe I spot a trail of smoke. Someone better call a big strong fireman."

"Zip it, Violet Lynn," she said, aiming a mock glare at me before turning back to Harvey. "I should be the Invisible Man. Detective Hawke barely knows who I am, so I could sneak in and out of places without drawing much attention."

Cooper shook his head. "Hawke knows a lot more about you than you think." He stabbed at the piece of beef on his plate. "And you can thank Parker's big mouth for that."

I flipped him off in between bites of buttery crust heaven.

"You're the Bride of Frankenstein, Zoe," Harvey said as if that were the final decision. "You have the hair for the role, not to mention the ornery temper." When she opened her mouth to disagree, he added, "Plus you scream a lot around ol' Frankenstein here."

"He has a point," I said and then dodged her elbow.

"I could be the Invisible Man," Cornelius offered, pushing up his shirt sleeves and baring his pale, bony wrists. "I have the perfect cloak to wear that was granted to me by a wise wizard from Transylvania who was on a quest to find his apprentice, which he thought might be me initially."

"When were you in Transylvania?" Natalie asked.

"That doesn't matter since we weren't in Romania at the time."

Aunt Zoe's forehead lined. "What changed the wizard's mind about you? I'd think you were an apt candidate for wizardhood."

"As did I," Cornelius said to her. "Especially with my advanced skill at cloak and dagger fighting."

I watched him chew for a moment, trying to figure out if he was serious or just pulling our chains. Knowing him and his eccentric past, though, this was probably a true story. "Were you not skilled enough in the wizarding arts?"

"I theorized that might be the problem. However, I assured him that as his apprentice I could be up to speed and performing spells in just under a decade."

"That's a long time for training, isn't it?" Reid asked.

"Not for a wizard."

Cooper took a swig of beer before saying, "I can't believe I'm going to ask this, Curion, but why am I not sitting at the table with a wizard tonight?"

"Unfortunately, it came to light that he was actually in town for a wizarding board game competition, and while I won his cloak with a lucky spread of four of a kind, the apprentice of his choice had mammary glands that were far more developed than mine." Cornelius frowned slightly. "And her gluteus maximus had a substantial amount of bounce, especially when she was on stage. I failed to measure up to his requirements on the physical level."

I sighed. "This was in Vegas, wasn't it?" Which was where Cornelius spent part of his youth when he wasn't in New Orleans learning bits of voodoo from his grandmother.

Before he could answer, Harvey piped in, "I once knew a top-heavy painted lady who had ample room for parkin' in the rear, if you know what I mean. Matter of fact, I had to be careful when I was easin' my rig between her pretty red—"

"Harvey!" I interrupted, squirming. "We're eating here."

"What? I was gonna say Corvettes." He snickered. "You got a dirty mind, girlie. I was talking about the parkin' lot behind her cathouse. She made good bank with the silver mine just up the road and invested her hard-earned cash in mint-condition Stingrays. She kept 'em parked in the lot."

"What's that have to do with Cornelius's wizard story?" Aunt Zoe asked.

He shrugged. "I thought we were talking about shapely ladies of the night."

"Were we not?" Cornelius asked, a crooked smile tilting his lips.

"We were talking about Cornelius being the Invisible Man," I said. "And you two know it."

"Corny's not invisible enough," Harvey said, returning his

attention to the food on his plate. "That's why he's the Mummy. With all of the funny gadgets he surrounds himself with, he can keep Hawke busy tryin' to unwrap everything and figure out what's underneath."

"I should be the Invisible Man," Natalie said.

"Nope," Cooper shot back without missing a beat.

"I would be great at hiding in plain sight," she countered.

"Have you looked at yourself in the mirror?" he asked.

"She can't," I said. "Because she's Dracula, remember?" At least that was the monster Harvey had assigned to Natalie right out of the gate.

"Zip it, Parker." Back to Natalie, Cooper said, "You're the opposite of invisible."

"You're biased," Aunt Zoe said.

"He's got his fuzzy pink love goggles on 24/7 around her," Martin added.

Cooper cast a hard glare at Reid. "My love goggles are camouflaged with flaming skulls at the temples, thank you very much. And we all know that Hawke has a thing for Nat." He returned to his previous point. "He'd like to hogtie her to his bed given half a chance."

"Hey," Natalie said, holding up her index finger, "that gives me another idea. How about if I—"

"Absolutely not." Cooper's tone added an exclamation mark to his refusal no matter what came out of her mouth next.

"Are we talking about women of the night again?" Cornelius said before taking a sip of his hard cider. "Because hogtying can double the cost."

"You know," Harvey chimed in, "I once knew a long-legged beauty out of Reno who offered a special rate for hogtyin' on hump day."

"Exactly how many ladies of the night have you known in your life, Willis?" Aunt Zoe asked.

Reid chuckled. "A stud like Harvey doesn't kiss and tell."

"You're being hard-headed, Coop," Natalie said, her chin jutting. "Just listen to my idea."

"I'm being level-headed." He glanced around the table, ending on his uncle. "Natalie is not going to be your Invisible Man."

"Of course not. She's Count Dracula." Harvey winked at her.

"She's the only one who can listen with her bat-like hearin' through the vents. And like you said, she can charm that turkey-hawk into doin' her biddin' with her eyes alone."

"I don't like her being involved at all," Cooper grumbled.

"Ah, come on, hot cop." Natalie leaned closer. "Look into my eyes and do my bidding," she spoke with a Dracula-like accent.

"No." He didn't budge.

"I just *vant* to suck your blood a *leetle* bit." She gnashed her teeth.

A smile crept onto the corners of Cooper's mouth. "Nat, that's not going to work."

"You *vill* like being my tortured henchman, Renfield."

"Fine, but I'm not eating any bugs." He looked over at Harvey. "And I'm not going to be your King Kong."

Reid laughed. "You are such a big ape, Coop. Always stomping around, beating your chest, and growling. Your uncle nailed that one."

I chuckled along with Reid. "Don't forget smitten by the pretty lady."

"Laugh it up, lizard breath," Cooper said to me.

I shook my head. "Like I told Harvey, I'm not the Godzilla type. Have you ever seen a curly-haired blond version of Godzilla with red lipstick? That won't scare anyone."

Natalie smiled. "They might die from laughing, though."

"You scare *me* first thing in the mornin'," Harvey said. "Especially when you wake up hungry."

"Yeah, but I do that on purpose so I can get the most bacon." I took a sip of beer. "I think I should be the Invisible Man."

There was a solid, "No!" from everyone around the table.

"Why not? I'm good at sneaking up on troublemakers. Just ask my kids."

"Not with the way you live, extra large," Natalie said. "And your kids are more into lightweight mischief than actual trouble."

"Extra large?" I frowned from her to Aunt Zoe. "I don't live that big."

"Big enough," Cooper said. "And you leave a huge mess in your wake for the rest of us to clean up, especially when you lock horns with an enemy."

Harvey scooped more beef pot pie onto his plate. "Sparky, you and Coop are the distractions and that's final. You're both big and loud in Hawke's world. There's not one-in-five ways from Sunday that either of you can be invisible when it comes to the law."

"What about Doc?" Aunt Zoe asked.

"He's the Wolf Man," I reminded her.

"How'd he get that role?" Reid asked. "I could be a Wolf Man." He howled toward the ceiling.

Harvey shrugged. "Doc has hair on his face."

Reid tugged at one corner of his mustache. "So do I."

I pointed at the old goat's beard. "So does Harvey."

"I'm older than the rest of y'all," Harvey said. "And I'm a big fan of ladies, which is why I'm the Creature from the Black Lagoon." He nodded as if his chin were a gavel, his word the final ruling. "But you can just call me Gill-man for short."

Cooper smirked. "I have a feeling this is going to be more like an Abbott and Costello meet the monsters type of shitshow before it's all said and done."

The sound of the front door closing had me looking toward the dining room.

"That must be the Wolf Man," Aunt Zoe said.

Doc rushed into the kitchen, his coat and boots still on, a frown lining his face from top to bottom. He zeroed in on me right away. "We have a problem, Killer."

Cooper beat me to my feet. "What's wrong?"

Doc's frown bounced from Cooper to Aunt Zoe and then back to me. "You guys need to see this for yourself."

"Doc, what is it?" Aunt Zoe was standing now, too.

"Outside. Now. Grab your coats on the way." He headed back toward the front door.

I hurried after him, with Cooper on my heels. Doc handed me my coat from the hall closet and then my stocking hat, waiting as I slipped them on.

"Ready?" he asked, glancing behind me. "Watch your footing when you hit the porch. It's a little slippery near the steps."

"Why is it slippery?" Aunt Zoe asked, pulling on her coat. "I salted it and the sidewalk earlier today."

"You'll see."

I grimaced back at her, but followed Doc outside. He pointed at a large dark spot on the porch when I joined him in the feeble porch light.

"What is that?"

Cooper bent down for a closer look, clicking on a penlight he'd extracted from his inside pocket. "It's blood."

I cringed, backing into Natalie, who steadied me while peering around my shoulder. "That's a lot of blood."

"Where's it from?" Aunt Zoe asked, now leaning partway over Cooper.

"A mule deer," Harvey answered, tugging his collar tight as an icy blast whipped around from the side of the house.

"How can you tell that?" I asked, tugging on my gloves.

He pointed toward the front yard. "There's the head."

I looked out as Cooper hit it with his light … and winced.

Sure enough, there was a mule deer head laying on top of the snow a few feet beyond the porch steps. One eye stared sightlessly up at the heavens.

"What fresh hell is this?" Cornelius asked.

"Oh, fuck," I whispered.

Another gust of bone-chilling air stole my breath away.

CHAPTER TEN

There really wasn't any calm, graceful way to handle finding a decapitated deer head chillin' in the snow outside the front door.

Greeting card companies didn't write caring words printed in pretty fonts to help with untangling the knot of terror that such a macabre sight instantly elicited. And no amount of yoga-inspired *oms* could divert me from the uneasy skin-tingling sensation that my neck might be next on the chopping block.

Or worse, the neck of someone I loved.

The freezing wind rattled the tree branches along with my knees through my sweatpants.

"Well, blow me down and call me shorty," Harvey said, shivering visibly in the pale light coming from the porch lamp next to the door. "Damn, it's colder than a witch's kneecaps tonight."

"You're missing a hat," Natalie told him, tugging her stocking cap lower over her ears.

"Who was the last one to arrive before me?" Doc asked, glancing from one of us to the other.

Natalie raised her mitten-covered hand. "That'd be Corny and me. I picked him up on the way. We got here about a half hour ago."

"This can't be more than ten minutes old," Cooper said, poking at the edge of the bloody area with the tip of his penlight. "It's beginning to turn slushy. In this cold, it'll ice over eventually."

"Blood freezes around thirty-one degrees Fahrenheit," Reid said almost robotically, still staring out at the deer head. "Where's the rest of the body?"

Doc shrugged. "I didn't see it, but I wasn't really paying attention until I noticed the head."

"Why would someone leave a deer head near our front step?" I asked, looking over at my aunt, whose worried frown matched Doc's. I wondered if her gut had a knot in it, too.

"More than the head was left," Cornelius said as he closed the screen door behind him. He straightened his tall, furry Cossack hat, and then handed Harvey the trapper hat he'd left inside in his haste to join the party on the porch. "Detective, you might want to shine your light at the porch beam above the blood." His voice had an ominous pitch, spurring another set of shivers down my spine.

Cooper aimed the small beam of light overhead.

Natalie and I recoiled another step, in tandem this time.

"Is that a headless doll?" she uttered under her breath next to my ear.

I cringed. "Criminy! Don't make this any creepier."

It looked more like a wadded-up piece of dark red cloth to me, stuck to the beam with some kind of a bone-handled knife.

"Reid," Aunt Zoe said. "Give me that walking stick over in the corner, would you?"

He grabbed it, but shook his head when she held out her hand for it. "I'll get it down, Zo. Step back."

We all took a step back and watched in silence as he whacked at the knife several times until it and the scrap of cloth came free and fell onto the porch beside the pool of blood. Reid lowered the stick and hooked the edge of the dark cloth, which was already frozen stiff from the cold. He held it out toward Cooper, who was now standing next to Doc down on the second porch step.

A drop of something dark and viscous dangled from the cloth, partially frozen in mid-drip.

Cooper spotlighted it, which was even redder close up. "That's a piece of hide soaked in blood."

A gust of wind thrashed around us, spurring a clattering racket from the cottonwood limbs, peppering us with bits of ice and snow. The bit of hide blew off the stick and landed mostly flat on the top porch step.

"That there's a hat." Harvey eased around the pool of blood for a better look. "It's shaped like an old-timey hat the kids wore in nursery rhyme books when I was a young'un. You can see the leather stitches through the blood."

Doc reached over the hat and carefully picked up the knife, holding it out for us to see. The bone hilt was about the extent of his gloved hand, from the top of his middle finger to his wrist. The blade doubled that length.

"That's an odd-looking knife," Natalie said. "The blade is all bumpy, like it was hammer-forged over a fire."

"It's a seax," Cornelius said.

"What's a seax?" I asked.

"It's like a dagger with a single-edged, straight blade that has a slight curve at the end. They were used a long, long time ago."

"Like how long ago?" Aunt Zoe asked.

He shrugged. "I've seen some in museums in Northern Europe that are estimated to be from the Germanic Migration Period. Others were from the Early Middle Ages."

"Damn," Reid said.

"But surely this one can't be …" I trailed off, chewing on my lower lip.

"Or it could," Aunt Zoe said, her brow doubly lined.

Cornelius bent closer to the knife. "It looks like the end is made from a …"

"Horn?" Harvey threw out.

"More like a tooth," Doc said, turning the blade back and forth. "Like a saber tooth from a big cat." He glanced up at Cooper and then Cornelius. "That's crazy, though, right?"

"It could be from a different creature," Aunt Zoe said.

"Like a walrus?" Natalie asked.

"I was thinking of something from another realm," she told her.

Natalie nodded slowly. "Ahh, an *other* creature."

"Yes. After all, we do have a *Scharfrichter* living here." Aunt Zoe wrapped her arm around me and pulled me in for a side hug. "One with a bounty on her head, according to Dominick Masterson."

"Ugh, don't remind me of that troublemaker."

Masterson always seemed to hinder more than help when it came to *others*. His ability to charm the common sense out of most everyone he approached, including my aunt in the past, made me avoid him at all costs. Not to mention that I had executed his pet Hungarian devil and sort of stole his good-luck imp, both without his knowledge.

"Did any of you hear any pounding sounds before I came home?" Doc asked as he set the knife down on the porch. "Or anything else from out here?"

We all shook our heads.

Natalie explained, "We were eating and drinking, you know, being loud and merry while we talked about being monsters."

"Monsters?" Doc turned to me.

"The classic ones, not *our* monsters. You're the Wolf Man, by the way."

One dark eyebrow lifted. "Okay. I guess I'll need to let my beard and fingernails grow."

"Nyce, did you see any suspicious vehicles on your way here?" Cooper asked, glancing up and down the street.

"No. It's like a ghost town out there."

"This is starting to feel like the setup for an old monster flick now," Natalie whispered.

"I'm fine with the wispy critters hanging out in town, so long as there is no uppity ghost in here," Harvey said, pointing at his own head.

Cooper shined his light around the yard beyond the deer head. "There aren't any tracks in the snow."

"Of course not." Harvey turtled his head deeper into his collar. "The snow is like hardpan, and the wind is busy whippin' around anything that's not frozen solid."

"This has to be some kind of warning for Violet." Natalie shared the same verdict as me. "Are there any words written in blood anywhere?"

"Or sigils?" Aunt Zoe added.

A short search around the porch with Cooper's penlight showed nothing. Just icicles and Addy's frozen pink glove waving up at us from part way under the porch.

"I'm going to circle the house," Doc said. "Can I borrow that penlight, Coop?"

"No. Wait a second." Cooper beelined inside the house. A few seconds later, he returned with a handgun and a bigger flashlight, the latter of which he held out for Doc to use.

"You brought a gun along for supper?" I asked.

"Sure," he said, as if I was silly for thinking of him coming unarmed to something so dangerous as beef pot pie. "Let's go, Nyce."

"Hold on, Coop." Reid stopped them before they'd made it off the porch steps. "Don't you want to take some pictures of the crime scene before you go tromping around?"

Coop hesitated, his cheek lines deepening. "How about you take some pictures of this area with your phone while Nyce and I go counter-clockwise around the house. That way we'll end up back here at the mule deer head after you've taken shots of the front yard."

They crunched over the salt-coated sidewalk, heading off around the front of the house.

Reid pulled off his gloves and dug out his phone. His years of investigating fires showed in the care he took while capturing multiple shots of the scene for later inspection.

"Shouldn't you be out there sniffing around, too, *Scharfrichter*?"

Harvey asked.

"It's too cold to smell anything besides the insides of my freezer-burned nostrils." Shivering, I huddled closer to Aunt Zoe and Natalie, trying to keep warm in spite of Father Winter's icy breath.

"Did you know that meat with freezer burn is still safe to eat?" Cornelius said, staring down at my nose in the porchlight. "And while cartilage is not always tasty on its own, it is high in protein and collagen."

I reached out and pushed him back a step. "Get away from my frozen cartilage, you freaky old mummy."

Doc and Cooper returned soon enough, along with another blast of subzero wind that sent shivers to the ends of my toenails.

Natalie took a step in their direction. "Did you find anything?"

Doc shook his head.

"We might as well go back inside." Cooper looked up at us from where he stood on the sidewalk at the base of the porch steps. "We've seen about everything we can in the dark. I'll come back at dawn to take some more pictures and get rid of the head before your neighbors notice it."

"Should we bag the hide hat and knife?" Harvey asked.

Cooper nodded, his focus on the pool of blood as he climbed the steps.

Harvey disappeared inside the house, followed by Aunt Zoe and Cornelius.

"Me being suspended puts a kink in getting to the bottom of this," Cooper said. "But I have a friend at a lab in Rapid who might be able to help me with investigating on the sly."

"I'm shocked," I told Doc as he joined us on the porch.

He put his arm around my shoulders. "Yeah, well it's not every night that you find a decapitated deer head right outside your front door."

I grinned in spite of the situation. "No, I meant I'm shocked Cooper has a friend. The deer head thing is just disturbing."

"Don't be jealous, lizard lips," Cooper said as Harvey returned with a couple of clear plastic storage bags. "We giant warm-blooded apes just get along better with the humans."

"Uh, has Coop's brain froze?" Doc asked me.

I chuckled, but then sobered at the thought of what the bloody remnants left for us really meant.

"Harvey, tell Doc about your monster mash," I said, and then headed inside, looking back through the frost-edged screen door as Cooper took the bags from his uncle and held one out for Doc to place the knife inside.

Then I closed the front door on the cold and grisly mess outside, taking a moment to breathe in a few calming breaths before shucking my coat and boots and returning to the kitchen.

A short time later, we had our wagons circled around the kitchen table again, including Doc, who was dishing himself up a serving of beef pot pie.

"So," Natalie said, resting her elbows on the table. "How do we figure out who left Violet those lovely presents and what it all means? It's not like we can run to the police and ask for help."

"What am I? Chopped liver?" Cooper glanced her way before returning to playing with the last few bites of his supper with his fork.

"More like tenderized," Reid said. "Your itty-bitty cop wings have been clipped thanks to this suspension."

Cooper hit Reid with a stony stare. "They're not itty-bitty."

"My grandmother had a pet crow," Cornelius said while scooping a second helping onto his plate. "It would often bring her gifts from the swamp that was just a few miles away. Once, it even gifted her with an eyeball." At my verbal gag, he added, "It was from an alligator, though, not human."

"That's still gross," I said, exchanging a grimace with Natalie.

"Have you tried eatin' gator eyeballs?" Harvey asked.

I wrinkled my nose, not even bothering with a response.

"Is there some reason behind this change of subject beyond simply spouting nuggets of nonsense?" Cooper asked Cornelius.

"Of course." Cornelius pushed the nearly empty casserole dish back to the center of the table. "My grandmother once explained to me that the desired effect of wing clipping is not to prevent flying completely, but rather to keep the bird from attaining full upward flight; therefore, stopping any roaming and the resulting vulnerability to possibly perilous situations." He glanced around. "Can somebody please pass me the pepper?"

My perplexity undoubtedly matched Aunt Zoe's, judging from her scrunched face. But she passed the pepper.

Harvey scratched under his beard. "Corny, I'm about as confused as a goat on shag carpet about your point with that yarn."

Cornelius picked up his fork. "It's simple. The detective can still achieve upward flight and roam free so long as he uses camouflage or the cover of night as a shield." He stabbed at a chunk of beef and crust. "The key is to convince the other constable into believing he has clipped his wings."

Reid tugged on his earlobe. "Sure seems like we used long division to come around to that answer."

Doc reached for his beer. "Yeah, but I like the direction Cornelius is heading." He looked across at Cooper. "You're going to have to figure out how to keep flying, even though you can't use your usual resources."

Cooper tapped his temple. "I have plenty of resources right here."

"That's real comforting," Reid joked.

I laughed, which earned me a squint from Cooper after he finished flipping off Reid.

"Zoe?" Doc said after setting his drink down. "Have you read any anecdotes in your family history tomes that share similarities with Violet receiving tonight's bloody gifts? I don't remember coming across anything like that in the book you let me read."

"The use of a beheaded creature left to give warning is not anything new," she replied. "But that bloody hide hat pinned overhead with a seax is unique."

I cringed. Would I ever be relaxed enough in this role that a decapitated head was simply business as usual? Lordy, I hoped not.

"You know what we need?" Harvey asked, scooting back from the table.

"How about dessert?" Reid eyed the raspberry lemon meringue pie sitting on the counter.

"You have a one-track mind, Martin," she said, getting up and pulling a stack of dessert plates from the cupboard.

He stared at her backside with a flirty grin. "Especially when it comes to my favorite treat."

Harvey grabbed the pie and brought it over, setting it in the middle of the table.

"We could try Edith again," Cornelius offered as he scraped his dinner plate clean. "She can be helpful when it comes to lost animals, as well as missing ghouls."

"That mule deer was not lost," I said.

"Who's this Edith?" Natalie asked.

"A wise spirit I've known for decades." Cornelius stood and began collecting everyone's dirty plates except Doc's, since he was still working on his meal.

"She helps him find things," I added.

"We don't need Edith, whoever she is," Harvey said, watching Cornelius carry the plates to the sink.

"I can go back through my notes and the older books written in Old German and Latin." Aunt Zoe set the stack of dessert plates on the table. "But I have to finish one of my glass orders first. It needs to be delivered on Monday."

"We don't need yer ol' books either." Harvey focused on Cooper, his chin jutting. "Do we, Coop?"

Cooper glanced toward his uncle, then did a double take. "What are you giving me the stink eye for, Uncle Willis? I already told you I'm going to come back in the morning and dig deeper into Parker's mess."

"It's not *my* mess," I growled.

"After that, I'll see what my *friend* at the lab can do to help us out with any prints on that knife and what kind of hide that hat is made of."

Harvey brought over a bunch of clean forks. "Come on, boy. You'd have better luck climbin' over a barbed-wire fence in a lacy weddin' dress."

"Now that I'd like to see," Reid said, chuckling.

"There's one place we can go that will help Sparky with this latest pickle, Coop, and you darn well know it."

"Ms. Wolff's apartment," Doc said, and then howled like her namesake.

Harvey handed a fork to Doc. "The Wolf Man pinned the tail on the donkey. We need those clocks. One of those tickers is probably busy as a bee right now, trying to let Sparky know that she's got trouble comin'. I'd bet my left nut on it."

"Leave your nuts out of this, Uncle Willis."

"You know I'm right."

"Maybe there is no clock for this particular situation," Cooper said, his gaze shifting from his uncle to me. "Have you thought of that possibility?"

I hadn't. Damn. I reached for the plate of pie Reid had dished up and was holding out toward me, grabbing a clean fork at the same time. "I guess we'll know one way or the other after Reid gets us into that apartment."

Reid nodded as he dished up another piece of pie. Meanwhile, I dug in and groaned in appreciation, giving Aunt Zoe two thumbs-up.

"That's a bad idea," Cooper said, waving away the plate of dessert offered to him, which was borderline insane, the crazy ape. Aunt Zoe had really nailed the balance of sweet and tart in every bite.

"It's a good idea." Reid handed the plate to Natalie instead. "As far as Detective Hawke knows, Freesia has ordered her semi-quarterly fire department inspection."

"Is it usually semi-quarterly?" Natalie asked.

"That depends on the owner's wishes and my amount of free time." He glanced at his wristwatch. "And would you look at that, I'm free tomorrow morning, afternoon, and evening."

Cooper sighed, looking at each of us in turn. "I don't like it. If any one of you is found out by Hawke, he'll throw a parade in honor of locking you up."

"Likin' it or not doesn't matter," Harvey said. "You know as well as the rest of us that Sparky needs those clocks. What woulda happened if her kids had been home and found that deer head outside?"

I winced at the mere notion. "That can't happen."

"Exactly." Natalie slapped the table. "Tomorrow morning, we're going in."

Harvey handed her a fork. "And then we're gonna figure out how to get them clocks out of there one way or another."

Nods went around the table, except for Cooper, who was still watching me.

"Hawke can't know you're in there," he told me.

"I'll wear a disguise." I thought about that time I'd dressed up for Hawke's interrogation. "Something without spurs that jingle jangle jingle this time."

Harvey snickered, settling in at his seat with his own piece of pie. "We need to find you a big lizard costume."

"Can't you think of a better monster for me?"

"Damn, Zo," Reid said, licking his fork clean. "You made pie times two tonight, and I can't decide which one tasted better."

"Have you ever tried stargazy pie?" Cornelius asked.

"That sounds romantic," Natalie said. "What's in it?"

"Potatoes, eggs, and fish—the latter with their heads popping out of the pie like shark fins as their dead eyes stare up at the stars."

Aunt Zoe coughed into her fist, her face one big cringe. "Are you serious?"

"As serious as the final act of a Shakespearean tragedy." He scooped up a forkful of meringue. "It's a Cornish dish that my great-uncle loved to eat in front of us children. I suspect our reactions were as rich as the pie."

"Fine!" Cooper said in a growly voice and crossed his arms. "I'll go to the station and distract Hawke while you guys are in looking for the clock that might belong to whatever killed that mule deer. Just don't go into the apartment until I give you the all-clear."

Harvey grinned at his nephew. "Boy, that makes me as happy as a possum in this here pie."

"What about collecting the rest of the clocks?" Doc leaned back in his chair, his plate clean. "Are you in this caper with us or not, King Kong?"

"Yes, dammit. But you guys have to do as I say so that none of you end up with a breaking and entering charge on your record." He scowled across at me. "Or worse."

"Hoo-doggie!" Harvey licked his lips with excitement. Or maybe it was just in anticipation of another bite of pie. "Looks like we're gonna have us some good-time caperin' fun after all."

CHAPTER ELEVEN

Sunday, February 10th (just after midnight)

U h, Killer? Is there a particular reason you're tiptoeing down to the basement in the dark?"

I paused a few steps down and looked up at Doc, who stood on the threshold leaning against the door jamb. The light over the kitchen sink backlit him, so I couldn't see his face, but I could hear the exhaustion in his voice.

I waved for him to follow.

He yawned instead. "Wouldn't you rather be heading up to our soft, warm bed?"

"Shhh." I thumbed in the direction of the dark basement below and whispered, "We don't want to wake Elvis." Or her hairless, honey-loving buddy, for that matter.

Daisy the imp tended to get huffy when woken in surprise. I'd learned that the hard way the morning I'd found the bugger asleep in Harvey's truck and tried to trap it in a bag. Silly me. A black eye and a bunch of scratches later, I'd limped back to my corner of the ring while the snarly little scrapper had scampered off into the trees.

Doc mimed zipping his lips.

"Leave the lights off and come down here." I used my flashlight to illuminate the steps for him. "I have something to show you."

He followed me down, quiet as a mouse.

It was cool under the house and smelled slightly damp, as most basements tended to throughout the year. I shivered in spite of the belt on my warm cardigan cinched tight at my waist. The cobblestone floor chilled my feet through my socks, making me wish I'd taken a moment to grab my slippers. And maybe a stocking hat.

I crept over to Elvis's two-story chicken condo and peeked under the old quilt covering the cage, keeping my flashlight turned away.

Daisy remained curled up next to Elvis on the fresh straw bed Addy had made for them before she'd left, same as when I'd checked on the imp earlier. Perfect!

Elvis fluffed her feathers suddenly, both eyes opening. I lowered the cover slightly and held my breath, not wanting to wake either the chicken or the imp at the moment. Not until I had a chance to show Doc my reason for leading him down here tonight.

After a blink or two, Elvis let out a soft warble, and then stilled again, her eyelids closing and beak drooping. I breathed a sigh of relief as she returned to the land of feathery dreams.

Chicken dreams—oddly enough, that was a hot topic in our house only last week. Addy was a firm believer that Elvis was a dreamer and liked to try to imagine the sort of fowl-brained images her chicken experienced while snoozing. Layne, on the other hand, wanted proof of dreaming. He tried to convince his sister to let him hook up some electrodes to Elvis's head while the hen slumbered to test her brain for activity during REM sleep. That went over like a sky-diving walrus. Addy feared the testing process would either give Elvis nightmares, or electrocute the bird and turn her into a mindless monster chicken. Aunt Zoe, the smartass, suggested we have Elvis analyzed by an Oregon psychologist she'd read about in a wildlife magazine who specialized in bird brain studies. This idea was immediately vetoed by me in spite of my children's cries of "please, please, please, Mom," since I'd likely have to foot the bill for any sort of testing by Doctor Birdbrain.

When all eyes had turned to Doc for his two cents, he'd grabbed his laptop and pulled up some science news video showing that not only do chickens dream, but they can also sleep with only one half of their brain while the other half remains alert, often keeping one eye open to watch for predators. Then Doc found a video starring various baby animals in the midst of dreaming, and nobody cared any longer what went on in Elvis's head.

Game, set, match. The Oracle won.

Behind me, Doc leaned against the workbench that held two big bags (one with food pellets, another with freshly chopped straw bedding) and a large container of granulated honey crystals that Aunt Zoe had picked up this week to sprinkle over the cat food Addy gave to Daisy. The imp wasn't into Rooster's food, so the lucky dog didn't have to share.

I joined him at the workbench, looping my arm in his.

"I haven't been down here in a while," he whispered. "Addy is doing a good job keeping it clean."

I nodded. "She figures I'm looking for a reason to give Daisy the boot, so she's trying extra hard right now to keep me happy on the imp front."

Addy wasn't far off the mark on her hunch. We didn't need another pet, especially one that had a reputation for causing chaos. I had plenty of chaos already in my life—five feet high of it and rising.

He sniffed. "Why does it smell like cilantro down here?"

I pointed my flashlight at a wilting bunch of the green plant hanging by a string from the wall next to the chicken condo. "Layne read in an old *Farmers' Almanac* in Aunt Zoe's workshop that cilantro has antimicrobial properties, so Addy put it down here to help keep the area fungus-free."

A low trill came from one of the dozers in the cage.

"That sounded like a cat purr." Doc glanced around. "Is Bogart down here, too?"

I shook my head. "It's Elvis or Daisy, I can't tell which. Both make that sound when they're happily sleeping."

"So do you, Boots." He elbowed me playfully. "In between your moaning."

I poked him back in the ribs.

"The chicken, the imp, and the killer," he said, chuckling quietly. "Throw in a few fencing foils and you guys could give the Three Musketeers a run for their money."

"You know, Candy Cane, if you weren't so pretty I'd kill you after mating."

"You talk tough for someone who closes her eyes when she swings an ax." He wrapped his arm around me and pulled me back against him, kissing the crown of my head. "So, what is it you wanted me to see, besides Addy's attempts to bribe you into keeping the imp for good?"

Earlier, after everyone had gone home for the evening and Doc had gone upstairs to change into his usual loungewear—flannel pajama pants and a thermal shirt—I'd collected the magic mirror from where Aunt Zoe had stowed it in the laundry room. I'd covered it with a towel and brought it down here for a late-night game of show and tell.

"A new trick Aunt Zoe showed me."

I stepped away from his warmth and tiptoed over to the mirror, which I'd leaned against the old dresser filled with Layne's mad scientist lab equipment in the corner opposite Elvis's pen. On top of the dresser, amidst the clutter of random tools and a remote control car battery, was a tiny aluminum foil hat with wires sticking out of it. Huh. I hadn't noticed that when I was down here before. It looked about the right size to fit a chicken. Apparently, Layne hadn't been joking about wanting to test Elvis's brain. I grabbed the tiny foil hat and tucked it in my sweater pocket for safekeeping.

Doc came over to help me carry the mirror to the chicken cage, catching the towel when it slipped off as he set the mirror on the floor several feet away—close enough to see, but not too close to wake up the cage's inhabitants.

"Why is your special mirror in the basement instead of Zoe's workshop?" he whispered.

I lowered to my knees beside it. "Come down here next to me."

He half-squatted, half-kneeled.

I carefully peeled back a corner of the quilt covering the cage, making sure to keep my flashlight pointed away from the sleeping duo.

"We need to be careful with this mirror," Doc reminded me, his tone grave. "I saw some bad actors trapped on the other side of the glass when I looked through it at Prudence's place."

Bad actors? More like freaky, nasty fiends and demons according to Doc's description after he'd returned to the safe side of the mirror.

"They were itching to get free," he continued, "trying like hell to latch onto me. Without Prudence, I might not have been able to stop them from following me back out."

"Don't worry. We're not going to do any mirror diving tonight." I tried to adjust the angle of the mirror's reflection so that he could see Elvis and Daisy. "Just some viewing from a safe distance."

"Like remote viewing?"

"No. This won't require any sensing of distant objects with your mind."

He wiggled his eyebrows at me, reminding me of the late, great Groucho Marx. "Have I told you how sexy it is when you talk paranormal terms with me, Boots?"

"Stay focused on the mirror, Romeo." I pointed toward it. "Tonight, we'll be doing some regular viewing with a small twist. Now, take a look."

I knew the minute Doc saw Daisy in the mirror simply by his quick indrawn breath.

"That, my dear Oracle, is an imp."

He leaned to the side, squinting slightly. "Will you move your light more to the right?"

"Okay, but I don't want to wake up Daisy."

"Why, Miss Big Bad *Scharfrichter*?" He winked at me over the mirror. "Are you worried about a repeat of the last time when you interrupted the tiny imp's naptime and ended up with a black eye?"

I flicked his arm. "Keep it up, wise guy, and I'll sic Daisy on you for Round 2."

"No, you won't. You love me too much."

I wrinkled my nose at him. "Dammit, you're right. Maybe I'll sic the imp on Cooper instead. Wait, better yet, Detective Hawke."

Doc's focus returned to the mirror. "You really nailed it when you said it's like a hairless cat, only bigger."

"Don't forget the longer, sharper claws." I stared at the sleeping creature without the help of the mirror. "And harder head butts."

"So, Zoe figured out this mirror trick to make Daisy visible to the rest of us?"

I nodded. "I don't know what it will do if it finds out Arcana here can see through its usual camouflage."

He grimaced. "If Daisy decides to break the mirror, that might let out something trapped inside of it."

"Yeah, that can't happen. We'll have to be careful."

His eyes met mine. "So very careful," he said, all jesting aside.

Part of me wondered what exactly he'd seen in that mirror, while the other part hoped never to find out. "Well, what do you think? Does Daisy look like what you'd imagined?"

A small smile tilted the corner of his lips. "It's no wonder you couldn't bring yourself to kill it at the school."

"Why do you say that?"

He pointed at the mirror. "Look how cute it is snuggled up next to Elvis."

I scoffed. "That thing is not cute. It's a menace to society. It's chaos on legs with pointy teeth and red beady eyes."

"The *Scharfrichter* doth protest too much, methinks." He chuckled softly. "Turns out that my favorite Godzilla is a big softy. Harvey might want to reconsider your monster identity. You know, Herman Munster was pretty lovable, same as you, although a bit clumsy. Come to think of it, he'd probably end up clobbered by an imp, too."

I squinted at him. "I wasn't clobbered by the little shit, just scratched a few times more than I'd have liked."

"If you say so, Killer." He returned to the mirror, leaning closer to it again.

I scowled at the imp. "Had I known when we were in the old school auditorium that Daisy would follow me home and hang out with our chicken in the closet half the livelong day, I'd have let the other monster in the room eat it for dinner."

"I don't believe that. Your heart is too big. Not quite Godzilla big, but larger than the average *Scharfrichter*, I'd bet." He glanced back and forth between the cage and the mirror. "I also think it's sweet how Elvis has become 'our' chicken. I never thought I'd have a family, let alone co-parent a chicken named after the king of rock and roll."

I smiled. "I hope you're not daydreaming about acquiring a whole flock, because I'm drawing the line at one pesky chicken."

He pulled the mirror a little his way, angling it more. "I'll take whatever comes with the Violet Parker prize package. Kids, cats, gerbils, dogs, chick—"

Daisy stirred, rolling belly up.

I froze, waiting to see if the imp opened its red eyes.

Elvis let out a series of soft clucks, which seemed to lull Daisy back to sleep.

"Whew," I whispered.

Doc was staring at the mirror, his eyes narrowed. "What is that?"

"What?" I looked into the other shadowed corner of the cage, wondering if Bogart the cat was slinking around; or if The Duke, Addy's gerbil, had escaped and snuck down here.

Doc took the flashlight from me and shined the beam closer to the two in the cage, lighting them up more.

"Do you see that?" he said very quietly, pointing toward the mirror.

I leaned nearer to hear him better. "See what?"

"That mark on the imp's neck. It goes partway down its chest, too."

I peered into the cage. I saw no mark, just brown raisin-like skin with wrinkles. "Are you sure you're not seeing a shadow?"

He nodded. "It's dark like one, but it has a reddish tinge to it."

"Like a blood bruise?"

"Maybe."

"The Bone Cruncher might have landed a hit or took a bite while it was chasing Daisy around the school."

"It's the shape of a hand, I'm pretty sure." He held his hand in front of the mirror, angling it to the side. "The fingers are spread wide and elongated, with a couple of tendrils twisting out from the fingertips like gnarled branches."

Goosebumps prickled my arms. "Doc, you better not be fooling around with me, trying to creep me out in a dark basement late at night."

"Trust me, Killer. I'd rather be fooling around with you if that were an option. Exploring your curves is one of my favorite pastimes." He lowered his hand. "Now quit distracting me and take a closer look at Daisy."

I inched nearer to the cage, scanning the imp from top to bottom. Its neck and belly were lighter brown than the rest of it, but otherwise, I saw no other noticeable color changes. "I don't see anything like a handprint. Nothing besides its wrinkled skin. Not even a slightly darker birthmark."

"Take a look at it in the mirror."

I turned the mirror slightly my way, angling it so I could see

Daisy. After a few blinks and a long squint I shook my head. "No mark. But I think I see one of my bottles of pink nail polish sticking partway out from under Elvis's rump."

I sat back, thinking about the first time Addy had given Elvis a pedicure and ended up with more polish on her hands and arms than the chicken's feet. A small wave of sadness washed over me. I missed my kids, darn it. I hoped they were having a great time with my parents, but it would be good to have them back in the same state as me soon.

Doc turned the mirror back his way. "It's still there," he said under his breath. "That's weird." He glanced toward the cage and then at me. "I don't understand why I can see the mark in the mirror but you can't."

"Maybe it has to do with you being an Oracle."

"Yeah, maybe." He reached over and lowered the quilt back over the cage. "I might try taking a look at the imp in the morning light. With your help, of course."

"Sure, but Daisy is still skittish around me. Maybe we can try to lure the little bugger in front of the mirror with honey."

If it didn't take the honey bait, I'd be happy to eat it.

He nodded and stood, lifting the mirror in one hand while helping me up with the other. "Let's go to bed. I'm too tired to think about chickens and imps any more tonight. I'd rather be under the covers with a curvy blonde glued to my side."

I followed him up the steps. "Does that mean I can warm my feet on your legs?"

"That depends on what you let me touch while enduring your frosty feet." He held the door for me at the top.

"Touch or rub?"

"A bit of both, Boots." He closed the basement door. "Should I take the mirror out to Zoe's workshop?"

"Nah. You can leave it in the laundry room for the night." I grabbed a glass of water while he carried Arcana from the room, staring out the kitchen window at the light coming from Aunt Zoe's workshop. She'd probably be up most of the night working out there.

"Violet," Doc said from behind me, his voice hesitant.

I turned to find him standing outside of the laundry room door, the mirror still in his hand. "What?"

"I had a thought."

Okay, but why was he looking so unhappy about it?

"Yeah?"

"I was thinking about earlier, after supper, when Cornelius told us about your experience with pendulum dowsing."

"You mean the wise and knowing Edith?"

"Yes." He took a step closer with the mirror still in hand. "He said that when you asked Edith about the ghoul being here with you, the stone just circled, not answering yes or no."

I nodded slowly.

"I've used pendulum dowsing several times in the past to test my own ghost radar." He moved to one of the kitchen chairs, setting the mirror on it.

"Did it work for you?"

"Yes, and that got me wondering."

Wondering what? I looked from him to the mirror and back. "Let me guess, you want me to use Cornelius's pal Edith while sitting in front of the mirror."

"No. Although that might be an interesting experiment."

"Or problematic. I don't want to accidentally let whatever is in there out, and you know how my luck runs when it comes to just about everything in this weird world."

"True. What I was wondering was if you would ..." He paused, then waved me over. "Just come over here."

I took a step closer, but then stopped. Something about the way he was watching me had my pulse pounding, and not in the normal, happy-to-see-him way. "You're kind of freaking me out right now, Doc."

He pointed at Arcana. "I want to look at you in the mirror."

I still held back. "Is this going to be a kinky thing? Because if it is, that mirror is a real libido killer. All I would be able to think about is what was watching from the other side."

He adjusted the mirror so the two of us could stand in front of it side by side. "Trust me, Killer. This is something different. Now get your scaredy-cat buns over here."

I moved closer, hesitating at the edge of his sightline in the reflection "What do you think you're going to see?"

"I'm not sure."

"If you see one of those terrors from the other side standing behind me, I don't think I want to know."

"I doubt that will be the case."

"There is a 'but' in there, though, right?"

"Yeah." He reached out and snagged my hand, squeezing it lightly. "Just humor me."

"Fine, but if my face melts off in your version of the mirror's reflection, don't blame me for the next weeks' worth of nightmares." I joined him in front of the mirror, staring at his reflection for a couple of seconds before focusing on my own. "Lord love a duck," I muttered, cringing.

"What do you see?" he asked, frowning my way in the reflection.

I tried to tame a couple of curls that were spiraling out from my head like TV antenna rabbit ears. "A woman in dire need of a brush."

"What else?" he pressed.

Behind us, the light over the kitchen sink lit the room in a soft glow. Beyond that, there were no bloody faces or glowing orange eyes, which was what I'd feared just off the top of my head.

"I see us. You look wild and rugged, while I look wild and rabid. Why? What do you see?" I waved at him in the mirror and smiled extra wide, tipping my head back and forth. "Do I look like one of those creepy clown head billboards that tower over a funhouse of frights?"

He didn't laugh. Not even a smile. Instead, he had a worried expression on his face that set free a colony of bats in my chest. "Hold still for a second."

I did as told as he turned on the overhead light, crossing my fingers there was no invisible, soul-sucking fiend with blood-rimmed black eyes and curly horns standing behind me. I blinked in the brighter light, wishing I'd saved my show-and-tell surprise for morning light when the ghosts had gone to bed and fresh coffee made the world cozy.

When Doc returned to my side, I raised my eyebrows at him in the mirror. "Do you see any of those freaky-ass entities hovering around me or what?"

He shook his head, his focus intense, matching the lines on his forehead. "No other entities."

I breathed a sigh of relief. "Can we go to bed now?"

"Yeah," he said, but sounded unsettled. "But tomorrow, we're going to need to pay a visit to your coworker up in Lead."

I turned to him—the real him, not his reflection. "Prudence?" At his nod, I scowled. "Why?"

He pointed at the mirror. "Because when I look at you in this mirror, I can see a handprint on the side of your neck and face."

I whirled back to my reflection, the bat colony swirling once again in my chest, but I saw nothing but my skin. "Are you screwing with me, Doc?" I whispered, slightly breathless all of a sudden.

"Once again, I wish that was the case. But unfortunately, no. And I mean that both ways."

He took me by the chin and turned my head to the left so that he could see the right side of my face in the mirror.

"For some reason that I hope Prudence will know, you and the imp share the same mark. The only difference is that Daisy's has spread slightly."

"The gnarled fingertips?"

"Exactly. Yours is only a handprint at the moment."

"Uhh, only? Isn't that bad enough?"

He held his hand up to my cheek while staring in the mirror. "There are dark reddish black fingers spread wide like this."

"Maybe it's just an allergic reaction of some sort." I licked my suddenly dry lips. "Maybe the imp and I are allergic to each other, like mortal allergen enemies."

Doc shook his head slowly. I wasn't sure if he was disagreeing with me or one of his own thoughts. "Four fingers, one reaching toward your mouth, one your nose, then your eye and ear."

I had a vision of a hand inside of my face pressing out, stretching my skin until it tore into bloody fragments.

"Holy shit!" I back peddled toward the sink. "What the fuck touched me?" I yanked a towel from the drawer and wet it, adding a squirt of dish soap.

Doc came up behind me as I scrubbed the side of my face, making my skin burn.

"Violet," he said softly, grabbing my arm and stopping me. "You can't wipe this off."

I scowled down at the dishtowel. "Was Edith right about the ghoul being here?"

"I don't know."

"How in the hell would it be able to leave an invisible mark on me?"

"I'm more worried about *why* it would leave a mark."

"Could you see anything on you in the mirror? Any other marks?" He'd been in bed next to me night after night. If it were going to rub off on anyone, it would be him.

He shook his head. "Nor on Elvis."

I bit my lower lip. "And you would be able to see something easily on her white feathers."

"Unless it's under her feathers, but I doubt that." He took the towel from me and tossed it on the counter, then pulled me into his arms.

I soaked up his strength and warmth for a moment, then leaned my forehead against his sternum. "If it's the ghoul, then why is there a mark on Daisy? I mean I can understand why I might have one after battling the asshole in Jane's office, but not the imp. Daisy wasn't anywhere near me at that time."

"I don't know."

"And why is Daisy's mark spreading?"

"I don't know that either."

"How soon until mine starts to spread? What if it reaches my eyes, or goes into my brain?"

"Sweetheart, I don't have any answers. I haven't seen something like this before, but I'm hoping Prudence will be able to help us. At the least, maybe she can clue us in as to why I can see things in *your* ancestral mirror that you can't."

"What the hell is this?"

He pulled back and tipped up my chin. "We'll get to the bottom of it, I promise."

I frowned up at him. "I don't want to tell Aunt Zoe yet."

"Why not?"

"She needs to get that order done. This will distract her. She'll stop working to try to find answers in our family history volumes."

"Fine, but if Prudence doesn't have any answers for us, Zoe will need to get involved. And soon."

I sighed. "You and I both know that Prudence is going to give me shit about being marked."

He chuckled, but there wasn't much humor behind it.

"Prudence will give you shit for having a shoe untied because she's jealous that you're still breathing and she's not. But you don't have to take her crap. You're a badass *Scharfrichter* in your own right."

"I'll have to play nice, though, at least until we find out what's going on with that damned mirror." I touched my cheek where the mark supposedly was. The skin felt tender and hot, tingly from scrubbing. "I wish I could wash it off."

He pulled my hand away and kissed my knuckles. "Come on, let's go to bed."

"Okay, but I'm not sure I can sleep now."

"Who said anything about sleeping?" he said with a wink and rubbed his thumb over my fingers. "Tish, I have just the thing to take your mind off the mirror, the mark, the imp, Edith the stone, Jerry's medium-for-hire that you told us about at supper, and even those clocks."

"What about Detective Hawke?"

He scoffed. "Get real, woman. I'm only human."

"Are you, though?"

"I think so." He pursed his lips. "Let's go see."

I shut off the overhead light while he returned the mirror to the laundry room. I spared one last glance out the kitchen window at where my aunt was working merrily away, clueless that her niece might have somehow allowed a ghoul to hitchhike its way into the house.

I groaned. As if an imp wasn't bad enough. At least Daisy liked Addy enough to behave. For the time being, anyway.

Addy …

Damn it. We were going to have to fix this handprint problem before the kids got home. I couldn't risk it somehow spreading to one of them.

Or both.

My hands trembled as I followed Doc upstairs.

CHAPTER TWELVE

I woke up at the wrong end of the bed.

It took some eye rubbing and head scratching to remember why my world had been spun 180 degrees.

Then it all came tumbling back, each memory thumping around in my head like tennis shoes in the clothes dryer. The clocks. The ghoul. Hawke—damn him. The mule deer head and the knife-impaled, blood-soaked hat made of some kind of hide. Ms. Medium Extraordinaire. The imp. The invisible handprint. Godzilla and the Wolf Man.

My thought train could have added more to the list, but I groaned to a stop and flopped back onto the folded chenille throw I'd wadded up and used as a makeshift pillow last night. I pulled my goose down comforter to my chin and rolled onto my side, curling into a ball.

My feet were cold again and my foot warmer was missing. I sighed and glanced toward the bedroom door, which stood halfway open. The smell of coffee coming up the stairs along with a whiff of bacon and eggs answered any question about Doc's whereabouts.

A glance at the clock on my nightstand told me a story about the current weather—it was darker than it should be for this time of morning. The wind whistled and whooshed outside the window.

I tried not to think about the frozen pool of blood on the front porch, hoping Cooper had stayed true to his word and gotten rid of the head already. Or at least covered it.

Closing my eyes, I tried to do a little meditating. But Prudence interfered, rearing her haughty head into my thoughts.

I decided to switch to what Cornelius called happy brain drills. Earlier in the week, he'd suggested a gratitude workout for the limbic cortex part of my brain upon wakeup as a means to make me more smiley in the mornings and less likely to snap like a "vicious turtle." Maybe if he would stop eating all of the cookies, I'd be less apt to bite.

Okay, that kind of thinking wasn't helping. Time to focus on things I was grateful for today … like Doc.

He had worked his magic on my worries and fears last night, only his remedy hadn't involved nakedness this time. Although his talented hands had played a part. He'd relied on an ancient art to ease my anxiety—massage. In particular, using Aunt Zoe's lavender-scented lotion and rubbing it on the soft tissues of my very cold feet, which explained why I'd woken up at the wrong end of our bed. He'd pulled the bottom of the comforter free of the mattress and had me lay opposite him with my feet up near his chest while he stroked and kneaded and caressed away my worries. I'd fallen asleep, and it had been lights out on all thoughts until this morning.

I looked toward the head of the bed and the pillows there. I couldn't even remember if he'd stayed topside or joined me down at this end of the bed.

I smiled and snuggled deeper under the warm blanket.

Let's see, what else was I grateful for?

Freshly brewed coffee in the morning was always nice.

My stomach rumbled.

And a hot breakfast. That made my list, too.

Especially bacon. And honey on buttered toast. Maybe even honey on bacon. I'd bet Harvey's left nut Daisy would really love that.

Daisy … How could Doc see that hand mark on the imp and me, but I couldn't?

I touched my right cheek. It didn't feel warmer than usual, nor tingly. The skin felt normal. I pinched it. No numbness. No weird texture.

Maybe the mirror was full of shit. Or maybe one of the fiends trapped inside of Arcana was showing Doc things that weren't there, trying to lure him back to the other side with the hope of helping me so it could somehow latch onto him and escape.

But why me and Daisy both? That didn't make any sense.

Unless … I sat up. Unless there had been something at the old school when I saved Daisy's life from the Bone Cruncher. Maybe we were both marked at that moment.

"If that were the case," I said to the empty room, "then Harvey might have a mark, too, since he was there with us."

We needed to get Harvey to come over and stand in front of the mirror.

Toasted bread!

I leaned toward the open doorway and sniffed. Yep, that was definitely toast.

I was grateful for cows—and their butter byproduct. And bees, since they made honey.

My stomach rumbled again, the hunger pains stronger. Speaking of honey, that imp better not have hogged it all.

Enough of this gratitude crap. I threw the comforter off me. Food was what I needed to make me smiley this morning. And Doc.

I rolled out of bed and grabbed my fluffy red robe. It crackled with static electricity as I slid it on. A glance in the mirror over my dresser showed the robe working its friction magic on my hair, sending electric charges that made some of my curls stick out like I was Frankenstein's monster in the midst of being shocked back to life.

I tried to pat a few curls into submission, but the robe sleeve rubbed more of my hair and the static electricity only seemed to be getting worse.

"Screw it," I muttered, stepping into my slippers. Doc had seen me at my worst, and then again during an even sorrier time than that, probably. A few wild hairs wouldn't raise his eyebrows.

I tied the robe over my pink polka-dot long-john pajamas as I tromped and crackled down the stairs and toward the kitchen.

"Good morn—" The sight of Cooper standing at the stove stopped me and my slippers in their tracks, along with all my happy food thoughts.

He wore a black sweatshirt, blue jeans, and white socks. And he was laughing. Actually laughing. If Bigfoot were standing at the stove wearing Harvey's Moon the Cook apron, I'd have been less bowled over.

My morning brain struggled to make sense of the sound coming from Cooper's mouth. Sure, I'd seen him laugh on occasion in the past, but that was usually during a high-stress moment. As in Mt. Everest high. Although he had been suspended yesterday, so this could be another example of him venting his tension—a burp of steam from a volcano before it blew its top.

I tried examining Cooper from another angle. There was a difference in him this morning beyond the laughing bit. No jaw muscle pulsed from gritting his teeth too hard. No vein bulged near his temple. No invisible ramrod appeared to be jammed up his backside. He looked … at ease, I would say, as if he cooked breakfast with a smile in Aunt Zoe's kitchen every morning.

I couldn't help but gape at him … and then blink a few times to make sure I wasn't hallucinating.

Meanwhile, Cooper flipped an egg in the frying pan. Then he grabbed a pair of tongs and plucked some strips of bacon from another pan and dropped them on a plate next to a couple of pieces of toast.

Huh.

Maybe I was stuck in an alternate reality that began with waking up at the wrong end of the bed. Or had I actually fallen through the looking glass last night when we were fiddling with the mirror and needed to find a tree with a door in it to return home? It was no wonder Alice struggled to find her way back to square one.

"Morning, Tish," Doc said, his voice startling me out of my stupor. He stood at the other end of the counter from Cooper, still in his long-sleeve thermal shirt and pajama pants, a mug in his hand. His eyes looked a little red, like he hadn't slept much last night. "Want some coffee?"

I nodded. "You sleep okay?"

He shrugged. "Well enough."

I pointed toward Cooper. "Am I dreaming about that?" I reached for the back of the chair next to me. The wood certainly felt real under my palm—cool and hard, textured grain, a little sticky in one spot undoubtedly thanks to my kids. Or Daisy and her honey. "Is it really King Kong laughing and cooking in our kitchen first thing in the morning?"

Cooper glanced my way and then did a double take. "Wow,

Parker! That hair." He whistled. "It's going to be hard to hear you over the volume of it all."

I glared at him. "Don't be getting my dander up already, you big ape."

He grinned and held his hands up in surrender.

Doc walked over with a steaming cup of coffee and set it down on the table in front of me. He took me by the shoulders and dropped a kiss on my forehead. "Hey, beautiful. How are you doing this morning?" His dark gaze searched mine, probably looking for shadows left over from last night's disturbing discovery.

"She looks like she rolled out of bed and ended up tangled in a trap net on the floor," the peanut gallery said.

"Nobody asked you, Chuckles." I muzzled the snapping turtle in my head and smiled extra wide up at Doc. "I'm grateful for Cooper." I tried to sound like I meant it.

Doc flinched at my expression, but held steady. "That's … uh … nice, I guess?" He ended with one raised eyebrow, apparently unsure.

I shrugged. "I'm going to sit now, drink some coffee, and try to make sense of my current life trajectory as I focus on other things for which I'm grateful."

"Ahh." Doc held my chair for me. "So, Godzilla and King Kong have something in common this morning—you're both trying Cornelius's happy brain drills. That should make breakfast interesting."

That explained Detective Sunnybunny's smile.

"Since when have you been interested in working on increasing your positive outlook on life?" I asked Cooper as he slid a plate of bacon, eggs, and toast in front of me.

"Natalie told me about Curion's cockamamie idea last night and suggested I give it a try." A frown flashed across his face. "Make that insisted I do it. Or else."

Insisted? King Kong must have been stomping around her apartment last night, beating on his chest about Hawke and the suspension, or the clocks, or the mule deer head, or … well, there were too many possibilities that might have pissed him off and my breakfast was getting cold.

Cooper pointed at my plate. "Eat up. We have work to do

today, and you're going to need your strength."

I started with the bacon. "What's this 'work' Kong is grunting about?" I asked Doc.

"That's *King* Kong to you, Peon Parker," Cooper grumbled, handing Doc another plate of food.

"Thanks," he said to Cooper and grabbed two napkins, giving me one as he sat down next to me. "I don't know. Maybe the big ape has a thorn in his thumb and needs your help pulling it out."

"I took care of the deer head." Cooper joined us at the table with his own plate.

"What did you do with it?" I asked, taking another bite of bacon.

"Do you really want to know?"

Actually, I didn't. But my bacon could use some honey on it. "What about the pool of blood?"

"Zoe helped me clean it up earlier, before she went up to get some sleep." He picked up his fork. "Your kids will never know that happened."

"Unless it happens again," I said quietly, crossing my fingers and toes that this gruesome gift was a one-time deal.

Doc scowled slightly as he broke open the yolk of his fried egg with his toast. "Which is why we need those clocks sooner rather than later."

"Yeah, about that." Cooper paused to sip some coffee. "I swung by the station on my way over here under the guise of needing something from my desk. On my way out, I overheard a conversation that could throw a monkey wrench in the works."

"You have monkeys on the brain," I said, getting up to grab some honey from the pantry. I had a feeling Cooper's sour news was going to need some sweetening.

"Apparently, Parker made Hawke nervous the other day when he ran into her coming out of Galena House."

Lucky for Daisy, there were several bottles of honey yet in the pantry. I returned to the table with a bottle. "For the record, I didn't pretend to cast any hexes or spells on the bozo. I just calmly explained my reason for being there."

"Good behavior or not, he's gotten permission to have extra security at Ms. Wolff's apartment."

I rolled my eyes. "You mean in addition to the regular police drive-bys?"

He nodded. "Now he has an officer sitting outside the building 24/7 when he's not home."

"Shit," Doc said, shaking his head. "We don't need this."

I raised my coffee cup. "I'll drink to that, especially after what happened last night."

This new move on Hawke's part seemed extra paranoid. I'd been able to enter Galena House for the last couple of months due to my status as Freesia's selling agent. Why the sudden freakout? Was it simply because I brought clients by to look at the place? There must be something more going on behind the scenes.

"Last night?" Cooper lowered his fork, his brow pinched. "You mean because of the deer head and blood on the porch?"

"No. I mean because of the …" I stopped and turned to Doc. We weren't going to tell Aunt Zoe about the hand mark on the imp and me yet—a decision I remembered almost too late. But did that mean I should hold off on spilling to Cooper, too?

"Because of the what?" Cooper pressed, lines crisscrossing his face.

Doc shrugged at me. "Your call, Killer."

"Listen, Parker." Cooper's voice lowered, suddenly edged with tension. Apparently, the happy brain drills were over for the day. "If I'm going to risk my neck to help Natalie and you get those damned clocks, you two need to tell me everything."

Natalie and me? Usually, Cooper focused on me alone when it came to his law-related frustrations. Why had he included her this time? What about everyone else involved in the caper, like his uncle who'd started this whole caper business? And Doc, who was sitting right here beside us?

I grabbed a piece of bacon, ignoring his hard stare as I squeezed a drop of honey onto it. Before I went into what happened with the mirror last night after everyone had left, I wanted him to tell me *everything*.

"Why were you suspended, Cooper?"

His gaze narrowed. "Quit changing the subject."

"I'm not, exactly. I just want to be clear on your true location up shit creek before giving you my hip-deep coordinates." I took a bite of the honey-bacon. Smoky and sweet—just how I liked my demons. I reached for more honey.

Cooper shifted and focused on his plate, taking a stab at his eggs. "I told you guys why last night."

Not quite. "You said the chief of police thought you could use some time to clear your head when it came to Ms. Wolff's murder case, but that was it."

He shrugged. "Exactly."

"Clear your head of what?" Doc asked.

He chewed without looking my way. "The whole mess with Parker."

I scoffed. "My mess is multi-leveled with twisty tangents shooting off to the left and right at every floor. Tell us what really happened."

"I don't …" he hesitated. "Why does that matter? All you really need to know is that I was suspended due to my association with you." He sat back and crossed his arms.

I drizzled more honey on my bacon. "It matters because I have a feeling that my visit yesterday isn't the only reason Hawke is more paranoid than usual."

Doc took a sip of coffee, staring at Cooper over the rim. "What happened at work yesterday?"

He scowled briefly at Doc, but mostly at me. "If I tell you guys, you can't tell Natalie."

"Why not?" I asked.

"Because you and your history at Galena House are part of the reason I've been sidelined."

I lifted my chin. "What's the other part?"

"There was a small … uhh …" he paused, half of his face scrunching slightly. "A small *incident* at work, which was actually the impetus for my suspension. It had to do with Nat."

How curious. I chomped on my smoky-sweet bacon. "Do tell, detective."

He returned to his food, finishing off his eggs before letting loose. "Not until you promise to keep your big mouth shut about this until I'm ready to tell Nat the whole truth."

"Why don't you want her to know now?" Doc asked.

"Because she's Freesia's handywoman."

Hmm, that didn't add up. "Bzzt. Wrong answer."

"Parker, you don't even know what the right fucking answer is."

"True, but there has to be more to it than that."

He shrugged. "I also spend the night at Nat's place somewhat frequently and I'd like to continue having that option in my future." He picked up his toast, focusing on me. "Mostly, though, I don't want to throw gasoline on the fire that *you* already lit under her."

Curiouser and curiouser. However, there was a snag for me. "I'm not sure I can hide something from Natalie if it's a big deal."

I'd hidden my relationship with Doc from her for some time last year, and it had been rough on our friendship when she'd stumbled upon the truth. After we'd bumped our way past that mess, we'd taken a vow of truth going forward.

"I have an idea," Doc said. "How about you delay saying anything to Natalie until Coop gives you the green light? Then you aren't hiding something, you're just waiting."

I chewed on that. "That's splitting hairs, but I might be able to pull that off, so long as Cooper doesn't wait too long." I held out my pinkie toward him.

He stared at my finger like it was last week's meatloaf.

"Come on, Cooper." I shook it. "Pinkie promise."

"Christ, Parker. Why do you have to make everything weird?" In spite of his grumbling, he reached over and locked pinkies with me.

"There," I said after letting go. "Was that so bad?"

He grunted his reply.

I motioned for Cooper to continue. "Let 'er rip. I'm all ears and locked lips."

"Hawke went to the chief for a restraining order."

"On Violet?"

He shook his head at Doc. "On Nat, claiming she's a risk because she has keys to everything in Galena House."

"Of course, she does," I said. "She lives and works there."

"The restraining order would be for only Ms. Wolff's apartment."

"Hawke doesn't trust her anymore," Doc said.

"It's more than only a matter of trust." Cooper followed a bite of bacon with a swallow of coffee. "He's jealous."

"Of what?"

Cooper's cheeks darkened slightly. "Of me. Because I'm

spending the night in Nat's apartment frequently."

"Did he say as much?" I asked.

"He called her a couple of crude names in the hallway that I found offensive."

Doc paused with his toast midway to his mouth. "How offensive?"

The lines were back on Cooper's forehead. "Well, first I told him that if he had an ounce of intelligence in his fucking head, he'd shut the hell up. Then, when he continued with his verbal assault of her character, I pinned him against the wall."

I leaned forward. That couldn't be all. A simple pinning didn't end in suspension, did it? "And then what?"

"I was pissed."

"And?" After a count of five, I added, "Don't make me torture it out of you, because I'm happy to get the thumbscrews out of the attic."

Doc glanced my way with two raised eyebrows this time. "Thumbscrews? You've been holding out on me, Tish. Think of the fun we could have in the bedroom."

Cooper groaned extra loud. "Don't start that Gomez and Morticia shit. I'm trying to eat here."

"They're an old family heirloom," I explained to Doc, batting my eyelashes at him. Then I dropped the sex-kitten act and returned to Cooper. "Finish your story."

He sighed. "I called Hawke a name or two."

"What names?" I pressed.

"A lousy detective and a no-good, rotten ..." He paused, squeezing his eyes closed before finishing with, "Snollyguster."

I laughed. "You, Detective High-and-Mighty Morality, actually used Prudence's trigger word on the jerk?"

She had planted that word in Hawke's head months ago during a temporary possession of Detective Hawke, telling me to use it when I needed to take him down a notch. In the past, when I'd used it, Cooper had chastised me.

"What can I say?" he growled. "I was weak in my moment of anger."

"And then what happened?" Doc had a small grin on his face as he ate.

"You know goddamned well what happened, Nyce. The

asshole barked."

I clapped several times, wishing I could have been there with a bowl of popcorn. "Was it loud?"

"It echoed down the hallway, clear to the chief's office." He shook his head. "Worse yet, Hawke kept barking. It was like he was stuck 'on' and I couldn't get him to shut up. I covered his mouth with my hand, but by then the chief had stepped out into the hall and caught us in the thick of it." Cooper blew out a breath. "Hawke finally quieted down after I let go of him and someone brought him a glass of water, but shit looked bad for me by that point. Hawke's face was beet red, his eyes all watery, his shirt pitted out. It's like he overheated or something when I triggered him. Jesus, what a fucked-up mess."

"And that's when you were suspended," I theorized.

"Yeah. Even though a couple of the guys stood up for me, explaining how Hawke spurred me on, the chief decided the best thing was for me to take a break and leave Hawke room to work his magic. Or not."

"What does 'or not' mean?" Doc asked.

"He said that if Hawke can't solve the case of Ms. Wolff's murder within the next month, then he will pull him off it and put me back on. But I have to give Hawke a chance first."

If only we could wait longer to get to those clocks, but my gut said delaying could end up with me dead. Or worse, my family. "How long are you suspended for?"

"A couple weeks at this point." He took a sip of coffee. "I can extend it with vacation time if there's still trouble with Hawke when it's over. I have a ton saved up."

That was no surprise. I couldn't quite see Cooper sitting on a beach wearing flip-flops with zinc oxide sunscreen plastered on his nose for even ten minutes.

"And you don't want Natalie to know about you defending her honor because why in particular?" I asked. It seemed to me like a great opportunity for her to see how much Cooper cared for her, since he was usually pretty unflappable in the face of … well, most everything, so long as he had his gun holstered at his side.

"Because I've been around Nat for long enough to know better than to tell her what Hawke said. Remember, I've met her cousins down in Arizona."

I frowned. "What do Claire, Kate, and Ronnie have to do with this?"

"Those women cut their teeth on cast-off spikes."

"Come on," I said, chuckling. "They're not that rough and tumble."

"Please. You get any one of them riled up, and you'd have less trouble lassoing a pissed-off bull than calming them down."

Doc chuckled. "They seem to be pros at stirring up hell with a long spoon."

"How do you know about the Morgan sisters?" I asked him. He'd helped me bail out Claire and Kate last Halloween, but other than that night, I couldn't remember him being around them again.

He pointed across the table. "Coop told me all about his last visit to Arizona."

Oh yeah, the vacation where Cooper had come home with new bullet wounds.

"Natalie won't back down from a fight," Cooper said. "If she finds out what happened with Hawke at the station that ended with me getting suspended, she's going to be hell-bent to take him down a notch."

"True." I'd seen her dole out some harsh punishments on ex-boyfriends who'd done her wrong. I squirted some honey on my fried egg. But back to the problem at hand.

All of a sudden, an idea popped into my head, which just might work if Cooper was game. "So, did Hawke get approval for that restraining order?"

"Not that I know of …" He frowned at my egg and then Doc. "Yet."

"That means we're going to have to make our move to get those clocks even sooner," I said. "Before he figures out a means to bar the way completely."

"Parker, didn't you hear me say that he now has someone sitting outside 24/7?"

"Yeah, but I might have a solution to circumvent that roadblock."

"What solution?" Doc asked.

"Well, what if Cooper has decided he's interested in buying Galena House from Freesia? Hawke cannot stand in the way of Freesia selling the place, and Cooper, being the pain in the ass that he is—"

"Get to the point, Parker."

"Well, you'd want to go through the house from top to bottom, giving it a thorough going-over."

Doc nodded. "Coop might even want to bring in Deadwood's fire captain to inspect some of the old wiring in each apartment."

"Exactly." I took a bite of honey-drizzled eggs and grimaced. Okay, so that combo wasn't so tasty.

Cooper took a sip of coffee, and then nodded as he swallowed. "You know, that just might work. Legally, he won't have a leg to stand on if I'm buying the place."

"Damned right," I said, taking a bite of my eggs with gusto. "Screw that 24/7 police monitoring crap."

"Good thinking, Parker," Cooper said, picking up a piece of bacon.

I paused for a moment to bask in the glow of a rare compliment from him, then returned to finishing my eggs.

"Now," he said, "what happened last night that you're dragging your feet about?"

Oh, yeah, that. I deflated. "Doc saw something in my family's mirror. Something alarming."

Cooper turned to Doc. "The mirror we took up to Prudence's place?"

He nodded and pointed at where the mirror was leaning against the wall next to the bowl of cat food. "That one right there."

I hadn't realized Doc had brought it out of the laundry room until now since it was partially hidden by the fridge from where I sat. What had he been doing with it? Or had Aunt Zoe brought it out earlier this morning to look at the imp again?

"What did you see?" Cooper asked.

I motioned for Doc to tell the story instead of me. When he was done, Cooper stared at me like he was trying to see under my skin. "Can you feel anything where the mark is?"

"Nothing at all." I looked at Doc. "I had a thought. We need to look at Harvey in the mirror. Maybe Daisy and I were marked at the old school when we battled the Bone Cruncher."

Cooper's brow tightened. "You think that since Uncle Willis was there, he might have it too?"

I nodded.

"Any idea what this mark means?" Cooper asked Doc.

"Nope."

"Did you ask Zoe? She's been studying up on those sigils, hasn't she?"

I nodded. "But this isn't a sigil, really. It's a handprint. Besides, we want to wait until she has her big glass order done and isn't under a dead—" The small creaking sound of the cat door flap swinging open made me stop and lean over to see who was joining us.

Cooper glanced around as the imp stepped through and then held the door flap up for Elvis, who was busy clucking as she waddled onto the linoleum. The two of them headed for the cat food bowl, neither bothering to look our way.

When Cooper turned my way with a raised brow, I held my finger to my lips and then pointed toward the bowl, mouthing to him, *the imp*.

He turned slowly in his chair to get a better view.

When the imp stopped in front of the bowl, its reflection was clear in the mirror.

Cooper's jaw dropped. "You've gotta be shitting me," he whispered, shooting a frown my way. "That's the little bastard who caused so much damage around Lead?"

I nodded.

"The bully that messed up your face?"

I nodded again, only frowning back at him now.

He snorted. "And here I thought you were a big, tough *Scharfrichter*."

I glared. "You try catching a pissed-off cat with nothing more than a cloth bag and your bare hands and then we'll see how you look when the dust settles."

He stared over his shoulder again. "It's uglier than I pictured, but the claws are about right."

The imp shifted to the side, letting Elvis move in for some nibbles even though she wasn't supposed to be eating Bogart's food.

"Can you see any kind of mark on its neck or chest?" Doc asked Cooper.

Cooper rotated slightly in his chair, taking a longer look. "No handprint. But those little beady red eyes remind me of Parker when she's had a rough night."

"Hardy har har," I said and took a sip of coffee, which could use some sweetening up. I reached for the bottle of honey, but then remembered the imp was in the room and stilled. Daisy would smell the honey as soon as I opened the bottle, so I waited.

As soon as Elvis pecked at a couple more pieces of cat food, the two of them scuttled and flapped toward the dining room, passing the table without even bothering to look in our direction.

"Can the chicken see the imp?" Cooper asked.

"I don't know," I said, leaning back to watch the two of them round the stair banister. "But those two are thick as thieves these days." I frowned at Doc. "They're probably heading up to our closet, dammit."

"Did you close the doors?"

"Yes, but the imp can open them without a problem." There wasn't really a way to keep Daisy out of any place the bugger wanted to go.

Doc walked over and grabbed the mirror, bringing it to the table. He set it in front of Cooper.

"You see anything on me?" Cooper asked, turning his face one way and then the other.

Doc shook his head and then waved me over.

I joined them, the three of us staring into our reflection.

Cooper winced. "Christ."

"Can you see it?" I asked, turning my cheek for a better view.

"No, but your hair takes up half of the mirror. Can you tune in AM radio stations with that?"

I flipped him off in the reflection, which made him smile.

"Seriously, though," he said, focusing on Doc in the reflection. "I can't see anything other than her normal face."

Doc moved behind me, holding his hand partway over my cheek. "It's right here. Slightly smaller than my hand."

"Is it just like the imp's handprint?" Cooper asked.

"No."

I touched my cheek. "Has it changed?"

"Changed how?" Cooper looked from me to Doc.

"The imp's mark seems to be growing," Doc explained. "Like small tendrils coming out the end of each finger." He leaned closer to the mirror. "Nothing has changed since last night, Killer."

"Good, I guess." I returned to my chair, watching Doc carrying the mirror back to its place against the wall.

"You need to have Curion look into that mirror," Cooper said, lifting his coffee cup. "If anyone would have a matching mark, it'd be him."

"Why?" I asked, trying to make the connection. "You think he has something to do with this mark?"

"No, he's just bizarre enough to have a mark of his own."

"Speaking of Cornelius," Doc said as he joined us again. "He and I paid a visit to your office yesterday after everyone had left."

"You did?" I was surprised neither had mentioned it. Then again, there were plenty of distractions last night.

Doc nodded. "We tried to make a connection with the ghoul in Jane's office, but got radio silence."

"Is that what your appointment was that made you late for supper last night?" Wait, Cornelius had arrived with Natalie before Doc.

"No. After our attempt, I met with the town archivist over at City Hall."

"You met with Weatherly?" Cooper asked. "Why?"

"I wanted to be able to dig deeper into the history of the buildings above the Hellhole and a few other locations around town, but I couldn't find anything in the library."

"Does he know what you're looking for?" I asked.

"No, but we made a deal—I have open access to him and the archives in the basement over there in exchange for me helping him with some long-term investment strategies."

"What's in the city archives?" I didn't realize there was a basement below City Hall, but that made sense.

"Insurance documents, archaeological finds, building blueprints, death registers, and tons more." Doc sat back, crossing his arms. "But there's something about Theodore Weatherly that you two might find interesting."

Cooper scoffed. "Weatherly wears the same white shirt and black tie to work every day and has driven that green 1975 AMC Gremlin since … forever. What could be interesting about him?"

"Nothing much," Doc said. "Besides the fact that I'm pretty sure he's not human."

CHAPTER THIRTEEN

According to Cooper, who'd suddenly decided he was in charge of the clock caper instead of Harvey and me, the first to-do item on my criminal agenda was to go to work. Boring!

I told him as much, too. I'd rather have joined Fire Captain Frankenstein and Natalie Von Dracula over at Galena House, clandestinely scoping out Ms. Wolff's apartment and counting clocks as they pretended to check the fire alarms. I really wanted to know which clocks were ticking away, telling me that trouble was in my neighborhood. Even more, I wanted to hear if any were cuckooing, letting me know someone or *something* was waiting at the metaphysical gate to be let into this realm. Unfortunately, neither Natalie nor Reid could hear them—it was a Timekeeper-only ability.

But Cooper was dead set on me staying far away from Galena House today. He wouldn't even consider letting me help my sexy Wolf Man and ol' man Harvey from the Black Lagoon distract the extra watchdog on Hawke's clock security team sitting outside the boarding house. When I asked Doc what he and Harvey had planned, Cooper told him not to tell me, so I would be clueless if later interrogated.

Grrrr.

Instead of having fun with the rest of the monsters, he'd insisted that the two of us play our part as King Kong and Godzilla, running our own diversion to sideline Hawke before he headed to the apartment for lunch—a relatively new change in his old routine of eating elsewhere.

This lunch location intel had come from Natalie, who'd told Cooper she could smell Hawke's food each day through her floor vent. I had a feeling that was 99 percent baloney. In fact, I'd go so far as to bet my purple boots that she'd been using Corny's hidden camera to spy on Hawke through the vent this last week and didn't want her cop boyfriend to know she'd been up to some illegal snooping.

I puffed my cheeks and released a slow breath, looking out Calamity Jane's plate-glass windows. The wind whistled through the door every so often as it gusted this way and that, as if confused about which direction to blow. I snuggled deeper into my thick, black turtleneck sweater, glad I had a pair of cashmere leggings on under my corduroy pants and knee-high boots for extra warmth.

At least the office was quiet, thanks to Jerry and Ben, my coworker, spending the day in Pierre, attending a state-required broker's licensing update course that offered Sunday classes. Mona had taken the day off, which left me sitting at my desk twiddling my thumbs. There wasn't much to do thanks to the North Pole ambience outside, unfortunately, so I had plenty of opportunities to think about how I really needed to NOT be at work. I had *Scharfrichter* things to do. I'd lost count of how many times I'd started to text Natalie and Doc, only to clear the messages prior to sending them.

My cell phone finally rang while I was pouring myself a third cup of hot tea. I spilled half of it in my rush to take the call, even though it was only King Kong on the other end of the line.

"It's done and ready for your monkey scratches," I said, in place of a greeting. I was referring to the fake offer letter for Galena House that he'd tasked me to create for my part in today's caper operation.

"Good. Hawke should be coming out of the station in about three minutes, if he sticks to his usual schedule."

"Does he always go to lunch the same time every day?" Or had Natalie's spy mission this last week picked up on a changed behavior?

"Yeah, like clockwork. He claims to suffer from low blood sugar if he doesn't stick to his eating schedule, and he gets really pissy when he's held up. Trust me, it's better off to let the bellyacher eat."

"Have you heard from any of the other monsters?"

"No, and you'd better not be trying to reach them."

"I'm not."

"Because you and I don't need any connection to them right now, especially a text or phone call."

"I know."

"Just to be safe."

"*I know*, Cooper. Sheesh. You beat your chest enough about this particular safety protocol after breakfast."

"Well, I wasn't sure you could hear through all that static in your hair."

"Keep it up, poo slinger, and I'm going to fry your ass with my laser breath when you walk through the door."

He chuckled. "It's so fucking cold outside I'd probably welcome the burn."

"You want to go over your lines?" I asked, tapping my pencil on the desktop.

"No, I know exactly what I'm going to say. I'm a professional investigator, Parker."

"You mean instigator, in this case."

"Shit, here he comes. Get ready to play your part. And don't fuck things up like usual."

"Real nice, Cooper. You could use some pointers from Winston Churchill on inspiring your troops."

I had a feeling he didn't hear me. If he followed the plan we'd made after breakfast, he was supposed to stuff his phone in his pocket while our call was still connected so I could hear him talk to Hawke and be prepared for whatever came my way afterward.

Pressing the phone to my ear, I listened to rustling sounds and muffled footfalls. Yep, I was definitely tucked away now.

I resisted the urge to tiptoe over and peek out the front windows. The police station sat a short block away on the other side of the street. Cooper had planned to park in the lot, which meant I might be able to watch as well as listen, but he'd made me swear I'd keep my butt in my chair so Hawke wouldn't catch sight of me with my nose pressed against the window and get suspicious.

There was a garbled shout through the phone line.

I held my breath.

"It's none of your damned business," I heard Cooper holler

back.

Another garbled sound, and then Cooper said, "Just go home and eat your lunch—while you still can."

"What's that supposed to mean?" Hawke's voice came through the phone, along with some swishing sounds.

"It means that you won't be eating at Galena House much longer."

"Hold up, Coop!" I heard Hawke call out.

The swishing stopped.

"What?"

"Is that some kind of threat?" Hawke asked.

"No threat. Just a fact."

"Bullshit." More rustling on Cooper's part, and then Hawke's voice again. "Hey, where you going?"

The line grew quiet. Cooper must have stopped.

"I'm going over to see Parker at work."

Oh, I really wished I could be looking out the window at that moment to see Hawke's face. Sometimes just the sound of my name turned his cheeks beet red.

"What for? You two going to plan another murder together?" There was definitely a snarl mixed in with that question.

"Careful, Hawke." Cooper sniffed, probably due to the cold wind I could hear whistling in the background. "You'd better make sure you can back up an accusation like that."

"Or what?"

"Or I'll see to it that you lose your badge when this is all said and done."

"We'll see who loses their badge, traitor," Hawke said. "What makes you say I won't be at Galena House much longer? You gonna go whine to the chief again about how I'm not paying Freesia enough to live there?"

"You weren't paying her anything at the time."

"I was there on police business."

"You were squatting. That's not police business. That's taking advantage of the owner."

"Whatever. Why are you going to see Parker? You better not be interfering with my case again."

"I'm putting an offer on Galena House today."

"What?!!"

"You heard me. Parker is my agent. She has my offer letter typed and ready for my signature."

"You're full of shit."

"Nope. I'm going to make an offer on the place, and if Freesia accepts it, I'm going to the chief tomorrow and demand that you and those clocks and everything else in that apartment be removed by the end of the week."

"You can't do that."

"Yes, I can. I'd like you out before the home inspector goes through the place from top to bottom."

"This murder case is still open."

"True, but you've been monopolizing that apartment for months. You've collected all the evidence there is, you've inventoried every single clock, you've interviewed everyone surrounding the case more than once. There is no reason for you to continue residing in that apartment. Freesia was too kind to kick your ass out, but I'm not."

The swishing sounds started again, followed by two sets of footfalls. They were both on the move.

"Just hold up a goddamned second," Hawke called.

"It's too fucking cold to stand out here any longer." More rustling came through the line, so much so that the connection crackled a little. "Keep your hands off me," Cooper warned, followed by sudden silence. "We're not in the station now. Nobody will come running to save your ass out here when it's twenty below."

"You know what your problem is, Coop?"

"Enlighten me, Sherlock wannabe."

"You get too close to your suspects."

"Natalie is not a suspect."

"I'm talking about Parker. For Christ's sake, you have dinner at her house most nights, and she's the one who killed Wolff. I'm this close to nailing down the proof to have her locked up behind bars for good."

I chewed on my knuckle, wondering how much of that statement was truth and how much was bluster.

"Parker has an alibi that has been doubly verified."

No lie there on Cooper's part. I did have a solid alibi.

"And now you're fucking her best friend," Hawke said,

sounding almost petulant.

"Careful, Hawke. I will finish what I started yesterday if you don't watch your damned mouth when it comes to Natalie."

"I understand, man. I get it. Nat is hot. Those lips and that ass." A wolf whistle followed.

"Did you hear what I just said, Neanderthal?" Cooper's voice had a sharp, steely edge to it.

"I'm not insulting your choice in women. I'm just saying I understand why you're bangin' Nat, but it's putting you too close to Parker. You can't see her for who she really is."

Cooper guffawed. "I see Parker clear as day."

I frowned at the sarcasm audible in his remark. What was that supposed to mean?

"Besides, it's a bad idea to put an offer on that boarding house," Hawke said.

"Why?"

"Because the place is haunted. Trust me, you don't want that property. There are too many bumps in the night there."

"You're saying it has ghosts?"

"Maybe."

"I thought you were a skeptic, Hawke."

"I was until I came up to Deadwood and met that witch."

"You mean Parker."

"Yes. She's put some kind of hex on me, I'm telling you. I think she has you under a spell, too, same as that boyfriend of hers."

Make that my fiancé, jackass.

"How else can you explain a clearheaded guy who deals in numbers and money falling for her and her crazy hair?"

I took a steadying breath, reminding myself that it would be bad to tie a police officer upside down naked from a tree limb and bat him around like he was a *piñata*, especially in sub-zero weather.

"I'm not under any spell, Hawke. What sort of bumps are you hearing and where?"

"There's a lot of rattling in the vents."

I covered my smile with my hand. That would be Natalie's doing.

"And every now and then I swear I hear that old-fashioned phone in Wolff's living room ring, but when I go out there and hold the receiver to my ear, the line is dead."

Really? Now that was interesting, considering I'd actually interacted with an *other* on that very phone. A rather rude *other*, demanding I let him through some metaphysical gate connected with the bedroom mirror. But he hadn't asked nicely, so I'd hung up on him. And then the gate had been broken by either him or me. I wasn't pointing fingers, but he was the one who'd been yelling at me right before it shattered.

"And those clocks," Hawke said, snagging my attention. "Sometimes they'll start ticking out of the blue. I don't like it, especially in the middle of the night. Makes a guy sleep with a loaded gun next to him."

Note to self—don't creep up on Hawke when he's sleeping.

Which clocks were ticking, dammit? I needed to know that to save my hide.

"I'll take that all under consideration when Parker and I finalize the offer."

"You're still going to buy the place?"

"Yep, and I'm still going to remove you from the premises as soon as possible."

"God, you're such an asshole, Coop."

I smirked. How many times had I had that same thought since meeting Cooper last summer? And yet here I was playing cops and robbers alongside him. Go figure.

"You should probably start packing up your shit, Detective. I think I remember seeing some empty boxes downstairs next to the evidence cage."

"The chief has the final say on this," Hawke snapped.

"True, but my poor old feeble uncle needs a place to live this winter."

I blinked. Was he talking about Harvey, also known as "The Mongoose" down at the senior center?

"Once the chief finds out that I plan to move Uncle Willis into Ms. Wolff's old apartment so I can help take care of him, I'm sure he'll swing my way on moving you to a short-term motel. After all, you have only one month to solve the case. After that, it returns to me. When I'm back in charge, the first thing I'm doing is kicking you off of it."

"Fuck you, Coop."

"Not tonight, Hawke. I'm washing my hair."

"I'm gonna go call the chief right now!"

"You do that and tell him I plan to pay a visit to his office tomorrow."

"Maybe I'll file a restraining order against you, too. Had you thought of that?"

"Good luck with that, but I have a feeling if Freesia signs my offer letter today, that will top your restraining order attempt."

"I'm not gonna let you get away with this," Hawke threatened.

"Sure you aren't." Cooper made a growling sound. "Jesus, it's too cold to listen to any more of your blustering. Screw you later, Hawke, I have papers to sign."

Hey! He stole one of Natalie's exit lines.

The swishing sound returned only to be drowned out by a loud engine. Through the front window, I watched a snowplow ease to a stop at the blinking light and then take a left on Pine Street.

Cooper must be close!

I ended the call and shoved my cell phone in my desk drawer right as the front door opened. The bells jingled over Cooper's head as he joined me inside, shivering in his leather coat and gloves, bringing a rush of cold, fresh-smelling air with him.

I popped up from my desk and smiled wide at Cooper. Meanwhile, Hawke stood outside the door glaring in at us, looking like he was just returning from an ice fishing trip in his snowmobile bibs, thick black police coat, and furry earflap hat.

"Hello, Cooper," I said loudly, not sure if Hawke could hear us or not.

Cooper cringed slightly. "I can't seem to get used to that smile on you."

"It's good to see you, too," I said, widening my clown-sized grin until my cheeks hurt.

"Is the asshole right behind me?" he said in a quiet voice.

I nodded. "Yes, I do have your offer letter here and ready for your signature." I held up the paperwork. "Have you decided on the official offer amount?"

"Yes, same as we discussed." He settled into the chair opposite my desk, taking off his gloves and stocking cap.

"Wonderful!" I took my seat and turned the fake offer paperwork his way. "Sign where I've indicated and I'll call Freesia.

She's waiting to hear from us."

That was true, but not for the offer to come through. I was supposed to give her Cooper's designated code word to let her know when Hawke was on his way so she could tell all the other monsters to clear out.

Cooper leaned forward and signed. I looked toward the front door. Hawke was huffing and puffing in the cold air. I knew that because I could see the steam blowing out of his big, stupid nose.

When I waved at him, he flipped me off and stormed away. My focus returned to Cooper. "Jeez Louise, the drama with that snollyguster."

"Is he gone?" Cooper asked.

I nodded, collecting the fake paperwork.

"Good. Phase 1 is done."

I smiled for real this time. "And from the sneer wrinkling Hawke's upper lip the whole time you signed the papers, I'd say he bought our story hook, line, and stinker."

"It's *sinker*, Godzilla."

"I know, Kong. It was a play on words. Listen, if we're going to keep working together, you're going to need to understand my sense of humor."

"That's 'King Kong' to you, Parker. And your humor keeps misfiring. It needs a total rebuild. Maybe you should have Natalie coach you on what's funny and what's not."

"Shut up." I crossed my arms. "What's next, Detective Bossypants?"

"You call Freesia with the code word and get them to clear out ASAP."

"You think Hawke will actually get hold of the chief right now or go to the apartment and pout?"

"I don't know, but either way, Reid and Natalie have had long enough to do their reconnaissance."

"You mean Frankenstein and Dracula." When he glared at me in response, I held up my hands. "What? It's *your* uncle who keeps insisting we use our code names."

He sighed, pushing to his feet. "Just make the call, Godzilla."

I pulled my cell phone from my desk drawer. "What comes next?"

"We reconnoiter tonight at supper," he explained, tugging on his hat and gloves. "And find out what they've learned before moving on to Phase 2."

"And what's Phase 2?"

He frowned slightly. "Figuring out how we're going to relocate those clocks to a safehouse right under Hawke's nose."

* * *

The afternoon dragged on and on.

Having to abide by Cooper's no-contact rule made for tedious hours alone, yet again, in the office.

After checking my cell phone for a text from Doc or Harvey or Natalie for the umpteenth time and finding nothing but crickets—undoubtedly because Cooper had told everyone they were not allowed to contact me either, damn him—I stuffed my phone in my purse, folded my arms on my desk, and rested my forehead on them.

I killed several more minutes grumbling about the big bossy ape and then decided to take a meandering stroll around the office to stretch my legs. My walk ended at the front windows, where I stared out at the swirling snow and the occasional plow that passed.

That exercise ate up ten minutes.

On my way back to my desk, I swung by Mona's and grabbed the thesaurus she kept in her top drawer. Plopping in the chair opposite my desk, I fanned through the pages and tried to memorize several new descriptive words I might use the next time Hawke wanted to trade barbs.

Fifteen snail-paced minutes later, I lowered the book and listened for any sounds coming from Cornelius's apartment overhead.

Silence. And then more silence.

Sigh.

Outside of the periodic whirring of heat from the floor vents, there was not a single creak to be heard throughout the building. The Mummy was either upstairs sleeping the afternoon away in his sarcophagus or roaming the cold streets in his sagging bandages, frightening any souls willing to brave the cold. Most likely, he was over at the Old Prospector Hotel, checking on the renovation work being done inside his haunted building.

Speaking of haunted, I peeked down the hall toward Jane's old office, the location where I'd had my last standoff with the ghoul. Doc had said that he and Cornelius hadn't made any connections with the entity when they were back there yesterday afternoon, but that hadn't stopped me from not only closing the office door on my way past it to my desk this morning, but also locking it. Jerry kept the spare door key in his desk in case I needed to go in there, but honestly, short of smoke pouring out from under Jane's office door, I wasn't going to risk stepping a toe in that room.

I glanced up at one of the cameras Cornelius had installed in the corner near the ceiling. The blinking red light comforted me like a closet light on a dark night. Cornelius may not be sitting at his monitors above me, but at least there'd be a recording if shit went sideways again with that freaking ghoul. Or if Jane's ghost made an appearance. I really missed her, along with the comfort of knowing she was floating around the office, watching my back.

Speaking of ghosts … that gave me another idea. I returned to my desk chair and tapped on the keyboard, waking my computer. If I didn't get to sleep at work, neither did it.

With Jerry out of the office, now was a great opportunity to search the internet for any information I could dredge up on Olivia Contraire, Medium Extraordinaire. Even if the cops were to check my browsing history afterward, there'd be nothing suspicious about doing some background investigating on a woman I was stuck dragging along with me and my clients from house to house.

A half hour later, I leaned back in my chair and growled at the ceiling. Nothing. I'd found basically zilch.

Her website was simply a placeholder listing her phone number and a claim to have decades of spirit interaction experience. More searching had led me to another woman with the same name, but the images linked with this particular Olivia were definitely for someone much older who was apparently enjoying a bohemian lifestyle in the south of France. Lucky her!

I gave up on finding fault with Jerry's medium and leaned forward again, scanning the bohemian's pictures as I daydreamed about lollygagging in the French countryside, eating cheese and croissants, and stopping at old manors and medieval castles along the way. My fantasies led me down another internet rabbit hole—

spending the night in a haunted Romanian castle with Doc. This tangent took me in yet another direction including several articles about archaeological treasures being found deep underwater in the Black Sea. I wondered if my brother, Quint, had ever visited that area of the world in his travels as a photojournalist.

The sound of the bells jingling over the front door jerked me back to my duty of holding down the fort.

I looked up from my screen with a happy-sappy real estate agent smile only to find my sister closing the front door behind her.

Speaking of family …

How weird. No, scratch that. I meant how unfortunate.

My smile soured into a scowl. "What are you doing here, Susan?"

She looked as if she were a fashion model filming a commercial for an ultra-hip Swiss ski resort in her black fur hat and boots with a metallic-red puffer parka splitting the difference. With her long, straight dark hair and her even longer legs adorned in charcoal gray ski pants, the image of a black widow spider came to mind minus the venomous fangs.

She sat down on the corner of my desk and pursed her bright red lips in a pout. "Can't a girl just want to spend some quality time bonding with her favorite sister?"

I cringed in anticipation of her fangs making an appearance, like they had during so many of our past interactions. "I'm your only sister."

"That we know of." She pulled off her hat and set it on the corner of my desk. "The way my birth father left Mom high and dry after knocking her up with *moi*, I could have several other half-siblings wandering around the country."

"True."

Susan was the product of my parents' temporary separation when I was very young and my brother was barely out of toddlerhood. In Mom's frustration and depression due to her relationship struggles with my dad, she'd gone to a bar one night, gotten stone drunk, and woken up in the bed of another man. A few weeks later she'd found herself pregnant.

Susan's real dad had been part of the rodeo crowd, traveling the West, sleeping with starstruck buckle bunnies along the way.

He'd wanted nothing to do with raising a kid.

Upon hearing of my mother's plight, my father had returned to her doorstep with flowers and an idea to try their hand at marriage again. He'd offered to adopt the baby—Susan—as his own after she was born. Mom had jumped into his arms that day, and the rest was happy history.

At least that was what Mom liked to tell us. I had a feeling the truth was more complicated, but dawdling too much in the past never did anyone much good. The same went for my history with my sister.

"Why are you really here, Susan? It's too cold for any of your games, so just tell me the truth."

She shrugged. "I brought Addy and Layne home. Aunt Zoe told me you were at work, so I thought I'd drop by and give you the latest goods I have on Rex."

I winced at the sound of my ex's name. "Didn't I tell you to stop trying to dig up dirt on that dickhead? It's not like your findings will remove him from my life. Rex is contracted to work up at the science lab in Lead for another year."

Rex Conner was my kids' biological father. Similar to Susan's dad, Rex had wanted nothing to do with my babies once he'd learned I was pregnant. The jerk had even signed a legal paper stating this way back when. But last fall, he'd shown up here at Calamity Jane Realty out of the clear blue and claimed he needed me to find him a place to live. Hiring me as his agent turned out to be a ruse, though. What he really wanted was to blackmail me into helping him get a work promotion by pretending to be his happy wife and a loving mother to his children.

Yeah right, that would happen when pigs sprouted wings and followed the birds south every winter.

After I'd put my foot down and told Rex where he could shove his happy family fairytale, he'd threatened to tell the kids he was their father. That was a truth bomb I'd rather not drop until they were older and better able to handle the emotions that came with having a dad who wanted nothing to do with them.

Threatening was all he'd done, though. So far. But I didn't doubt he'd come gunning for me as soon as the time was right for him.

This was where Susan came into the picture. Long ago, when

I was pregnant, she'd been screwing around with Rex behind my back. At that time, she'd claimed to have fallen in love with the philanderer, but in the end he'd jilted her, too.

Fast forward to the present. These days, I would like nothing more than to fly Rex to Jupiter and dump him off there; whereas Susan wanted good ol' revenge. With that goal in mind, she was now spying on him. She claimed it was on my behalf, but I was pretty sure she was trying to figure out when was a good time to plant a knife in his back for her own happiness. Metaphorically speaking, of course. Although I wouldn't put it past her to bury the hatchet literally and then flee the country, somehow leaving my fingerprints on the handle.

Susan leaned closer to me, her smile cold and calculating. "Have you considered that if I find something condemning enough on the bastard, I could make your dreams come true by having him kicked out of the Black Hills for good?"

I crossed my arms, staring up at her overplucked eyebrows. They seemed thicker today. Had she gotten new ones tattooed on or … I refocused on the situation at hand. "What's in this for you, Susan?"

Her smile flatlined. "I told you before to quit asking me that. I want to help my sister rid herself of a pesky cockroach for good."

"You didn't used to think of him as a cockroach. You were sure he hung the moon."

She snorted. "It turned out he was hanging up stinky wheels of moldy cheese."

"If this is personal, I don't want you dragging me into the middle of it."

"Of course it's personal, Violet. He fucked over both you and me. There is no way in hell I'm letting him break your children's hearts, too."

In spite of our rot-filled past, I believed she meant that. At least at this moment.

Susan had made it clear from the day my kids were born that she loved them. Although her concept of love was a half bubble off plumb, something I'd told our peace-loving mother repeatedly over the years.

Take that time Susan had tried to involve Addy in a shoplifting spree. It'd taken her a ton of apologies, some community time, and many hours of much-needed therapy to right that wrong.

More recently, Susan had stolen my identity; claimed my kids were hers; married a very rich, very old tycoon named Hooch who lived on an island in the Caribbean; and set me and the kids up as beneficiaries in the old guy's will before he'd keeled over.

Like I'd said—a half bubble off plumb.

That reminded me to ask, "What's going on with the St. Barts situation and Hooch's will?"

She waved me off. "Don't worry about that. I'm on top of it."

"Why do I have trouble believing you?"

"Because you've always been a doubty-puss."

I guffawed. "I've had plenty of good reasons to be."

She sighed. "Let the silly past die. You and I are going to have a bright future together. Especially after I get *our* revenge on Rex for all of the pain he's caused us."

Hmm. There were several things in her speech that gave me pause. "Your fangs are showing, Susan."

She gnashed her teeth at me and then slid off my desk, strolling over to the coffee maker. "Do you want to hear my latest dirt about Rex or not?"

I didn't, but I had a feeling Susan wasn't going to leave me be until she shared. "Okay, spill."

She picked up the coffee carafe and sniffed it, wrinkling her nose. "You actually drink this?"

"Yes, but you don't have to, so set that down and get back over here."

She returned, settling into the chair opposite my desk. "Well, besides those old pictures of you he was hiding," she started.

"Which we already talked about at length and decided that he was probably using them to show his boss that he and I were an item for many years," I finished.

The idea of Rex having my picture on his desk for his coworkers to see made me squirmy, but knowing I was merely a stepping stone to a raise took away any fear factor involved. Mostly, it all made me want to take the imp to his apartment and let Daisy loose on his narcissistic ass.

"I've been talking to some of Rex's coworkers and they all believe that not only is he married with kids, but that his family currently lives in New Mexico."

"What do you mean you've been talking to them? Where?"

She shrugged. "Here and there. That's not important."

"Susan, if Rex sees you in town, he's going to know you're stalking him again."

"I didn't stalk him before."

I raised one eyebrow.

"I just followed him now and then to make sure he was staying healthy." She sniffed, staring down at her fingernails. "And I'm not stupid. I know not to hunt here in your backyard. I simply got access to a list of his fellow scientists and their physical addresses, followed a few of the single males home, waited for the right time, and then casually ran into them out on the town, claiming we'd met at a past work party."

"And that worked for you? I mean, these guys are smart."

"Maybe they are, but they're still males with testosterone running through their veins." She laced her fingers together. "You didn't let me finish the news about Rex."

I waved for her to continue.

"After the third guy told me about Rex's fictional family in New Mexico, I decided to see if he'd gone so far as to list a physical address for his home. He did, and it turns out there is a house there. The title is in his name."

"Okay, so he's been living down there when he's not on location for his job. That's not exactly nitty-gritty news."

"True, but you might find it interesting to know that there is mail going there addressed to a woman named Violet Conner."

I blinked. "Violet?"

Susan nodded. "And here's the kicker. She has two children— a boy and a girl."

"You're kidding me." I sat forward. "Don't tell me they're twins."

"No, the boy is a year older than the girl."

"What are their names? And how in the hell did you find out all of this?"

"You have always underestimated me." She lifted her chin. "I don't know their names yet, but here's my theory. Rex put a backup family in place down in New Mexico to cover his ass in case his plan to manipulate you and the kids up here didn't work."

"That's kooky."

"I have a feeling the deeper I dig, the weirder shit is going to get when it comes to Rex." Susan stood suddenly. "Now, my mission here is accomplished and I'll get out of your hair, which looks very sophisticated secured in that coif today."

I narrowed my gaze, not trusting that compliment due to all her past insults about my curly mess.

"I need to use the restroom before I head back to Rapid."

I pointed toward the hallway. "Down there on your left."

She clomped toward the bathroom, shutting the door behind her. Meanwhile, I sat at my desk wondering what in the hell Rex was up to. Could a promotion really be worth the work of trying to blackmail me *and* setting up a fake family in case I refused to play ball?

Pounding at the front door made me squawk and jump to my feet.

I looked toward the door and found Detective Hawke standing on the other side, his nose pressed against the glass.

What did he want now?

He pointed at me and bellowed, "Don't you think for a minute that you're going to get away with this."

"With what?" I hollered back.

"I'm calling Coop's bluff. He's going to have to put his money where his mouth is."

Jesus, this guy and his threats were getting so old. "Hawke, how about you make like the dung beetle you are and roll away."

His sneer spread farther up his face. "Don't think you can hex your way out of a murder charge, witch." He held up his finger and thumb together in an almost-pinch. "I'm this close to bringing handcuffs along the next time I come to visit."

"Keep your sex toys to yourself." I sat back down, shooing him with my hand. "Now fly away, Hawke, before I put a restraining order on you for harassing me."

He flipped me off and then left in the direction of the police station.

I was still grinding my molars about the asshole's threats when Susan returned a short time later.

"I thought I heard you talking to someone out here." She grabbed her hat off my desk.

"Oh. Yeah. It was just someone passing by who wanted to

shoot the shit."

I would like to shoot Hawke-the-shit in the ass with a BB gun, given half the chance.

"I guess that's one of the nice things about a small town. I mean, if you like being friendly." She pulled on her hat. "Let me know if there is anything else you want me to do to help out, big sis." At my glare spurred by her use of an old insult about my size, she winced and corrected, "I mean just 'sis.' "

"Why?"

"I could use some more brownie points with the parents."

At least she was being honest about that.

Then it hit me. Hawke had no idea who Susan was. She was totally off his radar, unlike the rest of us monsters. And that meant …

Ta da! We had our Invisible Man—or rather Invisible Woman, in this case.

"Actually, Susan," I said, watching her put on her gloves. "I just might have a job for you."

CHAPTER FOURTEEN

I had a gut feeling the news about my choice for our final monster member was going to go over like a bloated hippo, especially with Natalie, who'd been avenging me for Susan's injustices for decades. To reduce my exposure to the initial uproar from my fellow monsters, I sent a message to the whole crew before leaving work, saying that I'd cast my sister to play the role of Invisible Man in our monster mash "play," careful to use obscure wording just to be safe.

After dropping that bomb, I pocketed my phone, locked up the back door at Calamity Jane's, and hurried to my SUV. Even though I'd rather give everyone a good hour or so to stomp and holler about my announcement, it was too damned cold and blustery to drag my feet. How Cooper had managed to stand outside long enough to argue with Hawke earlier without turning into a human glacier was a testament to the fire now lit within the big angry ape. Or maybe he was just too damned hard-headed to freeze.

My cell phone began to ping as I settled in behind the steering wheel. During the short drive to Aunt Zoe's, it didn't stop pinging either. Winning pinball machines made less commotion. I didn't bother to check the phone. I could imagine well enough what was being written in all capital letters with an overzealous use of exclamation marks.

I pulled into Aunt Zoe's drive and took a look around, determining who was waiting inside by the vehicles present. Natalie's rig was missing and so was Harvey's. That meant Cooper was most likely not present yet, thank the law dog gods! But

Cornelius was a wild card, same as he'd been since that fateful day long ago when he'd first walked into Calamity Jane Realty and told me he wanted to buy something haunted.

I shut off the engine and sat still for a few deep breaths, mentally refueling my tank of gumption before facing the storm of questions and reactions waiting for me inside.

Was I crazy to include Susan in this caper? A little. Maybe a lot. But I was more desperate than I was nuts. When it came down to it, I needed access to those clocks to keep my family alive. Danger loomed closer every day I sat on my hands and waited for Hawke to let me inside that apartment. Desperate times called for moments of temporary insanity, and in that way, adding Susan made sense.

I rushed up the sidewalk to the front porch, my shoulders hunched in the cold darkness. A glance toward the yard where the mule deer head had been left for me last night found only snow, no blood or other body parts. The constant wind throughout the day must have blown snow over last night's mess, plus Cooper had done a bang-up job of covering up the crime.

Doc opened the front door before I could reach for it, ushering me inside. I could see from the vertical lines between his dark eyes that he'd read my message. He helped me take off my coat, leaning down to whisper in my ear, "This could be a very bad idea."

Why was he whispering?

I heard a high-pitched laugh come from the living room and then remembered that Susan dropped my kids at home before stopping by Calamity Jane's.

Got it—little ears were back and listening.

I focused on tugging off my snow boots rather than holding his gaze. "If the bad idea you're referring to is Reid being in charge of supper tonight, that was Aunt Zoe's doing."

He waited for me to set aside my boots and look up at him. "How do we know we can truly trust your sister?"

"We don't. She and I probably should've sliced our palms and made a blood pact, but I always worry about an infection setting in on those sort of hand cuts. Not to mention that Lord only knows what pathogens are living in Susan's bloodstream after some of the partners she's bedded. You know, sometimes I wonder if she's even human."

"Violet, quit stalling."

I cringed. "That obvious, huh?"

"I'm worried about this addition." His serious expression made that clear. "What if ..."

Before he could finish, Addy and Layne ran in from the living room and wrapped me in hugs, both bouncing and shouting with excitement.

I took a moment to breathe them in, soaking up their much-needed love and smiles, and then I kissed each on the forehead. They smelled a little like cookies, which had me wondering how much my parents had sweetened them up over the last couple of days. Was sugar oozing out of their pores, for crissakes?

"How was your pre-birthday weekend with Grammy and Grandpa?"

"Grandpa went down the big water slide with us like ten times," Layne said, his hazel eyes sparkling. His dark blond hair hung partway over his eyes, reminding me it was time to schedule a haircut. "Then he hurt his back a little and took a break while we kept swimming."

"Yeah, and guess what?" Addy cried, her dimples deepened as her smile grew even bigger. "Grammy let us have ice cream and cake every night!"

That might explain why she was still bouncing, which was making her straight blond hair stick out all over. The static gremlins had gotten the best of both of us today.

Both kids continued to talk a mile a minute about all the fun they'd had with my parents. I kept up as best I could, smiling in spite of my clock caper, decapitated deer head, and invisible handprint troubles here at home. Their joy was infectious, but holy jumping *frijoles*, it might take a gallon of warm milk to get them both to sleep at a decent time tonight.

"It sounds like you might be all partied out now," I teased. "Should we skip having more birthday fun this weekend?"

"No!" they cried in unison.

Doc chuckled, although worry still lined his face. "Good, because I really need a party about now." His gaze met mine over their heads. "Your mom could use one, too."

"Addy and Layne," Aunt Zoe said from the kitchen archway,

a wooden stirring spoon in her hand. "Did you two finish unpacking your bags like I asked?"

They both suddenly found their socks very interesting.

"That's what I thought." Aunt Zoe pointed the spoon toward the ceiling. "Head upstairs and unpack. Dirty clothes go in the hamper. Supper will be ready soon."

They took off up the stairs, stocking feet pounding all the way to their rooms.

I grinned at Aunt Zoe. She looked comfy in her green flannel shirt and blue jeans, although a tad flushed. "You'd think they were small rhinos."

She pointed the spoon at me. "Did you slip on the ice and hit your head today, Violet Lynn?"

I touched my forehead for no reason. "No, why?"

"Because I can't think of any other explanation for why you would even consider including your sister in our caper."

I held up my right hand. "My rationale is solid, I swear."

"Oh, really?" At my single nod, she pointed the spoon behind her. "Then get your buns in here and explain your whys and wherefores to the rest of us." She spun on her heel and returned to the kitchen.

Who was "the rest of us," I wondered, hesitant to follow if the room was full of angry locals with torches and pitchforks. But then my stomach growled.

I turned to Doc. "What's for supper? It smells like hamburgers and French fries."

"Reid is making a cheeseburger and potato casserole."

"Oh my. That sounds wonderful." I glanced down at my work clothes. "Before I join you guys, I want to change into something looser."

"Okay, but first I need this." Doc caught my arm and pulled me in for a hug that warmed me clear to my toes. Then he eased back slightly. "Your announcement lit several fires, Killer."

"I know." I reached up and cupped his face with both hands, his short beard tickling my palms. He was my rock. I needed his trust more than any of the others. "I have a good reason for including Susan. Once I explain, you'll see why I asked her to help."

"If you say so." He tucked a loose curl behind my ear. "But

based on her history, you're dooming yourself to walk the plank simply by inviting her aboard."

"Ohhh, pirate talk!" I went up on my toes and kissed him. I tasted lemonade on his lips and went back for more. His return kiss steamed the cockles of my heart and filled me up with home-safe-home. "Ahoy, matey," I said when I came up for a breath. "String up the imp and hoist the sails. We have our heading!"

He winked and then turned me toward the stairway. "Go get changed, ya lusty wench, before I toss you over my shoulder and cart you up to our room where I can plunder yer wares without interruption."

"Why are you two talking about Mom's *underwears?*" Addy asked from the top of the stairs. She held Elvis tucked under her arm. Meanwhile, Daisy peeked at us from behind Addy's back. Both the chicken and imp were wearing sweaters my mom had crocheted for the bird—red for Elvis and pink for the imp.

"Because she has very pretty *underwears,*" Doc answered. Laughter edged his tone.

I aimed a wrinkled brow his way. What was he doing?

"I think so, too!" Addy said, bouncing a little on her toes. "My favorite are her purple flowery ones that match her bra. Which ones are yours?"

Don't! I mouthed to Doc and poked him in the chest. His grin was near bursting as he rubbed his hand over his beard.

I returned to my daughter. "That's enough about my underwear, Adelynn Renee. Are you done unpacking?"

"Yep." She came down the stairs still holding Elvis. The imp hopped down step-by-step after her, muttering something repetitive under its breath. "Mom, did you know that Daisy is potty trained?"

I met her at the bottom step. "No, I didn't." To be honest, I hadn't even given the imp's bathroom needs a thought.

"I think she's trying to potty train Elvis, too."

That painted quite a picture in my head, including an abundance of flotsam made up of feathers and toilet paper. "You witnessed this?"

Addy nodded. "I just caught the two of them in the bathroom taking turns on the toilet."

I looked back at Doc. "You ever heard of a potty-trained

chicken?"

He was still grinning. "No, but you Parker women keep teaching me new things every day." He held out his hand to Addy. "Come on, kid. Let's take your pals down to the basement and then we'll wash our hands for supper."

Addy hurried past me to grab Doc's hand.

I watched the four of them walk toward the kitchen. Doc must be assuming the imp was with Addy, unless he could see the pink sweater floating in the air. I doubted that, though. In the past, he'd not been able to see anything Daisy had on. It was as if the imp's ability to hide in plain sight included anything it touched, which seemed more like a magic trick to me than some supernatural power.

Magic—used that way, was the word spelled the old way? Or was it *magick* with a *k*? I sighed, deciding to leave the task of spelling to Cookie Monster over on *Sesame Street*.

Taking the stairs two at a time up to my bedroom, I pushed thoughts of the imp and Susan aside to focus on Reid's casserole. I could smell the cheese all the way up in my room, and I was feeling positively drooly about my immediate future.

A few minutes later, I was in the midst of pulling one of Doc's big sweatshirts over my head when my bedroom door flew open, banging against the door stop.

I gasped and poked my head out of the neckline like a turtle in time to see Natalie march inside. She closed the door behind her and leaned against it. Her dark pink cheeks matched her overalls, except for the white paint splotches. I'd have said she looked cute if her face wasn't so pinched and her eyes weren't blasting lasers at me.

"What in the hell are you thinking, woman?" she asked, crossing her arms with a huff.

I knew she was talking about including my sister in our caper, but I tried to throw some water on the fire in her eyes. "Well, I figured I'd be eating a lot of that casserole Reid is making, so I wanted to put on the loosest clothing I could get my hands on. I don't want anything getting in the way of stuffing my belly clear to the top."

Her nostrils flared. "You know damned well I'm talking about the Bitch from Hell. Don't tell me that you've gone soft on Susan after years of her screwing you over every chance she had. I mean, Christ, the dust hasn't even settled on her stealing your identity and leaving you tangled up in that dead guy's will."

I rolled up the sleeves on Doc's sweatshirt. "I know."

"Is it because she's taking your side against Rex? You do realize she's actually focused on revenge because that asshole won't take her back and she's feeling jilted again."

"Yes, I do."

She stepped away from the door and began pacing from the window to my dresser and back. "For the life of me, I cannot think of one single reason why you would trust Satan's concubine enough to include her in this caper."

I opened my mouth to explain, but she cut me off.

"Unless Corny's pendulum pal was right."

"You mean Edith?"

She nodded, pausing in front of the window.

"Right about what?"

She held her index finger up in the air. "Maybe you have been possessed by the ghoul. That's why Edith didn't give a clear answer when it came to you and spun in a circle instead. Something else has taken over your brain. That would explain why you'd even consider for a moment asking Susan for help after putting up with decades of her abuse." She turned to me, stepping closer, her eyes narrowed. "If you really are Violet Parker, prove it."

I scoffed, holding out my hands. "How would I prove that I'm me? I mean, if something is possessing me, wouldn't it have access to my memories?"

"Possibly." She chewed on her lower lip. "There has to be some test to find out if you are the one truly running things up here." She knuckle-knocked on my head.

I shoved her hand away. "You're being silly. I'm not possessed."

Her gaze was still squinty as she looked down over Doc's sweatshirt and my yoga pants. "Have you been feeling cold a lot lately?"

"Of course. There's a polar vortex outside and this is an old house. My skin looks like a plucked chicken's day and night."

"Are there any additional new voices in your head?"

"What do you mean *voices*? There is only one voice in my head, not multiples, and it's the same one I've always had."

She leaned forward and sniffed in my direction. "You smell the same."

I pulled the sweatshirt collar up and sniffed inside. There was a hint of my cherry vanilla lotion scent along with Doc's cologne.

"Have you smelled anything weird lately?" she asked.

I scowled at her. "Yeah, I smell you, pigpen. You're ripe with paint fumes. Now stop with this weird dog-style greeting and let's go eat."

She followed me out the bedroom door. "I just don't get why you would trust Susan for even a second."

"I'll explain my thinking after we eat when the kids are getting ready for bed."

"Fine." She hesitated at the top of the stairs. "But if that bitch pulls one of her usual stunts and we end up in jail, I reserve the right to knuckle-rub a bald spot on your curly coconut."

"Deal." I continued down, reaching the bottom stair at the same time the front door opened.

Cooper walked in, took one look at me, and snarled, "What in the hell are you thinking, Parker?"

"Jinx!" Natalie said, sliding past me to join his side and drop a kiss on his cheek. "It's crazy, right?" she said to him. "I think Vi's possessed," she added in a loud stage whisper.

"Who's possessed?" Layne asked from behind me.

We all watched him come down the stairs.

"Your mom is," Natalie said, giving him a sideways hug when he reached our level. "She was like a totally different person when you and Addy were gone, always whining and teary eyed because she missed you so much. Now look at her."

Layne stared up at me, shaking his head as if I had a sad, hopeless case of snuffle-itis. "Mom always wants a bunch of kisses after we get back from being gone, even if it's just for a single night."

"I know," Natalie grinned at me. "She's plumb bonkers. You'd think that one smooch was enough, but not for her."

"Hey, Coop," Layne said to the bristling law dog now focused on taking off his snow boots. "Are you coming to our birthday party next weekend?"

"I'm planning to." He shot me a withering glance. "I could do with some celebrating these days. Your mom has been extra tough on me while you were gone. It's a good thing you're home to take the heat off me."

I wrinkled my nose at him.

"Was she sore headed all the time about us being gone?" Layne asked.

"Yep. Imagine Godzilla with crazy curly hair, waking up too early on the wrong side of his bed and stepping on little Panzer tanks and Apache helicopters all the way to the john. That's been your mom."

"Really?" Layne frowned up at me. "Poor Doc. We shouldn't have left him alone with her."

I scoffed and then sputtered and then snorted, ending with a growl.

Cooper patted Layne's shoulder. "Your mom is having one of her episodes. How about you head into the kitchen and save us a couple of seats next to each other at the table?"

"You bet! I'll go pick out our chairs now."

Layne raced out of the room, leaving me alone to face the big ape's chest-beating routine again.

"Cooper, I'm gonna shove a bunch of bananas where the sun doesn't shine on you."

Natalie laughed. "Ohh, that sounds kinky. I like it."

"You're all hat and no hogs, Parker."

"He's got you there, Vi."

I wasn't sure what that meant exactly, but I got the gist. "Wrong! I'm all hogs, dammit."

Natalie laughed again. "You tell him, girl!"

"Including your sister is too damned dicey, Parker."

I nodded. "There are certain risks, to be sure."

"So many risks," Natalie said, piling it on thicker.

"You should have talked to me first," he said.

Natalie nodded. "And me, too."

"Why?" I said to Cooper. "So you could sing a long-winded, chin-music solo listing all the reasons not to include her?"

"Coop can talk the ears off a mule when he gets rolling," Natalie said, smacking him on the butt.

He frowned at her for a moment before continuing his rant with me. "You can't pull off a caper without proper planning, and introducing an outsider into the mix without running it past the rest of the team first is a rookie mistake."

"I went with my gut."

"That was clearly a case of indigestion," Natalie said.

I turned to her. "Whose side are you on, *best friend?*"

Pursing her lips, she shrugged. "Partly yours, but I'm sleeping with Coop, so a bit of both."

Cooper crossed his arms. "You do realize that all it takes is a single fuckup by any one of us and this whole house of cards will come crashing down."

I groaned, looking to the heavens for help. "I heard you the first time you told me that this morning after breakfast, and the second time at work when I finished my call with Freesia. So, yeah, I get it."

"Then why would you take a chance on including someone with a criminal history?"

Before I could answer that, the door opened behind Cooper. The three of us stepped aside to make room for Harvey, who was followed by Cornelius. Both were sprinkled with snow dust. They must have gotten caught at the wrong end of a gust.

Harvey pulled off his fur-lined trapper hat and then paused, looking from one of us to the next. His bushy eyebrows shot upward. "What's goin' on here? You three havin' some kind of secret meetin'?"

I shook my head.

"Are Zoe and Reid at it again in the kitchen?" he asked.

"No, but Layne is in there. And maybe Addy, too." I wasn't sure if Doc and she had returned topside or not.

Harvey nodded once, unbuttoning his thick coat. "Gotcha. It's a roundup for tall pockets only."

"Something like that," Cooper said, casting another squinty-eyed glance my way.

Cornelius pulled off his Cossack hat and sniffed the air. "That smells like a cheeseburger and potato casserole."

I gaped at him. How in the hell could he … Never mind. If I asked, he'd probably tell me Edith the stone had told him.

Harvey kicked off his boots onto the throw rug. "What exactly was it you three were tryin' to lasso before Corny and I got here?"

Natalie gave me a sideways frown. "What in the hell Vi was

thinking by inviting her sister to join the caper."

"Ahh." Harvey unwrapped his striped scarf. "Susan might be a li'l on the wily side, but I can see two perky points as to why she'd be a help with those clocks."

Two perky points? Ugh. "Listen, dirty bird, if you're going to start waxing on about her chest again, then—"

"Nope." He cut me off.

"What two points?" Cooper prodded.

"Firstly, I was referrin' partly to her long legs."

Cooper guffawed. "What do her legs have to do with this?"

"Nothin', but I'm sure gonna enjoy watchin' her strut her stuff." Harvey quirked an eyebrow. "Was she wearing tight pants when she paid you a visit?"

"Of course," I said, my upper lip wrinkling on its own accord. "She came out of the womb wearing painted-on pants and a low-cut top, I swear."

He grinned "Well, that alone wins her my vote for the Invisible Man position."

Natalie poked him in the shoulder. "So her legs were your two points?"

"Nope, just one. The other is her ability to lie without blinkin' an eye. Sparky was right. We need someone like that on the roster."

Cooper shook his head. "I still don't like it."

"What do you think about including Vi's sister?" Natalie asked Cornelius.

He unbuttoned his coat. "Is this the sister who had me confused for Violet's partner in coitus?"

I cringed. "I only have one sister, Cornelius, and you know that."

He shrugged. "What is her favorite color?"

"Black, I think," Natalie said. "Same as her soul."

"Does she have any abnormal birthmarks?"

Natalie and I exchanged frowns. "I can't remember any," I answered for the two of us.

"What does any of this have to do with her ability to help nab some clocks?" Cooper asked.

"You would be surprised." Cornelius handed his coat to me, as if I were his butler. "What's her zodiacal sign?"

"She's a Gemini." I handed his coat to Natalie, who tossed it over the stair rail.

"Ah, the twins." He nodded. "At their best, Geminis can be witty, fun, and enthusiastic."

"See," I said to Cooper and Natalie. "Nothing wrong with that."

"But," Cornelius continued, "they can also have a duplicitous twin."

Natalie nodded. "I knew it. A dark and evil twin in Susan's case."

"How dark and evil are we talkin'?" Harvey asked. "Like Elvira, Mistress of the Dark, kind of sexy with just a smidgeon of evil possibilities that get your blood flowin'?"

Cornelius stroked his pointy goatee. "I would say more like your garden variety of compulsive liars and back stabbers, with a complete lack of empathy and a tendency toward manipulation and impetuous behaviors that often wreak havoc and leave chaos in their wake."

"Oh, Christ," Cooper muttered. "I'm getting a beer." He pointed at me. "You had better have a damned good reason for exposing this operation to that much jeopardy."

"Trust me, Cooper."

His gaze narrowed to a tight squint. "We'll see."

Harvey rubbed his hands together. "Listen, you chatterbugs can stand here grousin' all night about the pros and cons of Sparky's sister, but my stomach is ringin' the dinner bell, so let's move this lynchin' to the kitchen."

CHAPTER FIFTEEN

Reid's casserole knocked my socks off. Why on earth Aunt Zoe would want to keep a man at arm's length who could cook finger-licking food was a mystery to me. I whispered as much to her during dishwashing after supper, earning an elbow in my side along with "Hush, Violet Lynn!" under her breath.

Doc returned from taking the kids upstairs so they could get ready for bedtime. "I recommend you get a new toothbrush," he said to me as he took a seat at the table with everyone else.

"Why?" I grabbed a towel from the drawer to dry my hands. "Mine isn't that worn out yet."

He was fighting a grin. I could see it tickling the corners of his lips. "I caught Addy brushing the air with it. Turned out it wasn't the air after all—it was the imp's teeth."

I groaned. "Damn it."

His grin surfaced. "She wanted Daisy's breath to smell minty clean."

"Are we sure she hasn't brushed the critter's teeth before?" Harvey asked, snickering.

"Well," Doc said, frowning my way. "Addy *said* this was the first time."

"Yeah, but she's a kid." Harvey leaned back in his chair. "Kids act before they think. Then they talk a blue streak to keep from gettin' in trouble." He pointed at me. "Maybe you and that imp have been sharin' slobber for longer than ya know."

I gagged a little.

Doc grimaced at me. "How many times have I kissed you since the imp moved in?"

"You might want to start gargling with bleach," Reid told Doc, laughing as he lifted his bottle of beer.

I dropped into the chair next to Doc. "Why does she always use *my* stuff?"

"Because you're her mother," Aunt Zoe said, stashing the clean plates in the cupboard.

Natalie loaded up a spoonful of ice cream from her bowl. "She's probably getting you back for not letting her have any ice cream for dessert."

"Did you see how she couldn't stop squirming while she ate? That kid is packed to the tips of her ears with sugar from a weekend of being spoiled by my doting parents."

Cooper draped his arm over the back of Natalie's chair. "Godzilla is such a mean mom."

"What flavor of ice cream did you say this is?" Cornelius asked while drizzling chocolate syrup on his full bowl.

He should add some honey like I had. It didn't take much, just a couple of dollops on the single scoop I'd dished up as soon as the kids were headed upstairs. It'd made the ice cream taste extra sweet and delicious.

"Just plain vanilla," Aunt Zoe said, returning to the table with a mug of hot ginger tea.

"I prefer Mexican vanilla to all the others." Cornelius capped the chocolate syrup. "It's bolder. Spicy and smokey. But too much gives me a little heartburn."

Harvey guffawed. "That sounds like Sparky's sister."

"Speaking of," Cooper said, focusing on me. "We're still waiting on your explanation for asking an outsider to help get the clocks without first going through the proper channels."

I shrugged. "We needed someone Hawke doesn't know. Someone who can be whatever we want—whether it be a distracting flirt or a total stranger. Susan fits that bill."

"And then some," Harvey added with a nod.

"We're talking about the same Susan I met at Christmas, right?" Reid asked Aunt Zoe.

"The one and only." She turned to me. "An anonymous identity is a beneficial qualification in this case, but we all know Susan's résumé is littered with deception and manipulation."

Natalie raised her beer to that. "The queen of lies," she

muttered before taking a sip.

Cooper glanced her way. "Trusting a criminal is always a bad idea."

"Try to take a step back and consider Susan's lies and scams from a Hollywood point of view," I said, glancing around the table. "You guys have to agree that if we need an actress to play any part during this caper, she has the legs to pull it off, more so than any of the rest of us."

"I'll say!" Harvey hooted. "Her legs go *allll* the way up."

I threw my napkin at the randy old owl before turning to Doc. "Can we trust her?" I repeated his earlier question. "We won't know without giving her the chance to prove otherwise."

"What if she plays turncoat on us?" Natalie leaned forward, her expression earnest. "You have to admit that if she's out to get the ultimate revenge on you, putting you behind bars for good is a great start."

"She won't do that to me."

"How can you be so sure?" she pressed.

"Because Susan is seeking Violet's admiration and approval," Cornelius answered for me, pointing his ice cream spoon at the jar of butterscotch topping across the table. "Could somebody pass that, please?"

"And my parents' approval," I added, a little surprised that Cornelius had picked up on my sister's aspirations without actually being at Calamity Jane's earlier today when Susan had stopped in. Then again, he did have cameras placed around the office. Maybe he'd reviewed the recordings before coming to supper.

Aunt Zoe nodded slowly. "It all makes sense. Her identity theft swindle fully broke your parents' trust in her, and Susan knows that."

Doc took my hand in his, running his thumb over my knuckles. "Didn't she tell you at Christmas that many of her past offenses were basically to get your attention?"

"Something like that."

She'd actually said I'd treated her differently than I did our brother. That I didn't adore her like I had Quint, hating her instead. But my animosity was only because she kept screwing me over and destroying my stuff.

"How do we know that she wasn't just showering you in more

bullshit at the time?" Natalie asked.

"There is always a chance she's playing another game with me, but like I said, we need someone Hawke doesn't know."

Harvey slapped the table. "As sure as a snake slithers, Susan is a good Invisible Man." He scooted back from the table. "Now, I need to go water the flowers."

After he left the room, Doc asked, "How much did you tell Susan about what we're up to?"

"Barely even this much." I pinched my finger and thumb together. "I told her I needed her help with relocating some important cargo, and if she did as I requested without making a mess, I'd let Mom and Dad know that she'd made amends for her wrongdoings. That I'd forgiven her."

Aunt Zoe let out a low whistle. "Wow, you really pushed all of your chips to the center of the table on this hand."

"I had to go all in." Lowering my voice, I added, "We need those clocks before whatever boogeyman left those bloody presents on our doorstep returns with more gruesome gifts for the kids to find this time."

Natalie grunted. "So, you're willing to sell your soul for Susan's help?"

"More like rent it out." I looked at the ceiling, where I could hear thumps now and then thanks to my children, and then returned to her. "When it comes down to it, keeping Addy and Layne safe is worth whatever it takes, including wiping the slate clean on Susan's past bullshittery."

The same went for putting up with Prudence's abuse in order to possibly find out why Doc could see a hand mark on me and the imp in the mirror. I prayed there weren't marks on the kids, too. My heart had thudded extra hard every time that worry had resurfaced throughout the day.

"Okay, Killer." Doc leaned over and dropped a quick kiss on my temple. "Susan gets my vote, too."

"Same here," Aunt Zoe said, frowning toward the ceiling.

Reid nodded as well. "If Zo's in, I'm in."

Her frown lowered to him. "Nobody likes an ass kisser, Martin."

"If memory serves me right, Zo ..." He let his words trail off and winked at her, and then laughed when she threatened him with her fist.

"I'm in," Natalie said. "I'm pissed off about it and will be waiting for Susan to screw us over somehow, but I'm in."

Harvey had already agreed with me, so that left Cornelius and Cooper.

"You okay with this, Cornelius?" I asked, watching him stir his ice cream and syrups together.

"Sure." He took a bite of the ice cream soup. "So long as you promise me that if we end up in the Deadwood jail, we'll hold a séance to chat up the ghost living there."

I cringed. I'd never live that down with the local cops. "Fine. Deal."

"That leaves you, Coop," Doc said.

Cooper squinted from Doc to me. "Parker, you're telling me that your sister signed on to this job without knowing the details?"

"Yes." I held up my right hand. "I swear, all I told her was that I'd be in touch soon with instructions."

He sat back in his chair, his squint easing. "Then I guess we'll see if she can deliver when needed. But if this goes south because of her, you're going to pay."

"How?" Natalie asked. "She'll be in prison. We might be, too."

"I don't know." His steely gaze stayed locked on me. "Maybe I'll write her a letter every day reminding her how she fucked things up."

"Aww." I turned to Doc. "Cooper just said he'd be my prison pen pal. Isn't that sweet?"

Doc grinned across the table. "It almost brings a tear to my eye, Coop."

"Come closer, Nyce. I'll bring a couple more tears to both of your eyes."

"I'm jealous," Reid said, sticking out his lower lip. "All I ever get from Coop are police reports. I want a love letter, too."

Cooper huffed and turned to Natalie. "You see what doing those damned happy-brain drills gets me? Nothing but smartass comments from these knuckleheads. I'm going back to being pissed off and grumbly."

"At what point did you stop?" I asked, earning a glare from Detective McGrumbles.

Natalie hooked her arms around his neck and nuzzled his

cheek. "It's all out of our love for you, hot cop."

He scoffed, but smiled a little as he reached for his beer.

I glanced back and forth between Reid and Natalie. "Okay, now it's Frankenstein's and Dracula's turn. What did you find in Ms. Wolff's apartment during your inspection? Did either of you see any ticking clocks that had a scene similar to what we found out front? Something with a decapitated head of some beast? Or one with a monster wearing a funky-looking hat like the one that had been pinned to the porch beam?"

"Or carrying a seax?" Doc asked.

"No, but there were so many clocks," Natalie said.

"And too little time," Reid added. "We were only supposed to be in there for an inspection, and the cop out front had checked his watch right before we went inside."

"I focused on counting first and foremost," Natalie explained. "I figured that was the most important detail needed for the caper."

"Same here," Reid said. "But I kept finding myself distracted by the craftsmanship on each clock. The amount of detailed carved into the wood is incredible."

Natalie nodded. "I didn't even think to pay attention to which ones were ticking until we were on our way back out."

Dang it. I understood the situation, but finding a clock belonging to this latest bounty hunter was the main reason I had wanted to go along instead of being stuck at work.

"How many clocks?" Aunt Zoe asked.

"We counted eighty-nine," Reid said. "Natalie told me some have gone missing."

Only eighty-nine?

"Back when I first met Freesia," I told them, "she said there were one hundred and thirteen clocks in that apartment. At least I think that was the number."

"So, twenty-four have been removed," Doc said.

"Where are the missing clocks?" Reid wondered.

"Did Hawke remove some?" Aunt Zoe asked Cooper.

He shrugged. "He may have, but I don't remember him talking about taking any himself, only harping that Parker was stealing them somehow. That's what spurred him to move into the apartment and lock down the place."

"Mr. Black took some," I said, remembering something about him needing certain clocks to "keep the balance."

"Where the missing ones have gone is not important right now," Natalie said, tapping her index finger on the table. "How in the hell are we going to sneak eighty-nine clocks out of that place? Some of them are smaller, but that's still a lot of clocks to move without someone seeing us."

"Or realizing they are gone," Cooper added.

"We're going to need a big movin' truck," Harvey said, rejoining the conversation as he slid into his seat at the table.

Doc shook his head. "There's no way we can sneak that past Hawke and his 24/7 police monitoring crew. Willis and I had enough trouble keeping the officer distracted today for a short time so he didn't follow Martin and Natalie inside."

"We have to get Hawke to move out of the apartment first," Aunt Zoe said.

Natalie scowled. "That could take weeks with the way he drags his feet on everything."

"And his knuckles," I added. "But Cooper has the Neanderthal thinking there's an offer for Galena House on the table now, so he can't dally too long."

"You should have seen him tonight," Natalie said. "Stomping around the place, pissed off and grumbling."

"How could you *see* him?" Cooper asked her. "Was he out in the hall?"

"Uh, yeah." She took a quick swallow of her beer. "I peeked down at him when he wasn't looking." Her bottle of beer wobbled when she set it down too quickly. "And I could hear him later through the vent."

She'd better be careful with that hidden camera. Cooper the bloodhound had a way of sniffing out criminal activity.

Then again, I had a feeling he'd met his match with her.

"Maybe two big-ass movin' trucks." Harvey leaned over to frown at Cornelius's dessert bowl. "What in tarnation did you do to your ice cream?"

"Parker and I can't be seen near that apartment," Cooper reminded all of us. "Even after Hawke's moved out."

"Right," I said. "So, we need to remove eighty-nine clocks within a short time without letting Hawke know we're involved."

"But how do we get the clocks in our possession without bonking him on the head and giving him amnesia so he won't go pointing fingers at Sparky or Coop?" Reid asked.

Aunt Zoe looked up from sipping her tea. "I do have a nice bat."

Reid shot a grin her way. "I said 'without' doing that."

"It's simple, really," Cornelius said in between spoonfuls of ice cream soup.

"Simple?" Cooper asked, his lined forehead showing his doubt about that notion. "Explain, Curion."

Cornelius's cornflower blue eyes shifted to me. "Violet, before I agreed to be part of this caper, do you remember what I asked?"

I chewed on my lower lip. "I remember you talking about stealing a brain."

"Come again?" Doc said, coughing out a chuckle.

Cooper crossed his arms. "There will absolutely be no brain stealing."

"Not that." Cornelius dipped his spoon in for more. "We can remove the clocks from under the detective's nose simply by employing a sleight of hand trick."

* * *

Monday, February 11th

My morning started out dark and shocking. The former due to the gloomy winter veil Mother Nature had draped over the Hills. The latter thanks to the sight of my hair hopped up on static electricity yet again. Pillowcase friction plus extra dry air equaled a headful of clown frizz for me. I might as well grab a red squeaker nose and call it good.

My cell phone pinged right before I stepped into the shower. The text was from Jerry. Apparently, his extraordinary medium was back for the day, and since I was the only one with clients scheduled, Madame Contraire would be riding along with me again.

"Lucky ducky me," I muttered, sending back a thumbs-up message. Then I covered my phone with a towel so I didn't have to look at it anymore and hopped into the hot shower to drown my clown hair into submission.

Doc and the kids were downstairs eating breakfast when I hurried into the kitchen a half hour later dressed in warm wool slacks and a long knit cardigan sweater. I was more concerned about keeping from freezing to death today rather than getting decked out for any kind of stylish success.

The kids were still in their pajamas, but Doc looked ready for work in dark pants and a button-up blue shirt. He must be skipping the gym today—or had already gone and returned.

"Morning, guys," I said, making a beeline for the coffee maker. I grabbed a travel cup from the cupboard. "Where's Aunt Zoe?"

"She ate earlier and is on her way to Rapid City to deliver that glass order." Doc joined me at the counter with milk for my coffee.

He smelled fresh from the shower, which conjured cheek-warming memories of the last time I'd stepped under the spray of hot water with him and my loofah sponge. Maybe I should tell Jerry I was going to be late and suggest Doc come home after dropping off the kids and join me for another round of back sponging. And front.

"She told me to let you know she's going to stop by your parents' place for lunch." He continued in a lower voice. "You are to let her know if you need her to give any instructions to your sister on the clock situation."

The caper, right. I nodded, blinking away my shower daydreams to focus on reality's weighty to-do list. "I'm running a little late. Jerry called and wants me to come in early. Can you drop the kids off at school?"

"Of course." He crossed his arms, leaning against the counter. "Any special reason you have to be in early?"

I wrinkled my upper lip. "More like a special person."

"Who?" he asked under his breath.

"A certain madame will be joining me again."

He groaned.

"That was my reaction, too."

I glanced at the table to see if the kids were tuned in to us, as they often tended to be when I least wanted them listening in on what I was saying. In the process, I noticed Arcana, the mirror, sitting out next to the dog and cat dishes.

Had the imp made an appearance for Doc this morning? Or

had Aunt Zoe put the mirror there before she left? Was Daisy still sporting the hand mark? Was I?

A whimpering sound near the basement door caught my attention.

I looked over and noticed Rooster sitting with his ears perked. As I watched, he glanced toward the mirror, letting out a whimper or two, then turned away.

Had he caught sight of the imp in the mirror earlier and hadn't liked what he'd seen? If so, I couldn't blame the dog. Not even a pink chicken sweater could make Daisy easier on the eyes. Maybe a wig and lipstick would help. I wouldn't be surprised if Addy tried that on for size next.

Crap. I'd better hide my tubes of lipstick and gloss, along with my new toothbrush, before heading to work.

Rooster stood, eased over to the mirror, and barked at it.

"Rooster," Layne called. "What's wrong, buddy?"

He barked once more at his reflection and then scurried into the dining room as if something had snarled back.

I stared at the mirror. Maybe it had. Or whatever was on the other side of the glass had. I shuddered at that dark thought and returned to Doc, asking, "What was that about?"

"Beats me. But he's been acting off since I let him out to take a leak this morning."

"Hmm." Putting worries about the dang dog aside, I leaned closer to Doc and went up on my toes for a kiss. "How about I give you some sugar as thanks for feeding the kids?"

"Sugar from you is my favorite." He met me halfway, warming my lips. "You even smell sweet," he whispered against my cheek as his kiss slid sideways. "I'll be back for more later."

"Gross, you two!" Layne complained. "Us guys are trying to eat here, you know."

"I think it's nice," Addy said, smiling at Doc and me as she reached for her glass of milk. "Mom was a lonely, sad old lady for a long time."

I scoffed. "Not that old, Adelynn Renee."

"She had no hope of ever finding someone who might want her and her two kids. But Doc felt sorry for her and came to rescue all of us."

Sheesh. Addy made me sound like an old hag living in a cave

deep in the woods. All I was missing were leaves in my hair, a gnarled stick cane, and a ratty wool shawl.

Doc grinned at me. "The sight of your poor old mom just tore at my heart. I couldn't help but hop on my white steed and race to the rescue."

"I think black horses are tougher looking than white ones," Layne said.

"Ohhh, I like the spotted ones best." Addy finished her glass of milk. "What about you, Doc?"

As the three of them discussed which horse made the best hero's mount, I put the lid on my coffee cup so it was ready for the road and grabbed a piece of toast already buttered and ready to eat. All that was missing was a little honey, which I grabbed from the pantry and drizzled on the bread.

When the kids moved on to what presents they hoped to get for their birthday this year, Doc turned to me. "The mark is still on the imp," he murmured for my ears only.

I frowned and swallowed a bite of toast. "That probably means mine is still there, too."

"I'd like to take a look before you leave."

I'd rather tuck it away in a dark cubbyhole in my brain and forget about it for the day, but, "Okay."

I picked up my coffee, opening the lid to take a sip.

"I'd like to check if the kids have a mark, too."

My hand began to tremble at the mere thought that they might. "How will you do that without them wondering why?"

He took the coffee mug from me and set it on the counter. "I was hoping you'd have an idea for that. Something to keep them from getting suspicious, especially Layne. He's too sharp to fool with vanity excuses."

True. Layne had studied a book once on how to read body language during an interrogation, gaining a skill he'd used on me on more than one occasion. Pulling one over on him required smoke and mirrors these days.

"Let's see." I glanced from the kids to Arcana. Well, I did have a mirror. What could I use for smoke? Oh! I knew how to make it happen.

"I think I got this," I told Doc.

I set my toast down and grabbed the mirror, bringing it to the table. "Okay, you two. Now that you're hitting the big double digits, I want you to look in the mirror and tell me who you look more like—your grandparents, Aunt Susan, Uncle Quint, or me."

"What if we look like our dad?" Addy asked, her brow wrinkled. "How will we know since you don't have any pictures of him to show us?"

Doc pursed his lips. "Good question, Squirt."

I bit back several responses that were not so nice about Rex. Instead, I smiled down into her earnest little face. "I can remember what he looked like." Hell, I'd just had a threatening visit from the jackass last month. "And you both have some of his traits, but you have far more from my family's side of the fence." Especially when it came to our ancestral line of killers and summoners. "Now, Addy, come look in the mirror with me and let's see."

After she joined me, I waved Doc over. "You've met my family, Doc. Be a judge for us."

He moved behind me, staring at my reflection.

I tipped my head to the side, giving him a clear view of where the mark supposedly was.

His brow pinched, and he nodded slightly.

Damn it. I'd hoped the mark would fade for some reason, but I should have known better. Supernatural shit was always sticky.

I tugged Addy closer and had her help hold the mirror in front of the two of us. Her straight hair draped down over her shoulders, so I pulled it up in a makeshift ponytail to give Doc a clearer view. "What do you think, Doc? Does Addy look like my mom? Me? Or Susan?"

He leaned closer. "I'd say a mix of you and Zoe, actually. Although I can see Hope, too, around her eyes."

Addy smiled wide. As soon as I had a firm hold on the mirror without her, she stepped aside and twirled around a few times. "I hope I end up as pretty as Grammy someday!"

I tried not to take offense at playing second fiddle to my mother, who'd always been a "looker," as Harvey called her.

Doc squeezed my shoulder. When I met his gaze in the mirror, he shook his head.

No hand mark on Addy. Thank God! Relief made my arms rubbery for a moment, the mirror tipping slightly in my loose grip.

But we weren't done.

I took a breath and got a grip again, then I waved Layne over. "You're next."

He shuffled closer and stood between the mirror and me, a big scowl filling his face.

"You look like Cooper right now," I joked.

Layne's gaze narrowed on me, suspicion behind his eyes. "Is he our dad? Is that why you two fight so much?"

Doc chuckled.

I made a face at Doc in the mirror before refocusing on my son. "No, Layne. Cooper and I fight because …" I paused, trying to pinpoint the exact reason. But there were too many.

"Because," Layne continued for me, "you both like to boss people around."

"He has a point," Doc said, clearly trying not to smile. "You both are alpha personalities."

I reached back to pinch his leg, but he stepped aside.

"What does the Greek letter A have to do with them?" Layne asked Doc.

I blinked, a little astonished he knew the Greek alphabet. Then again, he'd pretty much come out of the womb asking for some mother's milk and a dictionary.

"It means they both like to be leaders," Doc explained.

"Addy likes to be a leader, too." Layne stared at me in the mirror, his hazel eyes solemn. "Do I look like my dad?"

I stared back, thinking of Rex as I compared the shape of Layne's face, his eyes, his mouth and nose. There was only a tiny bit of Rex showing through, mostly in the way Layne's hair sat on his head. Otherwise, the kid was all mine, either due to my family's Summoner bloodline for males or simply because I won the gene tug-of-war battle over Rex.

"Actually, you remind me more of Quint when he was your age. His hair was a shade darker than yours when he was young, but you have the same dimples and jawline."

That spurred an instant grin. "Yes! Uncle Quint is big and strong, so maybe I'll be big and strong someday, too."

"Undoubtedly," Doc said, smiling at Layne in the mirror. "Especially if you keep swimming with me at the gym on the weekends. How about you give us a quick gun show before you head up to brush your teeth for school?"

Layne flexed his arms, earning a whistle and nod of appreciation from Doc. Then he raced up the stairs, followed by his sister who yelled for dibs on the bathroom first.

I set the mirror back by the pet dishes. "Well?" I asked Doc. "How about Layne?"

"Nothing on him either."

I rested my hand on my heart. "That's a huge relief."

He took me by the chin, tipping my head to the side. "But yours is still the same." He leaned down and kissed my neck where the mark supposedly was.

If only that would make this all better.

"Neither Addy nor Layne noticed the mark on you," he said. "Which was clearly visible with your hair pinned up."

"Okay, so only you can see the mark. We still have one other person I'd like to check." At his raised brows, I continued, "Harvey might be marked, too. He was at the old school with the imp and me when I killed the Bone Cruncher. If he has the hand mark, then that's where we got it."

"And if he doesn't?"

I leaned forward, resting my forehead on his chest. "I don't know."

"We should probably check Cornelius, too, just to be safe."

I nodded.

"Whether those two have the handprint or not, I think we need to go visit your *Scharfrichter* pal in Lead and try to find out why I can see the mark on you and Daisy in the mirror but nobody else can."

"And maybe she'll know what the mark means."

"Any informative answers about the mark would at least be a start to figuring out how to get rid of it."

I leaned back, meeting his dark gaze. "I really don't want to deal with Prudence right now. Especially on top of having to cart Madame Contraire all over the frozen tundra."

"I understand, Tish, but she knows a lot about mirrors from experience, and she's looked inside of Arcana. The sooner we can solve this hand mark mystery, the better."

He was right, of course. But …

I wrinkled my nose. "What if I don't like any of Prudence's answers?"

CHAPTER SIXTEEN

A short time later, I was turning into the parking lot behind Calamity Jane Realty when King Kong called. As much as I didn't want to hear Cooper's voice on this cold and dreary morning, I knew better than not to answer.

"Ooo ooo ooo?" I said in his language into the phone.

"What the hell is that, Parker?"

"It's ape speak for good morning." I pulled into my parking spot. "Now you need to roar back in Godzilla vernacular."

"I'm going to roar, all right, lizard breath."

"You sound pissy, Detective Kong. Did you do your happy-brain drills this morning?"

"Did you?"

"No, but I've moved on to the next level."

"Which is what?"

"Breathing like a lion."

He scoffed. "Sticking your tongue out and roaring during an exhale does not make you happier, Parker. Lion's breath exercises are for relieving stress and tension."

I gaped at my phone. "How do you know about the lion's breath technique?"

"My girlfriend hangs out with Curion more than you do. He has her roaring at me whenever I start talking about you and this damned caper."

I laughed.

"It's not funny. Let me roar at you early in the morning and see if you like spilling coffee down your shirt."

"You roared at me yesterday, remember?"

There was a moment of silence from him. "Yeah, but I should have roared louder."

"I might screech back, like Godzilla does."

He sighed. "Why did you call me, Parker?"

"I didn't call. You did." Natalie must have really flustered him this morning with her roaring. Or maybe something else had him sidetracked.

"Oh, yeah. I lined up a home inspector I know to swing by Galena House shortly. How soon can you get over here?"

Jeez! That was fast. Too fast for me.

"Shit, I can't. I have clients and a medium to take house showing."

"You're talking about that Contraire woman?"

"Yeah. Jerry had me come in early. We're going over the places he wants me to show my clients, and then we're going to practice his haunted house script along with Madame Contraire."

"Why do you need a script? I thought she's supposed to be legit."

"Legit or not, Jerry is in it for a sale, so he has something written up for us."

"Your boss is wacko."

"Yeah, well so is your detective pal."

"He's not my pal." Cooper blew out a breath. "Speaking of, I let Hawke know the inspector will be scouring the place today, and he's insisting on being here with us."

"Damn. I'd love to be there needling that big oaf."

"On second thought, it's probably better you're not here. We don't need you going off half-cocked and frying anyone with your laser breath."

"I'd only aim at Hawke."

"Yeah, but somehow you'd manage to hit me in the process and break my nose again."

I giggled.

"That's not supposed to be funny."

"Maybe all of that roaring from your girlfriend is tickling your funny monkey bone." I cringed at the sound of that.

"My what?"

"Uh, I didn't mean that sexually. Natalie and I don't talk about your monkey bone when you're not around. Although Natalie would probably be happy to talk about monkey boning. We usually just stick to analyzing your monkey brain."

Wait, what was I saying? Crap, that might get Natalie into trouble with him.

Silence came from the other end of the line.

"We talk about how big and impressive it is." *It?* I smacked myself on the forehead. "I mean your monkey brain is big, not the bone part. I really don't ever want to know the details about your …"

I stopped and covered my mouth with both hands. I needed to switch tracks and start again. Or go bury my head in a snowbank.

"Are we done here, Parker?" I couldn't tell if the slight vibration in his voice was from laughter or anger.

"Almost." I didn't want to leave our conversation on that squirmy note. "Where do monkeys go for a drink?"

Once again, silence.

"They go to monkey bars. Get it, Cooper?"

"Yeah, we're done."

"Okay, call me later, Kong."

"That's King Kong to you, Parker."

The line went dead.

Wincing, I leaned my head against the steering wheel. What was wrong with me? I looked up at myself in the rearview mirror. I blamed my hair, which was escaping its confines and starting to stick out here and there, damn it.

On second thought, it wasn't my hair's fault, it was Jerry's. He put a crimp in my plans with this medium of his.

God, why did I have to juggle Madame Contraire today? I scowled at my reflection. This was no time to play ghostly parlor games. I had a caper to help pull off.

After doing my own version of roaring in the rearview mirror with my tongue sticking out, I headed into work ready to face whatever awaited me. Or whoever.

It turned out nobody was waiting for me, client-wise, anyway. The couple had called Jerry during my drive in to cancel, which left me with one medium, one boss, and zero potential buyers. I tried to look at the bright side of being stood up—I could head over to Galena House to join Cooper, Hawke, and the home inspector as soon as Jerry gave me the opportunity to come up with an excuse to leave.

Unfortunately, he had a backup play in his gamebook.

"Grab the notes I printed and left on your desk, Violet. We're going to run through some drills with Madame Contraire."

In Jerry's sport-speak, that meant the three of us would be spending the morning checking out the houses on his list while practicing his script. Oh, what sweet hell.

Before we left the office and headed out into the cold, I slipped into the bathroom to make a private call to Zelda Britton, per my promise to Doc earlier before I'd left home. He wanted to get down to the bottom of this hand mark before mine started to spread like Daisy's was.

Zelda picked up after a few rings. "Hello, Violet. I hope you're keeping warm up there in the Hills."

Uh oh. That sounded like she was somewhere other than Lead. "Not really. I take it you're not home right now."

"No, Zeke had a consulting opportunity in California, so I decided to join him for a week." There was a shuffling noise on her end of the line. "Do you need to talk to Prudence?" she whispered.

"Yeah, unfortunately."

"She'll be so happy to have company."

I had my doubts about that. I couldn't remember a single time that Prudence had rolled out the red carpet for me.

"I would wait until you're home, Zelda, but this is kind of important."

"It's okay. I understand. You know where I keep the spare key. Besides, I'd appreciate you looking in on Prudence and the house to make sure everything is going okay while I'm gone."

Zelda's concern for the cantankerous dead slayer was sweet, but I had no doubt Prudence would be fine left alone there for months on end. That would give her plenty of time to come up with new ways to criticize my *Scharfrichter* work.

With a promise to send Zelda a text later about the state of things at her house, I thanked her for letting me stop by in her absence and hung up.

I wasn't dancing a jig about visiting Prudence without Zelda there in part because the retired librarian made delicious desserts for me every time I visited. The other reason was that Zelda's open mind to the spiritual world provided a clear channel for Prudence to communicate through her. Her kind demeanor and sweet voice also added a dollop of honey to Prudence's vinegar.

With Zelda gone, Prudence would need to use another channeler. Doc would volunteer without hesitation, but he had clients lined up all day. Not to mention that I feared the sight of him in the midst of her possession would cause me to have long-term, repetitive flinching reactions when it came to our sex life. Cooper and Natalie were busy, and Aunt Zoe was gone. That left Cornelius, but Prudence had made it clear last time that she was not fond of the terrors he kept locked away in his head and would prefer to kill him given the opportunity.

Well, crud. Maybe we would just have to wait until …

Oh! Harvey. Of course. He already had a link with her, although he really didn't like being used as her megaphone.

I called him anyway, desperate times and all that juju.

"Hey, Sparky. Make it fast, I'm in the midst of wheeling and dealing here."

"Where?"

"Hill City."

A knock on the bathroom door made me jerk.

"Wrap it up, Violet. The game clock is ticking."

I shook my fist at Jerry and hollered, "Almost ready."

"Where are you, Sparky?"

"I'm at work. Listen, I need a favor later."

"What kind of favor?"

"The kind that involves your ghostly girlfriend."

He growled. "Prudy ain't no girlfriend of mine. She's more like a shrewish ex-wife."

"Whatever she is, I need you to channel for me."

"I'm way too busy. Every day. Until I die."

"You're retired. Busy doing what?" Maybe he was at a doctor's appointment.

"Snaggin' a couple of movin' trucks."

"You're already doing that? Did you ask Cooper first?"

"That boy doesn't tell me when to jump. Or how high."

"When are you getting the trucks for?"

"This weekend. Your kids' birthday party is the perfect time to pull off this caper."

This weekend! There were so many "buts" that sprang to mind.

Jerry pounded on the door. "Violet, I can hear you talking on your phone. Hang up and let's hit the court."

I cursed under my breath.

"Kiss your momma with that mouth?" Harvey asked, snickering.

"No. I mean, yes." I sighed. "I have to go. Call me when you get back up here."

"You ain't the boss of me either, Sparky."

I hung up on his ornery ass, tucked in a few loose curls, and headed out to join my boss and his medium.

Four *supposedly* haunted houses later, I was ready to stick my head in a toilet, flush several times, and call it a day.

Dressed this time in a white and silver ice-princess ensemble, including glittery blue eyeshadow, mascara, and lipstick, the medium had Jerry eating out of her hand. If he waxed on about Madame Contraire's "all-star" spirit-channeling abilities anymore, I could start a candle-making business.

"Do you feel any spirits around us?" Jerry had whispered each time we'd walked into a house.

His inquisitiveness hadn't stopped there. Oh, no.

How Madame Contraire had been able to focus on sensing wispy folks around us was beyond me when Jerry had followed her from room to room, badgering her with questions like: "Can you sense their pain? Are they angry? How old are they? When did they die? How did they die? Are they friendly? Do they want to hurt us? Do they speak French? Will I feel them touching me? Should we try to talk to them in tongues? Will they give us a sign if they want us to leave? Can they smell us? Did they know Wild Bill?"

And so on, ad nauseam.

To be honest, his actions had left me scratching my head multiple times throughout the tours as I stood off to the side to watch. It was as if Madame Contraire had an invisible leash on him, and he was a bouncing puppy at her feet, desperately hoping she'd toss him a treat.

No wonder Mona hadn't liked the woman right from the start. She probably could sense that the medium was poaching on her territory, even though Mona claimed Jerry was nothing more to her than a boss.

I sighed, leaning against the kitchen counter in the small Tudor-style abode Jerry and Madame Contraire were currently frisking for ghosts.

To be honest, I still couldn't tell if Madame Contraire was playing games with us or being honest when she claimed to feel a presence in each house, because my ghost radar only "blipped" for Prudence. And for the ghoul in Jane's office. Oh, and for that little terror, Wilda Hessler, when she felt like playing spooky games with me and her half-burnt clown in a pitch-black elevator. I shuddered at the memory of that one.

I stood up straight at the sound of footfalls coming toward the kitchen.

"Violet, here you are." Jerry glanced around the tiny room that made him look like a mid-sized giant. "I thought you had to use the restroom."

"Oh, I did. I just came in here to check for any other messages from the clients who canceled this morning." I held up my cell phone. "There were none."

No messages, period. Darn Harvey. Maybe he was still in Hill City securing those trucks.

"Well, how about we—" His phone rang. He checked the number and grinned. "I'm going to take a time out. I'll be back shortly."

He stepped into the living room. Meanwhile, I heard the ceiling creak overhead. Madame Contraire must still be woo-wooing her way through the rooms upstairs.

Good. That gave me a few minutes to sneak a text to Doc: *Any word from Cooper about his home inspector outcome and Hawke?*

No, he replied within seconds. He must be between clients. *But I did check out Harvey in the mirror.*

Oh, really? Was he clothed or in his birthday suit?

Both, smartass.

I smiled. *Should I be concerned about losing you to him? I mean, he's pretty sexy according to the ladies down at the senior center.*

You should be concerned about what I saw in the mirror.

Crap, I texted.

And what I didn't see, he wrote.

What's that supposed to mean, Professor Cryptic? I held my breath as

I waited for his answer to appear.

There was no mark.

Crap.

You already wrote that, Tish.

It bears repeating in this case.

We need to go see Prudence.

I know. I groaned at the idea alone.

Pronto, Tish. No excuses.

I heard Jerry's footfalls coming my way. *Gotta go, hubba hubba.*

Why do you keep calling me that?

I'd called him that nickname just a few times now, and only when I'd watched him undressing. *More later!*

I pocketed my phone as Jerry returned to the kitchen.

"I have some bad news, Violet."

"How bad?"

Like he had an infected hangnail type of bad? Or that the Hellhole under Calamity Jane's had caved in and sucked the building down into the depths of Deadwood's version of Hades? In my world, either was equally possible these days.

"An old friend of mine is in town to look at some properties."

That didn't seem so horrible. More along the lines of a hangnail issue.

"So, I have to leave."

Shucky-darn, the haunted house tour was over.

"No problem. I can take you and Madame Contraire back to the office now." And then I'd head over to Galena House to see how King Kong fared with Hawke and the home inspector.

"Actually, I'd like you to finish up with Madame Contraire. I paid for another two hours of her time, and I'd like to get my money's worth."

"What do you mean, finish up with her?"

He shrugged. "How about you take her to Cornelius Curion's haunted hotel? See what entities she senses there." He patted me on the shoulder like a good coach would before sending me out to kick the game-winning field goal. "I'll catch up with you tomorrow morning on how this last bit went."

"But it's too cold for you to walk back to the office."

"I gave him this address. He should be here any ..." he looked out the dining room window. "Actually, he's here."

Before I could holler "Go team!" he was out the door.

Son of a peacock. Now what? The last thing I wanted to do today was babysit a woman who may or may not be an actual medium. I had caper details to find out, not to mention trying to get an answer from an uppity ghost who thought she was better than me about an ominous mark on my …

Hold on. I had an idea.

I fished out my phone and texted my bodyguard: *Meet me at Prudence's place ASAP, bodyguard!*

The stairs creaked.

I headed off Madame Contraire in the dining room.

"Where is Jerry?" she asked, looking behind me.

"He had to leave."

She frowned. "So, that means you and I are—"

"On our own," I finished for her. "If you're ready, I have one more haunted place I'm supposed to show you."

"Yes, of course."

She hurried out into the cold before me, heading for my rig as I locked the front door behind us.

I slid behind the wheel and waited for her to buckle her seatbelt before backing out of the driveway and driving toward our final destination for the day.

"Where are we going?" Madame Contraire asked me a few minutes later as my SUV chugged along.

"Jerry wanted me to show you another haunted location."

"Yes, you mentioned that already. But isn't this in the wrong direction? We're heading out of Deadwood, not toward it."

"Not at all." I smiled at her.

She winced at what she saw on my face. "Where are you taking me, Violet?"

"To a beautiful, century-old Gothic Revival–style home that overlooks the famous Open Cut gold mine." I cruised up the hill toward Lead. "You're going to love this one. The ghost usually delivers a big metaphysical bang for your buck."

* * *

The porchlight was on at the old Carhart house, which officially belonged to Zelda and Zeke Britton now. Actually, since

Prudence the ghost had lived there far longer than any of the living inhabitants, it should rightfully be called her place. Anyway, in the cold and growing-gloomier-by-the-hour afternoon, the porchlight seemed welcoming.

But I knew better. Prudence waited somewhere inside for us, and she didn't suffer fools well—if at all. I had little doubt that she'd let me know whether Madame Contraire was a real medium. I only hoped she didn't hurt the ice princess in the process of finding out.

"This is the place?" Madame Contraire said, a frown of disbelief on her face.

"Yep."

"It doesn't look haunted. It's so ..."

"Beautiful."

"Yes. It reminds me of the story of Hansel and Gretel. Add some pretty icing along the trim and stick some pieces of candy here and there and you have the old witch's house."

I sent her a raised brow look. "Are you afraid of being eaten once we get inside?"

She mirrored my brows back at me. "Are you?"

"Always." Or beat up.

But I had a feeling today was going to be different. Prudence and I would find a happy middle ground. Okay, so maybe "happy" was a little too optimistic, but at least cordial. If she helped me with figuring out this hand mark bugbear, I'd get to work catching some of the *others* on her to-kill list that she'd given me weeks ago, especially after I got those clocks out of Hawke's hands.

Madame Contraire's finely lined brows sank into a wrinkled frown. "You're kidding about being eaten, right?"

"Yeah, of course." I waved her off. "This ghost doesn't bite." She preferred to yank out the teeth of most visitors I brought along for show and tell. That reminded me, I'd have to nicely ask Prudence to leave the medium's teeth be and hope she'd refrain from repeating her past dental aggressions.

I reached for the door handle. "How about you give me a couple of minutes to open the front door and turn on a few lights. I'll flicker the porch light when I'm ready for you."

She continued to frown. "Okay, but I have to tell you, I don't have a good feeling about this." She touched her neck. "I sense something malevolent here."

"You mean here in the vehicle? Or there in your neck?"

There was a chance that Prudence already sat between us or in the back seat. She'd occupied my passenger seat before.

"I'm not sure if it's coming from you or the vehicle or the house."

"Did you sense it on me before we pulled into the drive?"

"A little, yes."

Hmm. Maybe she was sensing the tension that always bearhugged me when I had to visit this house. My panic-laced adrenaline rush wouldn't necessarily take a medium to pick up on, especially with how I tended to white-knuckle the steering wheel and clench my teeth the nearer I got to Prudence's lair.

"I don't feel any different," I told her.

Although, that wasn't quite true. I was missing my anchor in another potential Prudence storm—Harvey. He usually gave me the mental goose I needed to face whatever awaited me on the other side of the door. I'd also experienced a few gut twinges on the way here, but that I blamed on preparing to deal with Prudence's hostile personality. Bitter pills often gave me acid indigestion.

"You might not even realize what you are emoting. Many of my clients are unaware when their natural defenses are engaged."

Clients? "What do you do for a living?" Did being a local medium pay that well? Maybe if she were on television …

"I dabble in psychology."

Ahh. If she only dabbled, and she was not going by the title of *Doctor* Contraire, she must not be officially licensed to practice. Not that I knew much about that field. However, this new detail explained why she'd often ask the ghosts to talk about their feelings with her when we'd move from room to room in supposedly haunted houses.

"Why would my natural defenses be up?" I knew why I was holed up inside my castle walls, but I was curious to hear if she had figured out some of my *Scharfrichter* secrets.

"Because you have an issue with my presence during these mandatory ride-alongs. I just can't determine if it's personal or professional. Or a mix of both."

It was all of the above, along with a bit of teeth gnashing on

Mona's account for flirtatiously winking her long blue eyelashes in Jerry's direction.

"Tell you what, let's go inside and figure it out there."

I left her, hurried through Mother Nature's icebox, grabbed the spare key from Zelda's hiding place, and then returned to the porch. "Dammit, Harvey. Where are you?" I muttered, unlocking the door.

I tried to take a deep, calming breath, but it was too damned cold, so I stepped into the dark house and closed the door behind me, hitting the light switch. The Tiffany-style stained-glass sconces lit the foyer in a warm golden glow. The house smelled slightly sweet with a hint of cinnamon. I smirked. The witch's candy house, huh? Madame Contraire had nailed that one.

"Prudence," I called out, unwinding my chenille scarf and slipping off my coat, laying both on the side table along the wall. "I need to talk to you, and I've brought a woman along with me who claims to be a medium, since Zelda isn't here to act as your interpreter. I want to bring this medium inside now, but you must not hurt her because my boss might fire me if you do."

I took a couple of steps farther inside, peeking into the living room, careful not to step on the cream-colored shag rug since I was still wearing my boots. The burgundy leather sofa, matching chair, and ottoman were in their usual places, along with the coffee table and sideboard. If only Zelda was here to bring me some homemade, freshly baked dessert to make my meeting with Prudence sweet instead of what I worried would quickly turn sour.

"Did you hear me, Prudence? Give me some kind of sign if so. And *not* a painful one, please."

I turned back to watch the sconces for any flickering.

Nothing.

I shot a cringing glance toward the stairwell, afraid I'd see her standing at the top with blood running down her high collar—the sight Aunt Zoe and others previously had described upon seeing Prudence's ghostly form.

Still nothing.

"Okay, well, I'm going to bring her in anyway, because we don't have a lot of time for thumb twiddling." I headed to the front door. "Remember, no teeth souvenirs."

I was reaching for the porchlight switch when the door

slammed open, almost clipping me.

Madame Contraire rushed into the foyer, brushing past me along with a cold breeze.

I shut the door behind her. "I was just about to wave you inside. Did you sense that I was ready for you?"

She whirled around and rushed toward me, her eyes rolled back in her head, her blue lips gaping in a silent scream.

"Oh, shit." I recoiled against the door as she crowded in close, standing toe to toe.

"Hello, Prudence," I said, cringing. I should've offered Madame Contraire a mint before leaving my SUV.

"What have you brought into my home, *Scharfrichter*?"

CHAPTER SEVENTEEN

eez, Prudence." I shoved at Madame Contraire's shoulders, pushing the medium's body back a couple of steps. "Why do you have to make everything so difficult?"

"You know I do not like strangers in my home without my consent. Have I not made that clear in times past?"

"Oh, you definitely have." I focused on a spot above the medium's head so I didn't have to look into the spooky whites of her eyes. "I tried to call Zelda to give you proper notice, but she's not here."

"That does not allow you to trespass!"

"She told me to come and check on you and the house."

She scoffed. "I do not believe that to be true."

"Believe what you want, but I wouldn't enter this house without Zelda's permission."

Madame Contraire's blue lips opened and closed, but no words came out, reminding me of a fish out of water. Maybe Prudence was silently practicing her vowels.

"I also let Harvey know I was coming in case you used your ghostly telepathy to eavesdrop on his brain again, but apparently you didn't."

"Sharing mind space with the lothario must be suffered in small doses to maintain one's sanity." She lurched farther back, giving me more breathing room. "Now, elucidate why you have brought this charlatan to me."

"So, you're saying she's not an actual medium?"

"Why would you conclude she has that ability?"

"She's convinced others that she can interact with the dead on some level. She even charges for her channeling services."

"Truly? Let me take a closer look." Madame Contraire's chin dipped, but the whites of her eyes remained on me.

"I wish you'd close her eyelids while you're doing that."

"Quiet, *Scharfrichter.*"

"I mean the way you look right now would make the hair stand up on a faux fur coat."

"Silence!"

Fine. I held my hand between us to block the sight of her white eyes while she scoped out the inside of Madame Contraire's cranium.

Skirting around the medium's stiff form, I grabbed my phone from my coat pocket to see if Harvey had replied to my text.

Nope. The ornery bugger was probably avoiding me. Without Zelda around to bake anything sweet and delicious, there was nothing to lure Harvey inside Prudence's den. Apparently, there were limits to his self-proclaimed duty as my bodyguard.

I turned back to check on Prudence's progress in time to witness Madame Contraire's shoulders tremble violently for a few beats.

"Was that your doing, Prudence?"

"Hush, mooncalf."

I assumed that was an insult, although mild sounding compared to some of her past zingers. "Fine, but be careful in there. I need to return that vessel unharmed to my office in an hour."

The medium's chin lifted, and then her eyelids closed. "I am finished with this blowsabella."

Where did Prudence come up with these insults? Did she have some archaic thesaurus up in the attic that she pored over in her spare time? If so, I needed to borrow it for my next round of verbal sparring with Detective Hawke.

"And?" I prompted. "Is she a medium or is that a grift?"

"For a moment, I heard a voice whispering in the shadows." The medium's mouth stretched wide a few times. "But I could not locate an outright source."

"Is that normal? Whispering voices in someone's mind?"

"I would not know. I am a Slayer, not a doctor who practices trepanation."

"What's trepanation?"

She sighed at my ignorance. "Drilling a hole into the skull to assess the brain."

"Ick." I wrinkled my nose. "That's barbaric."

"Trepanation was practiced for well over 5,000 years, you simpleton." She moved toward the living room, slightly dragging one of the medium's legs along the floor.

"That doesn't mean it was a beneficial practice." I followed, dragging foot myself. Both feet. I'd really like to leave as soon as I could. The shadowy corners in this house always had me doing double takes.

"Is it possible that this vessel has been cracked open in the past?" Prudence asked as she lurched into the living room.

"You mean like she hit her head?"

"I am referring to a spirit that might have interloped at some time, and now this hornswoggler believes the slightest glimmer in her peripheral vision is a spectral."

I followed Prudence into the sitting area, hesitating at the opposite end of the sofa from her. After several past, painful meetings, I preferred to keep enough distance between us for me to make it to the door before she could catch me.

"Maybe, but I think people like the idea of there being something else out there," I said. "Something they can't see."

Most of my clients these days fit into that box.

I glanced around the shadow-filled room. Without Zelda and her happy-go-lucky aura onsite, the house reminded me of an old wax museum—ornate and elegant to the eye, but chilling to the spine.

"Fatheaded, all of these dabblers," Prudence said with a sneer. "It is my experience that unseen entities are best let be." She dropped clumsily onto the sofa cushion. "Now, why are you here, *Scharfrichter*?"

I pointed at the part of my face where Doc claimed I had the mark. "Can you see a reddish-black handprint here?"

The medium's eyelids remained closed. "I do not."

"Don't you need to open her eyes to look?"

She sighed heavily in response.

"Okay, well, you know the Oracle, right? The one I've brought here in the past?"

"Yes. That is a true medium. And more."

"Well, the Oracle was looking at the imp in my family's mirror, the magic heirloom we used to capture the *lidérc*."

"Never trust a mirror, especially a mystical one. It should be destroyed."

"Death and destruction are your favorites, I swear." I wondered if I'd turn so dark and bitter like Prudence with time. That was assuming I'd live long enough for that to happen.

"The remains should be secretly scattered to the wind," she continued. "Separated by vast distances."

"Right. Anyway, the Oracle noticed a dark handprint on the imp and then on me. The mark is in the same area on both of us, only the imp's mark has dark tendrils spreading out from the fingertips."

Prudence remained quiet, eyes closed and chin upturned, facing my direction.

"Do you have any theories on why the Oracle—and only with the aid of the mirror—can see these marks on us? And why they are even there?"

The medium's head tipped. "You have caught the imp?"

"Yes. Well, it sort of just came home with me."

She harrumphed. "You have allowed this vile creature in your dwelling?"

I nodded, debating on mentioning Addy's tendency to adopt stray pets, but decided to keep my daughter out of this.

She made another sound. It might have been a scoff, or maybe a snort, or both. "Did I not make it clear when you were here last how treacherous an imp can be?"

"Yes, you did, but this one is different. Now that I'm not hunting it, the thing is pretty docile."

"Imps are never docile. Clearly, it is planning a revenge, and you are a clodpoll to believe otherwise."

She'd called me that before, so I let it wash over the bow. Besides, Daisy was teaching Elvis how to use the toilet and letting Addy brush its teeth. Those were not the actions of a dangerous creature hell-bent on killing us in our sleep. Not to mention that since Daisy had moved in with us, I hadn't experienced the gut-tightening queasiness that usually alerted me of a presence requiring execution.

"I'm not here to discuss the pros and cons of having a pet imp. I need to know why the Oracle is seeing a handprint on the two of us, but only through the mystical mirror. Now, do you have any answers that do not include an insult?"

"No."

I sighed, walking over to look out the front windows. "Crikey. Back to square one."

"I might have an answer," she said from behind me. "But it will include at least one insult, if not multiple."

"Fine, insult away." I turned toward her, arms open wide to receive whatever she threw my way. "I need to know how to get rid of this mark so I can focus on getting the clocks."

"You are referring to the Timekeeper clocks?"

"Yep."

"Those that are under your charge now?"

"Yes, those clocks. The snollyguster constable has them locked away in an apartment that is being watched day and night in order to keep me from getting to them."

"This answer is simple. You must kill the snollyguster." She nodded once, albeit with a slight shoulder jerk in the process.

"Prudence, I can't just kill people."

"Whyever not?"

"Because it's morally wrong."

Not to mention that I had children to raise, which I could not do if I was locked away in prison for murder.

"Then I shall kill him." She jerked again, only this time her whole body moved.

As tempting as the idea was to remove Hawke totally from the equation, this was no solution either. "It's not that easy."

"It truly is. I simply stab a thin blade up through his neck on the inside of his jawbone." She used the medium's hands to demonstrate. "Then twist the blade this way and that inside the brain a few times and *voilà. C'est complet.*"

"Eww." I grimaced. "How many times did you execute someone that way when you were alive?"

She shrugged. "I lost count long, long ago." The medium's lips pulled up into a garish grin. "I am quite an astute Slayer, unlike you, *Scharfrichter.*"

"Hey, I can do the job when needed, so don't …" I stopped

there, reminding myself that I hadn't come to Zelda's house to compete in a pissing contest.

"You must retrieve the clocks," she said.

"I know."

"And you must kill the *Duzarx*."

"Yes, I remember." Although, I wasn't exactly sure where to find it yet, or what that creature looked like beyond it supposedly having a bunch of eyes and teeth.

"And the *caper-sus* before their numbers grow too many."

"Yeah, yeah, yeah." I also possibly had Kyrkozz-the-asshole and a deadly horde of troublemakers coming my way soon. I moved closer, standing across the coffee table from her. "But what about the mark on my face?"

"I will need to ponder on that, but I do not remember having heard of such a blight before, especially for one of our kind. It must be another example of your ancestral line's incompetence."

"Say what you will, but my line is still running strong."

"For now. However, if you do not slay that imp *today*, this may be the beginning of your end."

The medium's body convulsed violently all of a sudden, her eyelids fluttering. Her legs kicked straight out, her shins banging into the coffee table, shoving it at me. A gurgling sound came from her gaping lips.

"Prudence?" I reached toward her. "What are you doing? I told you not to hurt Madame Contraire."

"It is …" She spoke in the midst of teeth rattling tremors. "Not …" Her head fell back onto the couch cushions, as if her neck could no longer hold it upright.

I stepped closer, reaching out to her across the coffee table. "You have to let the medium go."

"I …" Her upper body twisted hard to the left, then to the right. "You …" Her back arched, lifting her partway off the couch.

"Stop this, Prudence!"

"Runnnn!!!"

Before I could do more than blink in surprise, the medium sat forward, her eyes open and black as night.

"Hello, *Scharfrichter*," she said in a low, velvety voice.

She pushed off the couch, leapt onto the coffee table, and launched straight at me.

For a petite woman, she tackled like a three-hundred-pound linebacker. She rammed into me, sending us stumbling backward until I tripped over my own feet. We fell onto the birch flooring, where the back of my head connected with a jarring *thud.* Her chin bonked my lower lip, mashing it into my teeth.

"Son of a … fuck!" I yelled, tasting blood. I shoved the medium off me, rolling to my feet barely in time to dodge the brass candle holder she'd grabbed from the mantel and swung at me.

I scurried around the chair, putting it between us. "Prudence, stop it! I can't hurt the medium."

She snarled and threw the candle holder at me.

I ducked and then winced as it crashed into the flower-covered, silk wallpaper.

"Damn it! Knock it off before you mess up Zelda's house."

Madame Contraire's face contorted in pain, her eyelids fluttering again, before closing.

"Not …" Prudence struggled to speak through trembling lips. Staggering sideways, she grabbed onto the white sheer curtains to keep from falling. "You must …"

The curtain rod buckled under her weight.

Riiiip!

"You tore the curtains, Prudence! How are we gonna sew that back together?"

The medium fell to the floor.

I started toward Prudence, reaching out to block another attack or help her up, I wasn't sure which. The uppity ghost had a history of flip-flopping on me when it came to violence.

As I rounded the coffee table, Prudence hopped up onto the couch arm and crouched there like a freaky gargoyle perched high up on a church, her black eyes staring at me.

I stopped short. "What in the hell is wrong with you?"

She shrieked and launched at me again. Her elbow clocked my jaw as we tumbled backward over the coffee table. Somehow, I landed on top of her. When I grabbed her wrists to hold her down, she started to buck and thrash and foam at the corners of her mouth. My knees clonked onto the floor several times as I squeezed her hips between my thighs.

"Prudence, stop it!"

Madame Contraire's body stilled, her eyelids closing. When they opened again, her white eyes stared blankly toward the ceiling.

"Violet, we have a problem," Prudence whispered in her mid-Atlantic accent.

"Criminy, you think? You're trashing Zelda's house."

Her blue lips quivered and stretched. "We seemed to have unleashed something."

My jaw throbbed along with the back of my head. "What are you talking about, Prudence?"

"I am not alone in here."

I glanced around the room, finding only long, winter afternoon shadows and a torn curtain. "In this house?"

"No, clodpoll! In this body." Her eyelids closed.

Her words sank in.

Oh, no.

I stared down at Madame Contraire's face, which was

twitching and contorting, as if something were alive under her flesh. What else was in there? Was it an entity similar to the terrors tucked away inside of Cornelius's mind? Multiple entities? Were they all running loose, tearing at the medium's brain to break free?

"Prudence? Are you in there still?" I whispered, my heart thumping hard enough for any seismometers in a ten-mile radius to register. "Are you battling something inside her head? What is it? Are there more than one? How can I help?"

Madame Contraire's eyes opened, her irises pitch black.

"Uh, Prudence?" I spoke hesitantly, hoping to be insulted rather than clocked again.

She hissed up at me.

Shit! I tightened my grip on her wrists. "That's not a very nice thing to do, whoever you are. Prudence doesn't like hissing in her house."

"*Scharfrichter!*" she rasped, her spittle flying in my face.

"Gross! Yuck!" I tried to wipe her spit off on my shoulder. "Good gravy, were you hiding under the frickin' porch when they passed out manners?"

She yanked one hand free of my hold with a strength beyond the medium's abilities. Before I could catch her hand again, she grabbed my shirt collar and rammed the top of her head forward.

I tried to jerk away, but I was too late.

Crunch!

Pain exploded in my eye and cheek. "Jesus!" Shooting stars filled my vision as I teetered to the side. "Your head is as hard as a bowling ball."

I held onto the bucking bronco underneath me through a wave of dizziness with nausea close on its heels. I tried to catch her hand each time she lashed up at me, but she managed to get several scratches down my neck, my cheek, and my forehead before I could capture it.

"Prudence!" I screamed after locking down both of the medium's wrists again. "Get a hold of this thing, dammit!"

The medium's eyes rolled up to show their whites again.

"I cannot …" Prudence said, her voice strained. She grunted. The body twisted and squirmed under me. "Hold it … for long." She undulated, almost slipping my grip. "Kill …" More grunting. "Her."

"I can't kill her!"

Madame Contraire was an innocent bystander here. Whatever was possessing her clearly had the upper hand.

Her body trembled from head to toe. "Then … runnnn!"

In a blue-lashed blink, the black irises were back in place.

"It is mine!" The medium's blue lips pulled back, showing her gnashing teeth.

What was hers? Madame Contraire's body?

She rolled to the side and tugged free of my hold, taking an open-handed swing at me that I didn't have time to dodge. She slapped my cheek hard, ringing my bell—actually, a bunch of my bells, judging by the raucous clanging in my skull.

I tipped slightly from the blow. That was all she needed to buck me the rest of the way off.

Rolling aside, I scrambled to my feet and turned to find her clambering up onto the arm of the couch again.

"What is it with you leaping at me like a goddamned monkey?"

I hunched slightly, raising my fists in the fighting stance Doc had taught me the last time we were sparring for fun at the Rec Center. Was she a professional wrestler in a past life known for tackling her opponents from the ropes?

She sprang at me.

I sidestepped in time to avoid her body slam and raced toward the staircase. Maybe, if I could lead her upstairs and shut her in a room, Prudence could take back control from inside the medium's mind. That would save me from having to knock her out and leave bruises as evidence of this fiasco.

A few steps up, she crashed into my back, sending me sprawling forward. My forehead and knees bounced off the stair steps right before she wrapped her arm around my neck and pulled me into a stranglehold.

"That's it," I croaked, struggling in her armlock. I managed to get a hand between her arm and my neck and broke the hold. "I'm done playing nice." I shoved her off me, sending her tumbling down to the bottom of the steps.

My whole head throbbed now. When I wiped my arm across my face, streaks of blood lined my sweater.

"Hell's bells!" I snarled, using the banister to pull myself up. I glared down at the medium, who was scrambling to her feet. "I'm gonna dot your eye, whoever you—"

"Sparky?"

The medium and I both looked toward the foyer.

Well, toot toot. Harvey had finally made it to the party.

He gaped at me. "Great googley moogley, girl! What happened to your face?"

"Harvey, get out of here!" I yelled, closing the distance between the medium and me.

Out of the corner of my eye, I saw him stagger to the side, falling against the wall.

When I reached for Madame Contraire, she turned toward me with a cry of pain, her body convulsing again. Her eyelids fluttered and then closed.

"Enough with you," she whispered, right before her body crumpled at my feet.

Carefully, I nudged her with my boot.

She lay still.

I nudged her again, wary of another attack, even though she lay prone on the floor.

No response. Not even an eyelid flicker.

Harvey joined me staring down at her. "You didn't do away with her, did ya?"

I frowned, and then I winced at the pain that came with using my face muscles. "No. But she tried to kill me."

"Yeah, it shows." He grimaced at whatever he saw on my face. "Is Prudy behind that nightmare you're wearin'?"

"No. She was on the inside, trying to stop whatever it was." From the still state of Madame Contraire, it looked like Prudence had succeeded in the end. But at what cost? I hoped she was still floating around somewhere. Worn out, but alive. Well, dead, but not missing like Jane's ghost now.

Harvey looked around the room. "Where'd Prudy go? I thought I felt her for a heartbeat or two there. She sort of made my knees rummy and knocked me sideways, but then she was gone. Left me winded, like when I play ring around the rosie with some of the friskier gals at the senior center."

"I don't know. She might have worn herself out battling whatever the hell kept taking the reins."

I kneeled next to Madame Contraire and carefully turned her

onto her back. Thankfully, her face still looked like it belonged on a porcelain doll. No scratches or bruises, only a few smudges of her blue lipstick and eyeliner.

You should see the other guy, I thought, wincing in dread of what I'd find staring back at me in the mirror.

Harvey offered a hand to help me to my feet. "It's a good thing I got here when I did, but I sure am sorry I missed the main bout."

"I'm glad you're here now." I took his hand, letting him tug me upright.

"You okay, Sparky?" He squinted at me. "Because you look like your face caught fire and someone tried to put it out with a crowbar wrapped with barbed wire."

"Isn't that just peachy keen. I'd like it to be on the record that I told Doc a visit to Prudence was a bad idea. But, oh no, he insisted we ask her about that stupid handprint on my face. And guess what? She was no help." I pointed at my face. "Now look at me."

Damn it! My bruises from the imp were almost gone, too.

He crooked his head one way then the other, closing each eye in turn. "You know, it ain't so bad if you don't take it all in at once."

I sighed. "What a clusterfuck!" Pain radiated from my lower lip the moment my teeth touched it to make the F "faa" sound. "Oww!"

I gently touched my mouth, tasting blood again. From the feel of it, I had a throbbing baby inner tube in place of a lower lip. That must have happened when the medium's chin had bulldozed into my chops.

"Look at the bright side, Sparky. You're still breathin', and Godzilla lives to fight another day." He patted me on the shoulder, which made me flinch. I must have landed on it during one of the medium's tackles.

I stretched my neck side to side. "You call this living?"

"It's better than dying." He hooked his thumbs in his suspenders. "Now, I wonder if Zelda has any sweets in her breadbox." When I gave him the stink eye for thinking about food when it was all I could do not to bleed out on her carpet, he held up his hands. "What? You're okay—mostly. And I'm hungry. Zelda always feeds me when I stop by. That girl has this ol' boy conditioned."

"I'm going to give you a knuckle sandwich after I quit bleeding."

He pulled out his hanky. "Come here. You have a couple of drops by your ear."

I winced as he dabbed away my blood, keeping my fingers crossed his hanky was clean.

"Not to change the subject," he said, "but I have some good news on the caper front."

Oh yeah, I'd forgotten about that worry. "Let me guess. You got the means to move the clocks?"

"Sure, but this is even better than that."

"What?"

"Detective Hawke managed to fall and break his arm."

"How is that good news?"

"If we get caught, it's gonna be hard for him to cuff you with just one hand."

CHAPTER EIGHTEEN

Madame Contraire woke from her trance, or whatever it was, as Harvey and I were in the midst of picking up Zelda's living room. She claimed to feel worn out, but was otherwise okay, besides a sore elbow and small lump at the top of her forehead. The initial sight of my injuries, however, made her screech and recoil.

Luckily, the medium didn't remember anything after the moment I'd left my SUV to unlock Zelda's front door—not walking up to Zelda's house nor talking to me in the living room. Based on that, I figured that tackling me multiple times and beating the crap out of my face took place during her temporary amnesia, too.

Thanks to her blackout, it didn't take much convincing to make Madame Contraire believe the ghost who resided in the house had taken possession of her body, and that was why she had no memory of any events. She also bought Harvey's story that I ended up with my many wounds due to a tumble down the stairs while holding onto a tray of dishes. Apparently, I'd been moonlighting as a butler in Harvey's story. He wrapped up his tall tale by saying my fall ended with me accidentally bowling her over at the bottom.

"Ah, so that's why I'm a little sore?"

A little sore? And here I was feeling like someone had played a drum solo on me with a set of croquet mallets.

"Yeah, that's why," I said, careful not to bite my split lip in the process of holding back several swear words.

After a glass of water minus the ice thanks to the ice boycott still going on in Zelda's house, Madame Contraire was ready to leave so she could go home and rest. She strongly suggested that I pay a visit to the hospital. I crossed my fingers behind my back and told her I would go straight there if she'd allow Harvey to drive her to Calamity Jane's. She agreed, seeming genuinely concerned about me as I walked her out to his pickup.

I waved goodbye.

"And good riddance," I mumbled through a thick lip. I really needed to get some ice on it. Hell, maybe I should just plant my whole face in a snowbank and call it a day, since Harvey had offered to pick up the kids after school.

I turned toward the house, sparing one last look at the attic window where I hoped Prudence was standing watch. There was no twitch of the curtain or any other sign from her, though, so I headed off down the road. Instead of the hospital, I went straight to Aunt Zoe's to patch myself up in the bathroom mirror before Harvey brought the kids home.

Aunt Zoe's truck was in the driveway when I arrived. I hurried inside, kicking off my boots by the front door. Head down, I started up the stairs and tried to brace myself for what I would see in the bathroom mirror.

"Violet, you're home early," my aunt said as I crested the top step.

I looked up to find her coming toward me down the hall.

She squawked at the sight of my face, and then cried, "Oh, baby girl," before covering her mouth. She hurried closer. "What the devil happened to you?" she whispered from the other side of her hand.

"I ran into some trouble up in Lead," I mumbled. My swollen lower lip really needed to hook up with a good ice pack.

"Sweet Mary Jane." Her hand lowered. Her eyes narrowed to a hard squint. "Was this Prudence's doing?"

"Actually, no. She was trying to stop it." I rubbed the back of my neck. "Listen, I'll explain later. Right now, I could use some ice and some pain pills and maybe a cloud to sit on while I try to duct tape myself back together."

"Come on, I'll patch you up." She pulled me in for a hug, which made me cringe.

"That hurts."

She stepped back, frowning as she examined my injuries. "What part of you doesn't hurt?"

I wiggled my toes. "Anything from the ankles down."

"Oh, dear. Well, suck it up, buttercup," she said with a kind smile as she nudged me into the bathroom. "Remember, you're a big, strong *Scharfrichter*."

"I hope you have some big, strong drugs."

"I do." She closed the door behind us. "Have you seen yourself yet?"

"No." I'd been afraid that would make me feel even worse.

"Well, you might as well get it over with."

I moved in front of the mirror. I looked like an abstract, flesh-colored Jackson Pollock painting. The sight made me whimper.

Aunt Zoe stepped next to me, her forehead wrinkled as she gently combed my hair back from my face. "I hope your opponent was the worse for wear."

I groaned. "I'll explain after we ice my whole head."

She kissed a spot above my ear. "You wash your hands and take off that sweater while I go get the med-kit from my workshop."

Almost an hour later, I'd told her the whole story. I started with the handprint visible on the imp and me in our family mirror, and I ended with how the clobbering I'd taken was all for naught, because Prudence hadn't given me any answers regarding the *what* and *why* for the marks.

In the meantime, I'd been cleaned, swabbed, wiped down with antiseptic, glazed with salve, bandaged, iced, fed pain pills, and dabbed with cover-up makeup wherever possible. Aunt Zoe had even added a lightweight stocking cap to help hide the lump on my forehead.

She stood back to inspect her work. "Well, there's only so much we can do short of having you wear a ski mask."

Lowering the ice pack I'd been holding against my lip, I stared in the mirror. "It's better already. You think the kids will believe I fell down some stairs?"

She shrugged. "Tell them they were concrete and ice-covered, and that your hands were full so your face took the worst of the fall."

"They're going to think their mom is a total klutz."

"Better that than a killer."

"Right. The longer we can delay that talk, the better."

She began to pack up her medical kit. "Violet, you should have told me about the handprint as soon as Doc saw it."

"You were busy filling a glass order that night. Oh, did you get that delivered?"

"Yeah, but you know this trouble is far more important than that sort of everyday life bullshit."

I sighed. "I was hoping to figure out some details before having to bug you."

She turned to me, her blue-eyed gaze unwavering. "I am your *magistra*. My sole purpose on Earth is to support you and your executioner endeavors at all times in order to continue our *Scharfrichter* line. We are a team until death do us part. Understand, baby girl?"

"Got it." I blinked away a sudden onset of tears. "But I'm sorry that your purpose is to take care of me. It should be about following your dreams."

She shook her head. "I'm not sorry. It's an honor, don't you see?" She caught my hand and squeezed it. "To play a part in history in such a way is an opportunity only offered to a few. I'm thrilled that the work I've put into learning about our ancestors— about their accomplishments and failures—is not only appreciated, but is being put to use. To have collected such knowledge only to pass it on to the next *magistra* without putting it into action would've been a letdown."

"You wouldn't rather have a normal life with Reid?"

She laughed. "As if anything involving Martin could be categorized as 'normal.' The man runs toward explosions instead of away." She let go of my hand. "I'll start digging through our family history books for anything about a dark handprint. Sometime later this evening, I'd like to take a look at you in Arcana and see if the mark is visible to me, as well."

"What if it's not? What if it's an Oracle thing? There's nothing about an Oracle in our ancestral stories, right?"

She shook her head. "If I find nothing on the handprint, then we may have to contact Mr. Black to find out if he knows anything about such marks. And if not him, maybe that Zuckerman woman he brought here to meet us will know. After all, she is supposed to be on our side."

A *thud* came from downstairs.

Aunt Zoe glanced at her watch. "I believe the kids are home." She smiled at me in the mirror. "You ready, Godzilla?"

"I think so."

"Are the pain pills kicking in yet?"

I nodded. "Let's hope my quicker-than-the-average-bear healing works in this case."

"This salve is from a recipe I found in one of our family history volumes." She held up the jar of green goop. "The *magistra* who shared the recipe also dabbled in alchemy and a sort of witchcraft that focused on the use of unusual flora to cure ailments. Let's hope it works the way she wrote it would."

"What?" I followed her into the hallway. "You mean you're experimenting on me now?"

She grinned back at me. "Of course. I'm the Bride of Frankenstein. Experimentation is how I came to be."

* * *

The kids took my face in stride. Apparently, they were getting used to me coming home with black eyes and scrapes. I wasn't sure I was setting a good example on how to raise normal, happy children. But then again, *normal* had been boring when I was trying to make a go of it down on the prairie, so maybe I should just keep my sights on *happy*.

Addy asked if it hurt when I blinked, which was a valid question since my eye was swollen partway shut, and then she asked if she could borrow my cell phone to look up some spelling words for homework. Layne wondered if I'd checked to see if my boots were too big, which would explain why I kept falling down stairs. Always so practical, that boy.

Rooster the dog, however, took one look at my face and barked. He kept barking, too, until I let him sniff my ear, of all things. Then he eased back to a soft growl and kept an eye on me until Addy shooed him out the kitchen door to take care of his doggy business.

The imp and Elvis passed by me without even looking when they came upstairs searching for Addy. At least I assumed she was the basis of their quest, since they danced around her feet until she passed out their afternoon treats. Then off they headed toward the dining room right before Layne let Rooster back inside. Fresh and frisky from the cold, the dog seemed to have forgotten about my face and made a beeline for his food. I hadn't seen Bogart today and figured the cat was curled up somewhere keeping warm, so there was no weigh-in on my appearance from the feline world.

When all the kid and pet commotion had settled down to a low hum, Harvey sat down across from me at the kitchen table. Both of us munched on molasses cookies that Aunt Zoe had made earlier, eating rather than talking about Prudence or the caper since the kids were hanging around while Aunt Zoe made snacks for them. I'd offered to prepare the snacks, but she'd insisted I rest and focus on icing my face. Once the kids left to eat in front of the television, she joined us and began going through one of our old family history volumes.

"We're about to have company," Harvey said.

"Oh, yeah? Who?" I asked between bites of sweet heaven. Nothing made a split lip and black eye feel better than soft molasses cookies.

There was a quick knock at the front door before Harvey could answer.

"Someone call 911?" Reid hollered from the other room.

The kids both called out hellos to him from the living room, and Rooster barked once.

Here in the kitchen, though, Aunt Zoe was glaring at Harvey. "Did you tell him to come early for supper?"

"No, but I ran into him at the gas station and yarned about Sparky's adventures in the ring up in Lead. He was frettin' that she might've suffered too hard a knock to the brain bucket, so he's here to take a look at her tongue and maybe stick a thermometer up her backside."

"*What?!*" I said, lowering my cookie.

Aunt Zoe chuckled at my expense.

Reid strode into the room in his dark blue fireman shirt and pants, skidding to a stop when he got a load of my face. "Hot damn! You weren't kidding, Harvey."

I turned to Aunt Zoe. "You said I looked pretty good."

"You always do, baby girl, black and blue face or not." She

reached over and patted my arm. "But I may be a little biased."

Reid came closer, extracting a small flashlight from his pocket. "Sparky, let me take a look into your eyes."

Aunt Zoe grunted. "Don't you think I know how to check if someone has a concussion, Martin?"

"You're not certified, Zo. Leave the skilled tasks to us professionals." He could barely hold back a grin as he spoke.

"Bite me, Martin."

"Now, now, Zo. I'm no Dracula, but if you name the time for ol' Frankie-stein, I'll do my best to nibble away at your softer parts."

Harvey snickered, which earned him a threatening finger point from Aunt Zoe.

Reid shined the light in one of my eyes and then the other before stepping back.

"Well?" she asked.

He examined my face up close for several beats, lightly touching on some of the swollen areas. His eyes were very, very blue this close, and he smelled like a fresh walk in the forest. My aunt really needed to try to put the past behind her and snuggle up with Reid every night in front of the fireplace.

"No concussion," he answered her. "But it sure looks like Sparky lost the fight." He stepped back and pocketed his flashlight. "Whose turn is it to cook supper tonight?"

"Cornelius's." Aunt Zoe returned to the book splayed out in front of her. She thumbed over her shoulder toward the refrigerator. "Grab yourself something to drink. He'll be here soon to start cooking."

"Cornelius is actually cooking?" I asked, wondering if maybe I had hit my head too hard and heard her wrong. "That man never cooks. He usually calls me and has me pick up takeout for him, and then just shows up to eat."

She turned a page. "Well, I'm not positive, but he mentioned something about an old family favorite."

"What are you reading there, Zo?" Reid asked on his return from the refrigerator with a can of soda pop.

"Violet, please explain to Mr. Certified Professional what I'm looking for here."

I pressed the ice pack to my cheek and told Reid the story

about the hand mark, giving a quick overview of my song and dance up at Prudence's place.

After he picked his jaw up off the floor, he turned to Aunt Zoe. "Don't you have a bunch of those big books full of family stories?"

"You know I do, Martin."

"How about you let me help you."

She looked at him over her reading glasses. "How can you help? There are no fires to put out here."

"Oh, I think there's always one or two hot spots when you and I share a room," he said with a cocky grin.

Her gaze narrowed. "Keep it in your flame-resistant pants, hose jockey."

He chuckled. "Zo, I know you have family books that you've translated."

"Yeah, so what?"

"I can read your writing, especially after all the love letters you sent back when you were pining for me."

"Those were not love letters. They were written hexes meant to turn you into a toad when read aloud. Unfortunately, I'm rusty on my hex crafting."

"Well, then it was lucky for me that I prefer to read romantic poems in my head."

"I'd like to read some of those love lines if you kept 'em." Harvey rubbed his hands together. "I'm always lookin' for new ways to make the pretty birds at the senior center flutter their lashes in my direction."

Aunt Zoe scoffed, but her cheeks had taken on a solid pink hue. "Martin, your pants are on fire."

He shot me a wink. "Like I said, there's always a hot spot when your aunt and I share space."

I started to laugh, remembering my split lip too late, and ended with a groan.

"Anyway, Zo. I can help you by searching for any reference to the handprint." When she continued to stare at him with narrowed eyes, he added, "For crissake, woman. I investigate fires for a living. Don't you think that kind of work involves some perusing of thick manuals?"

She sighed. "Fine. I'll be back." She stood and headed toward the dining room.

During her absence, Harvey told us how Madame Contraire had asked him all sorts of questions on the return trip to her car. He swore he'd kept a buttoned lip on the real story at Prudence's place, and that he'd changed the subject by asking her how she became a medium. Her story included a previous possession by a ghost during a séance she'd attended for fun with a friend. That was when she'd learned of her medium abilities and gotten into the talking-to-ghosts business for money.

It turned out Prudence had been right about the medium being cracked open in the past. I wondered if the ghost that jumpstarted Madame Contraire's paranormal career had been the hisser I'd met in Zelda's living room. The asshole who'd liked to climb on furniture and take flying leaps at me. Maybe that ghost had wanted to stick around for more wild and crazy times beating up the living.

When Aunt Zoe returned with an armload of our history volumes, Cornelius followed her into the room. Dressed in a black track suit with white stripes down the sides, he appeared to have jogged straight to our house from a track meet. I glanced down at the grocery bags he was toting and then up at his bare head. Who in the heck was this jock wannabe and what had he done with my Abe Lincoln doppelganger in a Cossack hat?

"Look who's here," Aunt Zoe said, setting the stack of family history books in front of Reid. "Get busy, hot shot."

Cornelius paused at the sight of me, leaning in for a closer look. "It seems you have something on your face, Violet."

"I ran into trouble at Prudence's place."

He grabbed my hand that was holding the ice pack and pulled it away from my cheek. "Hmm. It looks more like trouble came swinging for you."

"She did. It was a medium who had a mean old ghost hiding in her shadow. Somehow, Prudence and I accidentally lit up her dark corners, and the ghost took out its wrath on my face." I fished another cookie out of the cookie jar.

Cornelius stole it from me before I could get it to my mouth. "As H.P. Lovecraft once said, 'Do not call up that which you cannot put down.' Thanks for the cookie."

"A little late for that tip now," I said to his back as he headed for the counter.

Harvey stared at the grocery bags as if he had X-ray vision. "What's in the bags, Corny? That tan one has something about New Orleans on the side."

"It is a surprise that I believe you all will enjoy," he answered, blocking our sight of the loot with his body. "In the meantime, as you often tell Prizefighter Parker, take a tater and wait."

Reid chuckled at Harvey as he pulled one of our family books his way. "He used one of your own lines on you, Harvey. Hey, Corny, if you like to play cards, you should come to our next poker night."

Harvey snickered, leaning over to backhand Reid's arm. "Good thinkin', Martin. That would really throw ol' Coop off his game. I could use the extra winnin's to snag some antique cannon balls from a company I found out of West Texas."

I shook my head at his cannon fetish and moved the ice pack to the lump on my forehead.

Fifteen minutes later, Cornelius was in the midst of slicing and buttering what looked like short loaves of bread as the oven heated up, Aunt Zoe and Reid were flipping pages in the history books, and Harvey was off to take care of what he'd called his "leaky plumbin' problem." I decided to check on the kids, who'd gone upstairs to do their homework, but were a little too quiet for my comfort.

I was passing through the dining room when the front door burst open and Doc rushed inside.

"You're early," I said, glancing at the clock on the wall. "I thought you had a late client meeting."

"I did." He shut the door and dropped his briefcase on the floor before slipping off his boots. "But Addy sent me a picture of your face."

"What?" I might have frowned, but the pain pills were doing their job of making everything feel numb, so I wasn't sure. "How did she …" I remembered her wanting to borrow my phone earlier. "Ohhh. When did she learn how to send pictures?"

"Grammy taught Layne and me last weekend using her phone," Addy said from the top of the stairs. "She thinks it's good for us to know in case of emergencies, like when I saw your face today."

I pointed at my bruised mug. "This is not an emergency,

Adelynn Renee."

"Yes, it is." Doc hung his coat in the hall closet. "Thank you for letting me know about it, Squirt."

Addy smiled down at him, both dimples showing. "I thought you might want to worry about Mom, like I am."

She was worried about me? I looked up at her. "Sweetie, I'm okay. Truly, I am. Now go get your homework done before supper." I turned to Doc. "It was an accident, that's all," I explained for Addy to hear, since she was slowly backing away.

He pointed toward the downstairs bathroom. "I need to talk to you alone for a minute."

"Harvey still might be in there."

"Fine." He took my hand and gently tugged me upstairs and into our bedroom, closing the door behind us.

"Really, Doc," I started, but he held his finger to his lips and led me over to the closet. He opened the sliding door, pushed aside his shirts, and ushered me inside.

I hesitated, a little surprised not to find a chicken and an imp nestled up in either corner. There was a cat, however, curled up on the shelf above.

"Oh, there's Bogart," I said, reaching up to pet her head.

"Inside, Killer. Now." He nudged me forward under the hanger rod.

Ducking, he squeezed in behind me and pulled the door partly closed.

"This is cozy," I whispered in the shadows. "You come here often?"

"Yep." He leaned against the wall, partly stooping. "It's one of my favorite locales."

"Really? Chicken feathers, cat hair, and all?"

"Sure. It's where my girl proposed to me."

I wanted to smile, but I didn't want to split open my lip again, so instead I took his hand and rubbed my unbruised cheek on it.

He chuckled. "You've been hanging around Bogart too long. We humans prefer to hug and kiss, remember?"

"Yeah, but hugs and kisses hurt too much right now."

"I'll make it all better later tonight, Boots." Carefully, he drew me into a soft hug, his lips lightly touching my temple before he pulled away. "Now, tell me what happened, and don't leave out a single detail."

I pulled him to the floor first, since he looked so uncomfortable hunched over, and the full story was going to take a bit of time to spill. We sat in the semi-darkness, me recounting the earlier discussion with Prudence and then the battle afterward with the medium, him asking questions along the way.

When I finished, he leaned his head back against the wall. "This is all my fault," he said. "I pushed you to see Prudence about that mark."

"Not all." I grabbed his hand and laced my fingers in his. "I'm the one who thought it was a good idea to take a stranger with unknown channeling abilities to Prudence's place in order to kill two birds with one stone." I scooted closer to him, sending a couple of feathers flying. "I have no doubt that when Prudence rebuilds her strength and is ready to talk to me again, she's going to be all hisses, fangs, and rattles for me bringing that medium into her sanctuary."

"How were you to know Madame Contraire was harboring a malicious entity?"

"I should have been more careful." Shaking my head, I explained, "I guess I didn't believe she was legit, really. I figured that since Prudence was able to talk through several non-mediums in the past, she could use Madame Contraire to answer the question about the hand mark without any ghostly hiccups. Who'd have thought something so hostile was hiding behind all that glittery lipstick and mascara?"

He flipped my hand over, rubbing my palm with his thumb. "We need to talk to Prudence even more now."

"Why?"

"Because we need to know if she was able to drive out that entity, or if it's still in the medium." He stretched out one leg on top of my shoes. "You'll need to be extremely careful around the medium in the meantime. If that thing is still inside her head, imagine trying to fight it off without Prudence around to help."

"Good point. No more alone time with Madame Contraire, especially in a vehicle."

Doc reached out and gently cupped my jaw, turning my head this way and that. "I wish I'd been there to take some of the hits in your place."

"I can't believe Addy sent you a picture. She must have snuck a shot of me when I wasn't looking."

"She's a good egg."

"I'm sorry I screwed up your last appointment."

"Don't be. He wasn't thrilled about driving in this weather anyway. I offered to come to him if we could reschedule." Doc leaned forward and kissed the corner of my mouth that wasn't bruised. "Next time, call me as soon as it happens."

"But if you're busy …"

"We've had this conversation before, Killer. I don't give a damn about work. You and the kids are what matter now. Everything else can be readjusted to fit around you guys."

I wasn't sure what to say to that. A simple thank-you didn't measure up to the love that filled my heart and tried to leak out my eyes.

I sniffed and then shifted onto my hands and bruised knees, crawling onto his lap. "Doc, I'm afraid."

"I'm right here with you." He wrapped his arms around me. "What in particular are you afraid of at the moment?"

"This handprint." I pointed at where it supposedly was. "Prudence doesn't have any answers. If Mr. Black doesn't either, and this thing starts to spread, then what?"

"We'll figure something out. Maybe Masterson will have an idea of the source."

"God, I don't want to talk to that guy—or whatever he is. He's just going to harass me about his missing *lidérc*."

"We'll cross that bridge together if it comes to that."

"Doc, you have to promise me that you'll separate me from my kids if things go haywire, and something takes over my brain like what Madame Contraire experienced today."

"Violet, don't—"

"I mean it, Doc. You'll need to hide my kids from me and then take care of me if it comes to it." I drew a line across my neck, making it clear what I meant.

"Whoa! This closet conversation has gone way too dark."

"I do not want to hurt my kids."

He pulled me closer, resting his chin on my head. "It's not going to reach that stage."

"How do we know?"

"Because I won't let it."

I leaned away so I could stare up at him. "How can you stop something we know nothing about?"

"I will get to the bottom of this, I promise, no matter what it takes or who I have to deal with."

"Sometimes a *Scharfrichter* dies," I whispered.

"Not you, Killer." He hugged me, holding me close for several moments before kissing my cheek. "Now, enough of these dark closet thoughts. You're ruining one of my favorite romantic hideouts."

I buried my nose in his neck. He smelled nice, safe yet sexy. "You want to screw around?"

He chuckled. "Always, but I don't think you're up to it."

"Probably not."

"Besides, Cornelius is making po'boy sandwiches for supper, and I don't want Harvey to eat them all before we get down there."

I leaned back and gaped at him. "How do you know what he's making? He was all secretive with us."

"He had the French bread and some beignets overnighted from New Orleans and delivered to my office today, since he knew I'd be working and available to sign for them."

"He has beignets downstairs?"

"Yep, along with pecan pralines."

"The real deals?"

"Straight from New Orleans."

I scoffed. "Why didn't you say so as soon as you got home?" I shoved open the closet door and scrambled out. "Hurry up, or I'm going to eat your beignets."

"Don't even try it, Tish." He followed me, helping me to my feet and brushing the chicken feathers off my backside. "Lead the way."

We were partway down the stairs when the front door opened and Natalie shivered inside, followed by Cooper.

"Fudgesicles," she muttered, sliding off her coat. "It's colder than the Abominable Snowman's balls out there."

"Why would a yeti's balls be cold?" Cooper asked, closing the door behind them. "They're covered with fur."

Natalie scoffed. "Because it has to sit on the ice whenever it takes a break from chasing people through the snow."

Cooper turned toward us. I gasped at the sight of his black and blue, half swollen-shut eye.

"What the hell happened to you, Coop?" Doc asked.

Natalie helped Cooper ease off his coat. "A two-hundred-and-fifty-pound falling Hawke landed on him." She draped the coat over her arm and stared up at me. "Harvey told me you had some fun bebopping around the joint up at Prudy's, but from your messed-up face, I'd say a bunch of elephants trampled you on the dance floor."

"It's a good thing her wounds mend quickly." Doc towed me down the remaining steps, his gaze on the slow-moving detective. "Coop, however, takes a lot longer to heal. That's going to be real colorful for the next week."

Natalie nodded. "He's going to give the Northern Lights a run for their money."

"Head on into the kitchen, you guys." I took their coats from Natalie.

Doc led the way, waving for them to follow. "Cornelius is serving up some good grub tonight."

"What happened to Parker?" I heard Cooper ask Natalie behind me as I was hanging up their coats.

"According to Harvey," she said, "the boogeyman was hiding inside Madame Contraire's head. When Prudy came knocking, the sucker jumped out of the dark and started whaling on Violet."

"Christ," he muttered. "That's some crazy shit."

"I know. But on the bright side, babe, with you two both sporting black eyes, you'll make a great pair of matching bookends when we sit you together."

CHAPTER NINETEEN

Tuesday, February 12th

On a high note, the ham and roast beef po'boy sandwiches Cornelius made were a hit, and the beignets had us licking our chops for more soon after they were gone. I'd drizzled honey on mine, groaning with every bite. Layne had ended up with powdered sugar everywhere, including inside the back of his shirt. Addy hadn't fared much better considering I found some in her hair and behind one ear, making her goodnight hugs and kisses even sweeter.

On a low note, I'd had to double up on pain pills overnight and managed to only get a couple hours of sleep. This morning, I'd taken one look at the black-and-blue monster in the mirror and agreed with Doc's suggestion of staying home to rest.

I waited in my room until Doc left to take the kids to school, not wanting them to see me until I'd caked on some makeup. When the coast was clear, I slipped downstairs to grab some coffee before hopping into the shower.

A travel cup and a folded note with my name on it waited for me on the counter. One was hot and steamy, the other was full of fresh coffee with a dollop of honey. Ahh, Doc. I must have done something right in a past life to have won him in this one.

I sipped on my drink and soaked in the warmth of Aunt Zoe's kitchen while the snow and wind blustered outside. Pulling out my phone, I sent a text to Jerry saying I was feeling under the weather and needed the day off. He sent back a thumbs-up. There was no mention on his part about Madame Contraire, so I assumed that meant she'd woken up in far less pain than me and hadn't bothered complaining to him about our adventures at Prudence's place.

I shot a text off to Natalie next, telling her I was laying low for the day and would be happy to help her "paint." This was the code word we'd decided upon last night for me to come press my ear to the floor vent along with her.

Her reply came back in a jiffy: *Let's see how the King Kong vs. Mothra battle goes down at the dog pound.*

In other words, we were on hold until Cooper finished meeting with the chief of police to lodge his complaints about Hawke's "dumbassery" yesterday at Galena House—which was Natalie's word for the offenses that occurred during the home inspection.

The good news was that Cooper now had a solid reason to have Detective Hawke booted from the apartment by the end of the week—at the latest. It turned out that Cooper's black eye was only one of Hawke's screwups. The list also included badgering the home inspector, especially while he was checking out the attic and the roof; and then not heeding Freesia's orders by trespassing on her ladder when she'd told him to stay off; and that turned into reckless endangerment for Natalie, who'd been down below holding the ladder; and finally plain old battery, when the blowhard fell coming down from the roof and landed on top of Cooper.

According to Natalie, she'd actually been holding onto the ladder when Hawke's foot missed the rung on the way down, but Cooper shoved her out of the way and took the brunt of Hawke's fall. This was how Cooper ended up stopping an elbow with his face. An inch to the right and he might have arrived for supper with his nose bandaged.

As for Hawke's broken arm, he'd tried to grab a ladder rung on his rapid descent but missed. Instead, his forearm got caught between the rungs. That story ended with a cracked bone. I took another sip of coffee, cringing just thinking about Natalie's description of the sound of his forearm snapping.

I sent Natalie another text: *I'm going to hop in the shower. Let me know if the Mummy is able to turn the water into blood.*

That code phrase referred to another plan for today, one that King Kong's girlfriend, aka Count Natalie von Dracula, was hiding under her cape.

Last night after supper was over, she'd followed me upstairs to check on the kids and then into the bathroom, closing the door behind us. Once locked inside with me, she told me her secret plan to sneak Cornelius (or rather "the Mummy," as she'd called him) into Galena House in the morning while Cooper was at the station.

"How are you going to sneak him inside with the cops sitting outside watching the front door?"

She smiled. "Through the coal chute in the basement."

"Oh. That's going to make him all dirty. Isn't it hard to get coal dust out of clothes and carpet?"

"Really, Vi? That's the first thing you think of when I say I'm sneaking Corny inside?"

"Well, Freesia just had new carpet installed."

She crossed her arms. "I'd expect something more from you, like: 'Why are you doing this, my amazing best friend? With your big brain, you must have some master plan that is going to save the day!' Now I'm starting to wonder how hard you hit your head at Prudence's."

"Very hard, dammit." I motioned for her to turn around so I could finish what I came in the bathroom to do. "Fine, why are you sneaking Corny into Galena House?"

"Because Dracula and the Mummy are going to perform some monster magic and make it so the video feed in Hawke's apartment is accessible via a set of monitors in Freesia's place."

"To what end?"

"If we can record some footage of the apartment sitting empty, then we can switch out the actual video footage showing us sneaking inside the place with a loop of the recording."

"Oh! That's a good idea."

"I know, right? I told you, girl, I got your back."

"But isn't that illegal?"

"Possibly."

"And aren't you sleeping with a cop?"

"A suspended cop. He's not totally official at the moment."

"Does Cooper know about this?" I tried to avoid looking in the mirror as I turned on the faucet to wash my hands.

"Why do you think I'm sneaking the Mummy in while Coop is gone?" She turned to look at me. "As Harvey has said before, there are parts of the caper that King Kong doesn't need to know."

I shut off the faucet. "When did Harvey say that?"

She handed me the towel. "The same time he said we shouldn't tell *you* everything, either."

I gaped at her. "What aren't you guys telling me?"

"That's not important right now. What you need to know is that the Mummy says he should be done hooking up everything by the time Coop finishes at the station."

"What if Hawke comes home when you're setting this up?"

"He won't. He and his broken arm will be at the station with Coop and the chief the whole time."

"How do you know?"

"Because Coop told Hawke that he was going first thing in the morning to file his complaints. You and I both know there is no way Hawke will be able to keep his big beak out of that meeting."

"Man, I'd love to be a fly on the wall in the chief's office when that goes down."

"Me, too. Coop promised to tell me all about it when he was done." She rubbed her hands together. "Now, tomorrow morning, if I tell you 'the Mummy has turned the water into blood,' that means everything is done and we're recording live feed."

"Got it. And what if I want to ask about hearing anything through the floor vents?"

"We'll call that 'painting,' my lovely lizard friend."

We'd returned to the kitchen then, where Natalie had headed to the sink to help Doc with drying dishes, and I'd eased back into my chair where I tried to participate in the conversation without worrying about that freaky handprint possibly spreading farther up my face.

My phone pinged, bringing me back to the present.

Natalie replied to my earlier text: *The water is officially blood. Now go shower, Godzilla. I can smell you clear from here.*

I sighed in relief and gave her a thumbs-up. Before I headed upstairs, I texted Doc: *Any sign of King Kong outside the police station yet?*

He sent back: *No. How are you feeling?*

I'm alive. Going to take a shower, then I'll be even better.

Good. Send me wet and naked pics.

I chuckled.

Before I could reply, another text came from him: *On second thought, DON'T send me any pics. Your daughter knows how to access and send the photos on your phone.*

I winced and typed: *True. You'll just have to see the real deal in person later.*

I'm your huckleberry, Boots.

Loved your note with my coffee. Get to work!

I checked out the window while finishing my go-go juice, seeing smoke coming from Aunt Zoe's glass shop chimney. Rooster sat in the shop window looking back at me. He wagged his tail and bobbed his head. I waved back. All was well in Oz. Well, except for everything that wasn't, and that included the fact that upon taking a look at me in good ol' Arcana late last night, Aunt Zoe wasn't able to see the handprint on my face either. We'd checked on Cornelius in the mirror while we were at it, but Doc hadn't seen anything on him either.

On that so-so note, I set my mug in the sink and headed upstairs to try to wash away some of my troubles.

When I came back down, Trouble (with a capital T) was sitting at the kitchen table talking on his cell phone while his uncle Harvey cracked some eggs into a frying pan at the stove.

"What are you two doing here?" I asked, heading for another cup of coffee.

"Good morning to you too, Sparky." Harvey stared at me for a few seconds. "Huh. Your face looks more like a panda on that side this morning instead of a raccoon."

"Thanks, I think."

Harvey held up an egg. "Hungry?"

"Will there be bacon with that egg?" I asked.

"It's already broilin' in the oven."

I thought I'd smelled that upstairs, but figured my imagination was teasing me. "Then I'm starving." I poured my coffee, glancing his way. "You thirsty?"

"Nah. I had plenty of the rattle-and-roll stuff earlier before I picked up Coop at the station."

"Why were *you* picking him up? Does it have something to do with him taking a beating from Hawke yesterday?"

"I did not take a beating," Cooper said, horning into the conversation. "I had to drop off my rig at the station."

"Because you're suspended?" I rested my hip against the counter.

"No, because the engine light kept coming on. It needs to be checked out before I come off suspension." He set his phone on the table and pointed at it. "Natalie is listening."

"Hi, guys," she said. Her voice sounded tinny through the phone's speaker.

My phone pinged. It was from Natalie. I read her message, raising my cup to my lips: *Corny is here with me. Shh.*

Swallowing, I looked up to find Cooper eagle-eyeing me.

Crap!

"Is there something on my face?" I asked, trying to distract him from my phone.

"Yeah, about a mile of bad road. Same as mine." He pointed at the coffee mug. "I'll have one of those if you're pouring."

I pocketed the phone. "Sure, I'll pour if you tell me why you're here in my kitchen this morning instead of … I don't know, somewhere else doing the mambo-bambo monkey things you normally do when you're off duty."

This visit was not part of the caper plans discussed last night after supper. If I'd known I was going to have post-shower company, I would've at least tried to tame my hair.

One blond eyebrow lifted. "What off-duty 'monkey things' do you think I do, Parker?"

I shrugged and grabbed a mug from the cupboard. "Things like beating your chest, buffing your firearms, changing the batteries in your Taser, lollygagging at the shooting range, working on your currently illegible ticket writing penmanship, and maybe secretly window shopping for camouflage underwear."

A snort of laughter came through the phone. "She has a point about your lousy handwriting," Natalie said in between chuckles. "But Coop doesn't wear undies, Vi."

Cooper scowled at his phone. "Yes, I do."

"Oh, I forgot," she continued. "I'm not under oath. Okay, he does wear undies, but officially he prefers that I call them boxer briefs. I'm the one who wears *undies*."

"What kind of undies?" Harvey asked. "Does Coop like yours to be camouflage, too?"

"I'm not into camouflage shit," he bit out.

"I don't know if Coop has an undie preference," Natalie said. "Other than me taking them off."

Harvey let out a howl of laughter.

"Jesus, Nat!" Cooper scrubbed his hand down the non-bruised side of his face. "I'm in mixed company here."

"Please, Coop. It's just your uncle and Violet. In case you've had your head in the sand for the last month, they both know we're doing the wild thing."

"This is your fault, Parker," he said, his steely eyes using me as his target practice.

I set the cup of coffee on the table in front of him and held up my hands. "It wasn't on purpose, trust me."

"Coop is there this morning because he can't live without seeing you at least once a day," Natalie said, still snickering.

"Once a year would be more than enough," he grumbled, glancing toward his uncle. "I'll have some bacon, too."

"I'd already figured on that, curly wolf."

I dropped into a chair across from him and took a longer look at his bruises. "Why does your face look even worse this morning?"

"You can thank me for that," Natalie said.

"What do you mean?" I asked the phone. "Are you beating Cooper now instead of just roaring at him?"

"Did he tell you I was roaring?" she asked.

Cooper glared at me and held his finger to his lips.

I tried to think of a way to divert her focus from the lion's breath business. "Coop and I were talking about Cornelius's ideas for stress relief is all."

"Anyway," Cooper continued, "she wanted to make my bruises look worse for the meeting with the chief, so she added more color around my eye."

I leaned closer. "Damn, you're good, Natalie. I wouldn't have guessed."

"Bet your ass I am, toots!"

Harvey pointed the bacon-turning tongs at me. "You're a bit of a hard truth to look at first thing today, too, Sparky. Why are those scratches worse north of your neck instead of better? I thought you *Scharfrichter* folk healed lickety-split."

"Hey, I didn't know you two were down here, so I'm makeup-less at the moment." I pointed at my face. "This is the filter-free, post-trauma real deal."

"Your poor stallion must have a few more white hairs."

I glared at Harvey. "Careful, bodyguard, or I'll give you a matching face."

"Girlie, you're all a-gurgle and no guts."

It was too early for me to figure out what he meant, so I turned to Cooper. "You want to get any more digs in before you tell me what happened at the station?"

He shook his head. "I agree with Uncle Willis. Poor Nyce." At my growl, he held up a hand. "Wait. What I mean is, it has to be hard on Nyce to see you beat up like this. If it were Nat, I'd feel like shit for not being there to protect her."

"Aww, that's really sweet, Detective Love Muffin," Natalie said.

We both frowned at his phone.

"Anyway, what happened at the station?" I asked.

"Hawke has to vacate the apartment by Friday. He'll be relocating to a motel in town that rents rooms by the week."

"Yes!" I clapped my hands together. "Finally."

He crossed his arms. "Don't start celebrating yet, Parker."

"Why not?"

"Yeah," Natalie said, "why not?"

"Hawke saw this coming. He got the jump on us."

"What do you mean?" Natalie beat me to the question.

"He called a moving company out of Rapid City first thing this morning and rented a truck to move the clocks to a hidden location that only he and the chief will know about."

"*Ay caramba*," I muttered.

"Where is he having them moved?" Natalie asked.

Harvey looked over from the stove. "And *when* is he having them moved?"

"Hawke wouldn't tell me any details. Said it wasn't my business since I was suspended and off the case for now."

"He's a top-notch pedigree chump," I grumbled.

Harvey pulled out the tray of bacon from the oven. "We're gonna have to send that goose thunder-huntin' sooner rather than later."

I raised my eyebrows at Cooper. He shrugged back.

"What does that mean, Harvey?" Natalie asked.

He closed the oven door. "Move things 'round so as to leave

the big bird scratchin' his head."

That didn't really clear things up for me. "And how do we do that?"

"For starters, we need to split the wind."

Cooper sighed. "Speak English, Uncle Willis."

Harvey grabbed a stack of plates from the cupboard. "We need to move those clocks before Hawke tucks them under a rock, 'cause there ain't no way he's gonna kiss and tell on where he's storin' them once they're moved."

"I could torture the relocation details out of him," I offered. I might start with making him drink a fake potion that is supposed to shrivel his twig and berries.

Cooper pointed at his black eye. "Get in line, Parker."

"Well, we have to think of something, and quick." I looked down at the phone, wondering if the Mummy was still hanging out with Natalie von Dracula and listening in on our conversation. I cleared my throat. "Do you guys think Cornelius knows a voodoo spell he could put on Hawke that would work like truth serum?" I said loud and clear for the Galena House audience.

"Why are you talking so loud all of a sudden?" Cooper asked, his eyes squinty as he looked from me to his phone and back.

Damn the law dog in him. *Abort! Abort!*

"Uhh, my ears started ringing," I yelled. "It must be from hitting my head yesterday, I can't hear so … Oh wait." I paused, tipping my head to the side and then back upright. "Now it's clear," I said at a normal level.

His squint stayed locked in place, but before he could try to sniff out the truth from me, Harvey set a plate of bacon and eggs in front of him. "Eat up, boy."

I looked up at Harvey in time to catch a wink from him and slight head shake. Knowing Harvey, that gesture could mean all sorts of things, but my guess was that he knew about the recording operation Cornelius and Natalie were working on at Galena House this morning.

"Okay, you guys," Natalie said. "We all need to put on our thinking caps and ponder this for a bit. There has to be a way of getting the *where* and *when* details from Hawke."

"A legal way," Cooper added, picking up his fork.

Natalie blew a raspberry into the phone. "That's what I think of your legal beagle howling, law dog."

"You need to stay clear of Hawke, Natalie," Cooper said.

"I heard you the last five times you told me that already today, Coop."

"Yeah, but were you really listening, or just nodding with your fingers crossed behind your back again?"

I grinned, trying not to chuckle as I took the plate of food Harvey brought over to me and mouthed my thanks.

"Come on, babe," she said. "You know I listen to every single word you say."

He harrumphed. "You listen, but you don't do as I say."

"Of course not. These aren't caveman times and I'm not Wilma Flintstone."

"You're more of a Barney Rubble to Coop's Fred Flintstone than a Wilma," I said.

Cooper pointed his fork at me. "You're not helping."

Harvey sat down next to me. "Tell you what, Coop. I'll stop by the station and see if I can needle the truth out of Hawke." He laced his fingers together and stretched out his hands, cracking his knuckles. "I've watched plenty of *Columbo* in my time to know just how to poke him enough to make the sucker bleed."

"You stay away from him, too, Uncle Willis." Cooper gave me the stink eye. "And don't you even think about going anywhere near him, Parker. Hawke is just waiting for a reason to lock you up and throw away the key. Same goes for Nyce."

"Fine, Coop," Natalie said. "The four of us will keep our distance. In the meantime, I need you to run to Rapid City for me this morning as soon as you're finished eating."

"What?" He scowled at the phone. "No." He tore off a bite of bacon. "Why?"

"Because I'm busy painting and it's my turn to cook supper tonight."

"But my rig is in getting fixed."

"Your police vehicle is. Not your truck."

"You can take my pickup," Harvey said, thumbing toward the front door. "It's hot to trot and ready to roll."

Cooper shook his head. "But I'm busy."

"Doing what?" she asked. "You're suspended, remember? Unless you plan on shoveling the snow from a senior citizen's driveway like a kind local boy should, then you're available."

"Natalie, I'm always kind."

I scoffed.

Cooper reached over and stole a piece of my bacon as punishment.

"But I don't want to drive to Rapid this morning," he said. "It's too damned cold to leave town. Can't I just get something from Piggly Wiggly in Lead?"

"No way, King Kong. After Corny's meal last night, I need to up my game. I placed an order for pickup and gave them your name, so tally ho, the quarry has been sighted. I'll text you the details."

"Fine. But you're going to owe me big for this, Beals."

Harvey grinned. "That means he's gonna want to wear *your* camouflage undies tonight."

"I don't ..." Coop finished with a growl and stole a piece of his uncle's bacon, too.

"I'll pay up, babe," she said. "Don't you worry. Text ya later, monsters. Dracula is *out* ... of the coffin."

Cooper glared at his phone for a few seconds after she'd hung up. "That woman drives me nuts."

"She drives your nuts, all right," Harvey said, wiggling his bushy eyebrows at his nephew. "That's what you get for parkin' your big rig in her camouflage garage over and over."

"Come on." I wrinkled my nose at the dirty bird. "I'm trying to eat here."

"That's it, Uncle Willis." Cooper stole the rest of the bacon off Harvey's plate. "These are mine now." He pointed a piece at his uncle. "And you're coming with me to Rapid City whether you like it or not."

CHAPTER TWENTY

No sooner had Harvey and Cooper rolled on down the road, my cell phone started ringing.

I pulled it from my pocket, seeing Natalie's name and wondering what she had in store for me this morning.

"What's going on, Count Nat-ula? You thirsty for some fresh blood?"

"Always, and you're a vampire's favorite kind of candy."

I sat on that for a few beats, but still … "I don't get it."

"You're a sucker."

I grunted. "No, you're the sucker—for law dogs."

"That's not really a joke now, is it?"

"No. Why did you call? Is something going on in Hawke's apartment?"

"Not yet, but it will be soon. You need to get your buns over to Corny's place and check out his monitors."

"I don't understand. Aren't his monitors keeping track of what's going on at Calamity Jane's?"

"Not all of them. He's connected one to the camera feed in Hawke's place."

"How did he do that?"

She scoffed. "Does that even matter? I mean, if he were to explain that to you, would you be able to follow? Because I wouldn't."

"Maybe I would."

"Aren't you the one who struggles to even use the TV remote half the time?"

"That's because we have like four freakin' remotes to run one television."

"Violet, there are only three. One is for the ceiling fan."

"The struggle is real, Natalie."

She laughed. "Just get your ass over to Corny's place ASAP. Hawke got home a short time ago, and he's about to receive a visitor. You're not going to want to miss this."

"Who's the visitor?"

"You'll see. Take some popcorn and enjoy the show. Now, I gotta go—"

"Natalie, wait."

"What?"

"How did you know Cooper was gone? They only left a few minutes ago."

"Because Harvey texted me the all-clear."

"So, he *was* in on this." I thought back to the moment Harvey had delivered Cooper's food and redirected his nephew's focus away from me after my bungled attempt to ask Cornelius about potential voodoo spells on the sly. "Was going to Rapid City with Cooper part of his plan?"

"Of course. Someone needs to stall Coop long enough for us to take care of business here."

Wowzer. From my seat at the table, it had looked like Cooper leaned on Harvey to go with him, not the other way around.

"Damn," I said. "Harvey is good."

"He has his finger on the pulse of this caper, babe. Don't you doubt that for a moment."

I heard a low, mumbling voice in the background.

"There's a lighter in the drawer," she said to whoever was there with her. "Vi, I gotta go. Head to Corny's place now!"

After she hung up, I sat for a moment thinking about Cooper heading clear to Rapid City for takeout. That was about an hour there and an hour back. Make that three hours, if Harvey dragged his feet in the middle, which I expected him to do given the real reason for the trip.

I hurried upstairs to change into something warmer. After pulling on a pair of jeans and a soft alpaca wool sweater, I sent Doc a text that I'd be swinging by in about ten minutes to grab the spare key to Cornelius's place. Doc had an appointment earlier this morning that should have wrapped up by now, but sometimes his clients were there for longer than the hour he scheduled.

Why do you need the key? he sent back.

Keeping in mind that Cooper wanted us to be careful what we said in our messages, I wrote: *The show is starting soon. I don't want to miss the opening scene.*

You're cute when you're mysterious, Tish. Spill the beans, or I'm not handing over the key.

Maybe we can strike a bargain.

Like what?

I paused, checking inside the neck of my sweater to remember which bra I was wearing. Oh good, it had some color to it. *How about a flash of some skin in exchange for the key.*

I like the way you're thinking, Godzilla. Tell me more.

I'll whisper it in your ear when I see you shortly.

Pocketing my cell phone, I hurried back downstairs to grab my boots, purse, and coat.

"Where are you going in such a hurry?" Aunt Zoe asked.

She stood watching me from the kitchen archway, a half-eaten piece of toast in her hand and a smudge of soot on her cheek. She wore her old work jeans and a faded flannel shirt along with a blue stocking cap. Rooster sat at her feet staring up at the toast in her hand with his tongue hanging out.

"I need to go to Cornelius's apartment."

"Why?"

I opened the hall closet. "Honestly, I'm not sure, but Natalie said that some show with Hawke as a headliner is about to start on one of Cornelius's monitors."

Her forehead wrinkled. "I take it those two got the video feed up and running this morning."

"You know about that?"

She nodded. "Harvey called me earlier while he was waiting for Coop to wrap up at the station."

"The busybody is keeping Cooper preoccupied down in Rapid for the next few hours."

"He mentioned that, too."

Sheesh, Harvey was the master of ceremonies today.

"Did he tell you about Hawke already hiring a moving company?"

"No." She tossed the last bite of toast to Rooster. "What

company? For when?"

"We don't know, but Hawke is back at the apartment now, and I have a feeling Natalie and Cornelius are about to try their hand at getting some answers while Cooper is far away from the scene with a solid alibi."

Aunt Zoe held up a finger. "Give me a minute to wash up and grab my coat. I'm coming with you."

I went looking for Daisy and Elvis as I waited for her, finding the two of them plopped on the upstairs bathroom floor next to the wastebasket. The sight of Daisy using a nail file to buff the sharp tips off Elvis's claws made me stop short and stare.

"You've got to be fucking kidding me," I whispered.

Somedays this shit truly didn't seem real.

Taking a note from Hawke's preemptive playbook, I decided to beat the imp to the punch. I slowly entered the bathroom so as not to ruffle the feathers of either fowl or imp and fished out a bottle of one of my least-favorite colored nail polishes from the drawer. Twisting the lid slightly to make sure it wasn't stuck shut, I set the nail polish down next to Daisy.

"You can use that on Elvis's toenails, but don't touch my other polishes. Got it?"

The imp looked up at me, cringing slightly, its red beady eyes narrowed, its pointy teeth bared just a tiny bit. Then it slowly reached out to grab the polish. There was no hissing or snarling to go with the display of teeth, so I assumed I'd witnessed its version of a smile.

"And don't make a mess of things in here."

Daisy nodded once, slowly. I'd find out whether or not the imp truly understood me after I came home.

I backed out of the bathroom and headed downstairs. Aunt Zoe waited at the door with her keys in hand. "I'll drive since you're playing hooky today and we're parking near Calamity Jane's. I wouldn't want your numbnuts boss to see you driving around town."

"I'll duck if we pass him along the way."

She opened the front door. "It's going to be a cold ride. I didn't have time to warm up the truck."

I grinned. "I'll snuggle up next to you like I used to in the winter when I was little." I locked the door behind us and followed her down the porch steps. "I may not be as hot and hunky as Reid would be at your side, but I can blow warm air on your ear if you'd like."

She chuckled. "Zip your lips, Violet Lynn."

A short drive later, we were slipping and sliding across the parking lot behind Calamity Jane Realty. Mother Nature didn't cut us any slack on our way to Doc's backdoor, blasting us with lung-chilling gusts filled with tiny pellets of icy snow.

Mona's SUV was the only one of my coworkers' vehicles in the lot. Luckily, we didn't run into her on our race to Doc's office. I didn't want to try to explain my bruises to her yet. I'd save that for tomorrow when my face was looking better—at least I hoped it would be. Aunt Zoe's salve seemed to be hurrying the healing along, but nothing short of a miracle would make it all fade before I had to return to work.

I held Doc's door for Aunt Zoe and then hurried inside after her, shutting out the arctic-like weather. I leaned against the door for a few seconds to catch my breath.

"That cold wind knocks the salt and pepper right out of me," Aunt Zoe whispered in the shadowy back hallway.

The light came on overhead. "Look what we have here," Doc said, resting his shoulder against the wall. "Two Parkers for the price of one. Lucky me."

He looked smart and sexy in his coffee-colored pants and the black sweater I'd bought him when I was down in Rapid City last week.

"Hi, Doc," Aunt Zoe said, still shivering. She looked toward his front room. "You have a client?"

He shook his head. "Not for another hour." He dangled Cornelius's key out in front of him, his dark eyes locked onto me. "I was offered a deal in exchange for this, I believe."

"Yeah, about that deal," I said, closing the distance between us. I gave him my best attempt at a flirty fluttering of my lashes. "I'd like to propose a slight change in the terms."

He quirked an eyebrow. "Oh yeah? This better be good, Tish, because I was *very* partial to the original deal."

"You'll like this. Maybe not better, but I promise to add to the original deal later, if you agree."

"Sounds like I have nothing to lose."

"And a bit of entertainment to gain according to Natalie." I took the key he offered. "Come with us to see the show."

"What show are you talking about?"

"Grab your coat. I'll tell you when we get up there."

A shiver, curse, and race through Old Man Winter's ice box once again, then the three of us climbed the stairs to Cornelius's place.

We slipped into his apartment, careful to tread lightly inside since we were directly over Calamity Jane Realty and didn't want to snare Mona's attention.

I sniffed a couple of times. "Why does this place smell a little like rotten eggs?" I pulled the neckline of my sweater up over my nose.

Aunt Zoe stepped into the kitchen. "Maybe he boiled his breakfast egg for too long."

"I'll go crack a window," Doc said, heading into the living room.

I followed my aunt. "What are you doing?"

"This apartment is nicer than I'd expected. I like the updated layout." She looked around the clean kitchen counter and clutter free table. "Cleaner, too. Cornelius must be one of those neat and tidy bachelors."

I thought back to some of my past visits to his multiple dwellings, like when he was being haunted by that petulant little bratty ghost, Wilda, in his hotel suite. Or the time I showed up and found him sprawled out on his back on the kitchen table in front of me, trying to burn the crud out from one of his chakras—or was it to see with his third eye?

"More like a bizarre and mad scientist bachelor." I grabbed her arm. "Come on, his video nerve center is this way."

I led her into the living room where a bank of monitors was broadcasting real-time video of Calamity Jane's 24/7. On one monitor, Mona was typing away at her computer, her focus locked on whatever was on her screen. On another, Jane's old office sat empty and quiet, the door to the creepy closet with access to the Hellhole closed tight. Another monitor showed an empty back hallway where Cornelius had once seen a shadowy entity hovering behind me. A fourth monitor showed the front office from another angle, the corner with the coffee maker was the main focus at the moment. But the final monitor showed a different scene than usual—Ms. Wolff's apartment.

Doc joined me. "These four on the left all look normal."

I nodded. "Do you see any sign of Jane?"

He turned to me. "You do remember that I rarely actually *see* a ghost, right?"

"Yeah, but maybe something has changed in your Oracle brain. Or you hit your head and knocked something loose."

He chuckled. "You're the one who keeps getting hit on the coconut, Killer." He looked at the monitor on the far right. "I see Cornelius has been busy this morning."

"Where is that?" Aunt Zoe pointed at the last screen.

"It's the living room in Ms. Wolff's old apartment in Galena House." I leaned a little closer. "See the clocks covering the walls in the background?"

She whistled softly. "That's a lot of clocks for one *Scharfrichter* to monitor day and night."

"A lot of potential trouble is what I see." I sighed. "If we're able to get those clocks out of Hawke's hands, we're going to have to figure out where we can store them all."

"I have an attic," she said.

"No way. They can't be near Addy and Layne. I won't be able to sleep at night from worry."

"Not a single moving box in sight," Doc said. "Hawke must be paying the movers to box up the clocks."

"Yeah. I'm not sure if that's good or bad."

What would happen if they broke a bunch of them in the process of relocating them? How would I even know if they were broken since the clocks only worked when a traveler came my way?

My cell phone pinged in my pocket.

I checked who had texted—it was Natalie: *Are you in the Mummy's tomb yet?*

I replied: *Yes. Watching the play-by-play with the Wolfman and Frankie's bride.*

Good! We'll release the plague of locusts.

I reread her words a few times, then wrote: *I don't know what that means.*

Just watch. The Mummy says the Wolfman knows how to adjust the volume and switch views.

I showed Doc her message. He nodded and took a seat at the keyboard in front of the monitor showing Ms. Wolff's place. He moved the mouse next to it, clicking on a small box in the upper corner of the screen that caused a dropdown menu to appear.

A grunting sound came through a set of speakers next to the monitor.

"What's doing that?" I whispered.

Doc clicked on one of the menu items and then tapped a couple of keys. The monitor view changed to show Ms. Wolff's bedroom from high in the corner over by the closet. On the left side of the screen, Hawke was pushing one of the dressers along the wall, using his shoulder and good arm.

"What's he doing that for?" Aunt Zoe asked.

"Lord only knows with that buffoon," I grumbled. "Look at the pile of clothes and stacks of magazines and other shit he's left on the floor. The place looks like a pigsty."

Someone knocked.

I looked back toward the door, my heart stumbling for a beat or two, but then I realized the sound had come from the computer speakers.

Hawke stepped away from the dresser and stared out through the doorway that led into Ms. Wolff's living room.

"Who is it?" he bellowed.

I couldn't hear the reply.

"Tell Freesia I'm too busy for that shit right now," Hawke shouted back.

There was more mumbling in the background, then Hawke cursed and headed into the living room.

Doc switched the camera view so we could watch Hawke lumber past on his way to the front door.

After the detective passed out of sight, I glanced at Doc. "Can you change it up so we can see who's at the door?"

He clicked on a menu and then shook his head. "It looks like we can go back and forth between three stationary camera views— the bedroom, the living room, and the dining area. But I can't actually move the camera to follow Hawke around."

He switched the view so we could see the dining area with its walls also covered in clocks.

"Well," Aunt Zoe said, "at least we're able to see this much thanks to Cornelius and Natalie sneaking into the apartment to tweak Hawke's cameras."

"I have a feeling Freesia might be part of this somehow, too." I hip bumped Doc. "Did Harvey tell you earlier about them tapping into Hawke's feed?"

"No. But I'm not surprised they did. Between Natalie's daredevil nature and Cornelius's technical talent, it was only a matter of time before they teamed up to do something not so legal." He glanced at me. "I'm guessing Coop doesn't know about this."

"You're guessing correctly." I crossed my arms. "Cooper may think he's running this caper, but his uncle seems to be the mastermind behind the scenes."

Doc grinned. "Harvey is probably figuring that as long as you two stay clear of that apartment—and Galena House itself—and you both have an alibi, it's full steam ahead for everyone else."

"It's a good thing I dragged you two alibis here to keep me company."

"More like to keep you out of trouble, Killer." Doc's focus returned to the monitor.

Aunt Zoe leaned closer to the speakers. "Can either of you hear what's being said?"

I shook my head. "It's all mumbles right now."

Doc nodded in agreement.

My phone pinged.

Natalie was back: *The Mummy is at the Wolff's door.*

Doing what?

Stay tuned, you big reptile.

I pocketed my phone again. "That was Natalie," I said, watching the screen. "She said Cornelius is at the door."

Actually, he was already inside the apartment, according to the dining room camera. It showed him passing by on his way to the living room, leaving a trail of smoke in his wake.

Smoke?

"Where's he going?" Aunt Zoe asked.

Doc switched to the living room camera. "There he is."

Cornelius stood in the center of the room, waving a bundle of something over his head, leaving trails of smoke in the air.

I leaned closer to the screen. "What is that?"

"I'm guessing it's sage," Aunt Zoe said.

~

"What the hell are you doing with that?" Hawke's voice came through the speakers. "Trying to start a fire?"

"As I explained at the door," Cornelius said, "I have been hired by the owner to cleanse this apartment of wayward spirits."

Hawke stepped partway into view, the back of his head and shoulders making it onto the monitor. "What are you charging her for this wizard bullshit?"

"I don't discuss my fees with non-clients. If you'd like to hire me—"

Hawke scoffed. "I don't hire flakes."

"Ah, I see your dark yellow aura is currently ruling your mental state." Cornelius lowered onto the floor, sitting cross-legged while holding the bundle of sage in both hands in front of his chest. "It is dangerously close to the color of dull mustard."

"What's so bad about mustard? It goes great on a hot dog."

"I would suggest you spend a few moments clearing your ajna in order to see through the fear and resentment clouding your vision."

"My *what?*"

"Your ajna." Cornelius waved the sage around in a circle in front of his face. "You know, your third eye."

Hawke waved him off. "I don't believe in that psychic phony baloney."

"That is to your detriment then. Now if you don't mind, I need you to remain silent while I listen through my vishuddha for any entities in this room."

"What's a vishuddha? Some kind of hearing aid?"

Cornelius sighed at Hawke's ignorance. "It is the throat chakra."

"I can't believe Freesia is buying into this shit. Where's your Magic 8 Ball and Ouija board? Shouldn't we ask the ghosts in here to give us a message?"

Cornelius closed his eyes. "The sooner you let me tune into the spiritual ether, the faster I will finish my task here."

He began making circles with the bundle of sage again.

~

I waited, watching, wondering what Cornelius's goal was with this spiritual cleansing song and dance. How would it help us figure out the who, where, and when of Hawke's clock moving plans?

After about thirty seconds, Aunt Zoe looked my way. "What's that noise in the background?"

"Cornelius is humming," Doc answered first.

"That's what he does when we have a séance," I told her. "He hums while I close my eyes and think of a candle flame."

"Then the ghosts swarm the room and all hell breaks loose," Doc added. "And somehow I end up on the floor, battered and bruised, simply because I sat too close to Killer here," he finished with a grin.

I blew him a kiss. "I don't bruise you every time."

"You're right. Sometimes I take a beating from an angry otherworldly troublemaker who shows up at the party instead." He reached up and caught my hand. "Personally, I like your love pinches the best, *cara mía*."

"Ah, Gomez. Let's dig out the leather straps and red-hot pokers later tonight."

Aunt Zoe pulled the chair over from farther down the line of monitors and sat next to Doc. "I'd like to be in on one of your séances sometime soon."

"I don't think that's a good idea," I said.

"Why not?"

I couldn't think of an actual reason, it was more of a gut feeling. Or maybe it was simply because I'd worry about her too much and not be able to focus.

"Just because."

She smirked. "You'll have to do better than that to keep me away, Violet Lynn."

~

On the screen, Hawke paced back and forth in front of Cornelius. "Come on, man," he muttered. "Hurry it up."

Our resident Mummy with the smoking sage bundle continued to hum.

"I don't have time for this today," Hawke snapped. "I've got stuff to take care of here. Can't you come back after I move out?"

Cornelius opened one eye. "That depends."

"On what?"

"When you're moving."

"Soon enough."

He opened the other eye. "How soon?"

"You could come back next week."

"That will not do." Cornelius got to his feet.

"Why not?"

He held the smoking sage up right in front of Hawke's face. "Because you have a problem, Detective Sprock."

"It's Detective Hawke, not Sprock." Hawke pushed Cornelius's hand with the sage away. "Besides you standing in my way right now, I have no problems."

"Oh, but you do."

"If you're talking about your blond buddy at the real estate office, don't worry, I plan to lock that witchy problem up behind bars soon enough."

~

I growled. "I really want to blast that butthead with some atomic breath."

Doc chuckled. "Don't be going nuclear on us, Godzilla. Save your energy for the big battle yet to come."

~

"Witchy?" Cornelius repeated. "If you are referring to Jane the ghost, that wraith is not really a problem unless she grows angry and takes it upon herself to break my very expensive equipment."

"I'm not talking about any stupid, make-believe ghost. You're just playing on Freesia's fears to get money out of her. I should lock you up for ghost grifting."

"*Au contraire*, Detective Crock."

"I told you, it's Detective Hawke. Cement that in the brick you call a brain."

"There are definitely ethereal entities coexisting with us, including in this very apartment." Cornelius walked toward the camera, staring up at us for a couple of seconds as he waved the smoking sage through the air. "Regrettably for you, I can see the gossamer shadow of a phantom presence hovering behind you at this very moment. However, I cannot tell if it is simply the astral body of a being bridging the physical world from another location, or a displaced spirit clinging to your energy."

"That's a bunch of horse shit."

Cornelius shrugged. "Your fondness for excrement aside, I only speak of what I see. Believe what you will, but the reason I was asked here was due to this apartment's sinister past."

"Yeah, I know there's been a few murders here. So what? Are you trying to tell me one of those dead people are floating around me right now?"

"Not at all." Cornelius walked to another corner in the living room, moving the sage in a figure 8. "The being I am sensing is much older. And stronger."

"Riiiight. Let me guess, it's a demon." He howled, wiggling his fingers in the air.

"Not a demon." Cornelius pressed his ear to the wall. "Although, its presence is certainly dark and foreboding, smelling lightly of sulfur and decay. Have you not noticed that scent before?"

~

Aunt Zoe chuckled. "Damn, Cornelius is good."

I nodded, resting my hand on Doc's shoulder. "But how is tricking Hawke into thinking that the apartment is haunted going to get us the details we need on that moving truck?"

Doc reached up and patted my hand. "Patience, Tish. Cornelius usually has a method behind his show of madness."

~

Back on the screen, Hawke stood shaking his head. "I don't buy this crap, Curion. You may have others fooled with your ghost hunting games, but I think what happened down in New Orleans with your cousin was a crime, and you should be behind bars for your part in killing that girl."

~

I winced. That was pretty harsh.

Cornelius's cousin had been a medium who worked with him

at séances, same as what I did now. During one particular ritual, she opened her spiritual "channel" too wide and ended up possessed by a malevolent entity. When Cornelius and his fellow ghost hunters tried to extricate the entity, his cousin died in the midst of the ceremony. He hadn't told me how exactly she died, and I hadn't asked for details, not wanting to make him replay old nightmares.

~

To Cornelius's credit, he did not take Hawke's bait. Instead, he pressed his ear to the wall next to one of the clocks. "Do you hear that?"

"Hear what? Don't try to tell me you hear that particular clock ticking, because I'm pretty sure it hasn't made a sound for a long time. Most of these stupid things stopped working over the last few months, no matter how much I wind them up."

"Hmm. So, they are stopped until they suddenly start up again, as if on a whim, correct?"

"I guess."

Cornelius pointed at the clock next to him. "There is something behind this one."

Hawke walked over and yanked the clock off the wall. "No, there's not. Stop with the fucking games, Curion."

"I meant something inside of the wall, Detective Frock."

When Hawke started to correct him on his name, Cornelius shushed him. He held up his index finger and closed his eyes, placing his ear to the wall again. "There it is."

"You're just hearing that other clock over there ticking."

"This is no ticking sound," Cornelius said in an ominous tone. "It's a heartbeat."

~

Goosebumps spread up my arms. "Oh, he got me with that one," I told Doc and my aunt.

Aunt Zoe nodded. "Reminds me of 'The Tell-Tale Heart' story by Edgar Allan Poe."

Doc leaned his elbows on the table, resting his chin on his locked fingers. "I imagine Cornelius has experienced a few bone-chilling moments in his time to give him ample acting fodder."

~

Back on screen, Hawke bristled, clenching his fists at his side. "A heartbeat, huh? Fuck you, Curion. You're just trying to scare me out of this place sooner. Who put you up to this? Parker? Coop?"

"I can assure you, my mission is not to scare you or anyone else. In fact, I was told you would not be here this morning due to having to work at your constable job." He stepped away from the wall. "I am simply here to help Freesia locate the source behind the unease she experienced while walking through this apartment with the home inspector recently. It was an unnerving sensation that she claims to have felt one other time in the recent past while joining the fire captain during his testing of the fire alarms in here."

"Unnerving how?" Hawke pressed.

"She described it as a feeling of being watched, followed by sharp pains in her abdomen, and then dull aches in her joints."

Hawke snorted. "That was probably just gas and a touch of arthritis. This cold weather is a bitch that way."

Cornelius walked toward the bedroom doorway. "She claimed the sensation was strongest in the bedroom."

Hawke followed him. "There's nothing in there but clocks, dressers, some books, and a bunch of weird mannequin heads in the closet. Trust me, I've checked it thoroughly."

Cornelius paused in the doorway and looked back at the detective, pointing the smoking bundle of sage at him. "But have you searched the ether for malicious haints?" His voice was deep and ominous again.

"What's a haint?"

"A restless spirit who seeks to inhabit the living in hopes of gaining a foothold in the mortal world once again," Cornelius said before stepping through the doorway.

~

Doc switched to the bedroom camera. "Cornelius has Hawke on the hook now." He pointed at the screen. "Look at the way the detective keeps rubbing his neck. His shoulder is twitching, too."

"He's getting creeped out," I said. "So am I, a little."

Aunt Zoe snickered. "Cornelius is working toward winning an

Emmy at this rate."

~

Back in the apartment, Hawke dropped onto the twin bed, cradling his broken arm. "So, 'haint' is just another fancy name for a ghost. Well, I ain't buying your sideshow act, so wrap it up, Curion. I have stuff to do tonight."

Cornelius pressed his ear to the wall next to another clock. "I can hear the heartbeat louder in here."

"Knock it off," Hawke said. "This game of yours is getting old."

Cornelius walked to the dresser Hawke had been trying to move, circling the sage in front of it. "The smoke is chaotic here. Almost as if there is a force disrupting its natural flow." He turned to Hawke. "What are you storing in this dresser?"

"Nothing. We emptied it of the old broad's clothes and put all that junk in the evidence locker along with the stuff from the closet."

Cornelius opened the first drawer and sniffed inside. Then he closed it and opened the second, reaching inside. "What do these symbols and letters represent at the back of the drawer?"

~

I knew what symbols he was referring to. They were odd-looking markings written in black ink. Doc had found them months ago when we checked out the place in an effort to figure out why Ms. Wolff had a picture of Layne stuck in the dresser mirror in that very bedroom. The answer had led to me landing my Timekeeper job.

Doc had eventually figured out that the markings were poorly written letters. If I remembered right, he'd told me they were some derivative of Latin and said: *Only when the clock stops will your time be at an end.*

I just loved it when cryptic writing spelled out an even more enigmatic prophecy. Although I'd recently learned this was the Timekeeper's mantra, referring to the end for any traveler monitored by a clock, which could include a *Scharfrichter* such as myself.

~

"How should I know?" Hawke said. "The old broad was a little off her rocker, if you ask me."

~

Actually, Ms. Wolff had been completely off her rocker when Harvey and I had first found her. She'd been dead and shriveled up like a raisin on the floor in front of the rocking chair. That was an image burned into my brain that I would undoubtedly take to my grave.

~

"I can smell sulfur here," Cornelius said. He stepped back and pointed at the drawer. "How long have you been smelling this?"

"What smell?" Hawke joined him at the dresser, leaning down to sniff inside the drawer. "Jesus!" He flinched and took several steps back, pointing at the dresser. "That wasn't there before."

"Shhh!" Cornelius held his hand up in front of Hawke. He tipped his head to one side. "The entity is here in the room with us now," he whispered loud enough for us to hear.

"Stop fucking around, Curion," Hawke growled.

"You smell it as well as I do, Detective Hulk," he continued in a whisper.

Hawke plugged his nose. "It's Hawke, dammit," he said in a nasal voice. "I think you did something in here to mess with my head."

"You are correct about the fact that I did something—I burned sage to cleanse the apartment. Unfortunately, much like yourself, it appears your boogeyman does not want to be evicted."

"How come I've never smelled that in here before?"

Cornelius closed the drawer. "If I were to hypothesize, the nasal offense would be due to having now enraged the entity that is residing in this dwelling alongside of you."

Hawke glared at him. "What did you go and do that for?"

Fanning in front of his face, Cornelius stepped back from the dresser. "Have you been experiencing aches in your joints of late? Pains when you go up and down stairs?"

"Yeah, what about them?"

"I believe this entity has been attached to you for some time. In addition to the dark aura now shadowing you, the excessive paleness of your skin indicates the entity is consuming your life force."

"What? I'm not pale."

"And you're clammy." Cornelius reached out and touched the back of his hand to Hawke's cheek. "You've been feeling weak, correct?"

"Yeah, but it's because of Parker. She's put some kind of hex on me, I know it."

"It is not your nemesis who is feeding upon your energy," Cornelius continued. "It is the shadow hovering over your shoulder."

"This is batshit nuts."

"I suspect this drain on your *chi* is what caused your broken arm."

"I slipped coming down a stupid ladder. That has nothing to do with my life forces, or whatever it is that word means."

"Did you slip?" Cornelius's eyebrows raised. "Or did something cause you to misstep on the way down?" He waved in front of his nose. "I do believe the stench has grown stronger. We must be getting close to the binding strings used by this haint." He returned to the dresser and carefully set the sage down on top of it. He opened the third drawer down, then closed it. "I experienced this before in New Orleans and found that there was a connection between a physical totem and the spirit."

Hawke took a step back, coughing and then gagging, covering his mouth. "Maybe we should get out of here. Leave the thing be so it will calm its ass back down."

"Do you not understand the situation, Detective Flock?" He opened the bottom dresser drawer. "We must rid you of this malevolent spirit before it ..." He stopped suddenly, stepping back from the dresser while shielding his face. "Oh my. This is unfortunate."

"What is it?" Hawke asked, cringing visibly.

Cornelius lowered his arm. "Please tell me that *thing* in the drawer belongs to you."

Hawke crept over and peered down. Then he gasped and stumbled backward. "What the fuck is that?!!"

CHAPTER TWENTY-ONE

What do you think is in the drawer?" Aunt Zoe whispered, looking over at Doc and me.

Doc rubbed his jaw. "It's hard to tell with Cornelius. With his history and collection of psychic tools and whatnot, it could be anything."

I chewed on my knuckle. "It can't be any weirder than Prudence's collection of eyeteeth, can it?'

"Let's see if I can figure out how to get a closer view," Doc said, clicking on a dropdown menu. "I saw Cornelius zoom in while we were checking out Jane's office, but there's a chance Hawke's security cameras don't have that option." He clicked a couple more times, and suddenly our focus moved closer. "Got it!"

~

On the screen, Cornelius held his hand out toward Hawke. "Hand me that cloth, Detective Sloth."

"That's my shirt," Hawke said.

"Yes, well I need something with which to pick it up. Touching such an object like this without protection could result in death. Or worse."

"What's worse than death?"

"Being buried alive because your heart is beating so slowly it appears you're dead."

"Shit. Hold on." Hawke left the room.

~

Aunt Zoe scooted closer to Doc, squinting at the screen. "Can either of you see what they're looking at?"

"Not yet," Doc said.

I shuddered. I knew Cornelius was playing around, but I'd had too many harrowing experiences in that apartment to not imagine the possibility of finding an eyeball or an ear or even a whole shriveled-up head in that drawer.

Doc adjusted the zoom, pulling back for a wider view just as Hawke came back into the room holding a clear plastic bag and some dish towels.

~

"Here," Hawke said, holding out the dishtowels toward Cornelius. "Use these towels to lift that thing and I'll try to hold the bag." He struggled to pull the bag open, flinching as he jostled his broken arm in the process.

Cornelius took the towels and reached into the drawer, extracting what looked like a spindly, stick-like figurine about six inches long.

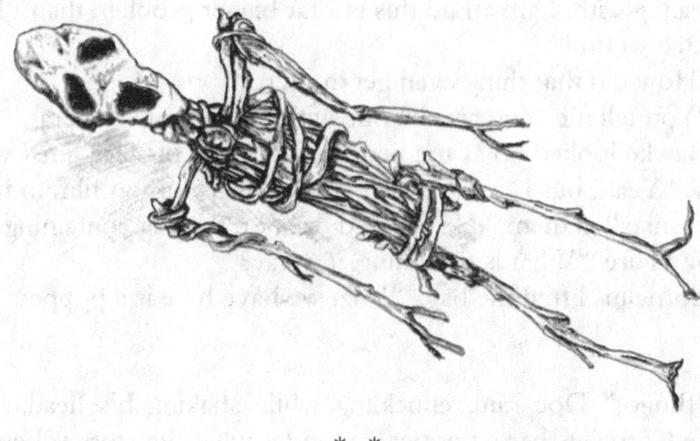

~

"What is that?" I asked, squinting at the screen.

"Let me zoom in again and try to focus on it." Doc clicked the mouse a few times. "Got it."

I reared back. "Jesus, that's some freaky-deaky weirdness right there."

Aunt Zoe was wincing when I glanced her way. "Is that some

kind of a voodoo doll made of sticks and twine?"

Doc nodded slowly. "I'm guessing it's a poppet."

What was a poppet? I knew the word from some British television shows, but I'd thought it was an affectionate term of endearment for a cute, young kid, like snuggle bug or pumpkin.

~

On the screen, Doc zoomed back out as Hawke struggled to hold the bag open for Cornelius. As soon as the stick figurine was inside, Hawke handed it off.

He backed toward the bed with his one hand raised as if to ward off the thing. "What in the unholy hell is that?"

Cornelius tossed the towels onto the floor and then held up the clear bag with the figurine in front of him. "Can you still smell the sulfur?"

"Christ, yes!" Hawke gagged. "You need to get that thing out of here."

Cornelius pointed at the bag. "This is quite concerning," he said, his ominous tone back in full swing. "Having seen what we are dealing with, I am afraid this is a far bigger problem than I had expected to find."

"How did that thing even get in there?"

"You tell me. You are the one with the security cameras."

Hawke looked up at the bedroom camera, his face lined with worry. "Yeah, but I haven't seen anyone show up on film in here since I installed them." He focused back on the bag containing the creepy figure. "What is that thing, anyway?"

Cornelius lifted the bag. "What we have here is a poppet."

~

"Bingo," Doc said, chuckling while shaking his head. "Of course Cornelius has a poppet. I wonder what the story is behind this souvenir. If it's from a haunted mansion down south or from some swamp dwelling in the bayou."

"What's a poppet?" I asked at the same time Hawke asked that question on the screen.

~

"A poppet is a magical item," Cornelius explained.

"Sometimes they can be used for good, other times not. The magic used is based on the law of similarity."

Hawke guffawed. "I've never heard of that law, and I've been a cop for a long time."

"That's because you are merely a constable. This is a law based on occult beliefs. It states that if an item resembles another item, the first one can be used to influence the other for good or ill." Cornelius pointed at the poppet. "Obviously, this is being used for ill."

"What is it made of?" Hawke asked. "Dried flesh?"

Cornelius stared at the poppet through the bag. "While that is entirely possible, I believe this one appears to be a dried root shaped to look like a man with a hat." He pointed at something on the poppet. "Look there. That appears to be bits of red pepper along with some grass."

Hawke plugged his nose and stepped closer. "Yeah, but why would pepper be on that thing?"

"I'm not sure," Cornelius said as he poked at the bag. "But I have heard of poppets that were coated in sulfur, red pepper, dried cat excrement, five-finger grass, masterwort, and foot track magic."

"What the hell is foot track magic?"

"The dirt from an intended's footprints is used to form a link between the poppet and the target for ill will." Cornelius lowered the bag. "Have you been watching where you have left your tracks of late?"

"Of course not." Hawke scowled. "What do all of those things mixed together on this poppet do?"

"Blended as such, it would allow someone to bind an entity to a person, and then give the entity the power to command that individual."

"That's crazy talk. There's no way it would work. Shit like that happens only in movies."

"Are you certain?" Cornelius asked, one eyebrow cocked higher. "As we discussed, this apartment has been the setting for many unsolved, mysterious deaths. Is it really surprising that a malevolent entity bound to the resident dwelling in these walls might be the cause of so much violence?"

Hawke sighed, rubbing his eyes. "Jesus, what a fucked-up day, and now this crap."

"Well, this surely explains the dark shadow hovering behind you."

Hawke's shoulders tensed. He looked over one shoulder and then the other. "How do I get rid of it?"

"We must not only cleanse this apartment, but also cut the strings binding this poppet to you. If we do not break the connection, this entity will follow you after you leave this apartment and stay with you until death."

"And how do we do that?"

"For starters, you need to start carrying a *gris-gris* bag."

"A what?"

"It is a small bag that you wear on your person day and night. In the past, some were made of goat skins with the hair still intact, and others made of leather from Morocco. In any case, these small talismans were filled with powders or dirt, along with trinkets or charms. Each item in the *gris-gris* bag has a purpose. There might be items for good luck, charms for protection, even dirt from the grave of an ancestor so they can watch over you."

Hawke kept eyeing the poppet. "Where do I get one of these bags?"

"I will need to make it for you."

Hawke sneered. "What makes you an expert?"

"As you know, I was raised partly in New Orleans by my grandmother, who was known to dabble in voodoo and other occult practices. She trained me to replace her at the helm."

Hawke began to pace, rubbing his shoulder above his broken arm. "How soon can you get this bag made for me?"

"It will take a few days to collect the items I will need."

"I don't have a few days!"

"If you are worried about this entity draining your life source after you move, do not fear. It will take at least another month, maybe even two, before the grim reaper comes for you."

"I mean I'm moving out, remember?"

"Oh, I had forgotten about that. When are you moving?"

Hawke dropped onto the bed. "The men are coming on Thursday to haul all of these stupid clocks away."

~

I clapped. "Yes! Now we know when he's moving the clocks."

"Damn it," Doc said. "This means we have less than two days to do something about getting them out of his hands."

"There must be a way," Aunt Zoe said. "We just have to put our heads together and figure it out."

~

Back on the screen, Cornelius stroked his goatee. "What men are coming? Is this some of your constable companions?"

"No, Curion. I'm talking about the movers."

"Oh, this is very bad." Cornelius set the bagged figurine on the bed next to the detective.

Hawke jumped up, recoiling halfway across the room from the poppet. "Why?"

"We must protect these movers so they do not also become bound to the entity connected with this poppet."

"What does that matter?"

"If they are bound, the malevolent entity will feed on them as well. You cannot allow this evil to spread. It must be stopped with you."

"Fine. How do we do that?"

Cornelius steepled his long fingers. "I could put a protective spell on them in advance, using a voodoo ritual my grandmother taught me."

"Let's do that, then. For me and the movers."

Cornelius nodded. "I will need to know who to protect."

"Well, I don't know the names of the guys who will be coming."

"Of course, however, I should be able to protect those from the company, so long as you can supply some sort of property belonging to it."

"Property? Like one of their trucks?"

"No, think smaller. Do you have a business card?"

"Oh, I do! Hold on." Hawke raced from the room.

Cornelius turned to look into the camera, his crooked smile in place. "*Voilà.*"

Hawke returned seconds later, a card in hand. "Here. Take this. The guy I met with last week gave it to me."

"Excellent. This not only gives me a name, but a fingerprint to use as well." He picked up the bag with the poppet, the small bundle of smoking sage from the dresser, and strode out of the bedroom.

Hawke followed on his heels. "How long will it take to put the protection spell on them?"

Doc changed to the living room camera.

Cornelius paused in the middle of the room. "Let's see. When will these movers be here?"

"Thursday around one in the afternoon."

"That should be plenty of time." Cornelius walked toward the front door.

Doc switched camera views again.

"Wait!" Hawke caught him by the arm in the dining room. "What about that funky bag you're going to make to protect me."

"I'll bring it by on moving day."

"What am I supposed to do in the meantime?"

"If I were you, I would sleep with this next to me on the pillow—not lit, of course." He handed Hawke the bundle of sage. "Burn it first thing in the morning as you walk through the apartment and last thing at night before going to bed."

"Okay," Hawke said, worriedly looking around the apartment. "Can I just sleep somewhere else?"

"Of course." Cornelius held up the figurine. "However, even though I am removing this poppet from the premises, it is still bound to you and can join you wherever you go until you start wearing the *gris-gris* bag."

Hawke cursed. "How much is this bag gonna run me?"

"Due to the direness of your situation and as a favor for the owner, I will help untether you from this troublemaker for free. Trust me, Detective Squawk, once these binds are broken, you'll start feeling much better again."

Cornelius left the apartment then, letting the door slam loud enough behind him for us to hear.

Hawke returned to the living room, looking around with a scowl on his face. "Fuck," he muttered, grabbed his coat, and headed for the door.

~

Doc sat back and looked at me with a grin. "Hot damn.

Cornelius and Natalie saved the day."

I laughed and gave him a hug. "We have our heading once again."

Aunt Zoe stood and stretched. "That was some impressive acting."

I snorted. "I think a lot of that was just Cornelius being his quirky self."

My cell phone rang. It was Natalie. I put her on speakerphone.

"He did it," I said in lieu of a greeting.

Natalie laughed. "Damned straight he did. The Mummy strikes again in *The Curse of the Poppet*."

"Now we just have to figure out how to get those clocks out before Thursday."

"I think Harvey already has an idea on that," she said.

I frowned at Doc and then Aunt Zoe. "Why does that worry me a little?"

* * *

King Kong showed up at Aunt Zoe's front door about a half hour before suppertime with a big box full of takeout food containers and a scowl on his face.

I held the door wide, ushering him inside, then looking out into the cold dark for any tagalongs.

"Did you come alone?" I asked, closing out the cold.

"Yeah." Cooper set the box down on the dining room table and then returned to the rug next to the front door to take off his snow boots. "Nat wanted me to bring this over here so you could help me warm it up before everyone else gets here."

I peeked into the box, sniffing. Even though everything in it was cold, I could smell chicken, maybe. Something tomato based, for sure. And baked bread of some sort. "It smells good. What is it?"

He pocketed his stocking hat and then hung his coat in the hall closet. "A mix of Himalayan and Indian food."

"Yip-a-dee-doo-dah! Your girlfriend really went all out." I rubbed my hands together. "I'm going to need to put on some pants with an elastic waistband to fully enjoy this meal."

He picked up the box and carried it into the kitchen with me on his tail.

"Where are your kids?" He put the box on the counter.

I pointed toward the ceiling. "Layne is reading a book he got through the library about Mayan glyphs, and Addy is playing dress-up with Elvis and Daisy."

Cooper paused, looking my way with both blond eyebrows raised. "Are you serious?"

"About which part?"

"I know Layne likes archaeology and history, and even though Mayan glyphs seem a little advanced for a kid turning ten this weekend, I'm not really surprised." He pulled out a couple of food containers and set them on the counter. "But the dress-up bit with a chicken and an imp—that's a rare sight, same as seeing two camels packed into a tiny car."

I guffawed. "That's not possible, is it?"

"Well, it wasn't one of those mini cars like Mr. Bean crammed himself into, but yeah. Don't worry, the trainer gave them lots of romaine lettuce and carrots as a reward after they got back out. I'm pretty sure the seats had been torn out." He lifted a couple more containers from the box.

"Addy has some old baby doll clothes that she thinks Daisy will look very pretty in since the imp painted its claws pink, along with the chicken's toenails today."

He paused in the midst of lifting another container from the box. "This shit just keeps getting weirder. What about clothes for the chicken?"

"Elvis has several sweaters that my mother has knitted for her. Apparently, Mom is appeasing her need for more grandbabies by making clothes for Addy's growing collection of pets. She even made a little jumpsuit with a sheriff's star on it for The Duke. You know, Addy's gerbil."

He shook his head. "Never a dull moment with you, Parker."

I opened one of the containers he'd set on the counter. It contained what looked like chunks of chicken in a rich, orange sauce. "What is this?"

"Butter chicken, I think." He reached over and closed the container before I could taste test the sauce. Then he finished unloading the box, tossed it into the laundry room, and returned to stare at all the containers stacked on the counter. "This had better be enough."

"It must have cost Natalie a small fortune."

"I think Curion split the bill with her. She said he had a hankering for chicken tikka masala and aloo gobi, so they went wild with ordering from the takeout menu."

Knowing Cornelius's love of sugary foods, I asked, "What did they order for dessert?"

"Indian honey cake."

I tried not to drool. "You had me at 'honey.' Adding the word 'cake' on the end only sweetens the deal."

He grabbed the bunch of paper napkins the restaurant had included with the order and took them over to the table. "You have a thing for honey lately, don't you?"

I nodded, opening and closing another container that had what looked and smelled like spinach with chunks of white cheese in it—saag paneer. "I can't get enough of it. Maybe I'm turning into a human fly."

"Or maybe embracing this killing business gave you a sweet tooth."

The next container had some kind of lentils in a red sauce and smelled spicy.

"Make that a bigger sweet tooth. I have a soft spot for peanut butter fudge ice cream." And if I kept eating beignets and Indian honey cake, I'd have a lot more soft spots, including a roll or two that wrapped around my middle.

Cooper returned and leaned against the counter next to me. "You know why Nat sent me to Rapid City, don't you?"

I slowly closed the container while wondering how to answer that. Did he know the truth behind his alibi run? Or was he fishing for answers?

"Well, I know that she wanted to up her game on the what's-for-supper front, especially after having to follow Cornelius's New Orleans feast."

His steely gray eyes narrowed to a tight squint. "Don't piss down my back and tell me it's raining, Godzilla."

I lifted my chin. "No stealing lines from old Clint Eastwood movies, King Kong."

"I've seen the video."

"*The Outlaw Josey Wales?*" I played dumb.

"No, *The Curse of the Poppet* starring Curion and Hawke."

Ohhh, *that* video.

"And I know that you and Nyce and Zoe watched it all go down from Curion's apartment."

I cringed. "Sheesh. Did you interrogate Natalie as soon as you got back from Rapid, or did she give you that information on her own free will? If it's the former, I think she is supposed to have the right to an attorney of her choosing."

"It was the latter. I came home …" He paused and shook his head slightly. "I mean, Uncle Willis dropped me off at her place with this load of food. As soon as I stepped through the door, she hit me with the details of what the two of them had been up to while I was gone."

Damn, Natalie was ballsy. I would have been nervous to tell Cooper the whole truth and nothing but the truth, even if I was sitting in a court of law under oath.

"In Natalie's defense, she was just protecting the two of us while Cornelius worked his magic at finding out some moving details that we really needed to know."

He let out a growly grunt and opened the cupboard door, lifting down a stack of plates.

"It was only slightly illegal, maybe." I continued to act as her defense attorney. I couldn't help it. It came naturally after thirty-plus years of friendship.

"It was very illegal," he corrected, setting the plates on the table.

"Nobody got hurt, though."

That earned me a scowl. "That doesn't make it right, Parker."

I shrugged. "Hawke homesteading in Ms. Wolff's apartment and holding the clocks hostage wasn't exactly right, either."

"You sound like Natalie."

"Great minds think alike."

He opened the silverware drawer and started plucking out forks. "If anyone sees that video footage, she and Curion could be in big trouble."

I took the bundle of forks from him. "If we don't get those clocks, we could be in even bigger trouble than some minor video voyeurism charges."

He huffed. "Video voyeurism is a federal crime."

"Yeah, but it's like a misdemeanor, right?"

"Sure." He pulled out a bunch of spoons. "But if convicted, they could go to prison for a year and pay big fines, and we both know Hawke would push those charges to the max."

"Cooper!" I took the spoons away, glaring up at him.

"What?" He glared back.

"I killed Ms. Wolff, remember?"

He frowned at me. "Yeah, but I saw how that went down, and she forced your hand. Not to mention that she wasn't exactly human."

"I also most likely murdered that big Juggernaut at the funeral parlor that night with a gigantic pair of scissors."

His frown deepened. "He was trying to kill Nyce, though, and you were just acting out of self-defense."

"Okay, how about this? I stabbed Calypso in the neck and reduced her to smoke and ashes right in front of you."

He shrugged. "She would have killed me if you hadn't."

"Exactly!" I set the spoons down on the table next to the forks. "Don't you see? If I don't get those clocks, there will be more deaths—and probably mine for starters. But maybe my kids', too. And Aunt Zoe, Doc, Cornelius, Natalie, your uncle. Hell, maybe even yours before it's all said and done." I returned to him, touching his forearm. "Cooper, I know you have been a good cop for decades, and you have obeyed society's laws to a T. So have I." At his skeptic look, I added, "Well, I have mostly. Anyway, my point is that these *other* beings don't follow our guidelines. They live outside of our ideas of morality and order. If we want to keep breathing, then we have to be willing to break some laws."

He sighed, scrubbing his hands down his face. "You sound like Natalie."

"Like I said before, incredibly brilliant minds think alike."

He smirked. "Your mind was just 'great' before, Parker. Don't get too big for your britches."

"Would it make you feel any better if you're in charge of making sure all damning evidence is destroyed and disposed of completely when we're done?"

"Maybe. But I'd really feel better if I could stop seeing dead people." He started pulling table knives from the drawer.

Oh. I hadn't expected him to give up on his obey-the-law

charge so easily. "Did you see a ghost today?"

I popped open a container of small triangular samosas, licking my chops. I'd be eating one of those babies for sure.

"No." He paused with a hand full of knives. "At least I don't think that guy was dead, but he smelled close to it."

I reached for another container. This one was full of basmati rice. "So, are you and Natalie still talking after finding out what she and Cornelius were up to while you were gone?"

He shut the silverware drawer. "That's not really your business, Parker."

"Yes, it is, you big ornery ape." I opened a container crammed full of pieces of naan flatbread. It smelled like heaven with a hint of garlic. "And you know what? I've got bad news for you, Kong." I ripped off a piece of bread and shoved it in my mouth. It tasted heavenly, too. "As long as you're sleeping with my best friend, and I'm engaged to yours, you and I will be sharing our private business. So, get used to it."

"That's King Kong to …" He stopped midway to the table, knives in hand, and turned back toward me. "What did you just say?"

I tore off another small strip of bread. "I said that so long as you're sleeping with Natalie and I'm …"

Oh, shit.

My cheeks warmed. "I, uh, meant to say, uh … that you and I are …" Damn it. I held up the strip of naan. "Have you tried this? It's really good. Here, have a bite."

He held out his hand to stop me from coming any closer. "You said the word 'engaged,' didn't you?"

"No, I didn't."

"Yes, you did."

"Do you have that on video? Because without proof, we can't be sure if you just misheard me."

He set the knives on the table. "I heard you clearly say you were engaged to my good friend."

"Isn't Doc your best friend? I mean, I know you two have become buddies, but aren't you besties now?"

"Men like me don't have 'besties,' Parker. I just have friends, okay?"

"If you say so." I thumbed toward the containers on the

counter behind me. "So, how do you want to heat these up?"

"With the microwave." He crossed his arms. "How long have you and Nyce been engaged?"

Dammit! "Shhhh." I rushed up to him. "Listen, Cooper," I whispered, glancing behind him to make sure we were alone still with no little ears eavesdropping. "That is not public news, okay? We're keeping it on the downlow for now."

"Why?" he whispered back.

"We want to give the kids more time to get used to Doc being in their lives."

"Makes sense. When did Nyce pop the question?"

"He didn't. I did."

His eyebrows raised. "No shit. Where were you? Out to a fancy dinner?"

"No. We were in my closet."

He snorted. "That's a strange place for talk of wedding bells to come up."

"It's a long story involving cookies and chicken talk. The point is, nobody else knows, so you need to promise me not to tell a soul until I give you the all-clear."

"What is chicken talk? Like *cluck cluck*?"

"Just promise me, Cooper."

"Fine."

"I mean it."

"I said 'fine.' I won't tell anyone."

"Not even if Natalie tortures you."

He grinned. "She can try her damnedest, but I'll take it to the grave."

I held up my pinkie finger between us.

His gaze narrowed, but then he locked pinkies with me. "Good enough?"

I nodded, stepping back with a sigh. Me and my big mouth.

"Now," he said, turning to the counter full of containers. "Can we get this damned food warmed up before Natalie shows up and gives me hell for not setting out the spread per her detailed instructions?"

CHAPTER TWENTY-TWO

We have a problem," Natalie said.

There was no food left to stow away in the refrigerator. We had devoured it all. I especially loved the Southern Indian honey cake. I'd been planning to eat two pieces until Addy begged me for the second one to take down to the basement as a treat for Daisy. Sigh. That dang imp.

But the lack of supper leftovers wasn't the problem to which Natalie was referring. Her worry was far more complicated.

After the dishes were cleaned and the kids were snuggled under the couch blankets in front of the television watching Aunt Zoe's copy of the Charlie Brown Valentine's cartoon special, all eight of us monsters gathered at the kitchen table to put our heads together and find a solution to this new clock conundrum.

"Time is running out," Natalie continued in between sips of hot chocolate spiced up with a dash of cinnamon and rum. "We have to figure out how the hell to get those damned clocks in our possession before Hawke's movers show up Thursday afternoon."

Cooper shook his head. "I don't think it's possible. Maybe we need to work on a way to collect them after Hawke has relocated them."

"You hangin' up your hat already, boy?" Harvey asked.

"I would agree with you, Coop," Doc said, "if Violet and the kids weren't at risk every day that she doesn't have a means to see what might be hunting her. We need those clocks."

Natalie nodded, giving Cooper a hard look. "And we need them ASAP."

Harvey snickered, elbowing me. "That girl is tryin' to saddle a tall horse."

"I take it you saw the video from this afternoon, Coop," Aunt Zoe said. She glanced at Natalie. "What did you call it?"

"*The Curse of the Poppet*," Natalie said in a Vincent Price wannabe voice before taking another sip of her drink.

Cooper grunted. "Outside of the potential voyeurism charge, if Hawke figures out Curion was playing him with that poppet doll, he'll lean hard into nailing him with some trumped-up, false reporting charge."

I looked at Cornelius, who'd been working his way through a stack of snickerdoodle cookies in lieu of some honey cake. He held out his glass of milk as if toasting a ghost. "In the business of seeking out the supernatural, I've been accused of worse," he said. "My attorney assures me that she always cringes when I call."

Natalie saluted him with her mug of hot goodness, and then turned to Detective Worrywart on her right. "Coop, I know you like to toe the line, but we can't on this one."

"I know we can't," Cooper said, arms crossed. "Parker beat me over the head with that before the rest of you got here tonight. But is it a crime for a guy to want to keep his girlfriend out of jail?"

"Nyce knows all about springing his sweetheart from the pokey," Reid said, sending a wink my way. "Maybe he can give you some tips, Coop, when that time comes."

Doc chuckled. "It helps if you get along with the detective who put her there, so you might need to find your way back into Hawke's circle of pals."

I glanced at the clock. We were spinning our tires here.

"Listen," I said, leaning my elbows on the table. "Maybe if we list all of the tasks needed to pull off this caper, we can figure out a way to get those clocks away from the big blowhard."

Harvey cleared his throat with purpose, drawing all of our gazes. "There's more than one way to eat corn on the cob." He pushed his chair back from the table. "You all sit tight for a few shakes. I'll be right back with the lowdown on how we're gonna strike pay dirt."

After he left the room, I turned to Cooper. "What does he mean by the corn on the cob bit?"

"How should I know, Parker? Uncle Willis wags his chin a lot. I pay attention when he starts talking about his favorite shotgun."

"Good ol' Bessie," Reid said, grinning.

"Don't forget about his cannon," I added.

Cooper cursed under his breath while Doc chuckled.

"I told you before," Natalie said, tapping her index finger on the table. "Harvey has this all planned out. He's a wise owl. You just have to trust him."

"Not much else we can do at this point," Aunt Zoe said.

"That wise owl of yours was part of the reason I ended up in jail the last time." I glowered at Cooper.

He shrugged off my glare. "I didn't see Uncle Willis holding Bessie at your back that night at the Opera House. You went snooping of your own free will, Parker."

"I could dig deeper into my voodoo toolkit," Cornelius offered, dabbing away his milk mustache with a napkin. "There might be a spell that would distract the detective. Some way to slow down his timepiece relocation efforts."

Reid frowned at Cornelius, and then me, and then the others in turn. "I don't know about the rest of you, but after some of the movies I've watched, voodoo seems like it should always be the *last* resort."

Harvey breezed back into the kitchen, holding onto several white envelopes. He looked down at the front of one and then handed it to me. It had the word *Godzilla* written on it in his handwriting. "This one is for you." He held another one out to Doc. "And here's one for your Wolf Man."

He continued making his way around the table, handing out envelopes with the assigned monster's name written on the front. After Harvey-the-postman finished his delivery route, he grabbed a beer from the refrigerator and then joined us again at the table.

"What's in this?" Cooper asked, eyeing it like it might need to be handcuffed and thrown in the slammer.

Natalie tore hers open and pulled out a folded piece of paper. "One—prep and load fake clock boxes," she read. "Two—paint trucks. Three—help load clock boxes on moving day. Four—distract the big bird." She looked up at Harvey. "By 'big bird,' I take it you mean Detective Squawk."

He nodded. "We'll have to find a place to paint the rigs without anyone else seeing you."

Aunt Zoe opened her envelope at the same time as Reid. "I

also have 'prep and load fake clock boxes,' " she said.

Reid nodded while reading his paper. "Same here."

"And 'paint the trucks,' " she continued.

Reid nodded again. "Yep."

" 'Help unload fake boxes in the big bird's storage location.' " She frowned at Harvey. "That's a different one, though."

Reid held out his piece of paper for her to see. "We must have the same list."

She leaned over, checking out his instructions. "Do you also have the task of talking to my brother about dressing in disguise to look and act the part of the moving company employee?" When he shook his head, she said, "Not quite the same, then."

"What do you mean by 'fake clock boxes'?" Natalie asked Harvey.

"The way I'm figurin', we'll need two sets of boxes. One will be for the real clocks, and the second set will have pieces of firewood sittin' in stuffin'."

"Where are we going to get enough boxes with so little time?" Natalie asked.

"Ox has a bunch that will fit the bill as official moving boxes," Reid threw out. "He's just about done unpacking from his move here. I'll swing by tonight and load them up in the back of my pickup."

"If we need any more," Aunt Zoe said, "I can swing by Piggly Wiggly. I often get boxes from them when I have a large glass order to deliver."

"See there, you two already put the lid on that jar." Harvey took another sip of beer. "We'll fill one of the two trucks with the fake clock boxes, and the other'n will be loaded with the real deals."

"I take it the box trucks look similar?" Cooper asked.

"Like your pa's beady-eyed and buck-toothed older sisters— slightly banged up and rattly in their joints, but close enough to be identical if you cross your eyes just a smidgeon."

"That is an inaccurate representation of my aunts," he told Natalie. "But they do tend to meddle and complain about their aches and pains more often than not."

"These two trucks are what we're supposed to paint, right?" Aunt Zoe asked.

"Yep. We need to have them lookin' close to the same as the trucks belongin' to that movin' company Hawke hired."

"Paint them tomorrow?" Reid confirmed.

"Hell, paint 'em tonight if you feel like stayin' up long enough to crow alongside the rooster."

Aunt Zoe aimed a gunslinger squint at Harvey. "Did you put me with this hose jockey to try to play cupid?"

He grinned wide enough to see his two gold teeth. "Not this time, shooter. You two need to work together because Hawke would be sniffing in the wind too much if I'd given you one of the other jobs."

"What other jobs?" Reid asked.

"Here's one." Doc held up his paper and read, " 'Figure out where the big bird is going to store the clocks.' " He looked at Harvey with raised eyebrows.

"We need to know where he plans to dump 'em, so that we can be there beforehand to unload the fake clocks," Harvey explained. "The longer he doesn't know gunpowder from pepper, the better."

"What if Hawke wants to follow the movers to the storage location?" Natalie asked him. "You know, to supervise in his usual annoying way."

"That's where your number four comes into play, Dracula. You need to wave your cape around and distract the big bird long enough to give us time to unload all those boxes before his big beak shows up and he starts pecking around."

"I don't like Natalie being the distraction," Cooper said.

No surprise there, I mused while pulling out my list. Anything involving potential harm for Natalie and Cooper started punching the panic button.

"She won't be alone flappin' her cape, King Kong. Look at your list."

Cooper frowned. "Is that what you meant with, 'Be a thorn in the big bird's side on moving day'?"

"Yeppers. You need to be at that apartment with Natalie, makin' sure there is no damage done to the walls and whatnot by the movers, since you're plannin' to buy the place. Wink-wink." Harvey tapped on the side of his beer bottle. "It also might not hurt to help pack those boxes to make sure those clocks aren't banged up."

"He's not going to want me to touch them," Cooper said.

"Aren't you the one takin' over the case if Hawke fails at findin' the murderer? Seems to me you'd want to remind him of that fact and insist on makin' sure those clocks are packed real good like."

Cooper grinned at Harvey. "A thorn in his side I will be."

"We can get Freesia in there, too," Natalie said. "She's good at running interference when Hawke starts sputtering and pointing fingers. With enough hubbub happening, Hawke will be up to his neck in ruffled feathers, unable to focus on any slipups the movers might make."

Harvey nodded. "Now you're ridin' alongside me, girlie."

"So, who's helping pack and move the boxes at the apartment besides Blake, my brother?" Aunt Zoe asked.

Harvey turned my way. "Read the first one on your list, Godzilla."

I unfolded the piece of paper. " 'Talk to the Invisible Man,' " I read. " 'Hire her as a clock packer and mover.' "

I looked up from the paper to see Natalie grimacing. "I still don't trust your sister."

I didn't either, fully. Her bites often left ugly scars.

"At least she'll be more likely to do as asked if she's working with my dad."

Harvey must have already thought of that, which was why he wanted Aunt Zoe to get my dad involved.

"I'm thinkin' that when Blake and Susan arrive dressed as the official movers," Harvey explained, "they'll let Hawke know the extra help hired to actually pack up the clocks had to cancel. That's when Count Dracula and King Kong can pitch in to pack."

"Us touching the clocks will make Hawke squawk and flutter even more," Natalie said with a nod. "But he'll be desperate for our help in the moment."

Harvey thumbed toward Cooper. "Especially with King Kong here heckling him."

"What else does yours say?" I asked Doc, leaning over to peek at his list.

"I'm supposed to create a fake manifest for the clock cargo to show Hawke." He glanced at Harvey. "I take it you want me to have it close to the same logo and look of the original moving company."

"Yessirree, with not a dime's worth of difference between them. Hawke's going to want some sort of proof that our movers are who they say they are."

Doc turned to Aunt Zoe and Reid. "I can help you guys prep and load the fake boxes tomorrow, too."

"You don't have any appointments?" I asked.

"One in the morning. I left the afternoon open to take care of some other stuff, but I can move things around."

"What else is on your list, Godzilla?" Natalie asked.

"Get hold of Mr. Black and see if we can have a few decoy clocks."

"We'll need those decoys if Hawke is feelin' overly prickly and decides to do some inspectin' at the storage unit," Harvey explained. "We'll put them in boxes up front and lead that law dog to those particular bones."

"What if Mr. Black is unavailable?" I asked.

It wasn't always easy to reach my fellow Timekeeper. He had a whole passel of *other* problems, it seemed, and I didn't ask too many questions about them because I had plenty to keep me busy scurrying for my life here.

"We'll cross that bridge if we come to it," Harvey said.

"What's on your list, Corny?" Natalie asked.

That was my next question, too. The cookie-dunker had been sitting and watching quietly so far, with his list on the table next to his almost empty glass of milk.

"I appear to be mirroring you, except my distraction specifies delivering a *gris-gris* bag to Hawke and performing more voodoo-related activities." He smirked at Harvey. "My grandmother would have enjoyed participating in this deception. Maybe I'll see if I can call upon her ghost when I arrive at the apartment in hopes of her joining us."

Harvey tee-hee'd. "The more we can ruffle that big turkey's feathers, the better." He finished his beer, setting the bottle on the table with a *clunk*. "Now, which one of you boys can do the best imitation of Hawke's voice over the phone?"

"How about this?" Reid spoke in a voice raspier and more nasally than Hawke's. "Coop, you know we go back a long way, and you have always wished you were half the detective I am."

Natalie giggled. "That sounds a little like Droopy Dog."

"It makes me want to pop you in the nose, Martin," Cooper said with a small grin. "But you suck at sounding like that ass."

"You think you can do better?" Harvey challenged.

Cooper nodded and cleared his throat. "Parker! Get that crazy hair over here, and don't be putting any more hexes on me, you nosey witch."

Chuckling, I flipped him off.

"Not bad, but how about this," Natalie said. She pointed at Cornelius with a heavy frown on her forehead. "Curion, this voodoo is a bunch of bullshit."

Cooper laughed. "Not even close, babe. And I'm glad for it, because knowing you, that voice would show up in our bed at night when I least wanted to hear it."

"What?" she continued in the fake gruff voice. "Me talking like your old partner during sex doesn't spin your sprocket?"

I cringed and giggled.

Cooper covered his face, shaking his head. "Oh, now you've created a real monster, Uncle Willis."

"How about you, Cornelius?" Aunt Zoe asked. "Can you imitate the blowhard?"

He took a sip of milk first. "What the hell is a poppet?" He wrinkled his upper lip in a sneer, like Hawke often did, and spoke each word with a bit of a growl. "What is a haint? Why do these clocks tick only part of the time? Why does Parker keep picking on me?"

Natalie clapped. "That was pretty close."

"Not bad," Reid agreed.

"Curion has the tone down," Doc said in a nearly spot-on imitation of Hawke's gruff voice, drawing all of our gazes. "But he doesn't bumble his consonants enough, which comes from being too lazy to enunciate." He turned to me, his dark eyes filled with laughter. "Parker, if you put one more hex on me, I'll throw your ass in the can for good."

"Winner, winner, chicken dinner!" Harvey cackled, pointing at Doc. "That means you have another task, Wolf Man. You need to call the moving company and cancel the job, but not before you find out where they're supposed to be movin' the boxes. We need that storage information."

Doc gave him a thumbs-up.

Cornelius was still eyeing Doc with a raised brow. "Well done, Tall Medium. It appears the ghoul isn't the only one capable of mimicking others."

The mention of the ghoul still fueling my nightly worries brought a chill to our warm after-supper glow. I touched my cheek where that mark supposedly was, wondering if there were tendrils growing from it yet.

Doc's hand touched my thigh under the table, drawing my focus his way. He smiled and squeezed lightly, whispering, "I got you, Killer."

I drew a heart on the back of his hand, and then squeezed it back. *"Merci, mon amour."*

He winked at me.

"What will you be doing during all of this grunt work?" Cooper asked his uncle, tugging me back into the moment.

Harvey hooked his thumbs in his suspenders. "Don't you worry about me, boy. I have plenty to do just supervisin' you all and makin' sure all of the knots stay tied."

Aunt Zoe tapped her index finger on the table. "This all sounds like it might work, Willis, but where are we going to put the real clocks after we do the switcheroo?"

"You leave that to me, too," he said. "The way I figure, the more you all are snowed-in about the details of the clocks' final whereabouts, the better you'll handle sittin' in that interrogation room playin' dumb—if it comes to that."

Cooper shook his head. "I don't like you possibly taking all the heat, Uncle Willis."

"I'm happy to have my buns warmed over the fire, King Kong, so don't worry your monkey brain about me. You just do your part to fluster the big turkey when he's flappin' around that apartment with his one good wing."

"Am I going to help at the storage unit?" I asked.

It wasn't on my list, but I didn't want to be sitting on my hands when everyone else was taking risks to help me get those clocks.

Harvey shook his head. "You need to stay as far away from all of this as possible, Sparky. But you can watch it all go down on Corny's video screen alongside the Wolf Man."

Doc draped his arm over my shoulder. "We definitely need to bring popcorn this time."

"But don't get too comfy," Harvey warned. "You two need to go out to a Valentine's Day dinner someplace local as soon as the clocks are on the move. Somewhere you are seen and heard by a few folks who might know Sparky's face. She needs a rock-solid alibi, since Hawke won't have her in his sights all day. She'll be the first one he comes barkin' at if he realizes the clocks aren't where he thought he put them."

"I'll take care of making that happen, Tish," Doc told me. "We'll bring the kids with us to make your alibi even stronger."

I nodded. A family Valentine's Day dinner then. Darn. I'd kind of wanted to have him to myself since it would be my first Valentine's Day with someone other than my kids since I couldn't remember when, but Addy and Layne would love to be included. And maybe this would get us one step closer to telling them about our engagement.

Harvey pointed at Cooper. "You should probably take Natalie somewhere public, too."

Natalie shoulder bumped Cooper. "We could always invite Hawke out to a romantic dinner, just the three of us."

He scoffed. "I'd sooner be taken out to a back alley and electrocuted."

"Please, hot cop." She pretended to fan her face as she fluttered her eyelashes. "Don't be telling everyone about our back-alley sex games. It's embarrassing."

Cooper just shook his head at her. "You need a good curry combing, wildcat."

Harvey turned to Cornelius. "As soon as the big bird leaves the nest, you need to slip back inside and clear out whatever you did when you tapped into his video feed. We don't need him figurin' out that we were watchin' all along."

"Freesia will be happy to help you with that," Natalie told Cornelius.

Freesia would be happy to do even more with Cornelius, if he'd only ask her. The wonderful woman had some kind of crazy crush on Corny, but she must not be wacky enough to catch his eye.

I looked around the table. "Do you guys really think we can

pull this off in just two days?"

"It's actually only about forty hours from now," Cooper corrected, frowning like he had his doubts, same as me.

Natalie slapped the table. "We can do this."

Aunt Zoe nodded. "We have to. It's our best chance."

"I love a good sleight of hand," Cornelius said before stuffing another cookie in his mouth.

"Unless something catches on fire in the next two days," Reid said, taking Zoe's hand in his. "I'm all yours, Zo."

She snorted and tugged free. "More working and less flirting, Martin."

"I'll do whatever it takes to help, *cara mía*," Doc said, lifting my hand to kiss my knuckles.

"Oh, Gomez," I said with a flirty wink back at him. "I'll be there by your side to the bitter end."

"Jesus," Cooper muttered, shaking his head. "I'm in if it means not having to listen to those two speak lovey-dovey shit anymore tonight."

Harvey coo-cooed. "That's it, then. It's time to get as busy as a hound in flea season."

CHAPTER TWENTY-THREE

Wednesday, February 13th

I called Jerry again the next morning after dropping off the kids at school, claiming to still be feeling blue. Actually, it was more like black and blue. My scratches were healing nicely thanks to Aunt Zoe's salve, but my bruises were a little too colorful to hide entirely.

My schedule was plumb empty thanks to it being the middle of the week in the middle of winter in the middle of a polar vortex, so Jerry had no issues with me taking another day to rest up before "hitting the court" again. I wasn't sure if he was dreaming up another outing for me with Madame Contraire or not, but I had my fingers and toes crossed she wanted to avoid me as much as I did her, and she'd do whatever she could to convince Jerry to let her ride along with Ben next time.

It turned out Mona was taking the day off, too, so Jerry and Ben would be holding down the fort. That made me even happier I'd decided to stay home. The office wasn't as fun without the flame-haired dynamo there to tease about the hearts that popped above her head every time Jerry walked past her desk.

I had my task list from Harvey in front of me on the kitchen table when I sat down with my cell phone and pulled up Susan's number. Before hitting the call button, I took a deep breath and counted to ten.

Her phone rang a few times before she answered. "Hey, big sis." For once, there wasn't a load of sarcasm behind those two words right out of the gate. She sounded more wary than snarky. "Imagine my surprise at seeing your name pop up. I don't think that's ever happened before."

I scratched some dried milk off the table. "You probably shouldn't get used to it."

She chuckled, but it sounded fake. "So, what has spurred this olive branch?"

It wasn't really an olive branch, but I wasn't going to split hairs. "I need your help on Thursday. No questions asked."

"Well, if I can't ask questions, how will I know what you need from me?"

"I'm going to tell you right now."

"Do I need a pen and paper?"

"No. Nothing can be written down."

"Ohhh, this sounds exciting."

"It's not a free trip to a tropical island," I started my explanation.

"That trip was far from free," she interrupted with a drip of acid.

"*But*," I continued, "if you meant what you said about doing me a favor to get back into our parents' good graces, this is your ticket."

"Let's have it."

I tried to be detailed without giving away too much. Threading a needle in a dark crawlspace would have been easier, but I stumbled through the basics of her to-do list anyway. Knowing, however, that Aunt Zoe had called my father last night and filled him in on the situation, and that Susan was simply to follow along under his guidance, made trusting her a little less worrisome.

Still, she could blow the whole caper up in our faces with a single slip-up, which I warned her about several times during my instructional monologue. I also wrapped up with a final caution. "If you blow this, Susan …"

"Sheez, I get it. Quit beating me over the head with your threats."

Okay, so maybe I'd added a teensy bit too much menace to my warnings, but I wanted them to really sink into her conniving brain.

I stood up from the table and went over to the coffee maker to grab another cup of joe. "One of the key takeaways here is that you need to completely disguise yourself in case you run into this jerk again in the future."

"I have the perfect pair of four-inch heeled, black boots just for this mission."

"Susan, you'll be moving boxes. Steel toes are what is needed here, not fuck-me heels."

"Fine, but you're no fun."

"I am fun, just not today." That led me to the next takeaway. "You must stay true to your role and keep the annoying detective convinced that you are *only* a mover."

"Got it."

"Until the very end of the job."

"Understood."

"That means no flirting, no scheming, no ass-grabbing."

She huffed through the line. "See, you're not even a little fun. But I've known that all of my life."

"The only reason I've *not* been fun around you was because …" I was digressing.

I closed my eyes and took a breath, focusing on the color white in my mind's eye—as in clean white sheets, in particular. According to Cornelius, who'd been trying to cheer me up last week when I was bemoaning all the snow around Deadwood that refused to melt day after day, white was supposed to inspire an overall peaceful effect. And good gravy, I could really use some peace today, along with plenty of love and happiness thrown in.

"Let's return to the takeaways you need to focus on."

Susan snorted. "It sounds to me like the clocks are the takeaways. No, wait. It's the moving truck that's the takeaway."

"That's not really funny."

"It is, too. It's called word play."

"Let's stick to working here, not playing."

"Boring," she said in a sing-song voice, and then sighed. "Continue."

"You're going to be working alongside Natalie."

Dead silence came from Susan's end.

"Did you hear me?" I asked, double-checking that the phone call hadn't been dropped. "Susan?"

"For how long?" she asked.

"Several hours."

"Can I change my mind about saying I'd do this?"

"You said that you would help me with whatever I need, *no questions asked.*" I emphasized that last part in my stern, motherly voice. "This is what I need."

She grunted, reminding me of Detective King Kong. "What is it with your obsession about not asking questions? It's like I'm some top-notch killer, and you're paying me to take someone out."

"You're a top-notch deceiver, and my payment for this job will be returning you to the land of our parents' good graces—especially Mom's. Trust me, the less you know—"

"The better I will be in the end. I get it, Vi."

I glanced at the Betty Boop clock on the wall. It was time to wrap this up. I had another call to make. "Do you have the details down? I'm talking about the time and tasks and clothing required to pull off this job."

"Yeah. Plus, you said Dad knows how it's all supposed to go down, so I can lean on him, if needed."

"And remember—not a single word to Mom. To keep her feeling holly-jolly and twirling around in her field of dandelions and honeybees, we need to keep her out of this."

"Right."

"Forever."

"I speak perfectly good English, you know. I understand what you're saying."

"Great."

"It seems weird, though, that your top-secret job for me would be moving a bunch of silly old clocks." She sniffed. "It's kind of boring. I'd rather be finding out a way to screw over your ex some more instead."

I hesitated, replaying her words in my mind to make sure she hadn't said "screwing your ex"—her old pastime. But that was *then*. I needed to keep focusing on *now*.

"Boring for you," I said. "But important to me."

"You have to make Natalie promise not to fuck with me, because I don't know if I can stay in character if she starts doing that freaky, demonic chanting under her breath when I'm near her. Or if she whispers in my ear about the messed-up shit she's going to do to me while I'm sleeping."

"Natalie will pretend she doesn't know you, as will her boyfriend, the other bossy detective who will also be at the scene."

"I remember Cooper from Christmas, Vi."

I squeezed my temples. "Just stick to pretending you're part of a moving crew and get the damned boxes loaded into the truck. When it's all done, I'll talk to Mom."

"Okay. Just don't fuss about this like you do about everything else. Stress never looks pretty on you. It makes your hair frizzier."

White sheets, white sheets, white sheets.

"Call me if you have any questions, Susan. Don't text. We don't need any kind of written trail on this."

"Trust me, I'm good at covering my tracks."

"I have no doubt about that."

"Will I see you on Thursday?" she asked.

"No. I'll be watching it all go down, though."

"Sounds kinky."

"Susan." I paused, trying to decide how to go forth with what I really needed her to grasp. I didn't want to beg, but ... "Please don't fuck me over on this. Succeeding at this task is not only important to me, it's extremely vital when it comes to my kids' futures."

"We're just talking about clocks, though, right?"

"Mostly. Goodbye, Susan."

"Catch you on the flip side, big sis."

I hung up with a knot in my gut. My sister wasn't the only wild card in this caper, but I'd put the whole crew at risk by including her. I really hoped she craved Mom's good graces as much as she loved easy money ... and sex with my ex.

I checked off that task from my list and moved to the next—getting hold of Mr. Black.

I hesitated before placing a call to Eddie Mudder, the owner of Mudder Brothers Funeral Parlor, who acted as the middleman between me and Mr. Black. If Hawke were to scrutinize my phone records, he might wonder why I called Eddie. Then again, it was no secret that Eddie had become sort of a friend of mine, and it wasn't against the law to call a pal and catch up. Besides, Jerry would tell Hawke that I'd stayed home sick, so maybe I was just hedging my bets and making sure that if my sickness turned into death, I had a reservation waiting for my corpse at the undertaker's place.

Eddie answered his phone right away. "Violet." He dragged

out my name, reminding me of Lurch from the classic *Addams Family* television show. "You're still alive."

"Funny, Eddie. Were you reading my mind? I was just thinking about contacting you to hold a place *on* your table for me."

He let out a deep-throated laugh that echoed on his end. It sounded like he was down in the basement of the funeral parlor. I could imagine him in the autopsy room where everything was metal and sterile—and possibly bloody at this very moment.

Ick! I tried to shut out my memories of huddling in his tall pantry-like cupboard in that room while my ex-coworker was nearly sliced to ribbons.

"I need to talk to Mr. Black," I whispered, for some reason.

"Okay," he whispered back.

I cleared my throat, continuing at a normal volume. "Do you have a phone number for him? I hate to bother you out of the blue like this, but it's urgent."

"No worries, Violet. He said that whenever you call, it would likely be an urgent situation."

Through the line, I heard the sound of water running and splashing in a metal sink basin. I closed my eyes, trying to stop my imagination from creating visuals for why a man who handled dead bodies on a daily basis would need to wash his hands.

The water stopped, then I heard a *creak*—I knew that sound. It was the hinges on the double doors leading out of the autopsy room. In a heartbeat, I was back in time to that night, outside of that same room, running for my life from the white-haired Juggernaut with the ghoulish and bulging eyes. Goosebumps peppered my forearms. Had I known then what I know …

"Let me head to my office," Eddie said, bringing me back to the here and now. "I need to grab the number Mr. Black gave me to reach him."

"Thanks, Eddie." I listened to his footfalls *clop-clop* on the linoleum floor, picturing his progress down that long L-shaped hallway I'd raced through to escape the Juggernaut. "How have you been?"

"Pretty good. I'm up for an award."

"Oh, yeah? For what? Best Funeral Parlor in the West?"

He snorted. "Don't be silly. It's for my music. It's an independent artist award. I've been nominated for the Best

Electric Organ Hip-hop Original Song."

"No shit?" Was there really such a category? Huh.

Eddie made the local funerals extra interesting by playing his unique organ music during the service. I'd never forget hearing "Staying Alive" during one of the Haskell family's viewings.

"That's wonderful news, Eddie! Congratulations. My fingers are crossed for you. I'll let Natalie know the exciting news, too."

"Thanks! She's been such a good friend to my family over the years."

Same for me and mine—well, Susan would beg to differ.

I heard the creak of a chair. "Let me see." Paper shuffling noises followed. "Ah, here we are."

"Do you want to read me Mr. Black's number?" I asked.

"I can't. He was rather adamant that only I can call, and then he'll come to you."

What was with these hoops to jump through? Mr. Black and I were supposed to be coworkers in Timekeeping.

"Okay. If you can contact him immediately, I'll keep my phone on me and wait for his call. Please let him know this is an emergency and I can't wait long."

"I sure will, Violet. You and Nat need to stop over some time and listen to some of my newest recordings."

"I would like that, Eddie."

And I meant that. What a lovely idea to sit and listen to music without worrying about clocks and capers and bounty hunters and dying. Actually, there'd probably be sprinkles of death in my thoughts, since I'd be sitting in a funeral parlor at the time.

We said our goodbyes and hung up.

I figured that I had a few minutes until Mr. Black called, so I decided to throw a load of laundry in the washer.

During breakfast this morning with the kids, Aunt Zoe had mentioned something about being low on clean towels, then she'd gulped down her coffee and zipped out the door to catch a ride with Reid. They had to pick up some firewood to fill the boxes they'd been taping together throughout the night out at Cooper's parents' place. With his mom and dad out of town on a mid-winter vacation in the tropics, Cooper had decided their house, which sat a few miles out of town, was the safest location to not only prep the fake boxes, but also paint the moving trucks in his dad's heated pole barn.

I threw in all of the towels and started the washer.

I checked my phone—no call.

Since I had a little more time, I folded the kids' clothes that I'd left in the dryer overnight, stacking them in the laundry basket to carry to their rooms.

Still no call.

Maybe Addy should teach the imp how to do laundry, and then Daisy could show Elvis how to match socks. We could get Rooster in on the action, having him retrieve the dirty clothes littering the floor in the kids' rooms and carry everything to the laundry room. I doubted Bogart would lift a paw to help. Cats made far better supervisors than laborers.

Chuckling at my own version of *Fantasia,* I pocketed my phone and grabbed the basket of clothes to take upstairs. I stepped out of the laundry room and stopped in my tracks at the sight of Mr. Black sitting at Aunt Zoe's table, drinking from my cup of coffee.

Apparently, cooties weren't a concern for his kind.

"I knocked, but you did not hear me," he explained in lieu of a greeting.

"I'm glad you didn't leave," I said, circling back to set the laundry basket on top of the dryer. When I returned, I took a longer look at my enigmatic partner in time. "You're wearing gray today."

As in a gray pea coat and a matching scarf over a navy linen shirt with a banded collar. His white hair looked quite a bit longer than the last time I'd seen him, and it was pulled back in a ponytail. Overall, he actually appeared quite jaunty, kind of reminding me of an old-time ship captain, instead of the grim reaper's hood-free cousin in all black clothing.

"And you are wearing bruises and scratches, *Scharfrichter.*" He took a sip of my coffee. "How did you come by those?" He sniffed the air, his gaze narrowing. "Was it a gift from the imp you appear to be holding captive in this house?"

I swung by the counter to grab another cup of coffee for myself. Usually, Mr. Black dropped brain bombs on me when he stopped by, teaching me far more than my brain bucket would be able to hold this morning without more caffeine.

"Daisy the imp is actually a guest here."

He frowned. "You jest."

"I do not." I sat across from him. "My daughter has adopted it, much to the imp's delight."

"I meant you jest about that moniker." He almost smiled. "I mean, truly, *Daisy*?"

I shrugged. "Addy's choice." I took a sip of coffee. "Did you know that an imp can be potty trained?"

He laughed. It was a deep, gravelly sound, as if his vocal cords had been rusted closed until this very moment.

I stared in surprise. I had no idea Mr. Black had the ability to make that sound, period.

When he quieted, I shook off my shock and added, "Even more surprising, the imp has taken quite a liking to Elvis, our chicken."

One white eyebrow raised. "It was my understanding that imps will eat chickens, given the chance."

"I believe you are correct, especially if the chicken is coated in honey."

He nodded. "Its elixir of choice." His forehead tightened. "However, blood is favored by the redcap."

I lowered my cup to the table. "By the *what*?"

"The redcap goblin. I noticed its territorial marking by the porch when I arrived."

The gears in my melon ground on his words. Redcap. Goblin. Territorial marking.

"Was that the visitor who left the bloody hide-stitched hat stuck to the beam overhead with some kind of ancient knife?"

He nodded. "The blood-soaked hat is a token signifying the goblin will return to finish the task."

"The task being what? I mean, it decapitated a poor mule deer and left the head in my front yard for the whole neighborhood to see."

"Killing *der Scharfrichter*, of course." He took another sip of coffee while I digested this newsflash. "Your kind is quite popular amongst the hunters, you realize. It is quite an honor to carry a Slayer's crest as a trophy for eliminating her."

Yeah, yeah, everyone wants to kill my kind. Whatever. I was more concerned about the so-called redcap goblin hanging out in my front yard.

"You said you noticed this goblin's marking before I even mentioned the knife and hat. What marking?"

Was it some kind of sigil, like what Daisy had been leaving at different sites?

"Besides the bloody hide hat and the decapitation, which are its usual warnings that your death will follow, redcaps tend to urinate in a hidden location."

I winced. "You mean something peed near the porch?"

He nodded. "But your kind would not be able to see it."

"Then how did you?"

"It is not discernable by sight, but rather smell. It has a distinct odor in its urine reminiscent of a harpy's scent."

"Harpy as in a half woman, half bird?"

He smirked. "Ah, humans. They do like to twist history to make it more entertaining."

"So, a redcap goblin peed by my front porch. That takes a lot of nerve."

"The telltale spray of urine indicates to other hunters that the redcap intends to kill the prey residing nearby. If another hunter dares to trespass, the redcap will come for them as well." He shook his head, frown lines crisscrossing his pale forehead. "They are gleeful killers, only content when they have an abundance of victims. Trust me when I say you do not want one of these goblins hunting you. Their long, boney, bloody fingers and fiery-red eyes will haunt you in your sleep."

I gaped. "But I do have one hunting me."

"Oh. Right." He grimaced. "Ignore what I said."

A guffaw of disbelief erupted from my throat. "Unless you have a lobotomy kit in one of your coat pockets, I can't just forget about that."

"At one time, I had a weapon that would work precisely for a lobotomy, but I lost it in a snowstorm."

Was he for real? Unfortunately, I believed he was—about both the lost weapon and the goblin's intentions.

"You should be fine, *Scharfrichter*. Just swing low when the goblin attacks." He finished my coffee with a final gulp. "Now, if the redcap was not the reason for you reaching out to me, what was?"

"Before we get to that, can you see a handprint on my cheek

that goes partway down my neck?" I turned my head to the side and pulled down my sweatshirt neckline, so he could have a better view of the area.

His dark pupils shifted into snake-like slits for a moment as he leaned in and sniffed near my neck. Then he sat back, his eyes back to normal. "I see only a few faded scratches and some bruising. I smell nothing on you beyond your soap, shampoo, the Oracle, clothing detergent, your children's scents, and some coffee you must have spilled, along with the honey you used as sweetener."

"Holy shit. You can smell all that?"

He nodded. "And more, but I don't want to make you uncomfortable."

What did that mean? Why would I be uncomfortable? I resisted the urge to sniff inside my shirt and instead focused on what he could see.

"The scratches and bruises were the result of an entity trapped inside of a medium." When he continued to stare at me without comment, I added, "Prudence and I accidentally almost let it free, but I think it's back in its vessel now."

"What sort of entity?"

I shrugged. "An angry one. Prudence was able to subdue it after a bit of a struggle."

It was quite more than a *bit*, but for some reason I felt the need to downplay the truth. This was probably a touch of Slayer ego stepping up to the plate, but the end result was that Prudence and I teamed up and won. I still hadn't heard from my fellow Slayer, but it had only been a little over a day, and Prudence and I often went without talking for weeks.

"Do you think this entity left the handprint on you?"

"No, the Oracle noticed the mark before the entity attacked me."

"Interesting."

"He noticed a similar handprint on the imp, too. But he only sees the mark when looking through Arcana, my family mirror."

"Yes, *der magischer Spiegel* that watches over *der magistra* while she works in her glass and alchemy shop."

Alchemy? I guess that was sort of on-point. "Right, that special mirror. Do you think you could take a look in the mirror and see if this handprint is also visible to you?"

He shook his head. "I should not look in that mirror."

I remembered when he joined us in Aunt Zoe's workshop a while back and saw it. She'd warned him not to touch it, but never explained why.

"Why not?"

"There is the risk of peering inside and never coming back out."

I couldn't recount how many times I'd looked into the mirror. "You're serious?"

"Very. Mirrors are unpredictable and often precarious."

I'd heard that before. "Do you have any idea why the imp and I have handprints on us?" I remembered another detail. "The mark on the imp is spreading, with tendrils growing out from the ends of the fingers."

His nostrils flared. "That is peculiar. I have not heard of such a marking, but I will ask *Frau* Zuckerman what she knows of this and relay her reply."

"Thank you." I sat back, wishing he'd given more help with my handprint problem. "As for why I needed to talk to you, we are going to take back the clocks tomorrow afternoon."

"You and your friends?"

I nodded. "We have a plan in progress. However, we need to have a few decoy clocks just in case." I spread my arms wide. "As you can imagine, it is not easy to find Black Forest clocks like these anywhere nearby, and the one I have for the *mardagayl* has to remain in my possession for now."

He stood. "How many clocks?"

"Three would do," I said, rising as well.

He nodded once. "You will have them by sunrise."

After the bad news about the redcap goblin and the handprint, I was happy to finally have something go my way.

"Perfect."

"Where will you be storing all of the clocks?" he asked.

"My friend, Harvey, has a location, but he's keeping it under his hat for now in case this caper goes south and I end up under investigation." I rubbed the back of my neck. "If I do end up in jail, I'll make sure Harvey reaches out to you through Eddie Mudder to let you know where to find the clocks."

He stared at me in silence for a few ticks of the clock overhead.

"If you are put in jail, it will not be for long."

"Are you going to bring me a nail file hidden in a cake?"

He smirked. "No, my fellow Timekeeper. You have a redcap goblin hunting you. It will free you from your trap in order to make the hunt more rewarding."

I shook my head. "If anyone could find the positives in having a bounty on my head, it would be you, Mr. Black."

He bowed. "Happy to be of service, *Scharfrichter*." He walked over to the back door, pausing to look back before opening it. "When you have those clocks safely in your possession, contact me through the usual channel."

"Why? Do you want to make sure none are damaged?"

"The clocks will be fine. You, on the other hand, need to learn how to use them to find these bounty hunters before they kill you first."

CHAPTER TWENTY-FOUR

Thursday, February 14th
7:25 a.m.

Doc made heart-shaped pancakes for the kids to start their Valentine's Day off with a smile. This undoubtedly placed him at the top of the list for the Best Breakfast Maker of the Year award in their eyes. However, since it was only mid-February, I still had time to knock their socks off.

For my breakfast, he made bacon and eggs, one of my favorites. He even added a dollop of honey to the bacon, making it extra sweet and savory. The same description could be used for Doc's long goodbye kiss, which he snuck in after dragging me into the dark laundry room and pressing me back against the closed door.

Thankfully, my lip had healed up nicely, along with most of my scratches. The bruises seemed to be fading quicker, too, this time. Maybe there was something to that special salve of Aunt Zoe's that I kept applying religiously, after all.

"Feeling frisky, Candy Cane?" I teased when his lips moved to my neck.

His hands slid under my cashmere sweater. "This new honey craze you have going is giving me some big ideas."

I pressed against him, getting touchy-feely. "I can tell."

He groaned, returning for another deeper kiss as his fingers tickled their way up my ribcage.

"You even taste like honey," he said against my lips.

I wrapped my arms around his neck, pulling away enough so I could kiss my way over to his ear.

"If you'll be my Valentine," I said under my breath, "I'll drizzle some honey on you later tonight and lick it off." I used his earlobe as a demonstration.

He sucked air through his teeth and groaned louder and longer. "Jesus, woman. You can't say things like that and expect me to go to work and talk rationally about retirement funds."

"You know, if this caper goes south for us, this might be our last conjugal visit for a while."

"The caper is going to go fine." His fingers slid over my bra, his thumbs getting distracted along the way with what they felt under the sheer, gauzy fabric. "Is this a new bra? It feels really soft."

I wasn't ready to show him his Valentine's Day present yet, especially not in the laundry room, so I distracted him by nipping at his earlobe and whispered, "What makes you so certain the caper will go fine?"

"Everyone finished what needed to be done yesterday." He pressed harder against my hips. "The trucks, the boxes, the manifest, the moving crew—everything is in place and we're set to collect those clocks come one o'clock." He bent down, capturing my mouth again for a long, slow kiss. "I can taste the honey on your tongue."

I wasn't surprised. I had gone a little overboard on the sweet stuff, adding another drop to each bacon bite. I pulled him down for a longer, more thorough taste, moaning as his thumbs lit up all the hot spots south of my neck.

When our lips separated, I said, "Maybe we should knock one off quick against the washer while the kids are upstairs getting ready for school." Maybe now was a good enough time to give him his Valentine's burlesque show after all.

It was my first Valentine's Day in forever where I had an actual partner for romance thrills, instead of me spending the evening with a half-gallon of peanut butter fudge ice cream and an old Humphrey Bogart movie on the television.

Doc glanced over at the washing machine and then back. "Why not the dryer?"

"The washer is heavier and won't bang against the wall." I reached for his belt buckle.

"I have to wonder at the thought you've put into that."

I chuckled. "I spend a lot of time in here daydreaming about dirty stuff."

"Wait." He caught my hand before I'd finished unbuckling his belt. "I hear someone in the kitchen." He leaned his ear closer to the door. "It sounds like they're getting in the fridge."

"Good grief." I adjusted my girls in their sheer straitjackets and fixed my sweater. "Is it too much to ask for five minutes of laundry room nookie in this house?"

"Damn." He ran his hand through his hair, blowing out a breath. "You're going to have to go out there without me, Tish. I need a minute to think deeply about something other than your lips, like maybe …" he glanced around the room, zeroing in on the shelf above the dryer. "Bleach and lint."

I giggled, giving him a kiss and a flirty squeeze before grabbing an empty clothes basket from the floor. He opened the door for me, hiding behind it as I stepped into the kitchen.

Harvey stood at the counter pouring creamer into a cup of coffee. "This ain't no time to be dillydallyin' with laundry, Sparky. We got us a bit of a situation."

I set the empty laundry basket on a chair. "What's wrong?"

"Ain't anything worth gettin' your face all pinched like that. We just had to shift things around a little."

"Shift what how?" Doc asked, joining us with a frown lining his brow.

Harvey looked from Doc to me to the laundry room to the empty laundry basket. Then back to me. A grin rounded his cheeks. "What was goin' down in the laundry room just now?"

"Nothing," I said too quickly.

"Nothin', my ass. You two sneakin' in some monster lovin' before school starts?" He winked at Doc. "Tell the truth, were you teachin' Godzilla the no-pants dance?"

Doc shrugged. "Tish tried to entice me into dancing the horizontal tango, but I told her that I was saving myself for the matrimonial polka."

I shot Doc a frown. Hinting at marriage in front of Harvey seemed risky. Most days, the ol' boy was sharp enough to stick in the ground when it came to figuring out the ins and outs of my romantic life.

Harvey snickered and returned to his coffee making, spooning some sugar into the cup. "You should've at least tried to take a peek at the box Sparky's kids came in before turnin' her down."

Doc laughed. "I'll save that one for next time." He came up behind me, wrapping his arm around my shoulders and pulling me back into his warm embrace. "Now, what's going on with the caper?"

Around 10 a.m. (T-minus three hours until caper time)

All was quiet inside Calamity Jane Realty.

Too quiet.

Having to sit at work while everyone else was busy preparing for this afternoon's clock switcheroo had me spinning in circles in my office chair to help pass the time.

I'd arrived at work to find out that Jerry was spending the day down in Rapid City, scouting out some potential new business properties to sell. He'd taken Ben along with him since he had no clients booked for today. That left Mona and me, which quickly turned into only me when Mona's clients showed up shortly after she'd arrived at work. She'd whisked them away to check out some homes in Spearfish and Sturgis, but not before taking a moment to pull me aside and ask me about the bruises around my eye that seemed to have relocated slightly on my face. She looked about as skeptical as Layne had when I gave her the icy steps explanation, which didn't surprise me knowing what she did about the horsing around with ghosts I'd done in the past.

"Was Jane's ghost anywhere near these icy steps?"

I shook my head. "I wish, but these were all new steps."

"Damn." She blew out a breath. "Well, I suggest that you have Doc and your aunt keep a closer eye on you when walking down these sort of 'invisible steps' in the future."

She gave me a quick hug and headed out after her clients.

Since Mona didn't plan on returning until later this afternoon, I sat alone, spinning now and then, watching every damned minute tick by on the clock.

I glanced up at the camera in the corner of the room and flipped it off, wishing that Cornelius was upstairs watching me on the screen instead of hanging out over at Galena House with Natalie and Cooper. Or maybe he was at Cooper's parents' place helping with the moving trucks. I didn't know for sure, because Harvey insisted I be kept in the dark on the finer details of today's events. He wanted my alibi to be rock-solid in case Hawke dragged me into the Deadwood Police Station for some finger pointing and more name calling.

I stopped spinning, closing my eyes until the dizziness ebbed.

I'd much rather have called in sick one more day and spent the morning cleaning the kids' rooms while Bogart watched in between her catnaps, eating honey by the spoonful along with Daisy, reading a book in the bathtub with Rooster sleeping on the bathmat—hell, even just hanging out with Elvis in my closet. Anything besides twiddling my thumbs at work. But Doc and Harvey had nixed my idea of calling in sick one more day. They'd both agreed it was important that I be sitting front and center at my desk, visible both on Cornelius's cameras and through the office's front window.

I tapped my fingers on my desk, frowning down at my cell phone, willing it to ring or ping or do something other than just sit there with a dark screen.

"Fuck this." I picked up my phone, pulling up Natalie's name, and sent her a message: *How is Frankenstein Jr. doing?*

Then I waited, fingers tapping again.

The necessary "shift" that Harvey had been talking about earlier in Aunt Zoe's kitchen had to do with Reid being called out to investigate a structure fire that had occurred overnight halfway down the road toward Hill City. Lucky for us, his son, Ox, had stepped in to take his father's place on the caper front. Coop and Aunt Zoe had briefed Ox on the situation, keeping the details sparse. Cooper had explained that he needed to take the clocks back because Hawke was stepping beyond his jurisdiction in keeping them so long. He made sure not to mention that I was involved at all, so that Ox wouldn't inadvertently say my name and send Hawke into a paranoid tizzy.

I frowned at my phone, still waiting for Natalie to reply.

Doc and I had both been wary of having another non-monster stepping in to help at this point, even though it was Reid's son, but Harvey assured us that this was merely a small pothole in the road.

"Trust me on this," he'd said. "Keep ridin' for the brand as planned."

That meant Doc was to meet with his client this morning at his office as scheduled. Lucky him for the distraction. Meanwhile, I was to sit at my desk waiting for my lunch hour when I could close up the office, run upstairs to Cornelius's place, and watch with bated breath as the scene at Ms. Wolff's apartment played out on the monitor.

My phone screen darkened. I touched it, bringing it back to life and then returned to my waiting game, adding another spin or two in my chair for something non-monotonous.

Finally, a few minutes later, a reply came from Natalie: *Who is this and how did you get my number?*

Funny girl.

I wrote: *I found your number in a grimy bathroom at a truck stop on the corner of Tart and Trollop in Hookerville.*

LOL! That's a good one. What are you doing, Godzilla?

I'm alone and plucking my nose hairs for shits and giggles.

It's good to self-groom. Your Valentine will appreciate your lack of fuzzy nostrils next time you swap spit.

I scowled at my phone and typed: *Answer my original question.*

So demanding. You've been hanging around King Kong too much.

Yes, I'd agree with that 100 percent, but I wasn't going to let her sidetrack me. *Quit stalling, Count Spudnut.*

Word on the street is that Frankie Jr. is doing fine. His pop would be proud.

Good. Is all well in Transylvania? I sent back, hoping she'd realize I was talking about Galena House.

We have a bit of a wet blanket situation in one of the lower chambers, but we're hoping it doesn't throw a pipe wrench in today's coffin opening.

I read that message two more times quickly, and then once very slowly. Still, I wasn't sure what she was hinting at, but I did get the gist that something was wrong with the caper as planned.

"Shit." I frowned out the front window, trying to figure out how to get to the bottom of what was really going on over at Galena House without outright asking.

Before I could come up with anything to write, another message came from Natalie: *Gotta go, Zilla. Stay warm over there on Monster Island.*

I read her cryptic message about the wet blanket situation once more. There was nobody I could call and ask without looking suspicious phone-record-wise besides Doc, but he was with his client for another hour, and he probably wouldn't have any answers for me anyway.

"Damn it." I opened my desk drawer, dropped my cell phone inside, and slammed it shut.

"Now what?" I closed my eyes and spun around and around again in my chair, wondering what shenanigans Daisy and Elvis were up to at home, and how long it might take to potty train a chicken. Would the imp's toilet coaching include flushing etiquette?

Creeeeaaakkk.

I stopped spinning.

My pulse hit the gas, making my heart rattle faster. I knew that sound. Jane's office door had just opened behind me.

I opened my eyes and turned slowly in my chair until I was facing the back hallway. At the other end of the hall under the fluorescent lights, Jane's ghost stood staring at me with a solemn look on her usually smiling face. As I stared back, her body wavered slightly. The gossamer glow surrounding her blond hair, pale skin, and Santa-red suit jacket and pants glitched and dimmed, darkening her clothes to more of a bloody burgundy.

"Jane?" I whispered, rising from my chair. "Is that really you?"

She lifted her arm and pointed at me, then her old office.

I started to take a step toward her but stumbled from dizziness. I reached out and held onto my desk, waiting for the rest of the room to stop moving.

Jane turned, staring in at her office. At least that was what it looked like from my end of the hallway.

Maybe it wasn't Jane's ghost. I'd been fooled before.

I grabbed the metal stapler from my desk, just in case I was seeing something else that had crawled out from the Hellhole under the office and wanted to play a closet door game of hide and go "creak" with me again.

11 a.m.–ish (Two hours until caper time)

Jane ghosted me, dammit.

One moment she was standing in the back hallway. The next, *poof!* She was gone.

I'd glanced away from her long enough to reach into my desk drawer and grab my phone, and when I'd turned back, she was no longer standing there. Or maybe she'd been "floating there." I'd been so surprised that I hadn't noticed such details.

For the last forty-five minutes, I'd been waiting, often pacing, to see if Jane would return, but so far nothing.

I'd tiptoed down the hall and listened through her locked office door a couple of times, but not heard anything on the other side. After my third check, I'd detoured into the bathroom and taken a long stare in the mirror with the hope that Jane would appear behind me and scare the crap out of me. That was when I'd begun to question my sanity. Did I really even see her ghost or was that handprint on my cheek now causing my brain to short circuit?

Several times as I waited at my desk for her ghost to reappear, I'd picked up my phone to call Doc only to stop, since I didn't know if he was still with his client. I'd even pressed my ear against the wall that divided our offices, but I couldn't hear anything on the other side of that either.

I stopped pacing to check the time again. Gah! The minutes were crawling by. Snails moved faster.

I walked over to the front door for a different view. Across the street in front of the courthouse, bare tree limbs thrashed about in the sub-zero wind. Some days being an Executioner felt just like those limbs.

Was Doc finished with that client yet? I could wait a few more minutes, and then send him a … "Ah, screw it."

I rushed outside into the icebox and jogged the few steps to Doc's office. The cold made my lungs ache, trying to flash-freeze me from the inside out. Holy-north-poly!

A peek inside Doc's front window found his office empty. His door was locked, too.

"Where are you?" I hollered into the frigid wind.

Cursing, I returned to Calamity Jane's, feeling even more alone than before. Why had he left without even telling me? It had to be something to do with the caper, I was sure—and so was the big fat anxiety ogre sitting on my chest.

Back at my desk, I pulled up Doc's number and sent him the same message I'd yelled into the wind.

Before I could set the phone down, a message came through

from my aunt: *The Wolf Man is with me. My old truck broke down and needed a mechanic.*

Her old truck? Her rig wasn't that old, only a couple of years. Besides, her truck was sitting in the drive at home, wasn't it? Maybe not. Maybe she'd had someone drop her off so she could shower or change, and then left again. But still, why would …

Oh! It wasn't her rig. It was one of the moving trucks.

Crap! If we didn't have two trucks, we were dead in the snow.

I wanted to call Harvey to find out what our options were without a second truck, but I couldn't risk it. Besides, I was supposed to be working, laying low on the caper front, but staying in plain sight for anyone to drive by and see.

I spun slowly in my chair. All I could do now was keep my fingers crossed that Doc could fix the moving truck and the caper would go on as planned.

I glanced toward the back hallway again as I circled.

Still no Jane.

With a sigh, I stood and walked over to the plate glass windows, staring at the frozen world outside. Across the street, I noticed some movement high up in the courthouse cupola.

I looked up.

Someone was standing in the cupola looking down at me.

Someone tall and gangly, wearing a red hat.

Red hat. That was …

My breath caught—the redcap goblin!

My palms began to tingle. Shit! I needed a weapon. Something bigger than a stupid stapler this time.

As I stared up at the bounty hunter, the goblin eased back from the edge, slipping out of sight behind one of the square cupola pillars.

A few minutes before noon (One hour until caper time)

For close to an hour I sat on top of my desk, the mace Doc had given me for Christmas in hand, my phone in the other. I waited and waited for that redcap to come for me.

Right after the bastard had backed out of sight up on the courthouse, I'd raced out the back door and sprinted through the parking lot to my SUV to grab my mace. Then I'd come back inside and locked down the office. Whether or not the deadbolt on the back door would hold back a bloodthirsty goblin was yet to be seen, but if the lock gave way, my mace would stop it in its tracks—I hoped.

What exactly was a "goblin," anyway? One internet site described it as a small, evil, ugly elf-like creature, which sounded more like an imp to me. Another site defined a goblin as a dwarf-to-human size fairy. Both claimed goblins were talked about in folklore from many European cultures.

The creature I'd seen up in the courthouse cupola was tall and lanky looking, at least from a distance. Plus, it reached high enough the other night on Aunt Zoe's porch to pin that bloody hat to the beam. It would've needed a stepstool if it were small. Unless it could fly.

I was thinking this hunter fell into the fairy category.

But, seriously, what the fuck did I know about goblins?

I had told Doc about the redcap last night after the kids had gone to bed. He'd reacted the way I'd figured—a few curses, some long hugs, and an order to carry my mace with me wherever I went. He'd even double-checked that I had the weapon in the back of my rig before heading off this morning to take the kids to school.

I glanced toward the back door and then checked out front again. Still no sign of the redcap.

Criminy, I wished Doc was sitting next to me right now, but caper duty called.

My cell phone rang.

Speaking of calling … I held up my phone to see which monster was on the other end of the line.

It was Susan. Uh oh. She was supposed to be the Invisible Man today, not calling me an hour prior to the caper.

"What's wrong?" I asked upon answering.

"I just wanted to let you know that I'm running about ten minutes late, but I'm on my way."

I cursed under my breath.

"It's fine, Vi. Just remind me where I'm supposed to go."

What? The band of anxiety that had been belted around my chest for the last hour constricted another notch. "Dad knows where to go. Isn't he driving?"

"Ahh, no." She sighed. "See, we had a bit of a problem this morning."

"What happened?"

"Mother happened. She was supposed to be going out to lunch with a widowed friend, but the friend is sick and cancelled. Mom stayed home, and when she found out we might be heading up to Deadwood, she really wanted to go. I mean *really*, really, and wouldn't take no for an answer."

"Damn it."

"Exactly. So, Dad had to run interference. He told her that he actually didn't want to come, but was just going to keep me company for the drive. Then he whisked Mom away for a romantic lunch."

I pinched the bridge of my nose. "This isn't good."

"But *not* before following me outside and giving me a final rundown of the plans for today."

"We needed Dad's muscles for moving boxes."

"Don't worry. I'm wearing some sensible shoes and can lift a box with a clock, no problem."

"There are going to be about eighty boxes with clocks."

"Woof! That's one hell of a clock fetish." She honked the horn. "Get out of the way, asshole."

"I need to get hold of Aunt Zoe or Doc and let them know we have a problem."

"No, you don't. There is no problem, and I already called Aunt Zoe and explained the situation. I just forgot to ask for the address and figured you'd be waiting by your phone."

"Susan, do you even know how to drive a moving truck?"

"Violet, I have driven a moving truck before. *And* I know how to drive a stick shift."

Oh yeah, I'd forgotten about that. Dad had taken both of us up on dirt roads in the Black Hills when we were younger, teaching us how to shift gears and navigate in tight spots.

"As for some muscle help," Susan continued, "Aunt Zoe mentioned something about an Ox being there to help. I'm assuming she was talking about a guy with that name and not the four-legged yoke wearer. Although if it is a beast of burden, we could pile boxes on the ox and save our backs some wear and tear."

I paced next to my desk. "Susan, this is no time to joke."

"I don't know. Moving boxes of clocks with an ox seems kind of funny to me. It sounds like one of those Dr. Seuss stories Mom would read to us when we were kids."

"Maybe we should call off this whole thing."

"No!" The intensity in her tone made me stand still. "I will make this happen, big sis. You have to trust me."

"Yeah, but see I haven't been able to do that since we were little kids, and even then when I tried, you'd still pinch me every chance you got."

"I know. I wanted your attention. Now I have it, so let me do this."

"Susan, if you fuck this up …"

"Christ, Violet. This is child's play compared to some of the shit I've done. I understand what's at stake—mostly. Maybe someday you can explain why these stupid clocks matter so damned much, but I'll wait for that. In the meantime, loosen up the ropes so I can run unfettered."

I blew out a breath. "Fine. We'll keep going forward." I listed off the directions to Coop's parents' place where the moving trucks awaited—at least I hoped Doc had both of them fixed.

"Oh, I know where that is," she said. "I'll be there in about thirty-five minutes, and I'm already dressed for the role, hat and all."

I had trouble picturing my sister in anything other than spiky heels, a slinky top, and tight pants.

"Be careful around Detective Hawke," I warned one last time. "He thinks I'm a witch bent on stealing those clocks. He's always on the lookout for another crime to pin on me."

"A witch, huh?" Susan chuckled. "This is going to be fun."

"No, Susan. You will not be having fun today."

"Toodle-doo, big sis. I'll see you when it's all over." She hung up.

I sat back down on the edge of my desk, frowning out the front window. The redcap goblin was turning out to be the least of my problems today. I just hoped that when Susan saw me next, there were no jail cell bars between us.

CHAPTER TWENTY-FIVE

Time was not flowing like a river. It was more like a trickle. No, better yet, a drip—and a slow one at that.

I sat stuck in a void. Life was happening outside of the office, but here at my desk, it was just me and my mace. A girl and her blunt weapon. A *Scharfrichter* and her bludgeoning daydreams about a goblin with a taste for blood and …

My cell phone pinged with a message.

Oh, thank God! Finally, some contact from the outside world. I stuck a sock in the mouth of my inner monologue demon and looked at my phone.

It was Doc: *Why are you sitting on your desk with your mace in hand?*

He was ten minutes late for our Valentine's Day date in front of the monitor for the one o'clock caper show. I looked up at the camera in the corner of the room. "You're upstairs?"

Another ping: *The door is open.*

"No further questions at this time," I told the camera and hopped off my desk.

I locked the front door and hung up the out-for-lunch sign in the window. One more time, I searched the courthouse and its cupola. Still no sign of the redcap goblin.

Grabbing my purse from my desk drawer, I headed down the back hall. I gave Jane's old office a wide berth, wondering again if I'd really seen her ghost or just imagined that part of my morning due to sheer boredom. I peeked out the back door—it looked clear. After a second check of the tree line just beyond the parking lot for the sight of a red hat, I made my exit and locked up behind me.

True to Doc's word, Cornelius's door was open a sliver. I raced inside his apartment and shut the door, leaning against it. Maybe I should deadbolt it and jam a chairback under the doorknob. No need to take chances in a frozen wasteland with a blood-thirsty troublemaker running around.

"You look like the devil is on your tail," Cornelius said from behind me.

I whirled around. "What are you doing here?" I thought he was supposed to be at Galena House running some of the voodoo poppet strings from there.

"I live here," he said with a shrug, as if we were discussing the current cold front, which he was dressed for in his Cossack hat and long wool coat.

"I know you live here." I glanced down at his chest and noticed a small leather pouch hanging from a braided twine rope around his neck. "Is that the *gris-gris* bag?"

He touched it. "Of course."

"What's inside of it?"

"Nothing special, just a copper button, a glass doll's eye, a small vial of grave dust, and three rat whiskers."

While the rat whiskers were interesting, the vial contents snagged me. "Whose grave?"

"It was marked as 'Unknown.' But I have a feeling she was known, just not a person anyone wanted to remember, judging by the warnings marked on her casket."

That painted a scene of digging in a grave on a dark, moonless night. "How do you know about the warnings? Did you see them?"

"One hears things in the wind if you listen long enough."

"Okay, Captain Cryptic. What will those items in the bag do for Detective Hawke?"

"Give him a false sense of security at best." He raised one black eyebrow. "Your aura has a silver shine to it today."

Silver had to be a good thing, didn't it? "Does that mean I'm about to strike it rich in clocks?"

"It means you have erratic mental energy."

I giggled a little too high and loud. "Well, that's a given for today."

"Or it could mean that you live a life of illusion."

I gave him two thumbs-up. "I'm living my best abracadabra

life, baby."

His brow raised. "It could also be a protective sign."

"Oh, I like that. I can use the extra protection these days." I held out my hands palms up. "Bring on all the silver you got, great aura goddess."

He frowned. "Or that you may be mentally ill."

I narrowed my gaze and poked him in the chest below the *gris-gris* bag with the spiky end of my mace. "Don't you have somewhere else to be right now, soothsayer?"

He nodded once. "Mental illness it is." Nudging me aside, he reached for the doorknob. "Let the Tall Medium know I've connected a fourth camera for your viewing pleasure."

"Mental illness my ass," I grumbled as I deadbolted the door behind Cornelius.

When I turned around, Aunt Zoe stood a few feet away next to the kitchen entryway. "Why are you carrying your mace?" she asked, eyeing the weapon suspiciously.

There was no need to lie, she was up to her neck in this *Scharfrichter* business as much as I was. "I saw a redcap goblin on top of the courthouse a little while ago."

"Doc told me about the goblin." She came closer and hugged me. "No rest for the killers or their hunters, it seems." Her arm still around me, she led me toward the living room, whispering in my ear, "You're safe in here. Harvey brought Bessie along and plans to leave her with Doc and you."

"Why did he bring his shotgun?"

"Because he's Harvey."

Normally, I'd scoff at this point in the conversation, but not after what Mr. Black told me about the goblin hunting me to the bloody end. "Good."

We came up behind Harvey, who was standing in front of the monitor at the end of the row, watching two men I didn't recognize pack clocks in boxes on the screen.

"What are you guys doing here right now?" I asked, glancing around the room, wondering where Doc was. "I thought you both were supposed to be with Reid at the storage unit that Hawke rented for the clocks."

Yesterday, Doc had called the moving company pretending to be Hawke. In the process of cancelling the moving job, he'd managed to charm the storage unit details out of the receptionist. As a fellow victim of Doc's charm, I didn't need to ask for the details on the "how" of it all.

"Reid is at the police station finishing up his report on the overnight fire," Aunt Zoe explained. "Harvey told him to stick around there and be chummy with the other officers, watching and listening for any signs of trouble for us."

Harvey looked back at me. "We might need him to play Frankenstein and make a big ol' distraction."

Aunt Zoe snorted. "Distracting is what Reid does best."

He winked at me, thumbing toward my aunt. "Especially when it comes to this one and her puffed-up tail."

She reached out and snapped one of his suspenders, making him flinch.

"Durn it, woman! You need to get off that gunpowder diet and focus." To me, he asked, "Did you hear from Mr. Black about those decoy clocks yet today?"

I shook my head. I'd kind of forgotten about them after Jane showed up at work, and the goblin and Susan hadn't helped with my memory.

"Oh! I meant to tell you," Aunt Zoe said, touching my shoulder. "I have three clocks that Mr. Black dropped off at the house sometime this morning. They're boxed and waiting in my truck."

"When did he stop by?" I'd stuck around as long as I could before heading off to work, waiting for him to show. "Did you talk to him?"

"No, but he left an ambiguous note on the door that said we should check the time in my shop. When I went out there, the clocks were sitting on my workbench. I boxed them up, same as the others, but I marked them with a tiny X on the corner."

Harvey rubbed his hands together. "Alrighty then. We have our decoys." He returned his focus to the monitor. "Look at that, Sparky. Your long-legged sister and her burly crew are busy little bees. They have the bedroom mostly packed already."

I leaned closer to the screen, recognizing the dresser where Cornelius had "found" the poppet. Sure enough, the walls were bare. Was that Freesia standing next to Hawke, watching as the packers worked their magic? I could see half of her on the screen, and only from the backside. I didn't see Susan, though.

Speaking of missing persons, I stepped back and asked, "Where's my Wolf Man? I thought he was up here, too."

"Right behind you," Doc said, walking toward us from the entryway, carrying two bags. "I forgot the food and drinks in my office. Someone locked the deadbolt on me up here. Luckily, I had the spare set of keys in my pocket."

I grimaced. "Sorry. That was me."

He eyed me for a few beats, his gaze searching.

I glanced away first, noticing the grease smudges and streaks on his green dress shirt. Those must be the results of him playing moving truck mechanic in the middle of his workday.

He lifted the two grocery bags. "You guys interested in a drink and some sandwiches?"

"Yes!" I answered with a clap. I grabbed Doc's arm and tugged him to the kitchen, leaving Harvey and Aunt Zoe back at the monitor.

Doc pulled a six-pack of my favorite diet soda from the bag and set the cans on the counter. "So, Killer, want to tell me why you were fondling your mace in the middle of the day?"

I chuckled. "I wasn't fondling it."

"That's too bad. I was hoping you were daydreaming about me," he said with a wink. "So, what was the deal?"

I took the can of soda he held out to me. "Would you believe it was a show-and-tell day at work?"

The scowl he sent my way was answer enough.

"In that case, I grabbed my mace after I saw the redcap goblin on the cupola of the courthouse a couple hours ago."

He stilled, his scowl deepening. "What did it look like?"

"Tall, gangly, creepy as hell with a red hat on its head."

"What was it doing?"

"Staring back at me."

"Christ," he said, pulling me into a long, yummy-smelling embrace, although I did catch a whiff of engine grease mixed in with his cologne when I buried my nose in his shirt. "I'm going to have to chain you up in the basement, Tish."

I leaned back and looked up at him. "Elvis and Daisy might like the company."

He cupped my jaw as his mouth dipped toward mine. "I'll

leave some honey for the imp after I finish sweetening you up."

He gave me another long Valentine's Day kiss, leaving me hungry for more than honey. But as soon as his lips left mine, reality returned, including the erratic thoughts that rode alongside a silver aura.

"I only brought two sandwiches," Doc whispered, returning to the food he'd laid out on the counter. "I didn't realize we'd have company."

I smiled as I took inventory of the lunch date meal he'd brought for us, appreciating his thoughtfulness when it came to remembering one of my new favorite sandwiches. "We can split the turkey with cranberries, stuffing, and mayo and let them share the ham, cheese, and what else is on this one?"

"Potatoes au gratin."

"Oh, yum."

"We'll order that one again another time," he said and grabbed some paper plates from Cornelius's cupboard.

We loaded the plates with sandwiches and a handful of honey-mustard flavored pretzels that he'd brought as a side dish. Food and drinks in hand, we headed for the living room. With chairs in short supply, I insisted that Harvey and Aunt Zoe sit, since they were going to be working later unloading clocks while we took the kids out to a very public dinner at Chuckwagon Charlie's.

For the next several minutes as we ate, I learned about how the night before had gone for Aunt Zoe, along with Reid's son, Ox, as they'd packed up fake boxes and loaded the switcheroo truck. Then Doc explained that the battery terminal had corroded on one of the trucks, which was the reason for it not starting. He'd fixed that and done some minor maintenance on both trucks' engines to make sure there were no other mechanical surprises once the caper got rolling.

I told the three of them about possibly seeing Jane's ghost and her pointing at her office, and then disappearing shortly afterward. None of them knew what to make of her actions, but they leaned toward the idea that Jane was back from wherever she'd gone, which was a relief. Mona would be happy to hear that.

On the screen, Doc switched camera views as we watched Hawke pace around the different rooms of Ms. Wolff's apartment, complaining extra loudly about his broken arm hurting him. He'd pause now and then to hover over the shoulders of our moving crew, keeping an eye on their work.

"Who are the two extra guys helping out?" I asked after finishing my half sandwich. I recognized Ox. Susan was easy to spot in her shapeless coveralls, in spite of the baseball cap pulled low over what must be a short, curly wig.

"They're two friends of Ox's," Aunt Zoe answered. "They helped him move up from Colorado and are here for a few more days. Both guys are your typical firemen—charming and happy to help out."

I glanced her way to see if there was a frown to go with her description of Reid's career cohorts, but she was watching the screen with a blank expression while finishing her sandwich.

"Those three boys really greased our wheels and covered our asses," Harvey said in between bites. "Your stallion here found out that the moving company had planned to hire some extra hands, which Detective Turkey-buzzard may or may not have known about."

"And they're getting the clocks boxed up twice as fast as we'd figured," Aunt Zoe added, dabbing her mouth with a paper towel. "Which means Willis and I need to get cracking." She popped the last two pretzels in her mouth and stood with her empty plate. "You ready, Mr. Creature from the Black Lagoon?"

"I told you, woman, it's just Gill-man." He gobbled down the last of his sandwich and followed her to the kitchen.

Doc and I joined them near the door as they pulled on their coats.

"You guys need anything else from us?" I asked, feeling a little guilty for sitting on my butt while everyone else did the heavy lifting. "We can come unload the actual clock boxes wherever you're taking them," I offered to Harvey.

"Nope, that's still a secret for the time bein'." Harvey yanked on his trapper hat. "Just watch for a text that the switch has been made. That's your cue to grab the kids from school and hightail it to the restaurant. Take your time eatin', though. We want plenty of local folks eyein' you both."

"Be safe," I said to Aunt Zoe and kissed her on the cheek.

"Where's the fun in that?" she said with a smartass grin.

Doc locked up behind them, then we grabbed the bag of

pretzels from the kitchen, more soda pop, and returned to the chairs in front of the monitor. Doc turned up the volume on the caper show as we chomped on pretzels, so we could listen to Hawke fret about how there wasn't enough packing material being placed in with each clock.

"At least he seems to be trying to take care with the clocks," I said, fishing out more pretzels from the bag.

"I'll bet a honey-mustard kiss that Hawke trips over a box before the show is over." Doc scooted closer and draped his arm around my shoulders.

"Come on, that's a given." I fed him a pretzel. "Let's make it fun, like a drinking game."

"What are you thinking, Tish?"

"How about we exchange a single kiss if he trips over one box."

"What if he trips over two?"

"We exchange two kisses *and* each of us have to take off our shirts."

He pursed his lips. "And how about three kisses for three boxes, plus thirty seconds of me getting to feel you up?"

"Only thirty seconds? You get so distracted with just light touching that we won't even make it to some serious groping."

He chuckled. "Okay, fine. A minute then. That should give me enough time to get past the 'giddy schoolboy' moment and focus on some serious caressing."

I held out my hand. "Deal."

We shook on it, and then we kissed on it.

"That was just a warmup, my little Valentine's vixen," he said, sitting back to watch the show.

I settled back into the crook of his arm as Natalie stepped onto the screen in Ms. Wolff's living room. Dressed in her old high school Golddiggers sweatshirt and paint-splattered jeans, she carried a towel in one hand and pipe wrench in the other …

~

"Well, I finished fixing your mess," she told Hawke, wiping her hands on a towel.

"How was I supposed to know that pipe would freeze?"

She crossed her arms. "Dude, Freesia and I both told you last week that you'd need to let the sink faucets drip during the deep freeze. I'm not sure how much clearer we could be. Maybe we should have drawn you an instructional page and handed out crayons to color it."

He cradled his sling. "Yeah, well, I was called away last night on a case and ended up getting a hotel room for the night up in Lead."

"Right," Natalie said, her sarcasm clear as a bell. "Because Lead is so far from here that you couldn't possibly have driven the three long and treacherous miles."

"Cut me some slack, Beals. My broken arm hurts and I haven't been sleeping well." He kicked at a bundle of bubble wrap. "So, uh, what are you doing later? Feel like hanging out at a bar or at your place?"

"She's going to dinner with me," a voice said from off screen.

~

"Uh oh," I said, reaching for more pretzels. "King Kong is back from Skull Island."

Doc took the small handful of pretzels that I offered him. "And judging from his tone, he doesn't want to share his favorite banana."

~

Hawke glanced in the direction of the dining room, then turned back to Natalie. "I don't know why you're wasting your time on old Coop. He was washed up a long time ago and just doesn't realize he's been hung out to dry."

"How's the packing going, Detective Broke-Dick?" Cooper asked, joining the two of them.

"It's going. Just calm down."

"What makes you think I'm anything but calm?"

"Your jaw is pulsing right here," Natalie said, touching the side of Cooper's face, which earned her a sideways glare.

"You're not helping," he growled.

"What are you doing here, Coop?" Hawke asked, his chin jutting. "This isn't your business."

"Oh, it is. I want to make sure nobody bangs up the walls since I'm going to have to pay to fix them." He looked around, his gaze holding on Susan for a few seconds. His frown deepened. "Don't forget that I'm taking over the case after you fail to solve it."

Hawke harrumphed. "I'm gonna solve it. You and I both know Parker killed the old broad."

~

"Shit," Doc said. "Your sister heard that."

I cringed, watching Susan, who was boxing up a clock—but she was also sneaking peeks at the trio standing center screen.

"Damn Hawke and his lack of a filter," I growled.

Now Susan would know that I was on the verge of being on the hook for murder. How she might choose to use that information against me was hard to foresee, but it would certainly trip me up when she did, and probably leave me flat on my ass in a puddle of trouble.

"I don't think the police chief would approve of one of his detectives making premature accusations of murder in public." Doc leaned down and kissed me on the temple. "Good thing we have this on tape in case we need it later."

~

On the monitor, Cooper said, "I doubt the chief would like hearing that you're running your mouth about a confidential case in front of John Q. Public."

Hawke waved him off. "These guys don't care. They're just here to stuff boxes and make some quick cash."

Cooper crossed his arms. "How do I know you didn't hire a few deadbeats off the street who don't give a shit about the quality of their packing job? These clocks could be one-of-a-kind pieces, for all we know. They should have been packed and moved long ago. Too bad your ego cut in line in front of what little common sense is left in your head."

"Relax, Coop. I have this all under control. Besides, I'll have the case solved before long. I just need to round up the remaining evidence."

~

What remaining evidence? More important, what did Hawke already have on me?

I thought when I'd completed the time loop procedures Ms. Wolff had forced upon me—some would even call it blackmail, given the circumstances in those final moments—that all evidence tied to me was basically erased. That was the deal we'd made. Cooper was there to witness it, too.

What had we missed and left behind for Hawke to cling to as evidence?

~

"What other evidence?" Cooper asked.

Hawke scoffed. "You think I'm an idiot?"

"The jury is still out for deliberation."

"I'm not telling you what I have on Parker. It's my case, and as soon as I can prove that she was the—"

"What in the hell is that?" Natalie interrupted, pointing at something behind Hawke.

He jumped and turned. "What's what?"

She shook her head. "Nothing. I thought I saw a dark shadow behind you for a second. That was weird." She shuddered. "Super creepy."

"Where?" Hawke spun around in a circle. "Do you still see it?" He brushed off his shoulders, as if clearing a layer of dust from his coat.

Natalie shook her head and looked at Cooper. "Did you see the shadow thing behind Hawke? It sort of just hovered there, like it was attached to him or something."

Cooper rubbed his jaw, appearing to seriously ponder her question. "I saw a flicker of something dark over one of his shoulders, but I just figured it was someone passing in front of the window and blocking the light for a moment."

"Fuck," Hawke said, his head whipping back and forth as he looked over one shoulder and then the other, before stepping closer to Natalie. "Where's your buddy?"

"Which one?" Natalie asked. "I have many in town."

"Curion. He's supposed to have something for me."

She shrugged. "He said he was going to be stopping over this afternoon but didn't say when."

Hawke backed toward the wall. "You need to call him." He tripped over a box, stumbling, almost falling on his ass before catching himself with his good arm. "Tell him to bring me that voodoo bag right away!"

"Okay, Detective Demand-asaurus." She pulled out her cellphone and walked off screen, smiling.

~

"That's one trip," I said, stealing a pretzel out of Doc's hand as I pulled his mouth closer to mine. "You really think Hawke will do that twice? I mean, with that broken arm, he should really be more careful."

"I definitely do." He leaned down for our one-kiss deal.

From the speakers, I heard Cooper say, "Watch where you're walking, Hawke! Jesus, you're going to—"

Crash!

"Son of a— Who left that stack of boxes there?" Hawke bellowed.

"And there's two," Doc said, his dark gaze drifting south to my sweater. "What bra are you wearing under that?"

I peeked inside of my sweater and then fluttered my eyelids at him. "Ooo-la-la. I think you're really going to like touching it."

He guffawed. "Please, Boots, that's a given. I like touching anything having to do with you."

I tapped on his chest. "You take your shirt off first."

"Why do I have to go first? This was your idea."

"Because you're a gentleman."

With a smile, he started unbuttoning his shirt. "You're such a tease."

"It's about damned time you got here, Curion." Hawke's voice interrupted our Valentine's Day game.

I turned to look at the monitor in time to see Cornelius stride across the living room, still wearing the Cossack hat and coat I'd seen him in earlier. He moved from the right side of the screen to the left in a heartbeat, disappearing from view.

"Where you going?" Hawke asked, struggling to his feet and then limping after Cornelius.

Doc leaned forward and switched to the bedroom view in time to catch Cornelius opening the top drawer of the dresser where he'd "found" the creepy-ass poppet doll.

~

"What are you doing?" Hawke said, joining Cornelius at the dresser. "Did you bring me that voodoo bag or not?"

"I have your *gris-gris* bag, but we have a more foreboding problem at the moment." He closed the top drawer and opened the second one down.

"What problem?" Hawke said, taking a small step back.

"The poppet is missing."

"Missing? How is it missing? I thought you took it home last night."

"I did, but when I woke up, it was gone." Cornelius slammed the second drawer shut and opened the third.

"Gone?" Hawke rubbed the back of his neck, his gaze darting around the room. "You think it just walked off?"

"My trepidation has far deeper roots."

Hawke leaned down and peeked under the twin bed next to him. "What the fuck is that supposed to mean?"

Cornelius turned to frown at Hawke. "I'm more concerned that the entity shadowing you collected the poppet from my apartment and brought it back here."

"That's impossible." Hawke walked over to the closet. "I've been here alone since dawn getting ready for the movers." He flicked on the light and looked inside, then turned back. "Well, Natalie was here, too, but not the whole time."

"Why was she here with you?"

"She was mopping up the floor, because the pipes froze and a water line broke, or something like that."

Cornelius held up his index finger. "What makes you so sure the pipes froze? It is just like a poppet to wreak havoc, especially when it comes to water."

Hawke returned to the dresser. "You think the poppet messed with the water pipe?"

"No. I think the entity caused the pipe to burst."

"Then why did it need the poppet?"

"It's a talisman infused with dark magical powers. With the poppet in its possession, it regained its strength."

Hawke nodded. "And it broke the pipe to show us that it was mad."

"Exactly." Cornelius turned and opened the fourth drawer. "Ah ha!" He reached inside and pulled out the goose-bump inspiring poppet figurine. "Look what we have here."

Hawke held up his hand, as if to ward off evil. "You need to burn that thing, dammit."

"I cannot burn it until the entity detaches from you, Detective. Otherwise, you could be injured in the process."

"Like injured how?"

"Your vitality drained, leaving you limp and wabbit."

~

"Did Cornelius say *wabbit?*" I asked Doc.

"Yeah. I think that means tired or weak."

"I haven't heard that word before outside of Bugs Bunny cartoons," I said, returning to the screen.

~

"Leaving me what?" Hawke asked.

"Limp and wabbit," Cornelius repeated with his back to Hawke.

Hawke lowered his hand. "What's a limpin' wabbit?"

Cornelius set the poppet on the dresser. "A lame hare with long bilateral symmetry hounded by one E. Fudd."

"Bilateral … " Hawke shook his head. "What's an *efud?*"

"That's not important right now." Cornelius lifted the *gris-gris* bag necklace from his neck, holding it out to Hawke. "Here, put this on."

Hawke took it and shook the small bag. "What's in it?"

"A copper button, a glass doll's eye, grave dust, and rat whiskers."

"Where'd you get the rat whiskers?"

"From a dead rat."

Hawke made a face. "That's gross."

Cornelius shrugged. "He didn't mind at the time."

"And this bag will get that shadow entity to leave me alone?"

"Yes, but it will take two or three weeks of you wearing that day and night. By the next full moon, you should be free." He picked up the poppet by one of its gnarled arms. "In the meantime, I'll take this home and secure it in a locked box so it doesn't cause any more water muddles."

"Can that shadow thing hurt me in the next few weeks?"

"You might feel drained as it continues to try to siphon your energy, but with time the symptoms will lessen and you'll return to your previous vigor." He paused and looked over at Hawke. "But beware of the rats."

"What? Why?"

"Because they will know you carry the whiskers of one of their fallen and might try to bite you."

Hawke watched Cornelius walk away. He looked back at the dresser again and shuddered. "I need to get the hell out of this fucking place."

Then he scurried out of the bedroom, slamming the door behind him.

~

"What the poppet!" I said mid-giggle, turning to Doc, who had tears of laughter in his eyes as he wheezed next to me. "We have that recorded, right? Because that was award-winning material right there."

"A limpin' wabbit," Doc said, swiping at the tears in his eyes. "*A lame hare with bilateral symmetry hounded by one E. Fudd*," he repeated Cornelius's words in between laughs. "Bugs Bunny and Elmer Fudd." He paused to laugh some more. "Where in the hell does he come up with this shit on the fly?"

"Only Cornelius could pull that off without even cracking a smile." I shook my head, amazed, still chuckling.

This was turning out to be a wonderful Valentine's Day after all.

Knock knock knock!

Someone was at the door.

We looked at each other and then the door.

"Who could that be?" I whispered, sobering. I pictured the redcap goblin with a bloody axe slung over its shoulder.

Doc shrugged and stood, heading for the door. I tiptoed after him.

"Who is it?" Doc called through the crack.

"It's Count Dracula," Natalie called in a Slavic accent. "Let me in. I vant to suck your blood."

CHAPTER TWENTY-SIX

I forgot to tell Doc about the fourth camera-view option, but Natalie remembered it when she swung by to let us know that Freesia was going to delay Hawke from following the moving truck by having him come to her apartment for a goodbye drink.

"So, she's taking one for the team," I said.

Natalie nodded and then showed us the view from the camera that Cornelius must have hooked up by the attic window, because we looked down on the moving truck from up high. Through the lens, we had an eagle's-eye view of Ox and his friends loading up the clock boxes. Susan was still inside packing, which we saw when we switched back to the dining room view.

"She's behaved so far," I said, watching my sister tape a box closed.

"Don't count your chickens," Natalie muttered. "I don't like that she heard Hawke say you killed 'the old broad' earlier."

"Same here," Doc said, holding out the bag of pretzels to Natalie.

"Well, so far I have one chicken." I dropped back into the chair in front of the monitor. "Cross your fingers Elvis is an only child."

Over the next hour, while Natalie and Doc kept an eye on the caper situation, I bounced back and forth between Calamity Jane's office and Cornelius's apartment. I repeatedly checked for voice messages on my phone and kept an eye on the office via the video cameras. Mona called midway through the afternoon to tell me she wasn't coming back in until tomorrow and suggested I close up shop early since it was so quiet. I was more than happy to oblige.

Thankfully, the moving crew had the clocks all boxed and loaded by four o'clock, before night fell and it was dangerous to be outside for too long. Freesia called Natalie to let us know that Cornelius was delaying Hawke even longer by insisting they do an entity cleansing to help with the removal of its evil tethers before the detective left Galena House.

Aunt Zoe texted right after Freesia hung up, giving me the go-ahead to come get the kids, whom she'd picked up after school and had ready and waiting at home to head to dinner.

The three of us locked up the apartment and my office, splitting in different directions: Natalie set off for the storage unit to help Cooper, Aunt Zoe, and the moving crew to unload the non-clock boxes as quickly as possible after Susan and Harvey switched trucks; I swung by home to get the kids; and Doc headed to the restaurant to secure our table since Valentine's Day was usually a busy night at the local restaurants and Chuckwagon Charlie's wasn't taking reservations today.

The kids bounced with excitement all the way into the restaurant. They hadn't gone out for a Valentine's Day dinner before, and they couldn't wait to see what the restaurant offered for dessert.

Doc had gotten us a booth, and we were early enough that it was only half crowded, mostly with couples older than us. It was impossible for the other diners not to notice us with my kids giggling and talking way too loud for a romantic atmosphere, even after they were seated at the table with Doc and me.

I kissed Doc hello, noticing that he'd changed into a clean dress shirt, and then slid into the bench seat opposite him, next to Layne. There was no way my children could share a seat if we wanted to keep harmony at the table.

"Come on, Mom," Layne complained, taking the menu the hostess offered him. "You promised you wouldn't slobber all over Doc during dinner."

I took the remaining menus and passed them out, waiting for the hostess to leave before explaining, "You and I made a deal that I wouldn't kiss him more than twice during dinner. There was nothing agreed upon about slobbering."

Doc chuckled. "Kisses are great, but I typically only allow slobbering from Rooster."

Addy smiled, her pink cheeks matching the hearts on her sweater. "We're not officially eating dinner yet, Layne, so they can kiss if they want to." She tilted her head sideways while looking at me. "It's good Mom finally has someone to smooch on besides us."

I had a feeling she would have patted my head like a good dog if I had been within reach.

"I suppose," Layne said. "At least she usually smells good," he added from behind the menu. "Right, Doc?"

Doc nodded as he perused the menu. "That she does."

"I think I can put up with a girl's kisses if she doesn't stink," Layne continued. "But Rooster's kisses are not so good."

Addy snorted, picking up her menu. "That's because he's a dog, silly, so he licks instead of smooches."

Layne lowered the menu and wrinkled his nose at Doc. "How gross would it be if Mom licked when she kissed?"

"Well," Doc said, leaning back into the seat with his arms crossed. "Let me picture that for a moment before answering." His dark eyes brimmed with laughter.

I hit Doc with a don't-you-dare glare. "How about we stick to figuring out what to order for dinner before the waiter comes?"

A little later, the menus were gone and we'd ordered our meals—steaks for all. When I'd suggested to Doc that maybe burgers for the kids would be just as good and less costly, he shook his head. "Nothing but the best for my Valentine's Day dates. Just make sure you guys leave room for dessert."

As we waited for our food to arrive, Doc asked the kids about their school day. Their answers were filled with tales of Valentine's Day candy and cards, fun times with word heart-themed puzzles and paint-by-numbers, and a history lesson on Saint Valentine.

"Did you know some books say Saint Valentine was a priest who performed secret weddings?" Addy asked, her eyes twinkling as she sipped on the strawberry lemonade I let her order. "The Roman soldiers and leaders didn't like that Valentine did that, but then he healed some blind girl and everyone started to like him."

Layne smirked. "How do you heal someone who's blind? I mean, maybe, with today's medicine and lasers we could do it, but back then? I don't think so."

"I don't know," Addy said, bouncing in her seat.

That lemonade may have been a bad idea, but sometimes a girl needed to feel special, particularly on Valentine's Day. I stared across at Doc, who looked so handsome as he smiled down at Addy. I tried not to let the hearts floating around in my head escape out my ears.

"But don't you think the idea of a secret wedding is romantic, Mom?" Addy asked.

Why, yes, I did, but I kept my lips pinched tight. Addy was on the verge of being ten years old and already lollygagged around in cupid land most days, daydreaming about happily-ever-afters. How were her teen years going to go? Would she have a broken heart every other month?

Doc nudged my leg under the table.

I looked at him. *What?* I mouthed.

He raised his brow. "Secret weddings are very romantic, wouldn't you agree, Tish?"

Uhhhh … "Sure, I guess."

Wait! Were we going to break the news to the kids about our engagement tonight? Right here, right now? My heart thudded extra-hard in my chest. Shouldn't we have talked about a strategy ahead of time?

My hands were clammy when I laced my fingers together on the table.

What if Layne threw a fit in front of all these people? I hadn't even checked with him lately about his feelings when it came to Doc being a permanent member of our family. They'd been getting along so well lately that I hadn't wanted to rock the boat. Would the idea of me marrying Doc screw that up?

My ears began to ring extra loud, muffling the conversations from the other diners around us.

Maybe now was as good of a time as any. At some point, we needed to let them know, because I really wanted to make things more permanent with Doc, and it was clear by my flub-up with Cooper that I wasn't going to be able to hold onto this big of a secret for long.

I started to pant, overheating suddenly. I fanned myself with my napkin.

This was going to be a big change for the kids. Even though Doc had been living with us for some time now, a father figure had been missing in their life for so long. Maybe it wouldn't really matter to them, but then again maybe it would flip everything upside down and shake it around. Addy would probably jump for joy, but Layne …

"Violet?" Doc said, pulling me back down to the table.

"What?" I said breathlessly.

He pointed at the waiter standing next to me, holding two plates of food. "One of those is yours."

"Oh." I blew out a breath. "Thanks," I said to the waiter, leaning back to give him room to set my plate down.

When he'd finished placing the plates of food all around, he folded up his serving table and promised to bring some more napkins along with the dessert menu.

While Doc helped Addy cut up her steak, Layne and I sliced away at our own. My little boy had claimed to be too old for my help with cutting, so I winced and watched him struggle with the steak, but kept my hands to myself. When he finished, he looked across at Doc with a victory grin on his face.

Doc leaned over the table, inspecting Layne's work, and nodded. "Nice job with your knife. You've been practicing."

Practicing? With a *knife*? The mother in me squeaked at that notion, but I stuffed a piece of steak in my mouth and kept quiet.

Layne nodded. "Can I try a katana now?"

"That's up to your mom," Doc said, staring across at me as he took a bite of steak. His gaze held questions, undoubtedly one or two having to do with my little freakout about secret weddings.

I smiled and rubbed my boot up and down his leg under the table, wishing I could explain that it wasn't the idea of marrying him that sent me spinning into a panic, mostly the fear of my kids' reactions, especially in a public place.

"Can I, Mom?" Layne asked, mid-chew.

"Don't talk with your mouth full, kiddo," I said, adding a dash of salt to my baked potato as I worked through my worries. "If Doc thinks you're able to practice swinging a katana without hurting anyone, including yourself, then I don't see why not." I turned and gave him a tough glare. "But don't you dare let me catch you taking a swing at your sister. Or poking our pets with it. I have no qualms about grounding you until you're twenty-one."

He scowled at me. "Mom, I would never hurt an animal."

"And your sister?"

He sighed. "I promise I won't even point it at her."

Addy clapped. "I want a sword, too!"

I frowned at Doc. "Why can't my kids ask for Barbie dolls and building block sets?"

"Because we're almost *older* now, Mom," Addy explained, chewing on her steak. "Like double-digits bigger."

"Close your mouth when you chew, dear," I said, trying to ignore the pang of sadness in my chest that my babies were definitely long gone.

We finished dinner and ordered a strawberry icebox cake for dessert, which was basically whipped cream and chocolate wafer cookies layered and stacked into a cake with strawberry jam gluing it all together. A handful of chocolate-dipped strawberries were strewn on the top of the cake, adding a pretty finishing touch to the lavish dessert.

Addy practically swooned when the cake showed up. "Oh. My. Molies!" she cried, clapping.

Layne sat up on his knees to be closer to the cake. "How do they keep the cream from dripping? It must be really cold." He reached out to touch it with his finger, but I caught him before he made contact.

"Experiment with your own piece, Professor Parker," I said with a wink.

Doc cut the cake and set a plateful in front of each kid. As they dug in, he plucked a chocolate-dipped strawberry partly covered with whipped cream from the top of the cake and held it out toward me. "Want a bite, sweetheart?"

His gaze smoldered as I leaned forward and took a bite, taking my time licking the sweet cream off my lips.

"You're being messy, Mom," Layne said, pointing at a piece of chocolate that had fallen on to the table.

"I like it when she's messy," Doc said and finished off the strawberry.

"Me, too." Addy grinned at me. A streak of whipped cream ran across one of her cheeks. Another small blob was stuck on a strand of hair hanging next to her ear. "She's more fun when she's messy. And not so bossy."

"I'm supposed to be bossy." I took the plate with a slice of cake that Doc held out for me. "That's part of my job description as your parent."

Addy scooped up a broken cookie with her fingers. "Maybe you wouldn't be so bossy if there were two of you."

"Two moms?" I chuckled, forking off a piece of cream-covered cookie. "You want to clone me?"

"No, you goof. I meant Doc." She chewed on the cookie, swallowing before adding, "You two could have a wedding."

I froze, my fork in mid-air. "A wedding?" The cake fell off my fork onto my plate.

"Yeah, a secret one." She smiled as she scooped up more cookies and cream. "Layne and I can pretend to be Saint Valentine."

I gaped at Doc.

He stared back with one raised eyebrow. "Will there be cookies and cream cake at the wedding?" he asked.

Addy snorted. "Of course!"

I turned to gauge Layne's reaction to her wedding idea.

He was frowning at his sister. "That's a dumb idea, Addy."

"No, it's not!"

"Why is it dumb, Layne?" I asked, trying to keep my tone level and diplomatic.

He swallowed his bite of the cake. "Because this cake won't work at a wedding. It has to be kept cold or the cream will melt. Wedding cakes have to be able to sit out for a long time."

Addy shrugged. "Fine, then we can have a white and chocolate wedding cake." She gasped, and pointed her fork at me. "Ohhhh! We need pretty purple violet flowers on the cake to match your name."

I turned back to Doc, my brows raised in question.

He nodded.

I lowered my fork and took a deep breath before diving into the truth. "It's funny that you two should mention—"

"Hello, Violet."

I cringed at the sound of that voice.

I turned my head slowly. Rex Conner, the no-good son of a bitch, stood at my elbow.

For a moment, I was sure I would spontaneously combust due to the flash fire that sparked in my chest and burned clear to my fingertips and toes. It was a wonder I didn't melt the damned icebox cake on the spot.

What in the fuck was he doing this close to *my* children?

"Can I help you?" I asked, my tone downright gravelly from the ground-up pieces of my back molars.

The asshole was dressed in fine, blue wool trousers and a matching suit jacket that covered a crisp white shirt. He looked fashion-photoshoot ready, like usual, with his blond hair slicked back and his dark blond beard perfectly trimmed. Jesus, the jerk probably used a protractor to line up those angles.

"I was just having a drink with a lovely coworker while we waited for our table upstairs at Charles' Club." He thumbed toward the bar at the other end of the room where a jaw-dropping brunette sat in a slinky pink dress.

Damn! If that dress got any shorter, her sugar cookie was going to get frostbit in this weather.

She waved at me as I stared. I waved back, but inside I was trying to keep the Godzilla-momma powering up in my chest from blasting Rex with a full dose of atomic breath.

"Good for you," I said, turning back to the kids' sperm donor. Keeping in mind that Addy and Layne might be listening in, I redacted all of the swear words lined up on the tip of my tongue and added, "Your date looks lonely. Maybe you should head back over there and keep her company."

He smiled, all charm and slithering slime. "Yes, I'm sure our table is almost ready with the wine perfectly chilled."

Was that a dig about me not being perfectly chilled? I had no doubt the urge to bite his head clean off showed on my face. I wrung my napkin in my hands under the table to keep from walloping him upside his arrogant mug with my plate.

"I just wanted to stop by to say hello to you," he continued, smiling past me at the kids. "And to tell you what adorable children you have."

That was it. It was time to drag him outside and use him for mace-swinging practice. I threw my napkin down on the table and reached for my plate.

Doc stood and grabbed Rex by the upper arm, looking chummy on the surface. "I'm so glad you stopped by, because I've been wanting to talk to you about a past agreement you signed that my friend, Detective Cooper, might be interested in hearing about after tonight."

Rex tried unsuccessfully to pull free of Doc's grip.

"Hey, you know, maybe your date would be fascinated by the details of this agreement," Doc continued. "Let's go see." He dragged Rex toward the bar.

"I'll be in touch, Violet," Rex called back to me.

Doc leaned over and said something in Rex's ear, but they were too far away for me to hear.

"Who was that, Mom?" Addy asked, mostly preoccupied with loading up a bunch of cream on a cookie.

"Just a past client," I said, taking a drink of water. I looked over mid-drink to find Layne watching me too closely for comfort.

He glanced around me toward the bar and then back at me. "Why don't you like that man?"

Dang the little Cooper Junior! I shrugged. "He's mean to kids. And he kicks puppies."

I hadn't actually witnessed him showing any cruelty to animals, but I wouldn't be surprised if he did, and I couldn't exactly tell my son that his sperm donor was the Grand Poobah of Dickheads Anonymous at this point in our lives.

"He's a bad man then," Addy said, her mouth full of the last of her piece of cookies and jam and cream.

I nodded. "How about we take the rest of the cake home and put it in the fridge for tomorrow, your birthday eve?"

That idea earned me two sets of sticky thumbs-up.

Doc returned to the table tight-lipped with a to-go box in hand. He must have read my mind.

Since we drove separately, Doc asked me to take the kids home while he swung by his office to grab some paperwork he forgot.

The house was dark when the kids and I got home. I wondered if the moving truck switcheroo had gone off without a hitch, but I didn't dare text or call anyone. Layne let Rooster out to take care of business, waiting by the back door to let him back inside since it was too cold for the dog to stay out for long. Addy went down in the basement to check on Elvis and Daisy, tiptoeing back up the stairs with a report that they were snuggled together in Elvis's cage, but she'd covered them with an old towel anyway.

Making sure the doors were locked just in case my redcap pal was wandering around in the dark, I herded the kids upstairs to clean up. This turned into me helping pick up their clothes and toys as they took turns in the bathtub to wash the sticky cream off their hands and cheeks—and out of Addy's hair.

By the time I came back downstairs, Aunt Zoe was home and sitting at the table talking in low tones to Doc, who was leaning against the counter.

"The kids are on their way down to watch some TV before going to bed," I warned them and then joined my aunt at the table. "Well?" I whispered, so the kids didn't hear. "Is everything taken care of?"

She nodded, reaching out to squeeze my arm through my sweater. "According to Ox, Hawke stopped by the storage unit long enough to tell them to close the door and secure the lock on it himself. Then he complained about the cold and hightailed it out of there."

I blew out a breath of relief. "And the actual clocks?"

"Harvey has them in a secure location," Doc said.

I frowned, not liking being in the dark. "Where?"

He shook his head. "He said he'll tell you later after the dust settles."

"Doc?" Addy ran into the kitchen, sliding to a stop in front of him. "Oh, good, you're here. Will you come help Layne fix the TV? He pushed the wrong buttons again."

"Did not!" Layne hollered back.

Doc chuckled. "I'll be back," he said, dropping a kiss on the top of my head on his way out of the kitchen.

Aunt Zoe took my hand in both of hers, which were still cold, probably from unloading boxes in the finger-numbing wind. "The clocks are safe, baby girl. Don't worry."

"Where is Harvey, anyway?"

"There's a Valentine's Day dance at the senior center tonight that he doesn't want to miss."

That would put him in the public eye, which was good. "What about Cooper and Natalie?"

"They were heading out to the Purple Door for some burgers and drinks, last I heard."

"That's not very romantic," I said.

"It was Natalie's choice. She mentioned something about kicking Coop's ass at the pool table."

Oh, so it would be a night of flirty pool playing with Cooper, one of Natalie's favorite things.

"And Cornelius?"

She grinned. "Freesia convinced him to stick around for some homemade butternut squash soup and molasses cookies."

I laughed. That girl had been trying to snare Cornelius in her web for some time. Maybe she'd finally found a way to his heart—through his sweet tooth.

"What about you and Reid?" I asked.

She pulled away from me. "What about us?"

"Aren't you two going out to dinner or drinks?"

She shook her head. "I'm bone tired. I just want to take a shower, down a glass of wine, and crawl under a soft warm blanket."

"I bet Reid has some soft blankets. And extra warm, especially if they're covering a hot fireman's body."

She stood. "Nice try, cupid, but some lovers are better off star-crossed."

I disagreed, but kept my opinion to myself.

She set her mug in the sink. "How about I hang out with the kids until they go to bed, and you and Doc take off for some Valentine's alone time?"

Tempting, but … "I hate to make you do that when you're so tired."

"Please, I'm not *that* tired. Go. It's been a stressful few days. You deserve a little fun."

"Okay." I'd take her up on that. "Oh, there's some strawberry icebox cake in the fridge, if you want something sweet with your wine."

"That sounds tempting." She walked over to the refrigerator and opened the door. "How was dinner?"

I thought about telling her that Rex had paid us a visit, but I decided to skip it for now and let her enjoy some wine and cake without a dose of acid indigestion.

"It was nice. I think the kids had a good time."

"I'm glad to hear it." Aunt Zoe shut the fridge door. "I'm going to take a shower." She gave me a quick hug on her way by and then headed upstairs.

I sat there in the quiet kitchen for a few minutes, wondering where Doc and I could go for more good times.

The doorbell rang, which surprised me because I thought the monster crew was supposed to be laying low for the night.

Doc beat me to the front door, holding it open for Reid, who was carrying a bottle of wine and a bouquet of pink, red, and white carnations.

"Where is Zo?" he asked me.

I pointed at the ceiling. "Taking a shower."

"Perfect! I can make myself at home without her threatening to fill my ass with buckshot." He walked by me, heading for the kitchen.

I followed him. "She was going to watch the kids for us," I said. "But if you want some time alone with—"

"Nope. It's better the kids are here." He reached for a vase from the cupboard over the fridge—one of Aunt Zoe's own creations—and took it to the sink. "You two go celebrate a successful caper." While the vase filled with water, he grabbed two wine glasses. "Zo and I will keep the kids company."

Doc joined us, looking over the situation. "What's going on?"

"You and Sparky are going to do whatever you want while Zo and I enjoy a night in front of the television with Addy and Layne. Hell, I'll even hold that damned chicken if it keeps Zo from sending me packing."

"You sure?" Doc asked. When Reid nodded, he turned to me. "Well, then, are you ready?"

"Ready for what?"

He disappeared into the dining room, returning with my coat. "Put that on and come with me."

He pulled his coat on, too, and then held out his hand. I took it, following him out the back door onto the porch.

I shivered. "What are we doing?" I asked as he led me down the steps and through the snow toward Aunt Zoe's workshop. Her window blinds were closed tonight, which wasn't normal.

"Taking a break," he said, opening the door.

"From what?" I stepped inside, stopping at the sight of lit candles on her workbench and the coffee table in front of her couch. A bottle of wine and a couple of glasses sat between the candles on the bench. The air smelled slightly sweet, a light mix of strawberries and vanilla, instead of the usual cinnamon air freshener Aunt Zoe used. "What's all this?"

"Part two of dinner and a movie with my Valentine." He closed the door behind us and locked it, before coming over to take my coat.

The heating unit built into the wall had taken the chill out of most of the room. A fire crackled in Aunt Zoe's glass furnace, which I could see through the open door. The various flames lighting the workshop added a little warmth and a lot of coziness.

I turned to Doc. "When did you set all of this up?"

"While you were helping the kids get cleaned up after dinner." He hung up our coats and then pulled me into his arms, slow dancing with me in the silence for a moment. "I texted my idea to your aunt from the restaurant." He twirled me around so my back was to him and hauled me close again, still swaying with me. "She was happy to take care of the kids and let us borrow her workshop for the evening."

Ahhh, so hanging with the kids wasn't a spur of the moment idea on her part. She could have fooled me with her performance in the kitchen.

I glanced up at him from the corners of my eyes. "Was Reid in on this?"

"No." He chuckled. "Martin is going to be a surprise for her."

I smiled, imagining how his sudden appearance might go over. "Reid was smart to include the kids in his plans."

"They'll make a good buffer." He twirled me back around to face him, wrapping his arms around my waist, swaying as he stared down at me in the shadows.

"Thank you." I went up on my toes and kissed his cheek. "Today was exactly what I needed for Valentine's Day."

He shrugged. "I wanted to do more. The caper took priority."

"I'm sorry that Rex ruined our dinner."

Doc shook his head. "He's such an ass."

I linked my arms around his neck. "I think I'm going to add him to Prudence's to-kill list and take him out of the picture for good."

He chuckled. "As much as I'd like to have him out of our lives, I have to wonder how that might affect your kids."

"What do you mean? They don't even know who he is."

"For now." He stopped swaying. "But they may want to know Rex in the future."

"Yeah, but I don't want—"

He held his index finger against my lips. "Just hear me out for a minute, Tish."

I nodded, but my shoulders were tight while I waited, ready to go on the defense.

"If you tell them that Rex is their father, that will take away some of his power over you."

That was true, but … "What if I tell them and they want to see him?"

"You let them see him."

"What if they want to actually meet him, and he doesn't want anything to do with them? He completely rejects them. Think of how hurt they will be then."

My heart ached at the idea of that alone, making me want to wrap my children tightly in my arms to shield them from even the possibility of being rejected yet again by that bastard.

"That is a sad thought, but a definite possibility," he said, tucking a curl behind my ear. "Here's the thing, though. I don't feel right stepping into the role of a father figure without giving Addy and Layne the option of knowing their real dad first."

Rex hadn't been their father from the get-go, though. He'd run from the opportunity, signing legal papers that cemented his lack of interest in a child before I'd even realized there were two little heartbeats pounding inside me.

"To be clear," Doc continued before I could get a bad word in about Rex. "I love that you are willing to let me be your partner in helping to raise them from here on out, and I'm all in on this, believe me. But I'm somewhat new to being around kids, and I'm a bit unsure on how to ease into this new role. I don't want to screw things up out of the gate, you know." He frowned slightly. "What if they don't want a stepfather? I mean, maybe they're more comfortable with me as a friend figure."

Tears filled my eyes at the thought he'd put into this, in addition to considering my kids' feelings. I looked down, resting my forehead against his chest while I blinked the tears away. I didn't want to get blubbery on our first Valentine's Day together.

That wasn't sexy at all.

"What are you thinking?" he asked, his tone hesitant.

"I'm thinking that I really love you." I sniffed and smiled up at him, watery eyes and all. "I'm also thinking that we have no idea how any of this is going to go, but I know that Addy and Layne have been looking for someone like you to come into their lives for a long, long time." I took a big breath and swallowed past the lump in my throat. "This is going to be scary for all of us, Doc. There will be bumps and, knowing those two, probably many fights along the way, but they already love you. Once we're married and we become a family of four instead of three, they will realize how lucky they are to have you there to help catch them when they fall."

He stroked my cheek. "I'm the lucky one."

"I think we're all lucky."

Well, except when it came to annoying exes, but since I couldn't legally kill mine, I needed to figure out some other way to deal with the asshole.

"As for telling the kids that Rex is their biological dad," I started, wrinkling my nose at just the idea, "I think having you around for a little longer first as an example of what a real father is supposed to be will help them navigate their emotions better. Plus, you'll be there for them to talk to about Rex."

One dark eyebrow raised. "Where will you be?"

"Sharpening my axe blade."

He chuckled and kissed me on the forehead. "Okay, then we need to break the engagement news to them sooner rather than later."

"I agree. What do you think of letting them have their birthdays first, and when things quiet down after that, we'll let them in on our secret."

He lifted my chin, smiling down at me. "Maybe we should have a secret wedding with just Addy and Layne."

"As much as I like the sound of that, Natalie will kick my ass for not having her there by my side."

"So, a small, sort of secret wedding."

I nodded. "Oh, and by the way, Cooper knows about our engagement."

His eyes narrowed. "How? Did he interrogate you again?"

I grimaced. "No, I just slipped up."

"To Coop?" He touched the back of his hand to my forehead. "Hmm. You don't feel feverish."

"I think he might have given me some truth serum."

Doc grinned. "Or maybe you two really do like each other a little."

"Maybe." I held my fingers out a smidgeon apart. "But only about this much."

"He'll grow on you."

"Yeah, like toxic mold."

He laughed and pointed at the couch. "Have a seat. The show is about to begin."

I walked over to the couch, which he'd covered with a big soft warm blanket, and dropped onto the middle cushion. "What show?"

"You'll see."

Doc popped the cork on the bottle and poured some wine into the glasses, coming over to set them down on the coffee table in front of me. Then he grabbed his laptop from behind the workbench and placed it on the table between the glasses.

He joined me on the couch, leaning forward to punch a few buttons on his computer. He grabbed a quilt draped over the end of the couch and covered our laps with it. Then he handed me my glass of wine and sat back next to me, putting his arm around my shoulder.

On his computer, the opening credits of *The African Queen* rolled.

"Bogart and Hepburn," I said, taking a sip of what tasted like a bubbly, sweet white zinfandel. "One of my favorites."

"Mine, too." He clinked his glass against mine.

We settled in for the movie, cozy under the quilt in the firelight. As the characters' affection for each other grew on the screen in the hot and buggy jungle, I finished my wine, set the glass aside, and leaned into Doc. A successful clock caper, a fun dinner with the kids, and a romantic evening with the guy I was bonkers about—I couldn't have asked for a better Valentine's Day.

Partway through the movie, Doc set his glass on the coffee table next to his computer and then smiled at me. "You know, we didn't follow through on our caper game."

"What do you mean?"

"During the clock boxing. Hawke tripped three times."

"Yeah, but the third time didn't really count because he actually tripped over Cooper's foot."

Since Natalie had been watching with us at that point, I hadn't wanted to bring up our flirty game.

"When he tripped and stumbled," Doc said, "he did kick a box, which made him fall."

"But only to one knee." Lucky for Hawke, Cooper had reached out and caught him mid-fall.

Doc paused the movie. "One knee or two doesn't matter, because there was a third box involved, and you know what that means?"

I did. And the way Doc was looking at me spurred my next move.

I pushed the quilt aside and stood, yanking my sweater over my head. "Something to do with this, right?" I asked, tossing the sweater his way.

He caught it without taking his eyes off my chest. "Damn. Is that a new bra?"

"Yep." I shimmied out of my yoga pants, kicking them aside. "It's a matching set. Happy Valentine's Day."

Doc's gaze bounced back and forth between the bra and panties, then he gaped up at me with a look of disbelief. "You've been hiding these from me all day, Boots?"

"Not hiding. We were just busy." And we needed to get busy again, because I was getting cold wearing nothing but my skivvies, and chicken skin was not very sexy.

He reached for my hand and then my hips, pulling me down so that I was straddling his lap. "Not that busy."

I shivered both from the chill in the air and the anticipation of what was going to happen next. I leaned forward, pressing against his chest. "You're warm."

"I'm actually hot now that I've seen my present." He adjusted the quilt over my shoulders before reaching inside to get a better feel of his gift.

I moved my hips against his, teasing a groan from him. "You're overdressed for dessert, Candy Cane."

"Lift up for a minute," he said, helping me onto my knees. He made short work of his pants, kicking them over by mine. "There," he said, drawing me back down.

"What about this?" I undid the top button on his shirt.

"It's cold. Maybe I should leave it on."

"If you want your minute of groping for Hawke's third trip, the shirt comes off. That was part of the second-trip deal."

He sighed, unbuttoning. "The kids were right. You're pretty bossy." He slipped his arms free and laid it on the end of the couch. "There, you happy now, woman? We'll freeze together."

I leaned down and kissed him, slowly, teasing another groan from him with my tongue. He grasped my hips, rubbing against me.

"I'm happier than I've ever been before," I whispered against his lips.

"Good, but that was only one kiss. You have two more to go."

He cupped the back of my head, pulling me back down for a return kiss that made my toes tingle. Or maybe the blood was having trouble reaching my toes with the way I had my legs folded under me, it was hard to tell.

When he pulled back, he stared up at me with a dark, hungry gaze. "That was two."

I beat him to the punch on the third kiss, wrapping my arms around his neck and sinking my teeth into his lower lip before taking his mouth and showing him how happy I was.

His hands slid up my ribcage. "That was three," he said when I came up for air. "Just a warning, I'm going to grope you now, and I'll probably go over the minute mark, because this bra is super sexy and the parts of you peeking out from under it is big-time fantasy material."

"Fine." I tipped my head back as his mouth trailed down my neck. "Ready, set, go."

I was breathless by the time he finished groping. And kissing. And licking.

He shifted us around so that I was laying under him on the couch. The soft blanket warmed my cold skin.

"I'm going to need a rain check on enjoying a more thorough viewing of the matching panties."

I ran my nails down over his shoulders. "Why is that?"

"Because I need to feel you too much right now."

He reached down and tugged my underwear free, holding them up in the candlelight for a moment. "They look risqué. I definitely approve." He threw them over his shoulder. His boxer briefs followed shortly.

"What about the bra?" I asked after he settled between my thighs.

"That stays on." He bent and licked me again through the fabric.

I moaned and arched into him.

He smiled down at me. "You know, it turns out that licking when kissing is one of my favorites. Rooster may have something there."

I wrapped my legs around him and pulled him close, skin on skin. "Shut up and lick me again."

"So bossy," he whispered.

Then he gave me my Valentine's Day present.

Make that presents, as in plural.

CHAPTER TWENTY-SEVEN

Saturday, February 16th (Two days later)

The weight of something crawling up the back of my legs pulled me out of a Winnie-the-Pooh dream where I was enjoying handfuls of honey straight out of the pot along with the chubby bear. I'd blame that dream on too much tequila, but I didn't drink any last night.

I opened my eyes slowly, focusing on the bedroom door, which was open a crack. Past experiences with cats and chickens in my room, along with gerbils and bats, had taught me to assess a bedroom situation before reacting.

"Tish, don't move," Doc said from his side of the bed.

I wanted to look his way, but I was on my stomach and that would involve pushing up and turning my head, aka *moving*, which Doc didn't want me to do for some reason.

"What's on me?" The extra pressure had moved to my lower back. "Please tell me it's not some version of a rodent."

"I think it's Daisy."

But the imp wasn't visible to him without Arcana's help, and the mirror was down in the laundry room last I knew. "Can you see Daisy now?"

"No, but I saw the closet door open and Elvis strut inside. The door closed and I figured Daisy was in there with Elvis, but then I felt something walk across my shins."

"That would be creepy under normal circumstances."

He chuckled. "It's creepy under any circumstances." The bed shifted slightly. "What is Daisy doing?"

"I can't tell, but she's moved between my shoulder blades."

"She?" Doc asked. "So Daisy is no longer an *it* for you?"

So it seemed. "I guess Addy has rubbed off on me."

"*She* it is, then."

The imp eased onto my shoulder. I turned my head as much as I could without moving my body and caught sight of Daisy's beady red eyes. "Now she's leaning down near my face, staring at me."

"Should I shoo her off?"

"You think that will work?"

"Maybe. I mean, if I could feel her on my legs, then …"

Daisy hopped off my shoulder, crouching on the bed next to my head. "Hold on, she's reaching toward me. Do I have something in my hair?"

The honey eating had been a dream, right? Or had I gone down to the kitchen in my sleep and dug into a jar for real? Honey anywhere on me would certainly explain Daisy's sudden interest this morning.

The mattress shook slightly again. "Not that I can see."

Daisy's hand moved slowly toward my face, giving me time to admire the pink nail polish on her claws. I looked from her weird little hand to her scrunched-up face.

"What's she doing now?" he whispered.

"She's holding her hand out in front of my cheek. It reminds me of someone trying to measure an angle using their thumb and index finger."

"That's weird."

"You're telling me." The imp was now focused on my cheek, her forehead extra wrinkly.

"Maybe you should just ask her what she's doing," Doc said. "Addy talks to her all the time, so she must understand some words."

It was worth a try. I raised my head off the pillow. "Daisy?" I said in my nice-mom tone. "What are you doing?"

The imp's gaze lifted to mine. "*Ootzcalel,*" it said in a raspy voice, before it reached down and lightly tapped a claw on my cheek.

Doc's hand warmed the middle of my back. "Did she answer?"

The imp stuck out her lower lip and tapped my cheek again in the same place. "*Ootzcalel*," she repeated.

I pushed up higher, resting on my forearms. "I don't understand, Daisy. Are you saying, 'Who's Calel?' "

"Kal-El is the name given to Superman at birth by his birth parents," Doc said.

"Well, I highly doubt Daisy is talking about Superman."

I glanced over at him. Prince Charming was propped up on his elbow, looking bewitchingly sleep rumpled enough to be despicably handsome. It was not fair that I started out each day hitting a solid seven on the wild-haired witch scale.

He shrugged. "Maybe she's been watching cartoons with Addy and Layne."

Daisy tugged on my hair. "*Scharfrichter*." When I turned back to her, she tapped my cheek again. "*Ootzcalel*."

"She tapped my cheek and said it again," I told Doc.

"What the hell?"

Creeeeaaak. The bedroom door opened wider.

"Mom?" Addy peeked in at me, her forehead puckering when her gaze landed on the imp. "What's Daisy doing in bed with you?"

"I don't know, birthday girl." I pushed up, sitting on the edge of the bed with my legs dangling, and held my arms out wide. "Come here and give me a hug, my beautiful ten-year-old daughter."

Addy raced across the room, jumping into my arms and knocking me back onto Doc, who grunted and chuckled.

I smiled up at her sparkling eyes and gave her a little birthday rib tickling, which made her giggle and squeal.

The imp hopped around on the bed next to us. "Addy-Addy!" Daisy rasped, and then she jumped down onto the floor and scampered over to the closet.

I let go of Addy. "Where's your brother?"

"He's already downstairs. Aunt Zoe is making huge pancakes for us." She slid to the floor and skipped around to the other side of the bed. "Doc, it's my birthday!"

"It is?" He sat up and grabbed his black thermal shirt from the end of the bed, pulling it down over his head. "What are we going to do about that, squirt?"

She wrung her hands together. "Maybe give me some birthday presents and then we eat cake later."

He reached under the bed, returning topside with a small box. "Would you look at that? The birthday fairy already swung by and left you something."

She gasped and clapped her hands. "Can I open it now, Mom?"

"It's up to Doc," I said, laying on my side to watch.

He nodded. "Go ahead."

She ripped open the wrapping paper, lifting the lid of the box to reveal a small beaded necklace with a tiny silver bell from the box. There were letters on some of the beads.

She looked up at Doc with a super bright smile. "It says *Daisy* on it." She turned to where the imp crouched by the closet. "Daisy, come here."

The imp eased over to her, warily eyeing the necklace Addy held out. "Addy-Addy," it said again.

"That's right, Daisy. Here, let's put this on you." Addy carefully slipped it over the imp's head. "Oh, look how pretty you are!"

The imp bounced around, the tiny bell making a soft tinkling sound.

"Addy!" Aunt Zoe called up the stairwell. "Time to eat."

"Thank you, Doc," Addy said, giving him a quick hug. Then she raced out the door with Daisy jingling behind her.

I crossed my arms. "You gave Daisy a bell to wear."

He stood and stepped into his flannel pajama pants, hauling them up. "Was it that obvious?"

"Could you hear the bell?"

He nodded. "Now your aunt and I will be able to hear Daisy coming."

"How did you know a bell would work for Daisy?"

"I didn't, but I figured it was worth a shot." He bent over and pulled another present out from under his side of the bed. "I need to give this to Layne so he doesn't feel left out."

"What did you get him?"

"You'll have to see for yourself." He walked around to my side of the bed and offered me a hand up. "Coming, gorgeous?"

"Are you kidding?" I took his hand, sneaking in a quick kiss after he pulled me upright. "Huge pancakes and birthday presents? I wouldn't miss that for all of the honey in the world."

"Who said anything about honey?"

I grabbed my robe and slid into my slippers. "That's not important right now." I fast-walked toward the door, smiling back at him. "Last one downstairs has to clean the feathers out of our closet next time."

* * *

Several hours later, Layne sat on the couch devouring a new history book on Hessian soldiers, one of his newer obsessions along with the Maya gods.

Doc had lost the race downstairs, but only because I cheated, which he swore he'd make me regret later tonight.

Meanwhile, the house was filling up with birthday guests and presents. Susan showed up with my parents, wearing jeans and a high-necked sweater, surprising me with something kid-appropriate for once. She greeted Doc without a single flirty wink and then followed me to the kitchen, carrying a big box containing the cake that Mom had made special for Addy's and Layne's birthdays.

I led the way to the laundry room where Aunt Zoe suggested we store the cake until it was birthday candle time. "What design did Mom do on the cake this year?" I asked Susan as she set the box on top of the washer.

"It's pretty cool." She carefully pulled off the upper half of the box. "Check it out."

One side of the cake had a temple made of stacked, frosted blocks. I couldn't tell if the blocks were cookies or squares of cake, but the temple looked like a blend of Egyptian and South American styles. Miniature plastic palm trees lined a path made of what appeared to be golden cookie crumbs, which led to a closed treasure chest.

"What's in the chest?" I asked.

Susan shook her head. "Mom wouldn't tell me. She said it's a surprise for Layne."

The other half of the cake had a chicken wearing a pink sweater dotted with red candies. I reached out and touched one. "Are those cherry sours?"

"Yep." Susan pointed at the feathers on the chicken. "She used a shaver and white chocolate to make the feathers look more real."

"Damn, she's good."

"I know. Remember that hippos-in-the-mud safari cake she made for Quint's thirteenth birthday?"

I moaned. "So much delicious chocolate inside and out."

She nodded. "I snuck out to the kitchen after everyone went to bed and ate a couple more pieces."

"I remember." I poked her in the arm. "And Mom blamed me for the missing cake in the morning."

"Yeah, I should have come clean on that." She carefully put the lid back on the box. "If it's any consolation, Dad figured out I did it. He lectured me on lying by omission."

"Good."

"Then he made me clean his workshop from top to bottom as punishment."

"I thought you did that for brownie points."

She leaned her hip against the washer, crossing her arms. "Why did that detective say you killed the old lady who lived in that apartment?"

Damned Hawke and his big mouth!

I shrugged, trying to play off an air of nonchalance. "He's full of shit, that's all."

Her gaze narrowed. "He was pretty bent about you. What did you do to him?"

"I just called him out on being an egotistical asshole." Which was the truth.

"But that doesn't explain why he thinks you killed a woman. Or why he also thinks you're a witch, which is what you mentioned the other day on the phone."

I chewed on my lower lip, wondering how much she needed to know before she'd let this go. "Okay, so I may have pretended to be a witch and put a hex on him once or twice, and now he's super suspicious of me when it comes to any crimes happening in town."

She grinned. "So you were serious about the witch stuff?"

I nodded. "It didn't help that I happened to be the first to show up at the old lady's apartment after her death. Harvey was with me when I found her."

"Oh, damn." She grimaced. "Was it gross?"

"Very." I sighed, shaking my head. "Detective Hawke came to town about then to help with the murder case. Unfortunately, our initial meeting occurred right after Rex had come to my work and demanded I act as his real estate agent, which had pissed me off. That's why the detective's misogynistic bullshit riled me up more than usual."

"What did you do to the detective?"

"I stomped on his pen and threatened to do the same with his balls. Our relationship went downhill from there."

She nodded. "A murder accusation, though? That's a long way downhill."

"Did I mention that he's a bit unhinged? And since I refuse to kiss his ass when he's strutting around in police-peacock fashion, he's got it out for me now." I crossed my fingers behind my back that this was enough information to appease her curiosity, and that she'd forget about Hawke's murder-filled rhetoric for the time being.

"Susan?" My mother called out in the kitchen.

My sister turned to leave, but I caught her sweater, stopping her. "Thank you for helping me out with moving those clocks."

She nodded slowly. "That was quite bizarre, you know."

"Yeah, and I appreciate you following through anyway."

She chewed on her lower lip for a second, then shrugged. "Well, I upheld my part of the bargain. Now put in a good word for me with Mom and Dad, as you promised."

"Will do."

We walked out of the laundry room together, which caught our mom's attention.

"What was going on in there?" she asked from where she stood by the table. Her gaze was wary, like when we were kids and she'd catch us pretending we hadn't been pulling each other's hair only seconds before she'd entered the room.

"We were admiring your cake," I explained.

The sound of Rooster barking in the backyard pulled my focus to the kitchen window over the sink. Someone must have let him out to take care of his doggy business, but what was with all of the barking? Rooster was usually quieter when he was outside, unless the kids were with him, which they weren't last I knew.

"I hope you two weren't fighting in there," Mom said.

"Because I poured a lot of good karma into that cake. We don't need either of your bad vibes soaking into the frosting."

"Jeez, Mom," Susan said, heading for the refrigerator. "Give us a little credit."

Rooster was really making a commotion outside, howling now, as well as barking. My fingers tingled with adrenaline. Something wasn't right, but I wasn't sure if the off-feeling was just a side effect from being in the same room with my mom and sister and not fighting with either of them for once.

I walked over to the window to see if the kids were outside. They weren't, and I couldn't see Rooster in the yard, either. Maybe he'd gone around the side of the house.

"I can't give you two any more credit," Mom told Susan. "You're both overdrawn, and my give-a-damn well is down to just a puddle."

I held in a sigh. "Mom, that's in the past." I walked over to where she sat and kissed her on the cheek, trying to sweeten her up before following through on my end of the deal. "Susan has apologized, and we've made peace."

She looked doubtful. "Apologized for what?"

I shrugged. "Everything."

"Oh, dear me." Mom pressed her hands to her cheeks. "I'm feeling faint. This must be a hallucination. Susan, what did you put in that mushroom coffee you made for me this morning?"

"Nothing, Mother." Susan set a bottle of sparkling water on the table in front of Mom. "You're fine and we're fine. Quit being so dramatic."

Mom's mouth gaped. "After three decades of you two fighting day after day, I have the right to exhibit a bit of drama about—"

BOOM!

Mom screeched like she'd been goosed.

I looked at Susan. "Was that from the backyard?"

She grasped Mom's shoulder. "I think so."

Rooster yipped a few times in between his barks. Out the kitchen window, I saw him race behind Aunt Zoe's workshop and head into the trees, snow flying in his wake.

Shit! Was he hurt? Jesus, had someone shot him?

Doc rushed into the kitchen. "What the hell was that?"

Aunt Zoe hurried in behind him. "Was that a gunshot?"

"Where are the kids?" I asked Doc.

"Upstairs," Aunt Zoe answered for him. "They're fine."

"Good." I grabbed one of Aunt Zoe's coats from a peg by the back door. "Keep them there, please." I turned to my sister. "Stay inside with Mom."

She nodded, clearly worried.

Doc beat me to the door, holding it open for me.

I grabbed his coat from another peg. "Here," I said, handing it to him as I passed by on the way outside.

He quietly closed the door behind us. "Your mace is still in your rig," he said under his breath.

I shivered in the cold wind that was whipping the snow from the backyard onto the porch. "Yeah, but there's an axe inside the door of Aunt Zoe's workshop." I searched the trees behind the shop. "I think someone might have shot at Rooster."

"Why would anyone do that? Especially in the daylight."

"I don't know, but he was barking like crazy, and then I heard the—"

"I nailed that son of a bitch, Coop!" Harvey's voice came from around the side of the house. "I know I did."

Creak.

"That's the side gate," I said to myself as much as Doc.

"You say you nailed it," Cooper said. "But where is it?"

The two rounded the corner of the house. Harvey had Bessie out and pointed toward the glass workshop as he tramped through the snow. Cooper's handgun was still holstered, but he was touching the grip.

"It took off up toward Mount Moriah." Harvey pointed at the hill.

Cooper looked up at the treed hillside. "How can you be sure you landed a hit then?"

"Because it was limpin' as it ran."

"What's going on?" Doc eased down the icy steps, offering a hand to help me.

I took it. "You didn't shoot Rooster, did you?" I asked Harvey as I stepped down.

The old boy stopped in his tracks and scowled from under his trapper hat. "Why in tarnation would I shoot your dog, Sparky?"

"I don't know. Maybe it was an accident."

Harvey snorted. "Your dog is fine and dandy. I shot your damned critter, though."

Oh no! I hurried toward Harvey, shivering in the blood-freezing wind. "You shot Daisy?" I asked in a low voice.

"I can't even see that one, girl." He pointed his shotgun toward the trees. "I'm talkin' about that redcap goblin varmint."

My breath caught. The goblin had been here? Just now? *Fuck!* My family had been outside a short time ago, carting in food and presents for the kids' birthdays.

"When I pulled up out front," Harvey explained, "I saw something slinkin' around in the trees over yonder." He indicated toward the foot of the hillside.

"What did it look like?" Doc asked.

"Tall, sunburned, and gangly with a red hat, same as what Sparky had described seeing on top of the courthouse."

I'd never mentioned a sunburn, but then my view of it had been fleeting.

He turned back to me. "I could tell that it didn't know I saw it. So, I drove on past the house and parked at the end of the road, sneakin' back through the trees. That's when I took a shot at it. Hit the sucker in the hip, I'm pretty sure."

"Why the hip?" Cooper wondered. "You should've aimed for the center."

"I slipped in the snow as I pulled the trigger."

"You weren't with him?" Doc asked Cooper.

"No. Nat and I were on the way over when he called me, claiming to have a visual on the redcap." He glared at his uncle. "I told you *not* to shoot, though."

"What was I supposed to do? Throw rocks at it? Hit it with a bully-boy glare? That thing is out to kill Sparky, not play patty-cake with her."

I turned to Cooper. His blackened eye looked extra colorful today, but the swelling was gone. "Are the cops on the way?" The last thing we needed was Hawke showing up and seeing Susan, recognizing her as one of the movers.

He shook his head. "I called in as soon as we pulled up. Told them a car backfired. That I was here when it happened, so call off the dogs."

"Where is that bastard?" Natalie called from behind us,

jogging toward us through the snow. She looked more like a paper tiger than a wildcat with her pink stocking cap pulled down over her braids and her rosy cheeks.

Cooper huffed at her. "Dammit, Nat, I told you to go in the house."

She flipped him off and focused on me. "The kids okay?"

I nodded. "And Susan is in there with Mom."

"Damn," she said, wiping under her nose. "If she'd been outside, Harvey could have taken out two of my headaches."

"Your dad was out front when we pulled up," Cooper said to me. "I sent him inside to keep the others corralled until we lock things down out here."

"Shit." I scanned the hillside leading up to Mount Moriah. "I had no idea the goblin was outside." Well, I had felt some tingling in my fingers, but nothing else. There was a lesson in this about letting my guard down. "Rooster was barking like crazy, but I figured he was chasing after a bunny rabbit or some birds."

Reid trudged toward us from the other side of the house, the fire axe he usually kept in his pickup in his hand. "Your uncle hit it, all right," he told Cooper.

"How do you know?" Doc asked.

"I went up through the trees a ways." He thumbed behind him. "That sucker lost a lot of blood. I tracked it part of the way up to the cemetery, but I'm dressed for a birthday party, not for a snow chase. Especially not in this weather."

Cooper grimaced. "That blood could be from another animal."

Reid shook his head. "It was black, not red."

"Maybe we should go hunt it down while it's injured and close by," Natalie said.

I didn't like that idea. "It's probably long gone." I shivered through another cold gust. "And it's too cold for us to be wandering around out here."

"Damned straight," Reid said. "Zo will have my hide if I let any of you guys chase that thing down in this freezing mess, and I can't have that. She's finally beginning to thaw out around me after I sweetened her up on Valentine's Day."

"At least we know we can cripple the bastard with some hot lead next time," Harvey said.

"Now we're talking," Cooper said, a grim smile on his face as he stared toward the trees.

"Violet?" My dad stepped out onto the back porch. "Everything okay out here?"

I nodded. "Is everything okay in there?"

"Seems to be."

"The kids?"

"Your brother is on the phone with them. He couldn't make it home in time for the party, but we brought the birthday presents he sent. You know how much they love to talk to their uncle Quint."

Yeah, I did, too. Quint was the perfect distraction from this craziness. Too bad he was so far away.

I checked out the tree line again. All looked cl— Wait!

Something was moving in the shadows, coming our way. Something small and …

Bark! Bark!

Rooster came galloping out of the trees with his tail wagging, carrying a piece of something red in his mouth.

"Rooster, come here," Doc said, patting his thigh.

The dog ran over to him.

"What do you have, buddy?" He played tug-of-war with Rooster, winning after a few pulls, and held up a piece of red-dyed leather.

"That looks like the hide hat that was pinned to the porch beam," Harvey said.

"How many of those hats does it have?" Natalie asked. "Did the bastard haunt a millinery during its last bounty hunting job?"

"One less now," Doc said, handing the hat over to Cooper.

"This thing looks like it was soaked in blood and then hung to dry," Cooper said.

"Christ." Doc aimed a worried glance my way. "That thing was just a short distance out there, watching and waiting."

"I know." I wanted to cram the red hat down the damned goblin's throat and then beat the bounty hunter into a puddle of black goo with my mace. But playing killer had to wait.

I took Doc's arm and pulled him toward the back porch. "Come on, we have a birthday party waiting for us."

As I climbed the steps, my dad stared down at me. "You got

this, Goldilocks?"

Dad knew all about my trade in killing. The Executioner genetic line had passed down through him.

"Not yet. But I will."

"That's my girl." He held the door for me and the rest of the crew.

Harvey brought up the rear. He set Bessie on top of the refrigerator and then came over to me as I was hanging up my coat. "I need to talk to Doc and you for two shakes." He nudged his head toward the laundry room.

"Doc," I called, waving him over from where he was talking with my aunt and Reid. "Harvey needs a quick word."

The three of us filed into the laundry room. Doc closed the door behind us.

"So, this is your love nook?" Harvey snickered. "Cozy."

"Zip it, old man." I pushed the cake back further so it didn't accidentally get bumped. "What's so urgent that we needed to talk right away?"

"I got a message for you from Prudy."

"Prudence?" I stepped back, leaning into Doc. "Did she talk in your head?"

"Yep, goldarn it. Any-hoo, she's got an idea about what was inside of that medium you dragged up to her place."

What was inside? Didn't he mean *who* was inside Madame Contraire?

"Accordin' to ol' Prudy, you might have a wee bit of a sorcerer problem."

"A sorcerer?" This couldn't be good. I crossed my arms. "You sure she said the word 'sorcerer'?"

"She talked in my noggin', so I heard her loud and clear."

"The *mardagayl* said she'd smelled a sorcerer on Ray Underhill when she came across him in the tunnel," Doc said.

"That's right." I looked up at him. "Could this be one and the same?"

He shrugged. "How did the sorcerer find its way into Madame Contraire?"

"When did it make its way in? We went to several supposedly haunted locations before I took her up to Prudence's place." I blew out a breath, turning back to Harvey. "First the redcap goblin spying on me from the trees and now this. Any more bad news you want to deliver, Mr. Harbinger of Doom?"

"Maybe, if ya ask me nicely."

I snapped one of his suspenders. "Spill it, old man."

"Prudy has the clocks."

"What?"

"She's gonna keep an eye on them for now."

"That's where you stowed them?" Doc sounded as surprised as I was.

"Yep. Reid's boy and his friends helped me unload them yesterday mornin', cartin' them up into the attic."

"Why the attic?" I asked.

"That's where Prudy wanted them."

"Was Zelda home?"

"Nope, but Prudy left the door unlocked for us."

I looked at Doc. "Why would Prudence want to hold onto the clocks?"

Doc shook his head, asking Harvey, "Was this her idea or yours?"

He shrugged. "Hard to tell who started the notion, but she was in on it before I ended it."

Doc rubbed the back of his neck. "What did you do with the trucks?"

"We took them back to my sister's place. Your aunt and Natalie will paint them white tomorrow, then Corny is gonna help me sell them to a friend of his in Nevada."

I wondered how Zelda Britton was going to feel about storing a bunch of ticking clocks in her attic. "So, I have to go see Prudence if I want to check on the clocks?"

"For the time bein'." Harvey hooked his thumbs in his suspenders, rocking back on his heels. "I figured that's as good a place as any right now. Hawke ran away scared last time he was up there with you. He ain't gonna think of findin' anything up in that attic but the boogeyman."

"It's a good idea," Doc said.

"Except for the Prudence part," I grumbled.

The laundry door opened and Cooper scowled in at us. "What's going on in here?"

"We're formin' a posse," Harvey told him, waving him inside.

"Get in here and shut the door."

Doc and I shuffled closer to Harvey.

Cooper squeezed inside. "What's this really all about?"

"I told them the trucks are back at your ma's place."

He nodded. "We'll lay low and let Hawke think those clocks are tucked away for the time being."

"Let's just hope he doesn't feel the need to check on that storage unit for a while," Doc said.

"He won't." Cooper aimed a hard glare my way. "So long as Parker doesn't do anything suspicious at Galena House."

I rolled my eyes. "You're starting to sound like Hawke. I just need to be able to show it to clients, that's all."

"Not anymore," Cooper said.

"Why not?"

"I want to put an offer on it. For real this time."

"No shit?" Doc said, wrapping his arm around my waist from behind.

"Why would you do that?" I asked.

We were done with Hawke being a problem there. According to Natalie, who called me at work yesterday afternoon when we were all supposed to be laying low, Hawke had stopped by first thing in the morning to leave the keys with Freesia. He was out for good.

Cooper snorted. "You need to up your real estate agent game, Parker. That's not very sales friendly of you."

"I thought you wanted something that was less busy with ghosts. Galena House comes with the possibility of wispy tenants."

"Hell, everything in this town is haunted. Besides, Curion thinks he might be able to help me say *adios* to any leftover ghosts with some sort of voodoo ceremony."

"You gonna have a place to rent to your favorite uncle in that ol' boardin' house?" Harvey asked, smiling wide enough for his gold teeth to show.

"Maybe." Cooper's gaze tightened to a squint. "If you can keep your big nose out of my personal life."

Harvey snickered. "Where's the fun in that, boy?"

"Okay." I fanned my neck with my hand. There were too many sardines crammed into this can. "I'll get the paperwork together when I go into the office on Monday." I'd taken the weekend off to hang with Doc and the kids. "What time in the afternoon works for you?"

"Make it Monday morning," Cooper said. "I might …"

The door opened, bumping into his back.

Natalie crowded inside, closing the door behind her. "What are all you guys doing in here?" She grinned. "And why does it smell like sugar and sex?"

"The cake is in here." I pointed at the box on the washer.

"If yer smellin' sex, it's because these two lovebirds use this as their makin'-whoopee room."

Doc laughed.

I sputtered, sweating clear to my toes now. "We do not!"

"Did Hope make the cake or you?" she asked me.

"Mom made it."

She clapped. "Oh, it's going to be so good. Remember that chocolate hippo cake she made for Quint that year?"

I nodded and turned to Cooper. "Does Nat know about your decision?"

Cooper's eyes widened. "Uhhhh."

Oops. Apparently, that was another secret from Natalie, along with him not fully telling her why he was suspended.

Natalie hopped up onto the dryer and snagged his hand, pulling him closer. "You mean about Coop agreeing to go with me down to Arizona while he's on suspension?"

"Arizona? Is your grandpa okay?" I asked, shifting the focus away from Cooper.

"Yeah. Everyone's fine—well, I'm not so sure about Kate. She's still preggo, and those hormones are flipping her brain back and forth between Dr. Jekyll and Mr. Hyde."

I remembered those pregnancy hormones too well, even after a decade. "Then why are you going down there?"

"Claire called and said she could use my help, so I'm thinking a dose of warm sunshine might be in order."

"You're goin' back to Jackrabbit Junction?" Harvey asked Cooper.

"Maybe," Coop answered, wincing as he spoke.

"What do you mean, 'maybe'?" Natalie asked, poking him in the side.

He grunted, catching her hand and not letting it go. "Last time

I went down there, I got shot.”

She lifted his hand to her lips. “Quit being a baby.” She kissed the back of his hand. “They were only flesh wounds.”

“I’m comin’ with you two,” Harvey told them.

“No!” Cooper didn’t even pause to think about it.

“Come on! I have friends down there. Any one of us could keel over before we see each other again. We need to muster as much trouble as we can while the sun’s still shinin’.”

“I know, that’s why you can’t go. You old guys are a pain in my ass.”

Harvey’s chin jutted. “Listen, boy, I have a driver’s license and my own rig. Either you take me along, or I follow on my own and give you hell when I get there out of spite.”

“Both options give me heartburn,” he told his uncle.

Natalie laughed and looped her arm around Cooper’s shoulders. “Come on, King Kong, let your uncle come along for the ride.”

Cooper sighed. “Fine, but he’s sleeping on the couch in the camper this time.”

“Oh, hold on,” Harvey said, turning to me. “Maybe I need to stay and play bodyguard for Sparky. That redcap goblin is still out there somewhere.”

“It is,” I said, “but you’ve slowed it down for a while.”

“I don’t know,” Cooper said. “For all we know, that thing could take ten direct hits like the one Uncle Willis gave it.”

“I could tell Claire that I can’t come for a couple of weeks,” Natalie offered. “Stay up here and help you guys hunt it.”

“No,” Doc said. “You guys should go. Reid and I are here, and Ox, if we need him. Zoe is no slouch with a gun, and Cornelius is pretty good too, for that matter.” He rubbed my shoulder. “Not to mention that we have a *Scharfrichter* here who could probably knock that goblin into next week with a crowbar, let alone her mace.”

“If you’re sure,” Cooper said. “I mean, I can be shot up here as easily as I can down in Jackrabbit Junction.”

Natalie laughed.

The door opened, bumping into Cooper’s back.

Cornelius poked his head inside. “Ah, it’s a monster mash. That explains why I smelled pickles earlier.” He pointed at the cake. "Mother Hope has sent me to collect the confectionery for an advanced screening by Violet's binary clones."

As my brain tried to digest his words, I could hear myself blink. "Mom wants what now?"

"Not a lick of that made sense, Curion," Cooper said. "I'm done here." He squeezed past Cornelius and out to the kitchen.

" 'Mother Hope,' huh?" Natalie repeated, hopping down from the dryer. "I can swing with that." She patted Cornelius on the chest as she slipped by him and trailed after King Kong. "Coop, wait up! We need to talk about Arizona."

"Pickles?" Harvey scratched his beard. "I once dated a girl who smelled like pickles back when I was a frisky hobbledehoy. Her daddy liked to dabble in some homemade taxidermy in their kitchen."

I shuddered at the macabre images that popped into my mind after having been in the back room of a taxidermy over in Central City. "Good gravy, Harvey."

He shrugged. "Pickle smell aside, that girl had a tongue like a frog."

"That's it. You're done here, too, dirty bird." I pushed him out of the laundry room.

Doc handed the cake box to Cornelius. "Be careful of the binary clones. They may become frenzied when they catch the scent of a sweetmeat."

Cornelius grinned. "As does Violet's long-legged littermate."

I held the door wide. "All right, fancy talker. Out we go." When I started into the kitchen after him, Doc caught my arm and pulled me back.

"Hold on a second, Tish." He closed the door.

I looked from the door to him. "What's going on?"

He reached behind the ironing board and pulled out Arcana. "I want to take a look at that handprint again."

"Right now?"

He set the mirror on the dryer and motioned me closer.

"Why do you want to look at it?" I joined him in the reflection turning my head to the side, same as before.

"I was thinking about Daisy's actions this morning." He tapped on the cheek close to where she had. "Wasn't she touching you right around here?"

"Yeah." My eyes widened in the mirror. "It was the same side as the handprint. Do you think Daisy can see it?"

"Maybe." He stared at me in the mirror for a few breaths.

"Well?"

He sighed. "Yeah, I think Daisy can see it. Why else would she be tapping you on that particular cheek?"

"Of course." I rubbed at the spot, wishing I could wipe the handprint off with enough scrubbing.

Doc tucked the mirror behind the ironing board. When he turned back to me, his brow was crinkled. "But if Daisy could see it all of this time, why hadn't she made a point of touching it before today?"

"Good question."

"Unfortunately, I might also have a good answer." He sighed. "Well, it's not good, but an answer, nonetheless."

My heart started to pitter-patter way too fast. "What do you mean?" I whispered.

"The handprint has changed."

"Like fading?" I hoped.

"No. You have a single dark tendril now spreading from one finger, the one closest to your mouth. It's tiny, but it wasn't there before."

I closed my eyes. "What the hell is going on?"

He pulled me into his arms, holding me tight. "We're going to figure it out together, Killer. Maybe Masterson can help somehow. Or even Daisy. And your aunt might be able to work out something from those sigils that will explain it."

"*Ootzcalel*," I whispered, repeating the imp's words. "What do you think that means?"

"I don't know, but it's got to be a clue. We just have to find the next one."

I looked up at him. "And the one after that."

He nodded. "Until we land on a fix."

The laundry room door opened wide. "Mom?" Addy said, stopping short at the sight of Doc and me hugging. "Awww, you two are my favorites." She came over and wrapped her arms around both of us.

"Addy, where are you?" Layne called. "We need …" He appeared in the doorway, and then his whole face scrunched.

"Sheesh, you guys. That's so mushy."

I held out my hand. "Come here, birthday boy. You know you want in on this."

"It's birthday *man*," Doc corrected.

Layne sighed. "Fine. Let's get this over with so that we can go open presents."

He grudgingly came over, and I pulled him into the fold.

"Are you happy now, Mom?" he mumbled into my side.

Happy? Well, there was a redcap goblin out there yet, a stupid handprint spreading on my face, a persnickety ghost holding my clocks hostage, a sorcerer looming, and a bounty still on my head, not to mention Rex and his bullshit, but …

"Yes." I stared up at Doc. "Happier than ever."

Doc leaned down and kissed my forehead. "Good."

"Me, too," Addy said. "Now can we go eat some cake?"

The End … for now

Ann Charles is a USA Today bestselling author who writes award-winning mysteries that are splashed with humor, romance, paranormal, and whatever else she feels like throwing into the mix. When she is not dabbling in fiction, arm-wrestling with her children, attempting to seduce her husband, or arguing with her sassy cats, she is daydreaming of lounging poolside at a fancy resort with a blended margarita in one hand and a great book in the other.

Facebook (Personal Page):
http://www.facebook.com/ann.charles.author

Facebook (Author Page):
http://www.facebook.com/pages/Ann-Charles/37302789804?ref=share

Instagram:
https://www.instagram.com/ann_charles

YouTube Channel:
https://www.youtube.com/user/AnnCharlesAuthor

Ann Charles Website:
http://www.anncharles.com

MORE BOOKS BY ANN

www.anncharles.com

The Deadwood Mystery Series

WINNER of the 2010 Daphne du Maurier Award for Excellence in Mystery/Suspense

WINNER of the 2011 Romance Writers of America® Golden Heart Award for Best Novel with Strong Romantic Elements

Welcome to Deadwood—the Ann Charles version. The world I have created is a blend of present day and past, of fiction and non-fiction. What's real and what isn't is for you to determine as the series develops, the characters evolve, and I write the stories line by line. I will tell you one thing about the series—it's going to run on for quite a while, and Violet Parker will have to hang on and persevere through the crazy adventures I have planned for her. Poor, poor Violet. It's a good thing she has a lot of gumption to keep her going!

The Deadwood Shorts Series

The Deadwood Shorts collection includes short stories featuring the characters of the Deadwood Mystery series. Each tale not only explains more of Violet's history, but also gives a little history of the other characters you know and love from the series. Rather than filling the main novels in the series with these short side stories, I've put them into a growing Deadwood Shorts collection for more reading fun.

The Deadwood Undertaker Series

From the bestselling, multiple award-winning, humorous Deadwood Mystery series comes a new herd of tales set in the same Deadwood stomping grounds, only back in the days when the Old West town was young.

The Jackrabbit Junction Mystery Series
Bestseller in Women Sleuth Mystery and Romantic Suspense

Welcome to the Dancing Winnebagos R.V. Park. Down here in Jackrabbit Junction, Arizona, Claire Morgan and her rabble-rousing sisters are really good at getting into trouble—BIG trouble (the land your butt in jail kind of trouble). This rowdy, laugh-aloud mystery series is packed with action, suspense, adventure, and relationship snafus. Full of colorful characters and twisted up plots, the stories of the Morgan sisters will keep you wondering what kind of a screwball mess they are going to land in next.

The Dig Site Mystery Series

Welcome to the jungle—the steamy Maya jungle that is, filled with ancient ruins, deadly secrets, and quirky characters. Quint Parker, renowned photojournalist (and lousy amateur detective), is in for a whirlwind of adventure and suspense as he and archaeologist Dr. Angélica García get tangled up in mysteries from the past and present in exotic dig sites. Loaded with action and laughs, along with all sorts of steamy heat, these books will keep you sweating along with the characters as they do their best to make it out of the jungle alive.